C000078328

Illthdar:
Guardians of Las

Rachel Garcia

Published in 2014 by FeedARead.com Publishing

Copyright © The author as named on the book cover.

First Edition

The author has asserted their moral right under the
Copyright, Designs and Patents Act, 1988, to be identified
as the author of this work.

All Rights reserved. No part of this publication may be
reproduced, copied, stored in a retrieval system, or transmitted, in
any form or by any means, without the prior written consent of the
copyright holder, nor be otherwise circulated in any form of
binding or cover other than that in which it is published and
without a similar condition being imposed on the subsequent
purchaser.

A CIP catalogue record for this title is available from the British
Library.

DEDICATION

To all the goddesses in my life, to which thanks must be given, for
without them this tale would never exist.

CONTENTS

ACKNOWLEDGMENTS

Endless thanks to Daniel, Danielle, Kit and Rebecca for their love, support, tireless hours of proofreading and feedback. A lifetime of gratitude is also owed to Jocelyn, Lisette and Emil for their creativity and inspiration.

CHAPTER ONE

D emons are real. Faeries are real. Gods and, in fact, most things humans take as fantastical tales, passed between parent and child—born from the imaginations of people who didn't understand the world—are very real and few know it better than them.

Their name is Sozo Abaddon and they are the kind of person who passes through—disassociated to the world around them. The drifter, a face no one can recall because it changes so often, who saw many places in their long life. Of all those, the spire of the Order of Mana was the last. *It was magnificent.* A beacon of comfort and protection to those who congregated around it.

The Order of Mana: a religious order in Illthdar; a world of celestials, demons and faeries. A place Abaddon thought they could attach to a worthy cause—do something besides wander. Finding purpose wasn't without setbacks. Abaddon spent a year recovering in their infirmary after an accident took their sight. They never imagined the people they met once released, or the course their life would take.

1

Even at the end, after the pain and suffering they all endured—the betrayal, hate and cruelty—Abaddon smiled. Somehow they were grateful. How could they have guessed the treasure they would find when teamed with their ragtag band.

Now, they stood upon broken ground. The towering spire of white swathed in crackling flames, visible to them by sound reverberations carried to their horns.
No one could have anticipated it would come to this from where they started three years ago.

How did this happen?

Like most stories, it is best to start with, "Once upon a time…"

For all who came before, though their means of arrival were different, the result was the same.

None could be faulted their reactions of confusion and horror—all variations on the same theme.

For Zercey, the youngest and last to arrive, it started like a dream that descended into a nightmare.

"When you get that letter, you better call me, eh?"

"Gulia, of course I will…" Zercey replied into the phone, crossing her fingers. Mousy brown hair, round-faced and acne-scarred, she was lacklustre in terms of looks, but everything in intelligence. Elida Stamos—though she preferred Zercey—was a nice enough girl, with a penchant for talking to herself. "It just hasn't arrived yet," she lied. Her lilac-coloured eyes slid to the bed. The University acceptance letter lay in the centre of the covers, an innocuous white rectangle against a green and pink background. Though she read it, she couldn't accept it.

"Okay, but the second it does, you're ringing me," Gulia ordered in mock sternness before excitedly changing to her favourite topic. *"Did I tell you about Antonio?"* Ignoring the loud groan from the other end of the line, she informed her friend, *"He told me I'm the one today. The One, Zercey!"*

"The *One*, one, eh? Gulia, he only met you two weeks ago. He doesn't love you and, in fact, one plus one to him is eleven." She sighed dramatically; her friend hadn't changed since puberty. "Oh, Gulia, when are you ever going to learn?"

"He said he didn't mean anything when he was out with that other girl!"

"Oh, my God, Gulia, you didn't even tell me about that! That just proves it. Run away now, or I swear you'll be crying into your wine before the end of the week!"

"Zercey, you're too cynical for eighteen. Love is all about taking risks; I'm telling you, Antonio is worth crying and fighting for."

Zercey threw her free hand up in exasperation. "You're delusional, and I'm going out. Gulia, think about what you're saying, and I'll talk to you later. Hopefully, you'll be sane by then."

"You sound like my mother. Love you, girlfriend!"

She looked at her phone and ruefully shook her head. "Love you too, Gulia."

3

A person could find snatches of green if they looked for it within the city where she grew up, but the reality was that civilisation claimed nearly all the space. It was only afforded life in flowerpots and token green-bits.

On her moped, Zercey headed out of town and down along the open roads, not strictly following the motoring laws, but she wasn't worried. Gulia's older brother was in the police force, and her destination was near.

Glancing in her rear mirrors, to ensure no one would have a stroke if they saw her, she slowed and slipped between some broken guard rails. She jostled and bounced along a worn, dirt path down the low hill. "Wheee!"

Terrifying as it was taking a path carved by a car crash, it made her feel more alive. When she first started coming, she held her breath as she walked her moped down the slope.

"Right, so let's see… Let's go this way…" She peered at a map to get her bearings. It was a bit tattered now, having been folded too many times over the summer. She used it to explore a new section of the woods each week to fill up her gap-year, and it did wonders keeping her distracted. If it wasn't for the self-study aspect she wouldn't have been on the hillside. Her nerve would surprise her friends and family if they knew. This was the last place that any of them expected a bookworm like her to go. She wasn't sure she was ready for University. Local or afar, the thought made her feel a tiny bit ill. "A lot," she corrected, feeling queasy at the thought. It shouldn't have. She told herself, "Cristiano and Domencio are doing okay. Why not you, Zercey?"

The little voice in the back of her head was all too happy to remind her. *"Because those two were always outgoing, and what do you think you're doing, Zercey, rolling in the dirt? Shouldn't you be dating, or whatever it is girls your age do these days?"*

Her last hope of getting out of it was being refused by every University she applied for, putting her fate straight into God's hands. The result of which took her to her sanctuary because God seemed to have different plans. To University she would go.

4

CHAPTER TWO

Five Orders made up Las city's Order of Mana: Crystal, Amber, Quartz, Jasper and Fluorite. While the Crystal Order bore compass talismans of gold to represent the yellow crystal, the other four branches were respectively decorated with their namesake stones: amber, picture jasper, smoky quartz and marbled fluorite.

Before the city came, the Order of Mana existed as a temple on the southern cliffs of Illthdar. Governed in those days by the Order of Crystal—a council of High Priests and Priestesses. Now, one ruled: High Priestess Chiyoko. A kitsune demon with blunt cut, shoulder-length hair, black pointed ears and a swishing sextuplet of fluffy tails sticking out of her long, yellow-hued robes. Tasked with directing the High Elders of the other Orders, she was a stern and mirthless woman. Rumours surrounded her like the vines covering the crystal of Vvekw with everything from: "She's a nogitsune in disguise," to, "She orchestrated the murders of the other High Priest and Priestesses."

If there was truth in it, the Order of Amber concealed it. Administrators and educators, the Order of Amber had two High Elders: Trenfal, a golden-haired, lios elf, with dull green eyes and a tanned face lined with wrinkles. His advanced age a curiosity among youthful appearances, forced him to declare, "I'm not as old as I used to be."

The second High Elder was Hok'jai the orc, whose official position was Historian and Keeper of Records, though he also volunteered a significant amount of time as a teacher. The pair worked as a unit, with Trenfal carrying a small roll of parchment and piece of graphite between his fingers, and Hok'jai holding a thick folder to place notes.

The Order of Quartz handled secretive affairs: chasing leads and conducting investigations. With the most members without teams, their chief function was following rumours and reporting the outcome.

One of the last Orders formed, their High Elder was Uwe, an aufhocker. Quick to flash a smile, he had no qualms about revealing many rows of shark-like teeth. With shoulder length, sandy brown hair and gleaming eyes the colour of dried blood, he was without physical flaw…on the surface. He survived by feeding on the life energy of others and often said creepy things like, "Not to worry, damsels. Of course, if you're scared, feel free to stick close to me. My bite only stings a moment." He liked watching men and women cringe with revulsion at his words, almost as much as he liked charming the silly things into bed and reminding them how much they hated him afterwards. A fashion slave to boot, Acolytes placed bets on his daily, off-duty outfit because he was never seen in the same thing twice. Others speculated, "He's got to be an incubus in disguise." As well as the popular, "He owns a brain-eating, demon shawl—that's the only explanation for why he's so off."

The Order of Jasper contained the military arm of the Order. The bulk of recruits ended up there led by Halbert Culvers, a taciturn half-blood arachne—though no one called him by his first name if they wanted to live. At six-foot-three, he was compared to a handsome golem—a male Galatea, so desired by the ladies it made Uwe's blood boil—but didn't spare him from rumours.

"He's just the half-blood."

"I heard he sleeps in a bed made of spider-silk."

As the tallest High Elder—Trenfal, the smallest stood at a

"Why is that weird? Do you think something happened on their island to drive them here?" Vyxen joined in.

"I can almost promise it," Scy declared. "I wonder what that something is."

Training new recruits wasn't a strict set up of trainees and Order Elders. Zercey suspected switching things around to impart general knowledge of all disciplines was so they never had the same kind of torture two days running.

During a day of endurance training, with the weather turning bitter, Zercey huddled around a small fire beside Abaddon, Scyanatha and Vyxen. "I'm going to die here," she said, blowing on her hands.

"I'll die with you," Abaddon agreed, scrunching further into their heavy, wool cloak, their colourless eyes glowing.

"You're exaggerating. It's not that bad." This came from a woman by the name of Magnilla. She was the one the others saw arrive the first day of training, accompanied by her brother, Thijs. She declared herself their group's leader moments after meeting, and wouldn't take no for an answer. "You'll get used to it," she added, rose-coloured lips pursing.

"Of course we will," reassured Scyanatha in a cheerful voice. Hailing from the Unseelie court, she was more used to abrasive personalities. She sat as close to the fire as the rest and said in a sympathetic tone, "Getting there is the hard part."

Vyxen was torn between wanting to strike back with all the passion in her small body, and keeping quiet so they weren't discovered by the opposing team. "Don't you have a fur coat you can never take off?" she questioned in a low voice.

Turning back to scan the icy hillside for signs of life, Magnilla shrugged. "You don't have to take my word for it." Her focus sharpened as someone appeared in the distance, but it was only a barefoot Nyima back from reconnaissance. "Don't forget, *you need me.*" The words were the echo of ones she'd spoken the day she chose them as teammates. "One of you is blind," she pointed at Abaddon, "three of you aren't even from this planet," she waved her hand in the direction of Vyxen, Zercey and Nyima, "and two of you are defenceless," she finished up looking at the spot between Zercey and Vyxen's shoulders. This familiar speech was followed by a list of skills and attributes that read like ingredients on the back of an instant soup packet, ending with, "That's why you need me. I am the future Alpha of the Thies clan and it's my duty to thing to decode came with special glasses, a marker or ring. "As soon as I find a Rosetta Stone, I'll get right on it," she said, sarcasm rearing its ugly head.

Vyxen clicked and trilled at the veiko until they settled down at the end of her bed. Then, she said, "I'm going to focus my energy on going back home. I can't live in Illthdar the rest of my life; I have family that depends on me."

"Ughhhh..." Abaddon groaned, climbing into the bed above Zercey's bunk and flopping onto it. Despite the theatrics, the wooden slats reacted with the minimum amount of creaking. "Order training is going to stink tomorrow."

"Uwe's going to murder me," Vyxen whimpered, burrowing herself under her blankets. A muffled, "Can't I defect over to you guys?" came from somewhere beneath the covers.

"Culvers is better?" Nyima questioned, doubtful. Given the choice, she'd rather tiptoe over some tiles, than tax her limited language skills to give orders in a war game. She eased down in bed, gritting her teeth as she shifted to a more comfortable position. "We do weapons and shooting." A seasoned warrior already she confessed more than once she'd never had so many injuries since being summoned to Illthdar.

"I reckon we'd be getting off lucky if he melted us down to make weapons." Zercey giggled, imagination running away with her. The sound cut off when she pulled a face and hugged her sides again.

"Would he really?" Abaddon sounded concerned.

"Zercey, don't be creepy," Magnilla scolded, pottering about fixing something to eat. With everyone weak, tired or injured, it was no trouble for someone as charitable as she to do a good turn. "No, he wouldn't, Abaddon."

"No," Zercey agreed, a wicked glint in her lilac eyes. "Of course he wouldn't, we're not metal. It would be wasted effort to try."

CHAPTER THREE

HA!"

To untrained ears, the exclamation might be confused for laughter. For the initiated, it wouldn't take long to register the excess force put into the vocalised expulsion of air.

"Again!" Elder Sora strolled through the ranks, every so often stopping to correct this person's foot or that person's grip. Divided by weapon types, Sora drafted additional Acolytes to provide further guidance for each section, while the plaid-shirted Culvers checked the ranks in his own time and was checked out in return.

"HA!"

"Lunge, repost! Again!" Elder Sora: tiny, blond, fierce and dressed in a bizarre uniform—in that it lacked every hallmark of something designed for battle. A short, leather wrap skirt and bodice, with steel plate overlay that matched her heavy boots, and no arm coverings. She looked like she was about to go dance in a mosh pit, not lead troops. Unlike Culvers, Sora had to bark for her voice to carry to the back row.

"HA!"

Faeries and demons had a complicated relationship with armour on Illthdar Isle. They wore it more like a fashion accessory than a utilitarian piece of kit. Half a breastplate, the other side of their chest exposed, and no one batted an eyelash. Gender didn't factor a different reaction, either. Finger gauntlets without hand-guards were also popular. Random spikes and bits of jewel fitted into cut-outs in a common step that took it beyond ridiculous. The amount of times things jammed in unfortunate positions was so commonplace it made the listing for the local betting board. If this was all it could be ignored, but some species went further into fetish-wear. Nipple-less breastplates, easy-access backs and bottoms were popular purchases among Acolytes and trainees; sex and violence commonly linked.

"Keep your point up." Culvers instructed someone a few paces away.
Zercey was quick to adjust the position of her spearhead. Thanks to a floral-smelling, healing salve provided by the Order of Fluorite handed out the morning after their failed capture the crown she only felt sore at the end of the day's training.
"Your feet are too close together." More advice filtered towards her and she adjusted her stance.
"HA!"
THWAP! Arrows struck bales of burlap wrapped hay; archers practising.

Across the enclosed yard metallic clangs rang. Trainees who proved they could handle wooden weapons moved onto using real ones. Abaddon, Scyanatha, Nyima and Magnilla were there from day one.
The sparring matches had spectators clustered around the rope ring, taking notes and waiting their turn as a new pair of sparring partners were announced. "Magnilla and Scyanatha! *En garde!*"
The French term made Zercey smile, it was proof some phrases translated into perfect Illthdarian.
"I know we shouldn't hold back, but I don't want to hurt or discourage you by going full force. You're not a Thies." Magnilla's projection cut the background chatter, determined to be heard by everyone whether they liked it or not.

37

Zercey paused practice to roll her eyes.

Scy's reply was smooth and regal. "That's kind, dear, but I shall manage."

"Again! Aim for the *other side* of your opponent!"

Sora's reminder drew Zercey back to her own exercises. She grimaced at the mental image. It was well suited, but the worst thing she ever killed was a rat that got into her aunt and uncle's basement—and she used poison. Aiming to put the pointy end through one's target left her feeling squeamish.

"HA!"

Of course, if the choice was between her or them, she didn't want it to be her. She shook her head, trying to delete the image like her brain was an Etch-a-Sketch.

"You're not fast enough, Scyanatha!" Magnilla shouted shrill suggestions between attacks. "You should hold your guard higher, like mine!"

Ugh! Zercey rolled her eyes as the sound of their blades meeting filled the air.

"Dear, we can't all hold our sword like a Thies." Scy's reply was a double-edge sword itself.

Along the path that split the courtyard loitered Acolytes from previous years. They clustered together in groups, assessing the merit and potential of combatants. Others called wagers between bawdy banter.

"A three coin on the blonde!"

"Three? Is that all? Damn, your ass gets tighter every time I see you."

"Like you'd know!"

"Take your lovers' quarrel to bed, no one wants a floor show. Besides, red there is an aos sí. She's bound to win."

"Lovers—fuck you!"

"Yeah! Have you seen how the ginger fights? My money's on her."

Zercey slowed. She really wanted to go and watch the others. If she had money she'd put it on Scy, and hope she got to see Magnilla's smug face eat dirt.

A shadow fell over her and she looked into the stern face of High

Elder Culvers. "Focus on what you're doing," he said, a glimmer of a smile turning up the corner of his mouth.

Busted. Zercey cursed under her breath and said, "Sorry, sir." She went back to repeating the exercises, conscious of Culvers watching her. His scrutiny lasted long enough that she felt a blush work its way up her neck and over her cheeks. Culvers had to be a good twenty years older than her, but damn, he was dashing.

From the side of her eye she noticed him nod, then march away, leaving her to continue working at the increased pace she'd put on for his benefit.

Sora bellowing, "Dismissed!" couldn't come soon enough.

Gathered in their barracks, the trainees had free time to rest and recuperate.

Faint cheers went up, with some leaving right away to take in the sights of Las's market, or hit the tavern for a well-earned drink. Some climbed into their bunks to sleep, while others set about cooking on the small stoves.

Zercey lounged on her bed, waiting for her arms and legs to stop feeling like they were made of jelly. Her eyes swept the room, passing over the remaining demons, faeries and otherworlders with little interest. She'd been in Las long enough to grow used to seeing fantasy creatures doing mundane things like washing their socks or picking their teeth.

"You have to pile the fuel in this section, make sure the door is secure and wait for it to reach the right temperature." Magnilla's confident instructions rang from over by the stove at their end of the room. The half-blood and demon she addressed wore matching annoyed expressions and backed away, leaving the business of taking care of it to her.

"It *is* better to let someone who knows what they're doing handle things," she said in a pleased voice, waving them off.

With thick, sleek and glossy honey-blonde hair, curled with a gentle wave; emerald green eyes, with rings of both blue and grey on the outer edges; natural rose toned, full lips; broad shoulders, an ample bust, slim waist and proportionally wide hips, Magnilla was a nineteen-forties poster-girl. Both of Zercey's brothers would have drowned in their own drool looking at her. Sporty, strong, talented, able to turn into a wolf and manifest wings, use both ice and fire magic, dual wield swords, make golems, speak to animals and all but keep forests alive with her presence she was perfect. Or so she implied. She was tolerable enough when silent, but had a habit of finding ways to highlight how much better she was at everything. She must not have been told no one was perfect. Of course, at the point where people were begging to tell her, she would say as much herself. Though, it was hard to tell if she meant it, or if it was just another way to highlight how great she was compared to everyone.

Zercey held suspicions about the powers Magnilla claimed to have. Plus, there was the fact if she could read minds and see into the hearts of others as she said—stating on more than one occasion that she had the "eyes of God,"—she wouldn't be able to stand being around anyone ever again. The dark thoughts she could inspire would drive her mad. Nor would she be able to look herself in the mirror. *I bet it's mostly bull.*

Scyanatha crossed into Zercey's line of sight, recounting a saucy story to a dwarf about some lord or other she knew when she lived in Scotland during the 60's—which 60's was up for debate. Tall and reed thin, with eyes the colour of a rich, red wine and hair like spun fire, she was a fountain of youth, as full of energy as she was information and stories. Part shape-shifter, part elemental manipulator, she could make beaded stones dance on currents of air, or turn them into lethal bullets. If she was of a mind—like one free afternoon a few days ago—she could sculpt stone into almost anything.

"How is that trinket coming along, Scyanatha?" Magnilla called, eyes on the contents of whatever she was cooking.

"She means the reproduction piece I showed you," Scy said in an aside to the dwarf. She raised her voice and replied, "As well as can be expected, dear. Thank you for asking."

"Um, d-do you need any extra, err, help, Scyanatha?" Abaddon offered in a shy voice. They perched on the end of their bunk, feet almost in the heater beside it, though they seemed fine with the slow roasting. They were in the middle of crafting something metallic between their bare hands. Their short, pink hair covered their eyes, but being blind, it made no difference. The glow from head, brows pinched with concern. "Will you be all right on your own?"

Zercey laughed, sardonic. She doubted anything she came across would want to eat someone like her. "Oh sure, I'll just take my fearsome veiko. If anyone comes at me Laurelium can chew their toes off, eh?"

Not having toes, the joke went over Bracken's head. "You should take your weapon."

Zercey's lips twitched with humour. One thing she'd learned was a lot of Earth concepts and jokes were alien to faeries. She and other half-bloods could say pretty much anything they liked without anyone noticing. "Oh yeah, I guess I can bring those along, too," she said, planning on bringing them anyway, just in case something decided she *was* worth eating.

"Zercey, if you keep teasing poor Bracken he will wind up bald," Scy commented, amused.

Bracken ran a hand over his mane and the women laughed. "It's almost soper," he said, naming the hour of the day when most sat down to eat. "If you wait until tomorrow I'll try and have a list of tutors for you."

Zercey nodded, realising her impulsive idea had its flaws. "Okay, I'm going to the brewery in that case." Scy waved and Bracken nodded their goodbyes as she left.

Heading to the brewery for lunch, she passed an Acolyte with a trainee, and listened with interest to part of their conversation. "One of them called the visiting diplomat, 'Dude'."

"That's nothing! You didn't see them the time they came back from a mission stark naked!"

"Damn, I wish I had seen that! They're a pretty lot!"

Zercey wondered who they meant. Rumours were common in the Order of Mana, along with stories how graduated teams fared on missions. Either because of their looks or propensity for mishaps and shenanigans, some were more notorious than others. However, the High Elders and High Priestess were one of the few topics that eclipsed them.

"Phanuel's been back and forth to port a lot of late," Abaddon commented during one metalaf—lunchtime. "Personally investigating a contaminated shipment of supplies."

"I didn't realise Phanuel knew outside existed." Zercey giggled, grabbing utensils for everyone and putting them on the scrubbed, wooden table.

The brewery—named so because it used to be one, but wasn't any longer—was a dim room, with high beamed ceilings with rows of long tables pushed together in a line, and benches on either side. It was reminiscent of a boarding school dining hall, complete with a stack of wooden trays and a line everyone queued in to collect food. Though, Zercey doubted there were goblin and orc lunch ladies in the schools of Milan.

"I suspect Trenfal has a crush on me." Magnilla changed the subject to her favourite: herself. She flicked her hair over her shoulder and sat down on one of the long benches.

"'Crush'?" Nyima echoed, unfamiliar with the Illthdarian word.

"Desire for," Scyanatha supplied, pouring cups of water for everyone from a jug and passing them out.

Nyima nodded her thanks for both and began eating.

At Magnilla's expectant look, Scy offered, "Why do you believe so?"

"I feel his eyes on me as I pass," she replied, lips tilting up in a knowing way. "I have a sixth sense when it comes to these things. However, if he wants to be with me, he will have to work hard and have the confidence to approach me—as the future Alpha of the Thies, I can only accept the best as my mate."

This was met with more silence, so Zercey changed topics. "Hey, did you hear about how a couple of water sprites started making out with each other to try to get out of spending time with Uwe?"

Vyxen perked up, pushing back her white hair. She was keen to learn anything to repel the persistent aufhocker. "Did it work?"

Zercey shook her head. "No, he ended up inviting both to his office."

"Why hasn't he been fired yet!?" Vyxen slammed her spoon down on the table so hard it made people look. "This is total sexual harassment!"

Scy explained. "I'm afraid you will find faeries and demons are more casual about sex and relationships. It's wonderful for those repressed and shunned, but not so for those uninterested in

With a mind to get Nurtis to safety, she crouched to his eye level and said, "I want to learn to read, but I can't by myself and I don't have time to go to school like you. I don't suppose you know anyone who could teach me?"

"You want to read our language!?" He bounced on his toes. "That's great! Maybe then you'll stop talking so funny!"

"Is it hard to understand me?" She felt the need to put more effort into emulating the antiquated style of speaking.

Nurtis shook his head. "No, but you talk fast and your words get really, really short." He held his hands up and inched them toward each other.

Zercey deliberated. "So, I should be saying olde shoppe, instead of old shop?"

"Yeah, it's much better to say it like that!" He paused, nose scrunched up. "But, you still say it kind of funny. Try like this, oh-elth-i show-p-i."

Zercey laughed at his drawn out pronunciation. "I'll keep practising," she reassured, patting him on the head. "But, I really want to be able to read it, more than speak," she hinted, hoping he'd take her to another grown-up.

"Hmmm, oh! I know!" He delved into a small sack secured at his waist and pulled out a bread roll. "This is a loaf, and we write it like this – " He looked around and found a stick. "Hluh-ah-af. Hluh-ahaf." He sounded each syllable out as he wrote down the word. "You try."

Maybe I don't need a tutor if I try it this way. Zercey took the stick and tried to copy the letters. "Luh. Ah. Fah. Lohahaf."

"Hlaf," he corrected.

"Hlaf," she repeated, and he nodded, showing off a gap in his teeth. Zercey beamed and laughed. "This is great. I'll try it. Thank you, Nurtis, you've been a great help."

"You're welcome," he replied, grinning and standing up. "You can keep the stick I found."

Zercey tested it in her hand. It was a little on the long side, but it was about the right diameter for a pencil. "I think I will." She stood also and tucked it into her sleeve. "Thanks again, Nurtis. I've got to go back, but can I walk you home?"

"It's there." He pointed to a familiar, tin roofed building on the far side of a low wall.

"There...?" *That looks like the place Hok'jai took me to when I arrived.* She looked at Nurtis. "Is your mother...Kess?"
He nodded, turning his head as a voice called his name. "There's mama, I gotta go. Goodbye!" He hopped the wall and pelted towards the building, leaving an amused Zercey giggling and shaking her head.

"HOW DARE YOU?!"
Sat on a low wall, Zercey jerked her head up from note taking and looked across the street. She spied an angry, red-garbed Ochsana with the blind and deaf minotaur, Parnach. A gentle soul, Ochsana was his champion as she faced off against a group of humanoid-looking teenagers.
"Toro, toro?!" She stamped her foot in disgust. It was a common taunt. Parnach couldn't hear, but it didn't stop Ochsana setting others straight. "You have no shame! Picking on those who are different! For shame!" She advanced, hand whipping back to strike.
"All right, that's enough." An Acolyte wedged his body between them, taking Ochsana's slap to his upper arm. Square jawed, he had a muscular frame and a draping of frost clinging to his forearms. "Chill out, everyone."
Zercey sagged with relief and left while she had the chance. Half-bloods standing against faeries and demons; she doubted she'd ever have the courage. Though, it reminded her of something Culvers said: *"They will underestimate you. Let them. Their arrogance is their downfall."*

On her way back to the barracks, a figure dropped down from the trees to block her path. Zercey screamed, "Oh, my God, don't hurt me!" Caught in her own feet, she landed in the dirt with a thud.
"They will underestimate you." Only if they're brain dead.
"Shhh!" Vyxen made quieting gestures and helped Zercey up. "Sorry I scared you, but you won't believe what I learned! It's pretty sucky, but you still won't believe it!"
"Whoa, wait, what's wrong?" Zercey's hands went to her hips, her brows furrowed in confusion.
"I was listening to the High Elders in the worship room," Vyxen

revealed, glancing over her shoulder. "They're going over the people graduating tomorrow."

The room of worship was a large, circular space that housed a massive, yellow crystal—the Order's purpose for being on Illthdar Isle. A semi-circular dome of windows that faced the eastern cliffs went from the ceiling to dirt floor. The crystal, half sunk in the ground was surrounded by a raised, wooden platform. Octagonal rods stuck out in all directions, with twists of thorny, multicoloured roses—known as worthy blooms—growing wherever they pleased.
High Priestess Chiyoko claimed a small space near the windows, complete with a kidney-bean-shaped desk. She debriefed teams and held meetings with the High Elders there. Rumours said no lies could be spoken while bathed in the crystal's warm glow.

Zercey's brow pinched at Vyxen's concern. "Were you caught?"
"No," she shook her head, "I don't think so." She drew Zercey to a quiet part of the street. "There's more. They're talking about something called a 'fire drill'." Her expression grew grave. "I don't think they meant they're checking a sprinkler system."
Zercey's face blanched, imagining the worst. She dragged Vyxen into a ditch by the side of the road which acted as a flood barrier. Concealed in the long grasses, she said, "Okay, what did they say exactly?"
"It sounds like hazing." Vyxen worried at her lower lip until she made it bleed. "New recruits get settled in their Order barracks and one of the other Orders 'attacks'," she said, forming air quotes with her fingers. "Since you guys are going into a different Order from me, I found out there are already people watching and listening in on the trainee barracks."
"And that's why you were waiting for someone to come by," Zercey replied, connecting the dots.
Given they had specialised training that day, it was likely trainees would pass their free time in the city.
Vyxen nodded, her face scrunching with disgust. "They want to make sure none of us are traitors."
Zercey thought about how they needed to act. "Okay, so we need a plan to get the others away from the barracks to let them know and

prepare."

Vyxen disagreed. "If there's too many people taken at once others'll notice, and if we keep going back and forth that'll do the same."

They grew quiet as a trio of Acolytes passed, chatting about how much money they lost in a betting pool over the colour of Uwe's Roman toga.

"These people need hobbies," Zercey commented, before turning her attention back to important matters. Without knowing who in which Order would be going after what group, there was no telling what kind of attack to prepare for.

"Everything?" Vyxen suggested, knowing it was a stretch.

"What we need is a red herring," Zercey mused. "Something to throw them off."

"Okay, what?" Vyxen shrugged in a helpless way.

Zercey mirrored her expression, out of ideas.

"Great," Vyxen replied, sarcastic. Silver eyes wandering, they lit on something and she bounced in place. "We could set something on fire!" She pointed to the street lanterns. At the look of horror on her friend's face, she was left to conclude, "Or maybe not…"

"Let's see what happens tomorrow," Zercey suggested, not wanting to go at anything half-cocked. "We may come up with something as people get ready to move."

Vyxen nodded her agreement. "Worst case scenario, I sneak into the lab and cow-tip a table."

Magnilla chipped hardened goo from the ballroom walls, complaining, "I understand us being held accountable for the whole thing going wrong, but it was the people in Quartz who brought the spells. They should be helping."

"We attacked," Nyima countered. Whatever reason for the Orders setting against them, the fact remained their group caused the mess.

Returning from the lab where they handed the refuse to Phanuel to dispose of, Abaddon parked a cart by the doors. When Magnilla came over to dump in armfuls they asked, "How much more is left?"

"Not much," Nyima answered, wiping her brow. They'd been at it for hours, though most of the damage was contained to one third of the room, with annoying specks to pick off further to the middle.

"We're very lucky," Abaddon said. "It could have caught fire and exploded."

"People could have died!" Magnilla exaggerated, annoyed on everyone's behalf. "Which is all the more reason why we shouldn't be the only ones held accountable." The lack of justice irritated her.

Cart loaded, Abaddon was quick to haul it away once more, leaving Nyima to endure Magnilla's ranting.

"Chiyoko has God to thank for the fact I'm so forgiving! I would have her head otherwise." She smoothed strands of blond hair away from her face.

Nyima had no comment. It was the safest thing when dealing with Magnilla. Otherwise she risked demonstrating a bit of head removal herself. She followed orders, and that was all she needed to know. She tried not to care about much else, including whether people got her name right. The Order assumed it was "Teysuht" because the word amplified her magic. By the time she knew enough words to correct them it was too late. So, in the grand scheme of things, who got punished for what stupid action was a small matter. She had greater concerns for Abaddon. They were jumpy and quick to avoid everyone at the first verbal confrontation. *They must be traumatised from some event in their past.* With the language barrier between her and everyone preventing sophisticated conversation, Nyima wasn't sure what she could offer Abaddon to help. Her own history gave her empathy, but that alone wouldn't do much unless she could speak of it. *I must try harder to learn this stupid language.* She might have taken the chance to practice with Magnilla, but previous attempts all ended with Nyima feeling shamed and embarrassed. No, she needed to find a better person to converse with, who wouldn't treat her like an idiot because she mixed up tenses or needed to pause and translate in her head before answering.

Some hours later, with most of the goo cleared up, the trio eased aching backs and rolled tense shoulders.

"If I never see a sticky trap spell again for the rest of my life it'll be too soon!" Magnilla tossed her scraper into the cart.

On the other side of the room, Nyima and Abaddon took down the ladder they used to reach higher spots.

"And I'm not about to let this go, either," she continued, when they said nothing. "I'm going to investigate and prove those guys were at fault—there's no way they'll escape justice, so long as I have anything to say about it."

"You do," Nyima murmured, too tired to attempt politeness. "It done now." She shrugged, expression conveying Magnilla should let it go. The words sounded closer to revenge than justice.

"I agree," Abaddon said, making their way to the door. "There's no more training, either, so we have to work with these people." They half-turned to look in Magnilla's general direction. "I-if you, um, antagonise them it could be bad." Changing the subject, their expression brightened. "But at least now we can rest for a bit."

"Actually, no," Magnilla decreed, faux regretful. "We need to take a turn on watch."

Nyima disagreed. "We not Acolytes. Ruined the test."

Magnilla was resolute. "*I* think we've passed and *I'm* not going to let anyone say otherwise. We protected our comrades and thwarted an impending assault from a legion with only *five people.* Under normal circumstances we shouldn't be punished for doing what we were trained to do!" Her emerald eyes blazed with righteous fury.

Abaddon smiled at the way Magnilla depicted their actions; it made them sound like heroes. Which was nice after spending the day feeling like failures.

CHAPTER FIVE

E lsewhere, the two-person search party fared better than expected. Zercey was terrible at disguising her tracks, even with the rain washing them away.

"I don't know if I want to laugh or feel sorry for her," Vyxen admitted, as she read the story of muddy smears, broken branches and a discarded rosebud. "Her night looks bad enough to be funny."

"I'm certain there will be much laughter when she tells it," Scy replied, taking the role of lookout.

"*Kaa,* I take it back. It was a bad night for all of us," Vyxen said in a grave tone. She raised her hand, showing blood on her fingers. Scyanatha's brow furrowed with concern. "Poor dear, but it doesn't look like much. Where to now?"

Vyxen placed her feet in faint imprints. "Well, it looks like she came this way, which is weird." She pointed to a spot away from the path. It was the first instance of Zercey not sticking to it.

"This cluster of rocks is a warning not to go this way." Scy paused by a cypress tree and held her hand up palm out. Her obsidian beaded bracelets slipped down her arm, clicking together.

"What are you doing?" Vyxen tipped her head to the side.

"Greeting the tree spirit," she replied, smiling. "Let's continue. The tree cover should make it easier going."
Vyxen paused to copy the gesture, and caught up.

Scyanatha was wrong. As the sky lightened, their pace slowed, hindered by thick mud. At times, they were forced to follow Baya and Laurelium into the trees or risk sticking. *At least we got rid of that annoying golem. "Sophisticated." The only way that could be mistaken for Zercey is if she were blind drunk and walked with a limp. It was fortunate the Acolytes on the wall weren't a bit interested in what we were doing. Pity. One was quite fetching.*
"It's times like these I wish I were an elf," she declared, as they shimmied up a tree to cross a boggy part of the forest.
"Huh? Why?" Vyxen was already leaping after Baya onto the next branch.
"They can levitate over running water, snow and mud." Scy spread her arms wide, crouched and leapt.
"Wow! Kinda makes me wish Phanuel wasn't such a douche-bag, so I could ask him about it, but he'd probably use it as a chance to say something dumb." Vyxen grinned, and descended the trunk. "It's drier over here."
"Yes, and there's few faery markers," Scy replied, pleased. "Greenwood forest is one of the safer locations on Illthdar, so it's unlikely the previous one was warning of anything malevolent. It could be a territory boundary."
"So, we're safe around here?" Vyxen looked about with interest. The forest looked no different to the one back home, and she knew hunting parties went in because she'd overheard Teysuht volunteering.
Home. Alaska felt a million miles away. Even with the weather cooling, it was too warm to fool her she was out in her woods. *Dad would have loved this. He'd have made it into one of his stories and thrown in a bunch of scary monsters—scarier than what I've seen already, that is.* Her mouth downturned and she shook her head. She needed a distraction before her happy-go-lucky mask cracked. "You know, Teysuht said it, but it's true. It's hard being human here. We're told we need to suck it up or we're no better than monster bait. My family hunts and gathers already, so I had a leg up over other people, but it's still hard sometimes."

"You're very good at hiding it, dear," Scy remarked, eyes widening at the small confession. "I would never have known if you hadn't told me."

They reached the crest of the hill and looked down at more trees with a small clearing. "Looks like Zercey headed that way." Scy pointed, marching ahead.

"Miigwech," Vyxen thanked her for the compliment, though it was a bittersweet. She'd been successful in throwing off the depressed and sobbing state she'd been in when she arrived like it was an old cloak. But, she hadn't forgotten the girl who wanted to go home. Along with other girls—and boys and the rest—who did, too. "Let's find her and help get her back on track!"

"Of course!" Scyanatha chirped. "And who knows, perhaps this is just what Zercey—and you—needed to encourage your mana to flow."

"I don't think I have any—not like how you mean," Vyxen replied. She'd been trying to do magic in secret, and failed. Despite wanting to go home, she also wanted to say she was a real faery, like Tinkerbell, when she got there.

"When children are first taught, they fail," Scy stated, pushing her way through some thick bushes, and pausing to help Vyxen. Above them, the veiko cooed and leapt to the east, helping them locate where Zercey's tracks disappeared and reappeared. "In a pinch miracles can happen, but control is achieved through meditation and practice."

Vyxen pulled a face. "Meditation?" She stuck her finger down her throat. "Me and sitting still aren't friends."

Scy tittered. "You may find the first time you access your power is by accident."

"That sounds more like me!" Vyxen giggled, waving to the veiko. "Yes, we're coming!"

The pair grew silent, as they helped each other down an incline, stopping to brush their hands clean at the bottom.

"What about you, Scy? What are your people like? What *is* an aos si?"

Scyanatha smoothed some wayward strands of red hair and smiled. "The aos si are better known as the daoine sidhe—" She paused when Vyxen's eyebrows lifted. "You know them? That's interesting," she added under her breath. "Anyway, my father's side of the family hail from Scotland—the same place your ancestors originate." She recalled Vyxen telling them she had a Native American mother and a Scottish father. "The lore surrounding my people is vast and not all stories are accurate." There was a pause as they navigated around fallen trees, pulled from the roots like weeds.

"So, what are *your* people like?" Vyxen reiterated.

"The falloy and puca are part of the Unseelie court," Scy replied, evasive. She was proud to be her parents' daughter, but she didn't want the politics that came with royal status. Not least because she sensed Chiyoko waited for it.

Vyxen opened her mouth, then stopped and dropped to her haunches. "New tracks."

Scyanatha stared where Vyxen pointed. "Whose?"

"These ones here met up with Zercey's there." Her arm swept across the area. "No struggle, but there was a meeting. Her feet sank in the mud."

Scy squinted at the spot, a memory of something trying to work its way up from the murky depths. The problem with being as old as she was she tended to forget things after a time unless reminded often. It was wonderful when bad things happened—sooner or later she wouldn't remember it—but when she needed information it frustrated. Tipping her head back, she noted how daylight filtered through the trees; it was well past metelaf and on the way to undernmete. They hadn't even stopped to nibble their rations. "Where did she go after?"

Vyxen traced the path and said, "That way." She looked at Scy, concerned. "Do you think she's okay?"

"We shall ask when we catch up," Scy replied, helping her up. "If we eat on the way we'll save some time." She opened the flap on her satchel and pulled out a cloth wrapped parcel.

"Oh, yum! Have you got any cookies?" Vyxen bounced on her toes like an overexcited child.

Scy laughed. "I have your granola bars, a few pieces of tack and some dried jerky courtesy of Teysuht."

"I call dibs on the granola!" Vyxen took it and broke it in two. "Here, it's good."

"Thank you, dear." They shared the rest of the food as they walked, passing a clay tankard of water between them. "If they stopped to rest, this should enable us to catch up."

"I hope so. I don't wanna be walking the woods in the dark, even if you did say it's safer here." Vyxen glanced around, imagining creepy things stalking her.

"Safer, but not safe," Scy corrected. "Greenwood has its dangers, like anywhere else." She paused and whistled to summon Munin, her corvazneo: a purple feathered, raven-like bird with glowing red eyes. "Look for a group of people," she said, waving it off again. Munin cawed and flew away, cutting through the trees and merging with shadows.

Vyxen faked a cheerful laugh. "That's reassuring!"

"It's not meant to be, dear," Scyanatha replied, tone reminding Vyxen that Illthdar wasn't a faerytale from her childhood stories. It was very real and *very* dangerous. "No matter what happens in the future, you must remember not to go off by yourself."

Vyxen's brows came together. "Err, *ehn*, okay." She shrugged, deciding it was better to agree, than argue. Behind her back she crossed her fingers. If a chance came up to go home, she'd take it. Even if that meant ditching Las and everyone she knew.

After a short conversation with Chiyoko, in which she agreed they shouldn't sit about, Abaddon and Nyima headed outside the mighty walls of the city.

Once, farmland fit inside the U that protected the north, east and west sides of Las. The city was little more than a playground estate, with plots of land to provide sustenance for those who lived and worked within.

War and illness brought people in droves to the gates, seeking sanctuary. The population swelled, and huts now stood wall-to-wall within. With a lack of trade goods and only a religious order as its main attraction, funds to build a secondary barrier weren't available. Warm, but overcast, the clouds threatened more rain to come later. Abaddon stretched their arms above their head, enjoying what might be the last humidity before winter set in for good. They had their hood on to protect them from the worst of the wind that tried to sneak under their cloak. "I hope everything goes back to normal soon," they commented, brows furrowing. They initially thought having Magnilla and Zercey make up would be enough, but they weren't technically at odds. To Abaddon, they both were who they were, yet Zercey seemed to be of the mind that Magnilla should be less than herself, because it didn't fit with her view of how someone should be. It was funny, usually, they were the subject of prejudice because of their species or gender, but among the women they were accepted, and Magnilla was the outcast because of her personality. *Very strange, but I enjoy not being on the outside for once.*

"It will," Nyima replied matter-of-factly, drawing them from their thoughts.

She sounds so sure. "How are you so sure? Isn't there something we can do to help?"

Nyima moved away from Abaddon. "Wait," she said, forming an orb of pure mana in her right hand. The gold glow was eclipsed by a shell of blue and she threw it towards a furtive figure appearing at the edge of the fields to their left. *"Teysuht!"* The orb split apart, turning into spears of ice.

The would-be thief turned tail and fled, screaming as he was caught by jagged edges. "People do as want," she stated, returning to their side. She waved a hand in the direction of the thief, to illustrate her point.

Zercey frowned at the non-answer. *It could be a sapling!*
Seeing her unmoving, Lerki put his hand in the centre of her back and urged her forward. "The shadows lengthen, and your hair still has not finished brightening."
Zercey blinked. *My what?* "My *what?*" She grabbed the trailing end of her ponytail and pulled it over her shoulder. She looked at Lerki. She looked at her hair again. She screamed, "What did you do to me?!" She fisted her other hand in the front of his poncho and yanked his face towards hers. "What in the *hell* did you do to me?!"
"I didn't do anything," he answered, voice soft.
"My hair doesn't change colour all on its own!" She wanted to keep screaming, but he looked like a beaten puppy. She drew in a breath and let it out, asking in a calmer voice, "Why is my hair turning green?"
"Resonance?" he questioned, shoulders rising.
Bullshit. "You're playing dumb. You just said my hair hasn't finished brightening." She released him, putting hands on hips. *Like a mother scolding a child.* "Lerki, why is my hair green?"
"Ah, I think—" he began, straightening up. He shook his head and tried again. "No, I *know* it is resonance."
"What's resonance?" She crossed her arms. *Santa Maria, what is this?*
"All venin hum in harmony with each other," he explained, green brows pinching. "If one separates for too long, they fall out of tune. Like plants without nourishment, they wilt and lose their colours. Upon return they resonate once more and..." he trailed off with an awkward hand gesture towards her hair.
"So, it's temporary," she concluded, calming. "That's a relief." Her lips quirked. "You could have just said that to start with."
"I did not think you would," he confessed. "When it started, I was curious to see how far it would go."
"Great. Non-human eyes and hair. Way to go me," she replied, cheer sardonic and lacklustre. "So, what are we doing next?"
"We—" Lerki began, but was cut short by a sudden commotion near the fire.
Whirling to face it, Zercey peered around him. The fire went out, and the rest of the venin scrambled to move pack animals and scurry behind trees.

95

"Something comes," he started, spinning to face her. He snatched her wrist and dragged her towards a large, knotted oak.

"Wait, what are we doing?" *We can't possibly be hiding behind a tree?!* She found herself pressed between the rough trunk and Lerki's less rigid, lean frame. One of his arms came around her shoulders and the other rested against the crown of her head. "L-lerki – " she started, a furious blush staining her cheeks.

"Shh, take a deep breath and hold it," he instructed in a low voice. The second she did, he pressed into her, hard. She could feel every line of his body, from his compacted torso, to his muscled thighs and the prominent bulge in between. She wanted to punch him. She wanted to squeal. All she did was widen her eyes at the feeling of the tree behind softening. Her body passed through with all the resistance of a warm spoon pushed into a tub of gelato. *Oh my God.* The spongy fibres parted to draw them in. Zercey glanced sideways, eyes going wide. The gradient circles of the tree's growth rings shifted and warped. It was like looking through a kaleidoscope. The rings wavered inward. The tree closed around them. It grew darker. In the dim, flickers of light appeared. *It glitters.* It was like staring into the heart of the universe. Then everything went dark.

In nearby part of the forest, Vyxen froze in her tracks. "What was that noise?"

Scyanatha stopped. "That is familiar, but I can't recall—" It sounded like someone rolling in bubble-wrap, then igniting a blow torch. "A fire elemental." It was the bubble-wrap that did it. Gaseous pockets erupted on the skin of some sub-species and set alight. "They tend to keep away from forests. I wonder why one is here."

"Ohh, yay! Any ideas?" Vyxen cheered, sarcastic, readying her bow.

"You distract it while I try to trap and smother it in rock," Scy suggested.

"Bait," Vyxen translated with a groan.

The popping-whoosh sound grew louder.

"How fast do you think you can do it?" Vyxen prepared to run. She signalled with her hands for the veiko to take sentry positions on either side of a small clearing ahead.

There came a tell-tale, egg-like stench of sulphur, wafting on a warm jet of air.

"Ew." Vyxen waved her hand in front of her face.

"Hmm," Scy estimated, looking around for resources and calculating available mana. "A couple of minutes." She erred on the side of caution. She also couldn't resist making Vyxen sweat a little by overestimating. Wine coloured eyes laughing, she asked, "Can you keep it busy that long?"

"Well, shit, I guess I'll have to," Vyxen replied, running into the open, as a briar thicket on the far side of the glade burst into flames. Notching an arrow, she whistled. "Hey, ash head! Over here!" She released the string. Her aim was excellent, but the elemental swatted it like a twig. "You've got two minutes!" She snagged a low tree branch and hauled herself onto it. She climbed higher when the elemental charged and body-slammed the trunk. There was nothing left of the elemental to reason with; another victim of *waste*. The fate of all who endured the mana famine too long. Consumption: a silent killer. Horrifying to watch, once it revealed itself. It had no cure. Mindless zombies trudged the fields, attacking until put down.

Symptoms began small: a shorter temper, more prone to violence. One could write it off as a bad day. A bad day which never ended.

Pain hit. Mind numbing. Crippling. Body bending pain struck without cause. When the torment ended, it didn't. Their minds were destroyed. Living corpses with a single desire: mana. They destroyed everything in their path to get it until their bodies burned out and collapsed. Dead.

Scyanatha entered the clearing. She traced a pattern with her finger in the air. Her gaze was on the elemental, but her attention was fixed on the earth. She sniffed back tears that wanted to cloud her eyes. She had no time to mourn. She could when it was at peace. She hadn't often seen faeries reach this point; she'd been trapped on the other side of the veil once the mana waned. Those few on Earth were friends or loved ones, members of the Unseelie court too stupid and arrogant not to see they risked their lives in a world with no mana. This elemental did nothing to deserve this. It was unlucky.

A panicked cooing caught her ear and Scy saw Vyxen dive from the tree, rolling in the long grass.

"Any time today, Scy!" She brushed hot embers from her hair and scurried away.

"Yes," Scyanatha murmured, waiting for the elemental to stomp closer. "I'm ready."

The ground still damp from the rain. Scy clasped her hands together, ripped them down and apart. A hole opened in front of the elemental and it fell in with a wet sucking sound, punctuated by slaps as it tried to climb out. Tearful, Scy swallowed the lump in her throat, clenching her fists and drawing them down.

The elemental flailed.

Opening her hands, Scyanatha mimed tucking a child into bed. A wave of mud rose over the elemental's head, covering all, but a hand. Its fingers uncurled, reaching out to her. "I hope you find peace," she whispered, covering it again. The grassy mound struggled, heaving shuddering breaths. It grew still. Scy put her hand to her mouth to hold back a sob. Arms wrapped around her waist.

"I'm sorry," Vyxen whispered, unsure how to console her.

Scy sniffed, gathering herself. "We are not to blame for this, we simply have to fix it."

"I know," Vyxen agreed, nodding solemnly. "We will."

A raven-like bird flew down and perched on a nearby rock.

"Munin? You found something?" Vyxen's eyes widened. "Zercey?!"

Scy smiled. "It seems things are looking up."

CHAPTER SIX

The entire Order of Mana, bar Quartz, gathered in the room of greeting. Feet shuffled. Someone coughed. Conversations overlaid raucous laughter. Others placed bets on why they'd been called. Weapons clinked against each other, along with whispered apologies. It was hot and stifling. Tempers frayed. Elders silenced arguments.

On the room's fringe, sequestered by the stairs stood Magnilla, Abaddon and Nyima.

Magnilla sighed, impatient. "This is taking forever. I thought it was urgent?"

Nyima shrugged. She inched away from the person beside her and flapped her hand in front of her face.

The jovial chatter stilled.

"I think Chiyoko is coming now," Abaddon murmured, as the crowd quietened.

Chiyoko stood atop the short flight of steps, bookended by the High Elders and Elders. She banged her staff against the floor for silence. "Outposts seven and four report forces gathering to the north in Greenwood Forest. Hundreds, poised like a blooded spear at the dragon's side. The Crystal and all in Las are under imminent

got the impression Seth spoke whatever thought was on his mind. "Who is Date?"

"He's a tengu in Quartz."

Abaddon nodded, familiar with crow-demons, but not that specific one. "He will be part of the sneak attack?"

Seth nodded, rolling one shoulder and making it crack. "Yeah."

The faint sounds coming from the forest grew. From the sentries came a combination of yells and horns blowing to sound the alarm. The horde arrived.

Acolytes screamed, rushing forward. It seemed like someone jumped in before given orders, resulting in an off-balance strike. Archers waited for enemies to get in range before loosing their arrows, but the uneven attack from their side meant they risked hitting their own people.

Weapons clashed. Faeries, demons and everything in between roared or screamed to the heavens. The valley filled with bloodlust and fury. Death walked the battlefield, claiming on both sides. Thunder clapped, and it rained hailstones and fireballs. Pits opened underfoot. Cracks split the earth. Stone slabs protected and crushed.

"GAAAAAAAHHHHH!" Abaddon's voice was unearthly, demonic. Heat pulsed and swirled around them with each rotation of their axe. They cleaved foes left and right, using the same tactic they had in the ballroom. This time with deadly precision. Blood dripped from them as they moved through the horde. They felt no peace, no hesitation. There was all consuming rage. It ruined and twisted metal, tore sinew and brought stone and bone to dust. The bloody ground marked their passage in shades of red, blue, white, orange and many others. They did not all bleed the same colour, but they all bled.

Sword in one hand, Magnilla used the other to direct and control her magic. Icy blasts made them slip. She finished them off with a leaping stab. She flicked blood off her blade so often it became a reflex. She didn't worry about her rear guard, that was Thijs's job.

Nyima lacked expression. Her movements controlled and economical. She flicked her fingers. Someone died. She pivoted to avoid attacks, brought a hail of ice on their head. They died. She didn't care for any of it. She followed orders and did her job. The ice was all she needed.

"Zercey!" Voices came behind thick foliage.

After passing out, Zercey woke to find the reason for the panic passed and her friends were closing in. The first to locate her was Laurelium, who clung to her legs like a koala.

"Scy?! Vyxen!" She shuffled forward with Laurelium still nuzzling and cooing.

The pair fought their way through the brush and Zercey blinked at the sight of them. Vyxen was covered in dust and had leaves stuck in her hair. Baya completed the picture, sat on her feet, hopping off when he got mud on his rump. Scyanatha had smears of mud staining her black, leather trousers up one side. Her faux-hawk braid was in disarray, with crimson strands going in every direction. "What happened to you?"

"Us?" Vyxen retorted, pointing at Zercey's hair. "What happened to you? What happened to your hair?!"

"We're well," Scyanatha reassured. "Tired and sore, and a few other minor troubles along the way, but otherwise fine."

Zercey managed to peel Laurelium from her back and answered Vyxen's question with, "It's a bit of a long story, but to sum it up the colour is only temporary. I'll be back to my mousy brown before you know it."

Laurelium pecked her shoes.

"You've been resourceful," Scyanatha noted, eyeing the dead fire. "How did you manage to make that without tools?"

"I'd love to take credit," Zercey replied, hugging them in turn, "but it wasn't me. Thanks for coming for me, by the way. I'm sorry I was such a douche last night."

"Yeah, you were," Vyxen stated, with a light punch to Zercey's upper arm. "And we guessed as much. We were following the footprints, so we knew you weren't alone."

As if realising it again, Zercey cast her gaze about, searching for venin to emerge and help.

"The rest have moved on," Lerki informed them, reappearing with dead branches for the fire. "I will see them later."

"I did wonder if it was the venin," Scyanatha commented. A smile tugged her lips as she added, "There are not many that travel at dusk in rows of three."

Lerki paused to take in her appearance, then laughed.

Vyxen looked around for the source of the whistling echoes.

"Ah, Falloy, clek-ni gou tavayma. Mygi-tone ra-fa keyntopy," he said, speaking the venin tongue.

Scy shook her head.

Taken aback by the peculiar language, Vyxen leaned over to whisper in Zercey's ear. "What did he say?"

"I know *of* you, but I do not *know* you. You will have to say it in Illthdarian, mister...?" Scyanatha's brows rose, waiting.

"You are wise. I think that's something that is good to have," he translated, ignoring her question.

Zercey took the time to introduce them. Gesturing with her hand towards each person in turn, she said, "Scy, Vyxen, this is Lerki; Lerki, this is Scyanatha and Vyxen. They're my teammates. So, I guess this is where we part ways?"

"Wind takes the rest on, but Earth has made a path for me that is different. I will follow, I think, to Las," Lerki replied, grinning. Reaching out, he plucked a leaf from Vyxen's hair and placed it into her palm. "A leaf like on my tree. It is very lucky; you should keep it."

"Huh, okay..." she replied, holding it up for closer inspection. It looked like a normal birch leaf, though one side was gold and the other standard green. Shrugging, she tucked it into a secret pocket of her outfit. "I don't think it's safe to travel at night," she said, pointing to the dark sky. "We might as well make use of that fire pit if there's any good embers left. We've been on the move since this morning trying to catch up with you and could use a rest."

"Sorry." Zercey grimaced. "I suck."

"Don't worry, dear. We received Chiyoko's approval to take you to the venin. In a way, this has made things easier. Returning with Lerki, she will make her own conclusions."

On hearing his and Chiyoko's names mentioned together, Lerki's smile grew strained.

Catching it, Scyanatha's brow quirked in silent question, as she presented Zercey with the white rosebud thrown away the night before.

Chagrined, Zercey said, "I really, really don't deserve you guys. You cover for me after my hissy fit, spend a whole day tracking my sorry butt down, you give me my stuff back...You guys are great friends."

"You can thank me with cake," Vyxen joked, giving her another hug.

"It's a good thing you collected wood, Lerki," Scy said, looking about the small campsite with a critical eye. "We've a little left from our provisions, but it will be a sparse meal."

"I have food," Lerki volunteered. "Dried logoi meat. I traded for it."

Zercey's brows furrowed, but she refrained from commenting. Logoi was a form of cattle kept by farmers. They were best described as the result of bison mating with moose: wide, large racks of horns upon a bulky, hulking, quadruped with split hooves. Lerki might have traded for it at some point, but he could have poached.

He went on to add, "And some dried honey sap berries. There is also," his nose scrunched up to indicate he didn't think much of the option, "pezzat greens."

The women chuckled at his clear distaste.

It was still dark when Lerki tried rousing everyone after a sparse meal and early rest. "Hey, hey, pst! Wake up."

Vyxen and Zercey woke, and scrambled for their weapons.

Scy was less frantic, noting the companions still slept. It wasn't urgent. "What is happening?"

Lerki swung into view from a tree, landed and said, "Something strange. Earth tells of many animals fleeing this way. Wind speaks of many cries from where they came."

"Huh?" Vyxen rubbed the sleep from her eyes, and checked to see if the others were as clueless as she.

"The elements say things like that a lot," Zercey explained, shrugging.

"They're not as off as you might think," Scyanatha said, crouching and closing her eyes. She steepled her fingers on the ground. "I can feel the tremors he's talking about." Dark red eyes opening once more, she looked towards her teammates, expression troubled. "Coming from Las."

"What are we waiting for, then?" Vyxen stood, stuffing supplies into her pack. "The sooner we get there, the sooner we can help."

Breaking camp and about to depart, Lerki paused. He made a strange humming sound and a creature that looked like a cross between a wasp and a spider appeared. It had six legs, multiple red eyes and a poisoned stinger on a yellow and brown striped body. It flew over and settled on his shoulder.

"Ohhh no," Zercey said, staring with wide eyes. She laughed, "You *cannot* bring that back to Las."

"My eitercopp? I can't?" He paused in bending to pick up a small shoulder sack with his cloak draped over it.

"We have a friend who is arachnophobic," Scy volunteered.

"Ah..." Lerki replied, nodding. "That is okay then; it is not a spider." Turning, he raised his glowing caterpillar lantern and said, "Come this way."

Zercey bit her lip and tried to contain her sniggers. She shot a look at Vyxen, who winked.

Scyanatha shook her head. "Magnilla will not be happy if she sees that thing," she reminded them. "It isn't funny, Zercey," she scolded, catching sight of the big grin on her face.

"Oh yes, it is," Zercey laughed and rubbed her hands together. Scyanatha ignored her, chalking up Zercey's bad spirit to jealousy.

"Kaa," Vyxen disagreed. "It's not funny, *it's hilarious!"*

"You had best keep it hidden," Scy cautioned Lerki. "Otherwise it stands a very good chance of becoming ash or a shattered pile of ice."

"It isn't a spider," Lerki protested, oblivious to the similarities.

"It's close enough. Trust me on this," Scy replied in a firm voice. She shook her head at her two cohorts, who tried to keep from laughing, with only Vyxen succeeding. Though, her shoulders could be seen shaking.

For a time, they travelled in relative and amiable silence, until they were spied by Quartz scouts.

"State your business!" ordered one, dropping from the trees and brandishing a dagger at Vyxen. Others appeared in the same manner, shoving pointy weapons in everyone's faces.

She rolled her eyes. "Oh, cut it out, Basil, you know who we are."

"You could be shapeshifters, posing as people who are supposed to be away on missions," he replied. He was quick to add in a slightly snotty and lisping voice, "And my name is *Basilisk!"*

"Oh, yeah, sure it is," Vyxen retorted, sarcasm biting.

"We sensed something amiss and returned early," Scy answered, batting a sword tip away with her hand. "Now, tell us what is going on here?"

Before any could reply, someone commanded, "Put those away, you idiots. If they were up to something, they would have done it by now."

"Finally, someone with sense!" Vyxen commented, tossing her hands in the air.

A man in black stepped from the shadows. He had black feathers for hair, slate coloured eyes and an impressively large nose. "We don't have time for this," he stated in a cross voice. He caught sight of Lerki and squawked, "And *you* were supposed to be back nearly a moon ago!"

"I'm sorry, Date, but Wind—" Lerki began, but Date sliced a hand through the air, cutting him off.

"Save it for Phanuel when he takes it from your wages. You ill-gotten son of a rot-log—you've been gone almost seven moons, or did you not notice? Did you think *we* wouldn't notice?" His brows pinched as he glowered.

Zercey crossed her arms and stared at Lerki. "You're an Acolyte? We could have done with that bit of information sooner." *This is why he knows Illthdarian.*

Lerki, for his part, had the decency to smile sheepishly. "I *am* sorry, Date," he apologised again. "It took longer than expected to resonate—" He stopped mid speech when Date repeated the cutting action.

"No time for this. Las is under attack and we're trying to find a way around the enemy forces. We've lost too many people as it is." He drew in a sharp breath before continuing. "The other Acolytes are holding the wall. The whole of Quartz is here, but we can't get into battle formation and wage a counter assault. This fucking forest is ruining everything, and Las will be overridden before daybreak."

"What resources do we have?" Zercey blurted, trying to think of something to help. "How come you keep getting separated?"

"There's spinner traps set all over the bloody forest," another Acolyte cut in, scowling. "We get turned around without notice. Next thing everyone's been yanked all over the place."

"We're locating and disarming them thanks to companions, but it's a slow process," Date explained. "My unit flies, so we've avoided tripping them, but others aren't so lucky."

111

"See?" Lerki directed to Vyxen. "I told you leaves from trees like mine are lucky. We could have walked into one, but we came without a problem."

Vyxen frowned and pulled the leaf from her pocket. "How reliable is that?" *Would it help me find a way home?*

"Very effective," he replied, before addressing the Quartz Acolytes. "Find gold birches and get as many leaves as you can, then find the rest of your people. The leaves are strong against traps."

"Gold birch," Scy exclaimed, raising a hand to touch her forehead. "Of course! It's an old remedy against illusions and disorientation."

"All right," Date said, nodding and turning to the remaining members of his party. "You heard Lerki. Get to it!" Moving closer he said in an undertone, "You better hope for your Fluorite ass you're right."

"I am," Lerki replied, confident.

Date addressed the women. "Which Orders are the rest of you in?"

"Quartz," Vyxen supplied, pretending to gag. "Scy and Zercey are Jasper."

"Beggars can't be choosers," Date muttered, shaking his head. "Jaspers are known for being reckless. What are your skills; anything we could actually use right now?"

Zercey replied for the group. "Vyxen's trained like you, and Scy shape-shifts, as well as earth and air magic." Sighing, she added, "And, my hair changes colour. If you can come up with something I can do with that I'll shake your hand."

"Earth knows," supplied Lerki, responding to Date's bland stare in Zercey's direction. "She is from Sungiphi—she has to be. Only one Zercey went through the veil, and she was a strong *Sancata*. With resonance, she may surprise us yet."

"Lerki, I'm five percent venin at best," Zercey pointed out, not holding much hope she would be anything remarkable. "The only surprising thing I'll be doing is not falling on my face."

Date nodded, hair feathers ruffling. "Like she said. What happens if she's just another barely-fae?"

Looking on the bright side, Lerki answered, "If not, at least I will not need to travel so much with another venin around."

"All right," Date responded, smacking his lips and rubbing his hands together. "Are there seeds in your bag?"

"Always," Lerki replied, cheerful and lifting the flap on his satchel. "What do you need?"

"Nothing yet. Just taking stock," he said, before addressing Scy. "You're Unseelie. How strong are you?"

"That depends on what you'd like me to do," she replied, a Mona Lisa smile touching the edges of her lips.

"Shift shape and blend into their ranks?"

Zercey made a giant X with her arms. "What?! No!"

Vyxen agreed. *"Kaa,* that's insane! What if she gets caught!?"

Scyanatha ignored them. "I can. Is there something specific you have in mind?"

Howls and wails ricocheted across the midnight painted plains. It was never ending. Soldiers fell, left groaning and twitching. Others returned to the safety of Las. Magic users dropped to their knees, mana spent.

On the waves came. Giants uprooted trees and swung them like mighty clubs. Whole battalions flung for miles. Others swooped overhead, firing arrows or unleashing magical blasts.

Minutes stretched to hours, and the rising moon crested its peak. On its descent the sky turned red, and the sun made gains on the horizon.

Citizens fled, heading for the Order. Beyond the tower, a sheer cliff with turbulent waters. There was nowhere else to run if the enemy breached the walls.

The Fluorite Order barricaded the doors and gathered around the crystal of Vvekw. They would give their lives for it and the High Priestess if they had to. Phanuel remained inside to lead, since Chiyoko's focus was the crystal. Culvers, Uwe and their Elders fought alongside the Acolytes outside. The whole of Amber Order got conscripted to serve as Chiyoko and Crystal Vvekw's guards. Chiyoko curled her fingers into claws, causing the blooms around the crystal to tighten. "They will not take it," she muttered. "They will fall before they have the chance."

"Jingyi!" Seth sprinted towards a figure in black and baby blue. He was trying to push himself up using a boulder, but it was slick with blood and he kept slipping. "Are you all right?" He looped an arm under his and pulled him up.

"I've got nothing left," Tundra replied, voice muffled by the half-mask he wore. He flinched, sky blue eyes trying to focus and ignore the pain. His leg was twisted in an unnatural angle. "How you doing?" he said, attempting to distract himself.

"My axe is broken, but otherwise I'm good. I'm doing better than you, dumbass. How the fuck did that happen?" He gestured at the broken limb.

"Giant clipped me," Tundra said, hopping a couple of steps. "A couple of wolves took it down before it could have another go."

"It's almost dawn," Seth noted, dark brown skin grimy with sweat. "How do you think Date's done?"

The pair moved to the wall, navigating around bodies and injured

114

Acolytes.

"If they've done anything, I haven't seen it." Sombre, Tundra scoured the torn landscape. The valley would never be the same after this. *Yesterday there were crops over there. People were farming. Now look at it.* "We're not going to be able to hold out much longer."

"I know." Seth shook his head, earring clinking. The image painted across the valley wasn't pleasant. In their efforts to protect the city, many exhausted themselves, succumbing to *waste*.

What started as a war against strangers was turning into one where Seth dispatched former friends and colleagues to the next life.

For Acolytes like Jingyi—better known as Tundra—who were skilled assassins even before they came to Illthdar, the challenge came in facing off against full-bloods. They had the advantage of being stronger, faster and all-around better. The reminders never stopped him from kicking their asses.

The sun passed over the horizon. The morning was bitter, with a foul stink in the air. Putrid.

Those that could, took refuge on the walls. Those that couldn't remained in the valley, battling futility or stared at the coldness of their own eternity.

Swearing profusely, having to stop to take out the odd charging demon or fae, Seth went about setting Tundra's leg. "We're not going to survive this," he muttered, losing hope. "The archers are almost out of arrows."

"So? We'll get slingshots and beat them back with rocks," Tundra retorted, clamping his jaws shut as his leg crunched. He held back the contents of his stomach through force of will.

"I can't believe you didn't want me to put you out first," Seth said, shaking his head at his friend's resilience.

"I was expecting you to be faster about it," he shot back, panting. "Help me, so I can sit on the wall. While I still breathe, I'm going to be fighting."

"You're a lunatic," Seth muttered, but helped him onto the battlements. Peering down, he observed, "Up here, no one can tell the difference between *consumed* and not."

"The archers focus on what's coming out of the forest. The more they take out at a distance, the fewer need to be hacked apart by the berserkers," Tundra explained, swiping his brow. The action didn't go unnoticed.

"You've got an infection, idiot. Why did you let me do the work on your leg? You could get blood poisoning. We need to move you where healers can treat you properly." He made to help Tundra up again.

"No." Tundra shook his head. "Let them focus on the worst cases first."

"You are one of the worst cases!" Seth hissed through his teeth. "Sheer pig-headedness!"

"Back at you," Tundra replied in a monotone. He jerked his head towards the fighting. "You're going back down there."

Seth clicked his tongue and looked away, guilty.

Tundra smirked. "I'm right. You just haven't figured out how to say it, or where you're going to get a weapon, so you aren't cannon fodder."

Seth rubbed the back of his neck, orange eyes smouldering like coal embers, in contrast with his dark complexion. Wagging a finger, he pointed out, "You're pretty annoying. Also right, but still pretty annoying."

Tundra chuckled.

Seth looked at the valley again. "I should sweep the place clean with a sandstorm; start over from scratch again with whatever remains."

"Is that how your ancestors did it?" Tundra said, referring to Seth's home in Egypt.

"I wouldn't put it past them; obviously someone in my line had the power. If I'm weaker than them, I'd hate to see how a full-blood does it." It was his last resort. Call up a storm and hope it was enough to take out whatever remained of the horde. "Let's do this."

Determined to hold her defensive line, Nyima was reaching her limits at the base of the wall. She'd thrown ice spears, blasted people in the face and flash froze body parts. She protected herself with icy walls and when she ran out of mana for that, a shield. She'd done everything she could think of with her power to stop them. Still they came.

Relying on her weaker melee skills, she manifested a jagged ice sword. The curves and hooks perfect for ripping into skin and

116

tearing through flesh. She struck, she moved on. She hit hard enough, so no one came a second time. *I will not die in this place! I refuse!*

Barefoot and ignoring the squelch between her toes, she picked her way through the thinning horde. A veteran, she could tell when the tide turned in her side's favour. They had a long way to go, but things were looking up.

She side stepped a shambling *consumed*, drawing her blade in an underarm strike. It caught the nymph in the stomach and stuck. Nyima walked forward and pulled, feeling the blade tear free. The nymph collapsed in a heap, gurgling. She wiped her brow and looked up, shading her eyes from the sun. Clouds gathered, bringing a chill to the air. "Ahh." She sighed with appreciation.

"HHHUUUUAAAAHHH!!" came the otherworldly cry of Abaddon. They showed no sign of slowing. One arm hung limp at their side, but they didn't stop. As testament to the carnage they wrought, long lines of blood splatter covered the walls behind them. It looked like someone went mad with the paint. They weren't alone, several others were also lost to intense blood-rage. Flagging, yet pushing forward, were Magnilla and Thijs. Unlike Abaddon, they'd grown weary with daybreak.

"Where do they keep coming from?" Thijs wheezed. The nearby remnants of a fire faery's maelstrom still burned, sending a fetid stink of roasting meat and brimstone. He'd been on their side, *consumed,* turning on their allies. An ugly way to die. *"I didn't think the forest could hold so many."* He projected the thought to Magnilla.

"There might be a portal or gateway," she reasoned, shaking her fur out. She'd changed forms some time ago, and her pale coat was covered in soot. The stretchy fabric from her outfit, designed to alter its shape to fit, was covered in splashes of multicoloured blood. *"If the city weren't in danger, I'd look for it now."* She shook her head once more. *"This is a disaster!"* It was hard to say where it went wrong. Trained as everyone was—though not to her clan's standards—they should have known how to hold rank. *It's not a lack of desire, but discipline,* Magnilla concluded. A free-for-all with everyone unleashing full force without thought or consideration for others. *"This would never have happened with our clan."*

117

The sky grew overcast and there came a rush of warm air, blowing towards the city like an indrawn breath. For a moment, the world stood still. Then a boom of thunder drowned out all other sounds. Some paused to cover pained ears. The gust of air returned, blowing outward at speed. Lightning split the sky, striking the centre of the horde. Screams rent the air. Unwilling bodies danced to a silent tune. They collapsed, twitching. And looming at the edge of the forest, came a massive, silver wolf. The fierce wind played with the rider's hair, twisting white locks about her head. Taking aim, she fired several arrows, hitting all her targets. Above, a flock of bird-men shot from the canopy. Loud caws blew down those still standing. Arrows finished them off.

"About time," Nyima commented, dropping to one knee. The Quartz Order sneak attack was late. Any longer and there'd be no one alive to sneak up on. She glanced behind and spied Abaddon staggering from a hit by a piece of discarded armour. "Abaddon, you well?" Muscles aching from exhaustion, she made slow progress to them.

"Yes," they replied in a dull voice, expression bleak. Thanks to the blow, they caught an overview of the valley. Gouges split the earth, like a massive clawed hand tore it asunder several times over. It was littered with broken weapons and bodies. It was unrecognisable to what they knew. The shock was enough to extinguish their blood rage. "Are you okay?"

Nyima's brows pinched. She didn't like that word. It had too many meanings and didn't exist in her language. Vague generalisations weren't helpful in her culture, where survival was the best quality one could have. "Yes." She had minor injuries, but nothing life threatening besides low mana.

"That's good," they smiled. "I think Scyanatha is up on the ridge." They pointed to where they'd caught a glimpse of the wolf and rider with their sonar.

"We see," Nyima replied, taking their arm and leaning into them for support.

As they crested the ridge, Vyxen called a greeting, proving Abaddon's guess true. Moments later, Magnilla and her brother arrived.

"I knew it was you," Magnilla declared, stopping in front of them. She retook bipedal form, grimacing a little as her body cracked and twisted. Her fur fell out in clumps and was blown away, catching Abaddon and Nyima's ankles. "What are you doing here?" She flipped her hair over her shoulder, tone reprimanding. Thijs changed shape at her side, though his shifting seemed more painful by his groans and moans.

"Rescuing the rescue party," Vyxen replied with a broad grin. "With a little bit of help from a returning Fluorite we met on the way." Looking at the carnage, she let out a low whistle. "You've been busy."

"Did you find Zercey?" Abaddon said, trying to look non-threatening. They knew they looked frightening covered in a thick layer of murky blood.

"Wow. You really cut loose," Vyxen noted, going for a compliment. "We found her. She's okay, but she's helping another group still in the forest."

"Good," Nyima commented, letting tiredness seep into her voice. She was more pleased to hear Zercey was well than she sounded.

"That's why we came this way," Scyanatha explained, speaking through her elongated snout. Having transformed into a steel wolf per Date's orders, she now lacked enough mana to change back. "We feared the worst with all the Quartz gossip." Taking in the view, she added, "I see why they're concerned."

"It's because there were too many and our forces didn't hold formation," Magnilla responded in a snotty voice. "Warriors of the Thies clan would have been better prepared and never would have broken pattern. We did the best we could with what we had."

"The majority of Quartz were convinced you wouldn't make it until morning," Vyxen said, happy to throw some of them under the bus. "You've done more than that; I'm impressed."

"Were lucky," Nyima said, not wanting to overstate anything.

"You were saying about why you came this way?" Magnilla prompted Scy.

"We need you," she replied, looking from Magnilla to Nyima, Abaddon and Thijs.

"Is it a gateway?" Magnilla hazarded a guess.

"*Kaa,*" answered Vyxen, "doppelgänger."

Doppelgänger had no plural—regardless of numbers. Left alone, they were harmless as anything in Illthdar. When they met others, they grew troublesome.

Doppelgänger had no form. Instead, they hovered like a black spectre, speckled with tiny flecks of light like stars at night. They expanded and contracted in size—one moment the size of a house, the next smaller than a teacup. Forever indecisive about what they were and what they wanted to be. For full-bloods, doppelgänger were lethal. They stole their victims faces, names and memories. Nothing was sacred. By the time they were done, they were you and you were nothing.

In Illthdar very few things terrified quite like a doppelgänger.

Date swooped in for a landing on top of the white wall. He drew in his midnight wings as his feet touched the gangway. Without breaking stride, he stormed over to Seth and punched him on the meaty part of his upper arm. Hard. "Do you have any fucking idea how hard it is to fly in those cursed storms you whip up!?"
Seth laughed. "You were barking, so I thought you wanted a reply."
"My ass you thought that," Date shot back, lips twitching.
"Well, since you're here now," Seth said, cutting out the jokes, "maybe you can convince this idiot to get some help." He directed Date's attention to where Tundra sat on a section of the wall hurling the last remaining potion bombs with a sling shot. His leg hung at a disturbing angle, but he didn't seem bothered. Unless one squinted and noticed the slight wobble in posture and beads of moisture on his brow.
"Gods damn it, Tundra, again..." Date sighed. He hit his forehead with his palm and dragged it down his face. "You're on your own. I need this idiot with me in the forest."
"Kinky," Tundra teased, trying hard not to move. "Go ahead, he was boring me anyway," he said, ignoring them flip him off.
Date grabbed the nearest Acolyte. "Take him to a healer," he said in a stern voice.
"Yes, sir!" The poor newbie didn't know whether to salute or not. Date sighed and turned away from him. "Seth, let's go."

It was a brief flight, filled with the sound of Seth gulping back nausea. They landed at the edge of the forest. Scyanatha and a small group stood a short distance away. "When she said friends, I should have guessed we'd end up with that one," he muttered, eyeing Magnilla with distaste.
"According to Abaddon, she's stubborn, but a good friend," Seth said, shaking out his arms and legs.
"Who is Abaddon?" Date looked, but none was the obvious owner of the name.
"The one who looks like they couldn't be bothered to take their clothes off before showering in the blood of their enemies," Seth quipped. Looking around, he grabbed a pair of sickles from one of the fallen. He strode up to the group and saluted with it, nearly cutting himself. "Afternoon."

"So, you're Seth Storm-Bringer?" Vyxen craned her head back. "You're tall." It was like looking up at her older brother, only less annoying. His dark skin was grimy, blood smearing his bare chest and arms. The leather straps were the only thing on his upper body and provided no protection. He had on trousers, gloves and heavy boots, but looked like the base model in a fantasy role play game before the player equipped armour.

"Some call me that," he replied, puffing his chest out. "And you are?"

"Vyxen," Date introduced at speed. "That's Scyanatha," he nodded to the metal wolf. His dark eyes swept past Magnilla, who stood all the straighter under his gaze in silent challenge. "I know you." Looking towards Thijs he added, "I can guess who you are." Her shadow didn't need an introduction and, Date suspected, if his parents might have forgone naming him completely if it could have been avoided. Moving on, Date addressed Abaddon. "Seth told me about you." He stopped and raised an eyebrow at Nyima. "But, I don't know you."

"Teysuht," she supplied, sticking to the alias for the sake of simplicity.

"Nyima," Abaddon corrected in a firm and loud voice.

Nyima was surprised; the pronunciation wasn't quite right, but the fact they remembered touched her.

"You're Seth's friend?" Abaddon's voice grew soft once more.

"Date Toshiiro of Mount Takao," he supplied, with a formal bow.

"Now we've done the meet and greet can we get going? I thought this was urgent?" Seth said, nudging Date as if it were his fault for the delay.

"I should call everyone 'hey, you'," he replied, rolling his eyes.

"Works with Jingyi," Seth laughed.

Nyima and Abaddon took rear positions; the former was tired and the latter less sure of their footing. Everyone else soldiered ahead at speed.

Date shook his head. "With luck, Lerki will have waited—"

"Whoa, Lerki?" Seth grabbed Date's arm to slow him. "When did he get back?"

"And who is he?" Magnilla asked in irritation. She crossed her arms as she walked and kept sneaking glances at Date to check if he was looking at her. She was annoyed at her introduction. It was beyond rude and when they had time, she'd teach him how to address someone of her status. The way he acted, it was like he couldn't care less who she and her brother were!

"A new friend," Scyanatha replied, jolting Magnilla from her thoughts. "A member of Fluorite."

"An old friend," Seth corrected, "who has a habit of getting sent on missions that he turns into long trips, but otherwise is very handy to have around." He scrubbed a hand over his chin and added, "One of these days, Phanuel's going to nail his feet to the floor."

"If I don't get to him first," Date muttered in dark humour.

Seth chuckled. "Tundra will need him before that."

"Is there a plan?" Magnilla complained in a nasal voice. "Or are you expecting your friend to have one by the time we get there?"

"*Ehn,* of course!" Vyxen said in a cheerful voice. It wasn't a great plan, but it was a plan.

"I expect by the time we get there, the only thing left to do will be to clean up whatever is left. Lerki was confident your friend Zercey would be able to handle it."

"He what?! Oh, for the love of—!" Magnilla shook her head and ran off. Thijs let out a short exclamation and chased after.

"That went well," Seth commented, sending Date a dry look.

"I expected that reaction much sooner," he replied, urging everyone else to pick up the pace and go after them. The wolves were in danger of ruining everything!

CHAPTER SEVEN

❝This is weird." One Zercey spoke and two more copied perfectly.

"This is weird."

"This is weird."

So weird.

They raised their right hand when she did. Tilted their heads in unison with hers. Even blink in time. They learned *fast.*

"So, if I do it, you'll copy me?"

"So, if you do it, you think I'll copy you?"

"So, you think I'll do it if you do?"

Very weird.

The plan was simple. She had to stand there and buy time. The doppelgänger couldn't steal anything important from anyone else if they focused on her. *Easy enough.*

Until one lunged and tried to choke her.

"The irony here hasn't escaped me!" She pried its fingers off and pushed it away. The second took the first's initiative and leapt on her back. Fisting its hand in her hair, it yanked hard.

"It's not irony, this happening was not unexpected!" the first one said, getting up.

"If my friends weren't here, you'd be animal feed!" Magnilla fired ice that scattered into particles, blowing icy fragments across the clearing.

"If you weren't wasting your efforts attacking them instead of me maybe you'd get somewhere!" another mocked, leaping towards a tree trunk and spring-boarding off to tackle one of the others.

Thijs barked, "Fuck all of you! Do as Magnilla said and go away! She's right. She can't beat them with us as hostages."

Affronted, Zercey snapped, "We're not—!" Her words cut off as she was yanked by the collar. A fireball shot past where she'd been standing. She twisted free and glared up at the smug look on Thijs's face.

With a nod to Seth, Date stepped forward and made a show of inhaling.

Lerki squeezed his eyes shut and covered his ears.

Seth punched the air at the same time Date released a deafening shock wave—known as a tengu bark. A fog bank dropped without warning, covering the area in thick mist.

"This won't stop them!" Thijs's sensitive ears hurt from the sound, and he sent another black look Date's way.

"Sure, but with this and Date's shock wave, she'll be down two out of three senses," Seth pointed out, lowering his arm. "Lerki, your turn."

Bringing his hands down, Lerki nodded and returned to his bag, finding what he'd been searching for. Slow and methodical, he went to his knees and dug a small hole in the ground. The contents of his palm went in, and he covered it over, knocking the ground with his knuckles. From the lump in the earth burst a massive, tangling bloom of large, hooded purple flowers. "Wolfsbane." He gave the common name for them, as Thijs coughed.

"Nyima, was it?" Seth turned to her, seeing an opportunity to get rid of Thijs and save the injured woman's pride. "He can't stay here. Can you escort him before he winds up in the infirmary? We've got enough injured, I'm guessing."

Thijs tried to protest, but wound up bent double, wheezing.

Nyima nodded, pushing herself off from the tree and grabbing Thijs's upper arm. "Come." Despite her fatigue, it wasn't hard to pull him along in his current state.

"Arrows, everyone," said Lerki, motioning for archers. Taking their quivers, he scraped the arrowheads against the leaves and stalks of the plant. Passing them back, he cautioned, "Careful, it is poisonous even to non-werewolves."

"So, we have to shoot all three of them?" Vyxen wanted to be sure, eyeing the points of her arrows. "We're not going to kill her with these, are we?"

"Oh, no, no, no," he replied, as his eitercopp crawled down his arm to sample the flower nectar. "It is not enough to kill anyone, unless they fell into water afterwards. It causes paralysis and stomach upset."

"Ah, nuts." Zercey snapped her fingers, feeling jilted.

"I believe Thijs would disagree with you," Scy observed, sending a reprimanding look at Zercey.

"Stronger senses, stronger reaction. Still would never kill them," Lerki reassured. He grew thoughtful and added, "Not this amount at least. Not alone."

"We can treat her with purified charcoal later," Date stated, as Lerki pruned sections of the flowers and tied them to everyone's clothing; it would keep the three Magnillas from coming too close. "We have to take those things down, and the only way we're doing that is by taking them out with her weaknesses."

How did this go so wrong? Any attempt she made to instruct the others, at least one doppelgänger would agree. By the warped smiles they marred her delicate features with, she concluded they knew. *Foul monsters.* They twisted her smile, her face and laugh. They limited her options, forced her to fight to their strengths. She could overpower them, but because the others wouldn't leave she couldn't go all out.

"You're a fraud."

To make matters worse, they wouldn't shut up. Their words distorted, coming far away thanks to that bark. It unsettled her not to hear the creak and crunch of the forest. It didn't last long, but by the time the buzzing stopped, thick fog filled the air.

"You're not worthy of anything."

Magnilla rolled her eyes. Their pathetic attempts to undermine her confidence made her laugh. "I'm not anything you say I am!"

More snide, mocking laughter echoed in the mist.

She twisted, trying to pinpoint and strike. "I've trained hard and pushed myself every single day to get where I am! I've sweat, cried, bled to become every inch of the person I am today! You have no right to censor me!"

"You?!" one questioned, voice burning with as much rage as Magnilla's. *"You're* the imposter! You've done nothing except be the greatest fake in history!"

"You're wrong!" They used the fog to their advantage, but she could still smell them. Or not, thanks to a stronger odour in the air. The mist shifted. *One's coming.* She slashed with her claws and heard a scream. A return slice from a sword had her crying out and clamping a hand on her arm.

"I draw *my* power from the moon, so *I* don't get as tired as someone who uses *mana,*" one mocked in a snide voice.

"I'm the best tracker there is with *my* senses," the other added, voice ringing with laughter.

They chimed in unison, *"My* clan is the best around; I will be their leader someday!"

Magnilla's blood boiled. "I'm not a brat! I've always been helpful!" The scent she caught earlier clogged her throat and she coughed. "I've always been very humble about my abilities! I've never used my status in my clan to show off!" Forcing down the itch in her throat, she charged at a hazy silhouette. "Gotcha!" She brought it to the ground, pulling her sword and impaling it through the shoulder in a single, rapid move.

"AGH! YOU BITCH!"

The second clone barged into her, knocking her off the first. Magnilla rolled away, leaving the sword.

The impaled clone struggled to get a grip on the hilt and pull it from their flesh.

The other clone leapt on Magnilla and they scrapped. Both bared their fangs, faces twisted into menacing masks.

The clone took a bite out of Magnilla's forearm and laughed. "You're just another pretty face brought up thinking she was the start and end of everyone's day. A self-important little princess, who only thinks of others in relation to how it looks for her." Magnilla screamed and headbutted it. "That's not true!" Bloodying its nose, she threw it off and shouted, "Don't call me a princess!" Clone-Magnilla snorted and spat a globule of bloody snot at Magnilla's feet. "You're nothing but a fake. A wannabe. Someone who's spent her whole life trying to convince everyone she's worth more than she is."

About to deny it again, the first clone got an arm around Magnilla's neck, choking her. Gripping their wrist and squeezing, they cut off her air supply.

Magnilla grabbed the clone, trying to throw it off. Dark spots danced in front of her eyes. She felt a sharp sting in her leg and everything went black.

"They're down!" Seth pulled back the mist. "Good work, guys! You got all three of them!"

"Thankfully." Zercey sighed with relief. She descended the tree, careful to look for hand and foot holds. The vantage point was needed to aim, but it left her arms and legs like jelly.

"There's no time to lose," Date declared, landing. His wings retracted, vanishing into the back-folds of his tunic, as he shouldered his bow.

Vyxen swung her way down from another tree, landing with a bounce. "Is it bad of me if I say I hope I got the original?" She winked.

Scyanatha shook her head, though her canine jaws pulled back in a wolfish smile. "Lerki, bind them all. I will carry the original home."

"I was about to," he replied, already in the process of fishing some ivy seeds from his bag.

Having little sound to give them a clear picture of what went on, Abaddon remained silent at the edge of the clearing through the event. Now it was over, they had no concerns about getting in the way, and came forward to help. "Um, I think you got them at the right time," they noted, lifting each Magnilla. "They were saying some things she really didn't like."

"How long do we need to wait for them to change shape?" Vyxen's silver eyes remained trained on the trio.

"Not long. Once they realise they can't stay as Magnilla and beat the wolfsbane, they will return to their original form—if you can call it that," Date replied, dark eyes hooded.

Seth raised his hand in question. "Doesn't that mean no one stronger than a half-blood in range?"

Date nodded. "Vyxen, Zercey and Seth will remain on watch. The rest of us must retreat."

About to follow them of the clearing, Lerki stopped. "You have your blooms, yes?"

"Blooms?" Vyxen's brows came together.

"The buds handed out, dear," Scy guessed.

Vyxen pulled the black one from a hidden pocket. "This?"

"Yes, yes those," he replied, bouncing on his toes. "Worthy blooms. Give them all to me, please."

"Hey, Date," Seth prompted, who grunted to indicate he was listening, "aren't you going to tell him why it's not okay to cheat?"

"You tell him if you have a problem," Date replied, waving a dismissive hand, getting comfortable between the roots of a tree.

"Cheat—?" Scy murmured, eyes glittering with restrained amusement. "Lerki, you can't intend to force them to bloom for us?"

"What?" His eyes grew round at the suggestion. "No, I was just checking them."

"Checking for what?" she teased, tail waving.

"To see if they are still growing. Some do not when they are plucked like this." He grew sombre. "I keep telling Phanuel, but he does not believe me when I say they need to be apologised to before they can bloom properly."

"Because it makes absolutely no sense," Phanuel declared, voice carrying through the thicket. He appeared soon after, hunched over and scowling with irritation. The man had more in common with a gremlin than an elf. The sun shining through the trees picked up the poor job he'd done with his hair. It wasn't just his roots that were brown, but some of the underside, too.

Trailing Phanuel was Culvers, ducking to avoid getting leaves in his salt and pepper hair. Grey eyes taking in the scene, he looked quietly impressed. "It looks like we weren't needed after all."

"But, it does look like there is a damsel in distress." Uwe detached from the shadows close to Vyxen, smiling at her.

She jumped, bared her teeth and made a point of moving to stand beside Date.

"I hope you behaved yourselves, gentlemen," he added, voice silky and absent of any embarrassment at Vyxen's reaction.

Date stood and saluted. "Date Toshiiro reports the forest is secure, all traps have been disabled and the last of the rebelling horde routed."

"And we found Lerki," Seth added in a throwaway remark. He chuckled when Lerki pouted.

Scy rounded off the report with, "And we completed our mission to bring Zercey to the venin."

Phanuel sighed long and suffering, shoulders stooping inches further. "Yes, we can see that."

Culvers strode past them and checked on Magnilla, nodding at finding her alive.

"I was on my way back," Lerki protested in a weak voice that trailed away. "I have the seeds you wanted."

"I needed those *six moons ago,* Lerki," Phanuel snapped. A vein on his brow pulsed.

As though sensing any mention of the elements would result in his premature murder, Lerki remained silent.

"What exactly happened?" Culvers' deep drawl got attention.

"Uwe's men weren't clear, and the last thing we heard came from Teysuht and that one's brother." He gestured to Magnilla.

"Speaking of him. He isn't going to like that we shot his sister." Scy's muzzle wrinkled at the thought.

"Thijs will have to get over it. He ought to be grateful she isn't dead and we don't have two Magnilla of the Thies clan clones running amok," Date said, snottily.

"Ehn!" Vyxen agreed, bouncing on her toes. "Everyone is super grateful that didn't happen!"

Zercey sniggered behind her, failing to turn it into a cough.

"Phanuel, she will need purified charcoal," Lerki advised in a quiet voice.

"Yes, I thought she might," he replied, noting the plants.

"You've done good work," praised Uwe. "As Culvers said, it looks like you didn't need us, after all."

"But, it's nice having Culvers 'round to look at," Vyxen said in an aside to Zercey, who nodded.

"If it hadn't worked, we would have," Seth admitted, stepping to the side, as the two doppelgänger began to shimmer, like a pond disturbed by a stone. "It was getting desperate and we were out of ideas." Pointing at them, he asked, "What are we supposed to do with these guys?"

Imogen was half-right. Zercey found Vyxen outside the Order's courtyard. To the east of the gate lay an overgrown path. Past dense foliage, the path grew narrow, then widened again. The Order stood on the southern cliffs of Illthdar, but according to Hok'jai, when the white royals claimed the island it changed from a humble church-on-the hill to grander architecture. With the renovation came the sculpture garden. That was long ago, and time wasn't kind. Statues were broken and missing limbs, pillars toppled and eaten away by rock mites. Weeds poked through the flagstones. The chessboard tile pattern was a smeary grey and dark grey. Raised flower beds were full of thorny plants and dead vines. Cobwebs clung to the corners of the dilapidated walls—larger than any Zercey knew. She shivered and rubbed her hands up and down her arms. She spotted her friend sitting on a wall surrounding one of the flower beds. "Hey, Vyxen."

Vyxen opened her eyes and smiled.

"Sorry, I just wanted to ask you something." She hesitated, getting the sense she shouldn't bring the topic up. "You know what? I can come back later if now's a bad time."

"Kaa, it's okay. I can't focus anyway." She tucked a strand of hair behind her ear. "What's up?"

Just go for it, Zercey. "Have you ever asked Magnilla about sending you back to Earth?" she said, rapid fire. She winced and added, "I mean, she says she has that power and—"

"She refused," Vyxen replied, blunt. She got up and spent a long time staring at her pixie skirt with clashing leggings and sweater, picking off microscopic bits of dust.

Zercey frowned. "Why, though? I mean, why did she refuse? Did she say?"

Vyxen shrugged. "She said she could do it but—" She swallowed and looked away again, hand fisting into the folds of her bright pink skirt.

Zercey's brows pinched and she reached out to comfort her.

"I'm okay." Vyxen smiled, but it didn't reach her eyes. "She said there was some sort of code, or rules she needed to follow," she finished, bitterness making her snipe. "She also ran on about all the things that could go wrong, but I wasn't interested. At the point where she said she needed a good reason I was done." Her silver eyes grew dark and cold. "I shouldn't have to explain how important going home is to me."

Zercey backed up, unprepared for how menacing she looked. "Sorry, I shouldn't have brought it up. Of course, you would have asked."

As quickly as the crack in Vyxen's mask appeared, it closed again. "It was a good idea," she said, cheerful once more. "I'll just have to find another way." A wicked glint came into her eyes as she said, "Besides, she probably made that one up for bonus wolf points to get one over on Abaddon and everyone else who portal jumped here." Before Zercey could even ask, she added, "I asked them, Teysuht and this other pretty Acolyte, Raemina, but they all came the same way we did: unwillingly."

"Is there anyone who would come here of their own free will?" Zercey doubted it. She looked at the creepy garden again for inspiration to a new topic. "What are you doing here, anyway?" She spotted a chandelier suspended from an iron pole. It dripped slow and steady into a sad water feature. In the centre half-dead flowers gave off a weak peach glow.

Vyxen pulled a face. "Meditating. Or trying—"

Zercey bent double, holding her stomach as she wheezed, "You can't sit still for five minutes!"

She snorted and said, "Laugh it up. I know it's hilarious!"

"Okay, okay." Zercey waved her hand, trying to calm down. "So, why were you trying to—" she snorted "—meditate?"

Vyxen gave Zercey's nose a gentle flick. "I'm trying to test a theory. For *science!"*

"All right," Zercey replied, humouring her, but unable to keep a straight face. "What was it?"

"Scy said people need to relax for mana to work." She could see why so many half-bloods had no power—they were stuck on Illthdar: the universe's least relaxing holiday destination.

Zercey shook her head. "I'll pretend I don't know biology and ignore how that doesn't make any sense."

"What can I say?" Vyxen's shrug was exaggerated. "Illthdar."

"Illthdar," Zercey echoed, copying her. "Had any luck?"

"I caught a quetzalli," Vyxen replied, half-hearted.

Zercey made a "pshing" sound like that wasn't anything new— Vyxen had a habit of collecting pets. She spotted a blue, bird-like creature with a peacock tail made of fire hopping about on the far side of the flower bed.

"See? I did. I named him Cypher."

Zercey giggled. "Maybe it's a sign?"

Vyxen raised an eyebrow in reply. "Just no, Zercey," she snickered.

"Okay, wanna make some cookies and hide under a heap of blankets, eating them until we're sick?"

There was a long pause, as though Vyxen were giving the matter great thought. "*Ehn!*" She all but pounced, grabbing Zercey's arm and dragging her back along the path, with Cypher hopping and making peeping noises as he followed.

CHAPTER EIGHT

Vyxen and Zercey couldn't anticipate the scene when they returned to the barracks.

A swarm of people clustered around Thijs, stood beside Magnilla's bunk. Arms crossed, he was stoic as they tried to flirt and feel his muscles, while Magnilla packed things into a cylindrical, canvas sack.

"What's going on?" Vyxen whispered, sidling close to Nyima.

"Leaving," Nyima replied. Her pose mirrored Thijs', lips pressed into a tight line, unimpressed by the news.

"Oh," Zercey voiced, trying to determine how she felt about it. She was unable to come up with anything other than, "Why?"

Looking her ethereal best again, Scy joined them. "Training, she said." Her deep red eyes gave no hint of her true opinion. "She was disappointed in her performance in the fight against the doppelgänger," she added, shrugging elegant shoulders.

"Let me make this perfectly clear," Magnilla barked, prideful. "I could have managed on my own! I didn't need you guys to interfere."

"Uh huh," Zercey intoned. She and Vyxen shared the same bland expression. *She could've handled it, same way she could open a portal to send us home.* If Magnilla could read minds, she ignored Zercey's.

"If everyone did as I said, I could have taken both out. It only got that bad because you kept getting in the way."

The people who'd formed a fan club for her nodded like sheep. Nyima and Scyanatha looked at each other, passing a wealth of communication while remaining silent.

The mood fell flat; a balloon void of air. Curdled worse than milk left out in the sun, there was no potential to recover from its plummet.

"Well. Great to see you're doing better," Vyxen offered in a neutral tone.

Typical Magnilla. Bringing the party wherever she goes. Zercey tried not to let her feelings show, but she was destined to lose.

"That's not what Lerki or any of the senior Acolytes thought."

"They have no idea what my powers and capabilities are," Magnilla rebutted with a familiar argument. Her green eyes glittered, hard and cool as her tone. "Thijs told me exactly the kinds of things that Date said—they clearly had no idea who they were talking about."

"Because everyone could tell you were winning," Vyxen snarked, shaking her head.

"You didn't even stop to listen to their plan," Zercey added, raising her voice, cheeks flushed. "You might not have been hurt if you had!"

The disharmony between teammates gave Nyima a headache. She, Abaddon and Scyanatha remained neutral during such conflicts. As much as she agreed Magnilla could tone down the posturing, it wasn't worth fighting about when she wouldn't change. Nyima moved to grab her wash things. *By the time I get back, they should have argued themselves out.*

"And that's another thing!" Magnilla boomed, anticipating triumph. "Their plan involved shooting me with a *poison arrow,* Zercey!" Her expression turned pitying. "If I were you, I'd be very, *very,* careful who you pick as friends; you don't have healing abilities like me. If they wanted to use you the same way, you'd be dead."

Zercey's face drained of colour. "You don't know that..." The argument was weak and she knew it.

"These are the same *geniuses* supposed to test us for final graduation. Five of us against all the Acolytes of Quartz and they *lost!"* Magnilla's lips twisted with scorn. Her tone biting and incredulous, she added, "Are you saying you actually believe they're better strategists than me?"

Beside her, Thijs nodded. "At best, they're presumptive and arrogant. At worst, they're petty and vindictive. In both cases they're dishonourable louts, who had no business butting in." Jutting his chin upwards with clan pride, he added, "None of them could even hold a candle to Magnilla in a fight head on." His eyes drifted over his sister's form, making a slow and lingering sweep as he noted, "She is the most desired woman in our clan. That's why she's the strongest and best." He continued to stare until the atmosphere grew uncomfortable. Snapping from his self-inflicted trance, he grabbed Magnilla's bag, saying, "Magnilla, let's go."

With an air of finality, the pair walked towards the door. "Well, have a nice trip, anyway!" Vyxen called from the windowsill. She did a one-handed clap for a wave, insincere smile on her face.

"Don't push your luck," Magnilla snapped, twisting to look over her shoulder.

Vyxen's smile and eyes widened with exaggerated innocence. "Who, me? What did I do?" She placed a hand on her breastbone and looked around the room.

Scy hid a smile and shook her head.

Magnilla turned, placing her hands on her hips. "I may forgive you, because Date's team doesn't represent Las, but do well to remember the alliance and support the Thies clan provides Las is directly linked to me as their representative." At the blank looks she sighed.

Thijs patted her shoulder, hand sliding down her arm as he stepped in front of her. "The Order of Mana benefit greatly from us being here. Magnilla intentionally chose to work her way up—that's just how good of a person she is—but it's still truth. We'll send a substitute while she's away, but our father may not be so willing to turn the other cheek, and Chiyoko is aware of it."

A gust of frigid wind blowing in their wake, the pair exited. The door was left ajar, allowing everyone to hear their comments as they stomped down the stairs.

"I have never, in my life, had to deal with so many difficult people!"

"I know, sister. They'll learn what's good for them in the end."

As Scyanatha pushed the door closed, Zercey blew a raspberry. Inspired by the obnoxious pair, she sang a line from *Regurgitator*'s *My Ego,* off-key. Her performance was met with polite applause. She rolled her eyes and jumped onto her bunk. Several arrow fletchings were scattered across the covers. She crossed her legs and examined her work.

Vyxen wasted no time stripping the sheets from Magnilla's bed and raiding the chest, pouting when she found it empty.

Peace and quiet returned to the barracks. People went about their business—the show was over.

"Would she really have?" Abaddon queried, drawing rest from their thoughts. They'd moved to a corner of their bunk during the discussion, until they felt safe to come out.

"Really have what?" Zercey replied in an absent manner, failing to keep her focus on splitting feathers.

"Been given, um, the t-title of Elder...to start with?" Abaddon's

brows came together, recalling all the failures their group had. *Would Chiyoko want an Elder who needed training?*
"Anything is possible," Scy stated, stretching out on her bed. She waggled her fingers as she spied Nyima returning from the wash room. "Squeaky clean, dear? I'd never have guessed you were the type to avoid anything." Her lips went up in a teasing smile.
Nyima rolled her eyes and replaced her wash things in her trunk, nudging Vyxen aside. "That Magnilla's."
"I know," Vyxen replied, with a wicked grin.
"You will get catched one day," she pointed out, guessing Vyxen planned on hanging anything of Magnilla's from the oak tree in the courtyard.
"Not today," Vyxen sighed, slamming the lid shut. "She didn't leave so much as a hair behind."
"I wonder how Chiyoko chooses High Elders," Abaddon said, moving over for Vyxen to sit beside them.
"Politically," Scy replied, having examined the placement of people in charge. "She has allegiance in mind."
"Ew, who'd wanna align with Uwe?" Vyxen pretended to gag.
Zercey laughed. "Them." She pointed to where another group of Acolytes discussed who was better in bed.
"Double ew!" Vyxen grabbed Abaddon and hugged tight. "Save me!"
The others made noises of amusement and settled into conversation that meandered in a companionable way from one topic to the next, with little disagreement.

146

Having slept in the Jasper barracks, Vyxen made her way down with the others, almost bumping into Date and his friends when she reached the second-floor landing. "Good morning!"
Stepping back, he questioned, "Is it?"
"Isn't it?" She grinned, knowing she was teasing, but enjoying the moody look on his face.
Date snorted. "Perhaps it is." He opened his mouth to say more, but a hand clamped over it.
"Don't get him started," Tundra said, shoving him into Seth's waiting arms. "Chiyoko's making an example of him."
Seth's hand replaced Tundra's and he said in a loud voice, "What's that, Date? Sorry, I can't hear you. You seem to have something blocking your fat mouth." He was dressed in long red robes with silver trim. The slits in the side revealed grey, yogi-style pants underneath when he walked.
The pair chuckled as Date shot them black looks, unmoved. He was dressed in black again, but today's outfit was a short-sleeved tunic, with a longer-sleeved, navy one underneath. He also had on a pair of baggy breeches in the same shade. High top boots and a thick belt with matte finish completed the look.
"It's nice to see no one is worried," Scy commented, gesturing for Tundra to take the lead. He sorted his crutches and made a reckless descent.
"Be careful! You will break your other leg." Lerki hurried after him, smiling briefly to the rest.
"Whatever, mom, I said I'm fine!"
Abaddon and the women stifled their amusement, as everyone followed.
The group split at the bottom of the stairs, with those involved in shooting Magnilla and her doubles summoned to the room of worship.

Vyxen and Zercey lined up beside Date, Lerki and Seth.
Chiyoko's tails swished, reminding Vyxen of an angry cat. *Don't*

smile. Don't smile! She fought hard and lost.

"Is something funny?" Chiyoko paused, brown eyes zeroed in on Vyxen.

"Nothing!" Vyxen shook her head briskly. "Nothing, nothing! I swear nothing!"

Chiyoko's clawed fingers came towards Vyxen's face. She sucked in a breath, but all Chiyoko did was tuck Vyxen's hair behind her ear.

Moving back, Chiyoko's face was unreadable. "Good." She turned elegantly. "Now, back to business." She paced in front of them, staff tapping on the floor with every other step. "The Thies heiress departed for her clan. While she's gone, you will write and send letters apologising for your insulting and reckless behaviour."

Date, lips twitched when her back was turned.

"The strategist of the most excellent plan will write to Lord Rhett and Lady Chastity, apologising for injuring their child. He shall also write to Princess Magnilla begging forgiveness."

With a sweep of his hand, Date bowed deep in acknowledgement.

"The rest will write formal apologies for their part." That done, Chiyoko flicked her hand towards the door. "Out."

"How you aren't dead yet, I don't know," Seth told Date the second they were out of Chiyoko's hearing.

Date ignored him, opting to send Lerki to fetch paper and quills from his trunk, so they could write the hated apology letters.

"I'm writing mine," Zercey said, determined to show she'd learned enough Illthdarian to manage.

"Neat! Can you do mine, too?" Vyxen clung to her arm and looked up with a winsome smile.

Zercey laughed and shook her head. "You're incorrigible. Okay, but If I have to write the god-awful things, you're going to sit with me for moral support."

"Ehn! Done! Deal!" Vyxen slapped her hand into Zercey's giving it a firm shake. "No take backs!"

Filling the ranks on the battlements of the white wall, Abaddon was joined by Nyima and Tundra.

Because of the injured, the Order instigated a buddy system. Along the wall at key points people wearing a variety of bandages stood beside frightened newbies.

Nyima glanced over her shoulder, taking a break from keeping a lookout. Her gaze flitted over her companions, hesitating on Tundra before moving on.

Tundra sat on one of the low parts of the wall, designed for archers. Wearing black and baby blue again, and with black hair and blue eyes, he looked matchy. The incongruous part was the wood cast on his leg. "Damn thing itches," he declared, trying to work a finger into the gap.

"Would a scratcher help? I could make one," Abaddon offered.

"If it'll fit, I'll take it," he replied, checking the space between cast and skin. There was barely enough room to allow his pinky. "Lerki should be along in a bit. I'll see if he can do something."

"Humans, very fragile," Nyima noted, shaking her head. "How you can survive?" She let out a bemused exhalation.

"You'd be surprised," he said, a boyish smile on his face. "People can do any number of things, if they're shown how."

Nyima kept his gaze, nodding slowly. "I see."

He ducked his head to hide a smirk, concentrating on scratching his other itch. A shadow fell over him and he said without looking, "You're blocking the light, Lerki." A pair of cream coloured boots came further into his field of vision. "Not better."

"Tundra, you will hurt the tree if you force it," Lerki said, crouching to observe the damage. Gone were his tan and brown leather trappings. Instead, he wore a blue-green shirt with ruffled edges, that hung open in the front, showing his jewellery. Purple breeches puffed over his knee-high boots. A crisp, dark green coat stopped short of his calves. The final piece was an ocean coloured scarf, with fluorite pin.

"It's getting cut off in three months," he argued back in a mild tone.

Shaking his head, Lerki used magic to encourage the plant to make more openings for Tundra to scratch himself raw. He stood, eyeing the injury and making a whining sound in the back of his throat. Tundra shot him a look. "I'm fine, let it go."

"What happened?" Nyima looked between the pair, curious. As chatty as Tundra was during their shift, she realised very little of what he said was about himself. She kept doing a double-take whenever her gaze landed on him; he looked so much like he belonged to one of the tribes of her home-world it was uncanny. *But none of my people would speak in such a way that everything is a word game.* It was...fun.

"He was very unwell when I got to him," Lerki replied, pulling her from her thoughts. "He should have seen a healer before then." He wrung his hands and shook his head.

Standing next to Tundra, it was clear to see Lerki had a good couple of inches on him, though a lot less muscle. Nyima imagined the height difference between Lerki and Seth was so small it could be overlooked if one didn't pay attention. Date was very much the shortest. They all had an easy way about them that spoke of their close links, which she found appealing. They were an interesting group, and it seemed her friends found something in common with at least one other person.

"Seth said it was blood taint, but he was glazed when I saw him," Lerki continued, shaking a reprimanding finger at a laughing Tundra.

"You a healer?" He didn't look much like one, but she had little reference.

Tundra laughed harder, and Lerki waved his hands back and forth. "No, no, not at all," he replied, panicked at the suggestion. "I know about plants and bodies and how the two work together."

"Taint and glazed would be equivalent to blood poisoning and shock," Tundra offered for clarity. "It was fine. I was fine. It's no big deal."

154

She nodded, taking his statement at face value. "You know poisons," she said to Lerki, surprised when his expression grew stony.

"I have a strong immunity to most," he admitted in a grudging tone. "Because of this, Phanuel sends me to collect what others cannot."

"Why does he need poison?" Abaddon questioned suddenly. Feeling all eyes on them, they stammered, "W-we're supposed to guard or get shards back. So, um, why would he need something so underhanded?"

"Maybe he coats the crystal in it to keep sticky fingers from touching?" Tundra suggested, shrugging. "You'd be surprised how many people try to snap pieces off during the holidays." He twisted his finger through one of the holes in his cast and scratched. Pulling back sharply, a stiletto of ice was thrust under his nose. He lifted a brow in question.

"Take," Nyima said, by way of explanation.

"Thanks, but that's going to melt on warm skin," he smiled, turning down the offer. "Besides preventing random acts of vandalism, Quartz uses sneaky shit to get their jobs done. Uwe would want a stock on hand for any possibilities."

"You done this?" Nyima questioned, having heard he was an assassin before he came to Illthdar.

"Somewhat." He broke eye contact with her. He clapped and said to Lerki, "Anyway, nothing new here."

Nodding in easy acceptance, Lerki asked, "Is there anything I can collect and return when I next pass through?"

"You hear rumours?" Nyima's sudden question had Lerki stopping dead with surprise.

Tundra drew his good leg up onto the ledge, using it as an arm rest. He put his chin on his forearm and gave Nyima a thoughtful once over. She looked more like a blue-skinned, belly dancer than a warrior, with the bare feet, yellow ribbon skirt and bra, but no one that held the wall against the horde was a pushover. She didn't speak much, but she made it all count. *She's pretty cool, and it's fun teasing her. She's a good sport.*

"Ah, Wind talks of many things, but I do not ask about what does not concern me," Lerki replied, the opposite of helpful.

Tundra decided to give his own answer. "I do." When Nyima looked at him, he smiled and said, "What are you after?"

She tilted her head, eyes narrowing a fraction. He'd been making statements like that all morning, and she was starting to think they had more than one meaning, if Abaddon's coughing was any indication. "Magnilla's clan is allies to Order of Mana?" She stuck to the facts.

He nodded, adding a, "Yup," out of respect to Abaddon missing the non-verbal. "Why are you asking?"

She forwent details about the declaration Magnilla made before she left—because she'd be in danger of wanting to stab herself. "Curious what they get," she replied.

Abaddon didn't like where the conversation seemed to be going. "If she w-was here, we could ask her. She would tell us."

"She's not." Nyima's reply was whip sharp.

"Being direct doesn't always give the answers you're looking for," Tundra agreed, grabbing his crutches and getting off the wall. "I haven't heard, but seeing how Date's been bitching up a storm about her, he might know."

Nyima nodded, she could believe that. Date was heard telling all and sundry he was the fourth son of some lord. It stood to reason he would have information of that kind.

"He might not care enough to find out," Abaddon argued in a gentle voice. "He was sharp with Magnilla and Thijs."

"If you really want to know, ask him direct. He's a blunt instrument that way." Tundra chuckled.

"He should have been Jasper and you should have been in Quartz," Lerki declared, giggling. "You like to tiptoe."

"I was *trained* to tiptoe," he corrected. "There's a difference."

"A difference to what?" called Scyanatha from the covered stairway.

"Hi, Scyanatha." Abaddon waved in her general direction.

"Going for the jugular is always better," Tundra continued, warming to his theme.

Nyima agreed. "Quick death is better."

"More fun, too," he replied, smirking.

"Much," Abaddon said, hearing Nyima hum in the affirmative.

"Hello, dears!" Scy appeared at the top of the steps, holding up a basket. "It's undernmete," she said, smiling.

"You lived on Earth. Can't you just say 'lunch' for all of us clueless half-bloods?" Tundra joked, craning to see what she had for them.

"I could, but I wouldn't have nearly as much fun," Scy teased, winking. She placed the basket beside him. "We have hot cocoa and cold sandwiches." She put her hand out and added, "We haven't been properly introduced. Scyanatha."

Tundra took her hand in a firm grip and shook once. "Tundra—err, Jingyi." He let go straight away and grabbed some food from the basket. Scy was a flirt, he wouldn't deny that. Tall and with a mane of red hair that looked like spun fire when the light touched it, she had temptress written all over her. *Way too hot to handle.* He'd put good money on her being the sort to expect lovers to be at her beck and call. He preferred something more casual. He glanced at Nyima.

"Did I hear you speaking about Magnilla?" She looked around the group, but no one would meet her ruby-eyed gaze. She shrugged and added, "It's only that, I was having a nice chat with Navya and she said the Thies clan are having trouble with territory disputes. They sent Magnilla here to act as an emissary, but also to make sure the other clans didn't try to kidnap or murder her." She poured herself a cup of cocoa from a metal pot, sipped it and said, "Isn't it nice of Lord Rhett, making us her bodyguards?"

CHAPTER NINE

Rounding the corner from the old oak tree, Vyxen did a slow count from twelve. Reaching zero, she hugged her stomach and bent over. *I don't know if I want to laugh or cry.* All Illthdar conspired against her. Even Zercey hit sore spots.

Hearing a peep, she reached down to stroke Cypher's downy body. Baya took the opportunity to get a piggy-back and climbed up, cooing.

Vyxen's reaction was between a laugh and a sob. *I need to get out of here before anyone sees me.* She couldn't take any concern. Her mask would crack for sure.

Most of the time it was an effective way of dealing with things. She wasn't sure how she kept up the poker-face, but it was harder of late. All anyone talked about was Magnilla. Vyxen either reeled from slapping betrayal or tried not to die from inappropriate

Seated on the floor by their bunks in Jasper barracks, Nyima and Scyanatha picked over a cheeseboard with fruit, nuts and other bits. Scy blocked the heat from the stove with her back, and Nyima faced her. The room buzzed with sounds of other people sat on bunks, eating, chatting or sorting personal chores.

"Vyxen didn't think much of it," Scy commented, discussing the day's events. She shrugged one shoulder and added, "I didn't expect her to. She doesn't dwell on what-ifs."

Nyima hummed, having expected as much. "Little sister?" she questioned, referring to Zercey. If the answer was positive she'd be shocked.

"Zercey was...Zercey," Scy answered with a short titter. "Seth was helpful, but Date was borderline hostile. Lerki did not say so directly, but strongly implied his friend is nursing a grudge."

"A rumour, still," Nyima stated in a low voice. She didn't want to spread gossip. "To be wary is best."

"I agree," Scy sighed, picking up a grape and popping it in her mouth. Once it was gone, she said, "I wish we didn't have so many internal conflicts, it's undermining our efforts to form a cohesive unit."

Nyima remained still for a few moments, then nodded. "Yes." Another pause. "They will share their hearts and make peace." A small amount of head bobbing as she worked out another sentence. "If cannot, Zercey must learn to be adult for it."

"Zercey's still a young human," Scy defended, with some additional consideration. "Though they're not much different in age, Vyxen's more focused on her goals." She hoped the two would balance each other, but so far all they did was feed the other's need for mischief. "They've become good friends, but Zercey is far too passive. While Vyxen is liable to fling herself into hell if it got her what she wanted."

Nyima exhaled on a short laugh. "Yes. Hope to be they will balance each other." She scowled at her poor language skills, though Scyanatha seemed to understand.

It wasn't often the two were alone without a younger one wanting to bend their ear. Nyima was a good sounding board, until she caught up and gave answers. Scy was excellent for giving advice on plenty of subjects. She had an opinion on everything, and everyone.

With that in mind, Nyima had a few questions of her own. "The men; what are you thoughts?" She leaned forward to snag a piece of cheese in a casual way.

Scy's lips curled up in a sultry smile. "Seth is adorable. Like a little puppy, and I wouldn't mind tickling his tummy." She laughed as Nyima blushed. "You asked, dear."

"Not like that."

Scy laughed again. "It's the only way that matters when speaking of attractive people." She sobered at Nyima's stern glare. "Jingyi or Tundra—whichever he goes by—is sharp and observant. He has an interesting outlook and an easy way about him." She stopped to greet a lilac haired woman, carrying a spear. "Good evening, Raemina, dear." She picked up a clay mug and sipped from it before saying, "Lerki is mysterious. I sense he is hiding something, but that's also how venin are. The only one I worry about is Date." She shook her head with pity. "He is not a happy man, but he is quick witted. It was clever thinking to disguise Vyxen and I as an orc wolf-rider."

"That was how," Nyima murmured, having been curious. As for the men, she agreed. "They work well." Her brows came together, adding, "They are friends with us too fast. Why?"

Scy hummed. "I've been too busy to enquire, but it looks suspicious." She added as a joke, "Our winning personalities and good looks only account for so much." Her expression turned calculating. "What did you think of Tundra? He's very built for one so young."

Nyima blushed and looked away. "I did not see," she lied.

Scy laughed. "I'd work on that before someone else asks you about him."

"He fights well," Nyima amended. "He is nice."

Scy pouted at the lacklustre reply. "So I heard. It didn't sound like he meant training to be a 'Guardian of Las'," she said, making brief air quotes.

"He talks of others more," Nyima explained why she hadn't learned much. She wanted to. He was a curious person, in looks and personality. "The company was good." If she were honest, it was the most normal she'd felt since she became an Aetumuh. She had to remind herself throughout the day it didn't matter what she learned because this wasn't her life. It wasn't permanent. That didn't stop a little voice in the back of her head from pushing questions past her lips. "How are your morning?" She turned the subject back to Scy before she began teasing again.

"Long stretches of blandness, punctuated by moments of frustration and distress," Scy summarised in a throwaway tone. "That is why I am trying to pump you for something juicy to sink my teeth into before I leave on a mission with Vyxen."

Nyima's blue lips quirked in amusement. "Ah, you gossip for purpose."

There was a peal of bell-like laughter. "I'm trying too hard," Scy admitted, placing her cup to one side and standing.

"You care," Nyima replied, smiling.

Nodding, she said, "Thank you Teysuht—or, Nyima, is it?"

"Nyima," she replied, taking the chance to reaffirm her real name.

"I wish you said sooner," Scy said, with a slight head shake. "It wouldn't be so hard a habit to break, but I shall try, Nyima. No one should have to give up their name. Have a good night."

"You're just in time," Vyxen greeted the moment the door shut behind Scyanatha.

Turning, Scy noted Date and Seth accompanied her.

"I was coming in to get you," she said, waggling her finger and grinning.

"I hear there is an encampment with a shard?" Scy said, listening to the mission brief as they descended the stairs.

"It was confirmed last night," Date replied in a confident tone, lacking the scorn from when she last saw him. "Lerki's waiting for us," he added.

Scyanatha nodded. The team size was the right side of successful.

"The plan's pretty simple too," Seth said. "Date will go overhead to distract them, while I sabre-rattle and make them think we're coming from another direction. Lerki cuts off their escape and you make the earth move, Sweetness. Meanwhile, Vyxen snags the crystal piece in the chaos."

"Long as you keep them busy and not derp it up everything will be great!" Vyxen smiled at him.

Date reassured her, "If it gets bad, I'm to dive in and get you out. Lerki and Scy will take care of the rest while Seth pulls back."

Seth balled a fist and punched his palm. "Then, BOOM! I bring down the hurt and everyone escapes. Praise be to Seth!" He postured and Vyxen giggled.

"What sort of companions do you two have?" Her question followed them outdoors, as they met with Lerki. She waved to the little eitercopp on his shoulder.

"A p'ake called Adil," Seth replied.

"A sasah," Date said. "Her name is Inoshi."

Vyxen made a fizzing sound and her shoulders hunched.

Feathery eyebrow raising, Date demanded, "What is it?"

"Nothing!" Vyxen replied through her sniggers. "I just pictured you with a corvazneo or something."

Tall and manly Seth with a fluffy, golden antlered alpaca was amusing enough. The dark and brooding tengu paired with a baby-pink jackalope was more than she could handle.

"You're not the first," he noted, as they trekked into the woods, with Lerki and Ka-Teamose taking the lead. "It isn't worth getting into how and why. She's the one I kept in the end. Now shush. We don't want to be discovered."

166

With dense tree cover and foliage concealing them, Date, Lerki, Scy, Seth and Vyxen took their positions. Both Date and Lerki were in the trees. Scy hunkered down, crawling on hands and knees to peer through a thorny bush that kept snagging her hair. Seth and Vyxen took positions opposite each other, waiting for their respective cues.

Vvekw's shard was secured to the ringleader's belt in a small pouch.

With everyone ready, Date leapt from his perch. The pleated back of his tunic parted to reveal ready-made slits, allowing his wings to spring forth. Clipping branches and twigs, he grimaced at the tight fit.

The sounds attracted the thugs huddled around the leader.

Ill-fitting skin hung in heavy wrinkles over his wide shoulders and gaunt, grey-green limbs, the leader was a sight to behold. Limp algae clung to his back and shoulders like a ratty poncho.

Heads turned Date's way. Arms raised spears and aimed arrows in his direction.

Scy closed her eyes and focused on the earth. *Rise up. Let's play. Do you know leap frog?* The rocks and pebbles glimmered with golden sparkles. The ground lifted and fell, bouncing the bandits like they were on a trampoline. She stood and drew her swords, smile challenging.

"WHHHHOOOAAAAHHH~~!!" came Seth's deep and bellowing battle cry as he charged. Axe raised, he met the leader head on. *This guy's huge!* Taller and broader than Seth, the demon wielded a crooked, fanged claymore with one hand. Seth swung. Metals clanged. He pushed forward, roaring in the demon's face. "Come on! That's all you got!?"

Above, branches shifted, as Lerki hopped from tree to tree tossing fistfuls of seeds. "Just in case." Wherever he went, the sound of things growing at speed and weaving a latticework of tree limbs in his wake followed.

Vyxen kept her body low to the ground and plunged into the mayhem. *This is my chance!* In the dark she was difficult to spot with a black hood drawn over her tresses, cloaking her in woven twilight. With the two combatants dancing their duel, she had to keep on her toes to weave with them. She sucked in a breath as a wayward swing cut the top of her hood off. Her luminous, white locks tumbled free.

"Oi!"

 Spotted.

"Behind you!"

"Shit." Vyxen grabbed the pouch, as the mountainous man turned.

"YOU!" He grabbed at her, while she tried to snap the thin cord holding the bag to his hip.

"Hey, asshole! Don't forget about me, shit for brains!" Seth leapt on his back and clung for dear life.

The demon thrashed, trying to throw him off.

Reeling back in panic, Vyxen yanked the pouch free and was snapped up by a pair of arms.

"Got you." Date's voice filtered to her ears and she clung tight, even as he told her, "Hang on tight and don't get motion sick."

"Li—" Before she could enquire why, he spun them like a maple seed pod, only up.

BOOM!

The sky grew thick with thunderous clouds, that turned the area from grey to red.

Date took them high above and Vyxen looked down. "...It's raining *fire!"*

"He's not called the storm bringer for nothing," Date replied, settling her more securely in his embrace.

It occurred to her that Date was much stronger than he looked.

"Did you get it?" he asked, and she nodded.

"Yeah, I have it," she replied, breathless from the roller coaster ride.

"Great work!" He swooped, heading for the trees, nodding to Lerki

168

on the way past. He drew his wings in, flapped a few times and settled on a branch.

"Wow! Is it easy flying? How do your wings work? Are they hollow like a bird's? How much can you carry?" Vyxen went into nosy enthusiasm mode, peppering him with questions.

"Not now," he replied, rolling his eyes.

Vyxen grinned. "You'll have to some time, Grumpy Birb." She gave his cheek a playful poke.

Initially befuddled at being called a grumpy youth, Date scowled and repeated, "Not. Now."

Lerki leapt from a tree branch and knocked the ground with a fist, like rapping on a door. The wind carried his murmurs to them, but they didn't catch the exact words. A wild, dizzying array of plants shot from the ground, twisting and weaving all over. They rushed towards the bandits and their leader, wrapping around like a lover desperate to greet their sweetheart after a long absence.

Sheathing her swords, Scy bounded towards them, with Seth trailing.

He laughed and clapped Lerki and Date on their backs in a victorious mood. "Did you see that?! They didn't even see us coming! Boom! Bringing the pain in record time! We've gotta brag to Tundra he's the one always holding us back, man! He'll die!"

"Or he'll kill you for the insult," Date guessed a more accurate scenario.

"Bullshit!" Seth laughed. "He likes me!"

"The only reason you're still alive, I'm sure."

"Well, Chiyoko should be happy to see this!" Vyxen pulled the yellow crystal from the pouch and held it up. "Is it the real deal?"

"The Elements are pleased," Lerki replied with a tired smile, staggering.

"Uh oh!" Seth commented, recognising his friend's disposition. "Let's get back before you pass out, Lerki. You stretched yourself with those seeds."

Lerki nodded mutely, slinging his arm over Seth's shoulders for support.

"Thanks for the cover, by the way, it was just what we needed," Seth added.

Lerki smiled once more.

"You got rid of the clouds, right, Seth?" Vyxen glanced over her shoulder and added, "And why fire? In a forest of all places?!"

"Water sprites hate it," Seth replied, winking. "If I used normal rain it would have been ammo."

"Illthdar," Vyxen said, throwing her hands in the air.

"Job well done, everyone," Scy complimented, taking point back to Las.

CHAPTER TEN

❝What I don't understand is why water sprites were so far from water." Scy tapped her two-pronged fork against the side of her bowl.

With the injured recovered and repairs completed, meals in the brewery returned to more specific catering, necessitating individual groups returning to cooking or eating at the *Alewifery*.

"What's that, Scy?" Vyxen mumbled, trying not to spit crumbs.

"Oh!" She didn't realise she spoke aloud. "Water sprites prefer large bodies of water. They don't move beyond them unless they must."

"Who you stole the shard from?" Nyima heard the recount once they got back.

Scy and Vyxen nodded in unison.

"Weird," Zercey commented, twisting a lock of green hair around her finger. "Could it have been the shard that drew them away?"

"The big one was a gremlin," Scy disclosed. "I am of the belief he drew them in."

"That's what that massive man was?!" It was the total opposite of what she'd thought a gremlin was. "Would water sprites even make good escorts through a forest?" she added, with a doubtful eyebrow raise.

"No. This is why they couldn't be mercenaries," Scyanatha admitted. There was too little information to solve the puzzle, which irritated her.

"What are the chances they were coming here?" Zercey asked. "Either to surrender it or attack us?"

"The report stated not," Scy replied, gathering the plates into a neat pile and placing silverware on top.

"Shard has this much power to draw sprites from water?" Nyima wondered, curious about the crystal.

Scy hummed, nodding.

"Does Chiyoko know?"

"Ehn, it was mentioned," Vyxen answered, relaying what she recalled from the debriefing. "If she was bothered, I couldn't tell."

"Something must be wrong, then," came Abaddon's soft observation. "She doesn't hold back what she thinks."

"Well, Phanuel sent Lerki back out almost as soon as he was rested," Zercey offered. Her cheeks turned pink when everyone looked at her. "He wanted to take a little time to resonate with me before he did. He told me then," she said, trying to make it sound like no big deal.

The concept of being in another person's company for more than just the fun of being around them was strange. It didn't help she kept hearing not nice stuff about him. Aside from the obvious comments centred around his looks and possible sexual prowess— which turned her cheeks scarlet—there were mentions of his species being on the dumb side. They were idiot sub-nymphs. They wandered with their heads in the clouds and no purpose to their actions. Zercey snorted. *Prejudice rears its ugly head no matter what planet you're on.*

A faery across the room threw a dark look in her direction, then returned to talking too loud with their own friends. "...unclean half-bloods."

"They're impure bloodlines and should be eradicated. No respectable member of the Seelie would contaminate themselves with them. Quality over quantity."

The pomposity made Zercey's lip curl.

"Demons are worse," their friend replied with a contemptuous sniff of her nose. "Corrupt to the core—their existence alone is proof of their foulness. Did you know they're born from the souls of people who have been evil for multiple incarnations? It's their own fault they're so disgusting. They shouldn't be allowed to join anything, let alone a religious order."

I wonder if celestials weren't so reclusive there'd be more open prejudice towards demons. Good thing they live on—what was that place called? Serenite? No, that's where Magnilla's from. She clicked her fingers. *Shinar! Bet they'd start on with the birthmark thing again. Imagine treating someone badly because of something so minor. Illthdar!* She sighed.

"If what Date said is a clue, we might not see him again until spring," Vyxen remarked, pulling Zercey's attention from the bigots. She bounced up and gave everyone hugs, intent on heading back to her barracks.

"How's the meditation thing going, by the way?" Zercey asked as Vyxen reached the door.

Vyxen laughed until she bent double. "Like a deflated balloon! I'll let you know if it starts blowing up. *Baamaa!"*

"Meditating?" Scy prompted, once Vyxen left.

"I like doing th-that," Abaddon volunteered. "It's calming."

"That's why she's doing it. She said Scy mentioned it."

"Oh, yes," Scyanatha replied, recounting her previous advice.

"J'retkohc have not strong power," Nyima offered in observation. "My young people. Only who become Aetumuh. Is a sacred rite;

must have inner strong first."

"The *Aetumuh* of *Vaosynlr,*" Abaddon recalled in an echoing tone. Nyima nodded, humming an affirmative.

"The who in the what?" Zercey prompted Nyima.

She raised an eyebrow at the phrasing, though her lips twitched with amusement. She lacked the language to explain, but tried her best. "When time is right. When go from *j'retkoh* to grown. Must train body and mind. Is painful. Tiring. Sometimes end up hurt."

Zercey's eyes widened. "Puberty for you sounds intense. And here all I had to worry about was having my period start in the middle of class."

Nyima didn't know what "puberty" was, but she had the sense she'd been misunderstood.

Jumping to the next person before her first period could be discussed in all its bloody glory, Zercey prompted, "Abaddon, what about you?"

"Hm?" Their brows knitted together. "What about me?"

"What was puberty like?"

"It was...it happened." Abaddon struggled to articulate themself. They resorted to a twisted grimace. "I didn't enjoy it much."

"Oh...right," Zercey replied, drawing conclusions about the many torments they must have gone through. "Yeah, sorry, I wasn't thinking."

"It's okay," they reassured. "It was strange at first, and uncomfortable getting used to my body changing, but I'm more comfortable with how I look now."

"I hear that." Zercey nodded in understanding. "I don't have the slightest idea what your changes were, but if body hair and mammary glands were on the list—" She groaned and put her head in her hands, trying not to think about the horrors of being a young teen. "—And, oh my God, all the stupid things I said and did when my hormones were all over the place! Ugh!"

"That sounds a lot like what I had, but with horns," Abaddon joked.

Having more context now, Nyima concluded Zercey *had* misunderstood. She hadn't experienced any of what they were talking about. She didn't bleed and hadn't gone through much physical development, besides growing taller and gaining a small pair of breasts. There were no embarrassing things said or done; her people always kept occupied with tasks or simple survival. She wanted to ask what "being hormonal" was like, but thought she'd sound like a bigger idiot than usual when trying to express herself. "We have mission—*a* mission—tomorrow," she said, changing the subject and correcting herself mid speech.

Zercey turned to her. "To that cave place?"

Nyima nodded.

"Me, too," she replied. "I don't know why, unless they need bait." She laughed, awkward.

"Do you know who else is going?" Scy asked, curious. A team of two was guaranteed to fail.

Zercey and Nyima indicated they didn't.

"I'm on wall duty again," Abaddon said, and Scy smiled.

"So am I. We can have a nice chat while we look at the scenery." Abaddon chuckled. "I-if you think so..."

Vyxen skipped down the spiral staircase, still giggling about the "meditating" comment.

Mid-way she stepped closer to the wall to let Tundra and Seth pass. Tundra hopped, using his crutches to miss a couple of steps. The movement made his low V-neck tunic gape, exposing a significant potion of his chest and abs.

Vyxen would have enjoyed the view, but he had a black leotard on underneath. *Spoilsport.* At least Seth provided some eye candy on the battlefield. Though off, he wore head to toe bright coloured robes. "All this magic and they can't even put in an elevator!" she joked, laughing.

"It's a good workout," Tundra replied, puffing and looking sweaty. Behind him, Seth waved.

"Hi, Seth." Vyxen smiled.

"Sneaking back?" When she nodded, he said, "Us too."

"Oh?" Vyxen asked, waiting for an explanation.

"Nothing important," Tundra said. "Date got a letter."

Seth grimaced. "He was laughing, so you'd think that'd be okay but, it's Date, so..."

Tundra snorted.

Vyxen was left hanging for a translation for the non-verbal, unable to tell if he found it funny or predictable.

"The Thies clan wrote personally?" she guessed. *That was quick.* "They never bothered with anyone else."

"No," Seth drew the word out, rubbing the back of his neck, "it wasn't from them." He slapped Tundra on the back, causing him to stumble. "Anyway, we've gotta get gimp face to bed. Goodnight!"

Vyxen's eyes narrowed at the abruptness, but she replied, "Okay, night." She tracked their movements as they headed towards the men's Jasper barracks.

"Gimp face?" Tundra's voice filtered down.

"Did you want me to call you three legs?"

"You're an idiot."

Her lips spread in a grin at the mocking banter. *They're fun. And cute.* Snickering, Vyxen continued until she reached her own barracks. *Here we are: home.* She stopped and shook her head. *This isn't home!*

Quartz had some interesting—even cool—people. Some were friends, but it was a place to sleep and eat. *Home is Alaska, with my family and—* She yanked the door open and went in. *This isn't home.*

The following morning, Seth was waylaid on the way to duty by Queline.

"Aunty! It's been seven years now!" he said, trying not to whine in the open street.

To the amusement of those passing through, Queline gave a reprimanding lecture, going into tangents covering her and Seth's shared history.

"I'm not some scruffy little monster! You don't have to worry!" She paused mid-tirade. "I didn't think you were a monster!"

Seth shook his head. "Maybe, but you probably thought something unpleasant." He sighed and held up his hands. "I promise I won't get into any trouble, if that'll make you feel better. I broke that habit ages ago, you know."

"You were pulled in to see the High Priestess again," she pointed out, long ears twitching with triumph. "How is that not getting into trouble?!"

"Uhh." He paused and scratched the back of his neck. "Technically—"

"Don't 'technically' me. You were!" She wagged a finger at him.

"Technically, that was more Date's fault than mine. I was there only because he came and got me." If he was in trouble, then Date was coming along with him.

"That Toshiiro!" Queline grumbled, panic abating at the news. "Uwe should pluck him like a chicken for all of the times he's gotten everyone into trouble."

Seth chuckled. "He always means well, and he did this time, too. They needed me. He wouldn't have brought me if he didn't think so." He concluded his defense with, "That's one great thing about Date: he knows the strengths, value and potential of people around him."

Defeated, Queline sighed and shook her head. "Just, don't get in too deep, Seth, okay? It was too much work getting you here; I don't want to see that go to waste." She always fell back on that when she was at a loss what to say.

Poor woman. Queline was the closest thing he had to family, besides his teammates. She took a great deal of responsibility for him, even now he was nineteen and grown. Queline and Bracken were great inspirations, and the main motivators why he joined the Order. More than anything, he wanted to make them proud.

"And it won't," he reassured, feeling a bit like a spectacle. A large fellow getting the grilling of his life by a talking bunny was something worth staring at, no matter how much he'd like to avoid it. "I don't even think Chiyoko was *really* that mad. We did get off with just writing letters. That's one of the mildest punishments to date." The only time he felt more ridiculous was when he was first given Adil—small as the p'ake was at the time. Granted, he wasn't nearly as bulky in those days either, but he was always tall for his age and he hoped for something more intimidating than a sentient marshmallow. *That was a spring month; Sphene, I think.* Seth tried to remember where on the colour wheel they were now. "Is it Zoisite? No, that's too late. Or too early. Queline, what month is it?"

"Eh?!" Taken aback by the abrupt topic change, she answered, nonetheless. "Zoisite. Why?"

"Already?!" Seth blinked in surprise, counting each month off aloud. "Covellite, Prasiolite, Diopside, Sphene, Beryl, Spessartine, Garnet, Rhodochrosite, Alexandrite, Sapphire, Topaz, Zoisite." At his realisation he told Queline, "I can't believe the year is basically over."

"I was thinking it should have snowed already," Queline replied, showing her large incisors in a grin. "It looks like the strange weather will continue. It'll be bad for the crops next year if we don't get enough ground water." She worried her lower lip. "As if the heatwave last year wasn't bad enough."

"Okay, Auntie, stop!" Seth knew the signs of an approaching worry spiral. "You can't see the future, so don't try. We survived this year and we'll survive next. It isn't anything you can solve by worrying."

"You're right," she said, patting his arm. "Now, what is it you're supposed to be doing right now?"

He knew she wasn't asking because she didn't know the answer.

"B-but, you—I—" He gestured to the pair of them. "You stopped me on the street!"

"A good Acolyte does his duty," she replied, winking. "Go!"

Laughing, Seth ran to meet with his patrol partner for the day: a pretty half-blood called Imogen O'Day. The second he finished saying hello, she vaulted onto his shoulders.

"You make a good stand. Let's go!"

Okay? "Bit excited to be let out?" he joked, as he walked through town with her balancing on him. The girl was crazy in a fun, spontaneous kind of way. He felt self-conscious, but at least it wasn't permanent—unlike for those in Uwe's entertainer's guild, if the rumours were true.

"The cage has six sides and I climbed them already," she joked in response. "And there wasn't enough padding to practice tumbling."

Other tricks Imogen pulled on rounds were firing a bow with her feet and doing flips down a staircase like a slinky.

Seth did something more constructive by helping move stones for a new family in the Sanctuary to erect a wall around their hut. Working with his hands reminded him of home, in Egypt. He worked by instinct, placing and mudding until the surface was clean and smooth. *I was doing this when I fell into Illthdar.*

The ground crumbled. He fell. He thought he'd landed in a tomb at first, but when his eyes adjusted to the dark he saw trees. *So many trees.* He later learned it was Greenwood forest, but for someone raised in a desert, it looked like paradise.

As the days grew into weeks, it dawned on him that Illthdar and paradise weren't even distant cousins. It was purgatory clad in a shiny wrapper.

Queline caught him, after first losing him and then having a fight with a nest of heafodbollas—nightmare creatures with white bodies that looked like human skulls. She dragged him to Las and dumped him straight into a bath. For weeks after the heavens alternated between raging storms and perfect calm. Some believed it was due to the lack of mana, but he already knew it was him.

Throwing herself into work, Vyxen arrived at the wall before anyone else. Cypher tagged along, hopping around her legs. As a chill wind blew, she blew on her hands to keep warm. It was harder when the weather got colder; it reminded her of home. She should be hunting and trapping with her older brother, collecting furs to sell and meat to store. So much needed doing all year round, but it was when the temperature plummeted it became a race against time. Nervous energy made her jittery. She *needed* something to do.

"Salutations, Vyxen." Scyanatha waved.

"You're up early," Abaddon added, as the pair came onto the battlements.

"Boohzoo," Vyxen returned, looking around with surprise. It wasn't shift time yet, the last lot of guards still leaned against the wall, fatigued. *That'll be me in a few hours. This part of the job is so boring!* "You're early, too."

"One of the w-women in our barracks woke everyone having a flaming nightmare." Abaddon's deliberate phrasing transmitted the message with ease.

"Is she part phoenix or something?" She didn't realise fire fae bedded alongside ice and water. "Poor them," she said, face wreathed with sympathy. "And poor Nyima, too."

"It was quite startling to those of a cold disposition," Scy confirmed. "I believe they left to escape the heat. They hadn't returned when we left."

"Culvers cleared everyone out, so he could construct a better sleeping area for her." Abaddon's shoulders hunched as they added, "There's not a lot of space, and people were mad."

"Better cramped quarters than burning in our beds," Scy replied. Vyxen shuddered at the thought and changed the subject. "Did you hear about the letter Date's supposed to have got?"

Quartz barracks buzzed with descriptions of an ornate scroll, and others said it was delivered by footmen. Hearsay. Queline was the Order's herald and delivered correspondence.

"Do you mean the part about the feathered delivery person, or where Date broke the seal and it unravelled across the floor?" Scy countered, lips twitching with amusement.

Vyxen shook her head. "According to Seth and Tundra—I saw them on the stairs—Date was acting weird about it, so they went to see if he was okay."

"You could ask him," Abaddon pointed out. "He might tell you. I, um, h-heard that he likes people to be direct."

She shrugged, not really interested in the gossip mill, even as a diversion from her own troubles.

Scy's gaze grew shrewd as she took in the exaggerated gesture. Tengu were an interesting species, even among all the others Vyxen could be curious about. It was odd she chose *not* to question him. "How is your meditation going?" she asked instead.

"Bad." Vyxen giggled. "I was hoping I'd suddenly grow fairy wings and throw glitter that makes people fly."

"I could teach you some tuning techniques," she offered, engaging smile on her face.

"Couldn't hurt," Vyxen replied. "Maybe I'll get the power to open portals, so I can go home."

Abaddon's brow creased with pity, and they turned their back, so Vyxen wouldn't see.

"Anything is possible," Scy said in a tactful manner. She didn't want to explain portals were ritual based, not a power. "Faeries travelled through the veil in the past, it might be possible to again one day."

"We need a crystal detector," Abaddon commented, turning around and scowling. "If we had one we could restore all of Vvekw much sooner."

"That'd be nice," Vyxen sighed, slumping against the wall.

"Vvekw isn't a normal mineral," Scy said, regretful. "Even if we used companions capable of sniffing out concentrations, we could wind up finding nothing more than a mana spring."

"Good morning," Tundra called, grunting as he came up the steps and cutting through the melancholic atmosphere. Once there, he propped his crutches against the wall and seated himself on the ledge. Noting the lack of personnel, he remarked, "There's something happening if we're this short handed."

"Have you heard anything?" Scy queried with renewed interest. He was usually good for gossip.

He shrugged. "I might have, but I'm not too sure."

"Any of your other friends coming to join us?" Vyxen asked, leading him to volunteer more details. "Like Date, for example?" She didn't bother being subtle.

He shook his head. "He's doing rounds. You'll see him sooner or later."

"We heard he got a letter; what about?" Scy prompted.

"Just some preening, gold crested pheasants with their feathers ruffled," Date said, voice cutting loud enough for anyone to hear. "I'll read it aloud to prove it."

"Don't," Tundra cautioned. "Your version of dramatic reading is nothing anyone wants to see this early in the morning." He ignored Date's answering snort to address the others. "Only he thinks it's interesting."

"You don't know him like I do," Date countered, lowering his voice to normal volume. Jaw muscles twitching, as he clenched and unclenched them, he said, "And I don't think it's interesting; I think it's comical."

Tundra shook his head and didn't reply.

Having interpreted the movement to indicate the conversation was finished, Date produced a folded piece of vellum from a hidden pocket. "The names used are particularly funny: 'Oh lingering apparition,'" he quoted, "'You are too small and insignificant to be a spiteful spectre to our mountain family. Exorcise yourself from our memories, ghost.' He couldn't be bothered to put a signature, but I knew he would write."

"Wow, riveting," Vyxen remarked, sarcastic.

Date snorted and returned the paper to his pocket. "No, it isn't," he admitted. "I've clearly irked them, however, and that makes me happy."

"You're like the pith of a grapefruit," Tundra pointed out, talking over the mocking laugh in return. "You're not happy, you're bitter. You're just going to keep waving that thing around at every available opportunity you can get, until one of us gets so fed up— probably Seth—and tosses it in the nearest fire."

"How often do you get letters?" Abaddon asked, sensing this was routine.

"Every few months. Usually because he's annoyed some people and news travelled," Tundra answered in a bored voice.

Scy hummed, nodding slowly. "That makes a lot of sense." As Date was about to leave to finish his rounds, she stopped him. "Since you're here, can I get your thoughts on something?"

"Hmm?" His eyebrow rose. "What?"

"Do you have any idea what could have gotten water sprites to follow a gremlin?"

"Anzu's looking into it," Date answered, naming a water sprite in Quartz. "I know what you mean. They're not what you'd call a natural alliance."

"If it's anything like the movies," Vyxen remarked.

Date sent a quizzical look to Tundra for clarification.

"A performance," he supplied.

Date nodded his thanks, as the rest continued to chat.

"I thought you might worry if you knew," Scy said to Vyxen. "Seth must have known what he fought. Not only did he know about the sprites, but he knew about the gremlin, which multiplies when wet."

"Ugh!" Vyxen looked horrified. "It's exactly like the movies!"

"Seth has been here longer than some expect. He also comes with some added life-experiences that most half-bloods don't have when they become Acolytes," Date revealed.

"Is that good or bad?" Vyxen wondered, recalling what little she

184

knew of Seth. She didn't pay attention to the answer, losing herself in a horrifying thought. *How long has he been here? Will I have to be here as long before I get home?*

Zercey had a free morning and no clue what to do. Having tidied her bunk and trunk, she looked at Laurelium. "It's been awhile since we went out."

The companion cooed in response.

The worst of the valley was put right, though the grass still had large bald patches. Those wouldn't be filled until the coming spring, short of nymphs making themselves sick using magic. They were willing, until ice faeries pointed out the snow would cover their work before the end of the month.

People did their utmost to collect and return keepsakes of the fallen, but there were still items found by companions. The pile was sitting in the research room adjoining the requisition office.

Waving her hand in the general area, Zercey said, "Go bring me something." She added under her breath, "Without a limb attached this time."

Veiko made good sentries, scouts or—in Vyxen's case—therapy pets. They were the most common creature in Las and plenty of Acolytes had one. Other Order companions were the mana storing p'ake and messenger floydrake—tiny dragons the size of hummingbirds with a shocking amount of firepower in their small, crimson scaled bodies.

Sitting within the shadow of the wall, Zercey watched Laurelium jump and flap about in the valley below. It wasn't the ideal place for veiko: they preferred trees or water. With an absent hand she pulled strands of hair to her lips and chewed. It was back to its usual brown shade since she wasn't resonating with Lerki any longer. *Resonating. Ha! Guila would ask if that's a euphemism!* She wasn't sure it wasn't in some way. The hair colour was disturbing now she knew the result. "No wonder he makes such a fuss about it," she said to herself. "He probably freaked out the first time his hair turned not-green." She had a feeling that, for full-blood venin, it was a bit more than accustomed vanity.

186

"You'll catch cold like that," Seth said, standing over her.

Zercey looked into his grinning face. At this angle, his orange eyes looked like two burning coals. *So pretty.* "Oh hi, Seth," she greeted, standing. "I was already cold to start with, the only thing left is to get colder."

He chuckled and shook his head.

At a sudden thought knocking her on the side of the head, she asked, "Say, how did you get so good at using your powers? You're a half-blood, aren't you?"

"I think so," he answered with a shrug. "I don't really know." Bouncing his head side to side for a moment as he thought, he opted to explain. "By the time anyone found me, I'd been wandering for...a few months, maybe? I'm not sure, it felt like forever."

Zercey whistled, impressed. "Wow! I can't imagine what that must have been like. I would've died on the first day eating something poisonous—almost did, actually."

"I don't know how I did it, either." Seth shrugged and shook his head. "I was a mess in every way a human can be. I couldn't even understand the language when Queline finally managed to catch and drag me in."

Zercey pressed her lips together to hide a smile. She couldn't imagine the fleet-footed borrower dragging anyone anywhere.

"With how many languages we humans speak, it makes sense that some of us wouldn't understand any of it." She could think of several people in Jasper Order who struggled just as much as Nyima. She'd heard a couple formed study groups to help each other learn.

"I've been here at least seven years now," Seth disclosed. "That's plenty of time to become fluent."

"Seven years!" she gasped, shocked. "And you've not been able to get home the whole time?!" The Order was touting Earth like the golden carrot, but if people were displaced for years, how could they guarantee anyone going home? *I can't mention this to Vyxen.*

She'll be crushed. Changing the topic, she asked, "What are you doing out here? I don't see Adil anywhere." She tried to spot the fluffy alpaca.

"Taking another walk. I just finished patrol, but didn't feel like heading in yet," he volunteered. "I turned him loose on the world first thing this morning. He'll probably come back with someone's shoes later. He's notorious for things like that. He stole someone's feather duster last week. Why he thought I needed one, I have no idea."

Zercey laughed, as he continued to list the number of strange and peculiar things the p'ake dropped into his bewildered hands. "Oh, God," she gasped, wiping tears from her eyes. "Stop, I can't breathe!"

Seth chuckled. "Companions are a bit kooky, if you haven't noticed."

"I didn't think anyone else went through that." The amount of junk Laurelium brought her was ridiculous.

"No one's ever really alone in anything. We just think we are when we're in the middle of it all. Once we're on the other side we realise there were other people beside us the whole time," Seth stated.

Zercey grew sombre. She could tell he wasn't referring to companions. "I wonder if I'll ever get to that point," she remarked. "Being on the other side of the learning and able to say stuff like that with confidence." She cheered up and slapped him on the bicep. "You're a surprisingly strong guy, and in ways more than muscles."

"Well, thank you," Seth said, puffing his chest. "That's satisfying to hear." Pausing, he jokingly asked, "Wait. Does that mean you thought I was all brawn before?"

Zercey laughed again and shook her head. "No, but you could pass for it," she teased, as Laurelium waddled towards them with a dead mouse in its beak. "Another one? Gee, thanks, Laurel. I love you, too," she remarked, accepting the gift. "Ew, it's still damp. Just where are all these things coming from?"

"Looks like a glaring of trekadisk made itself a home nearby," Seth commented. "I'll swing by and tell the others. They're one of those companions everyone wants because they have a useful skill. Like cats, they follow their prey everywhere it goes."

"So, we can use these to catch them?" That seemed kind of stupid on the part of the trekadisk. She made a show of putting it in her pouch, making a note to get rid of it later.

"Yup. Well, I've done my good deed for the day," Seth teased, waving. "I think I've earned something to eat."

"See you around," Zercey laughed and waved, turning back to see what else Laurelium would bring.

CHAPTER ELEVEN

Nyima stood by her trunk, peering at the contents like they would provide the meaning of life. The swathes of fabric and bangles wouldn't help her. *Although...* She pulled out a bone one. The design was blackened with ash, and a large crack marred the surface. A grief stricken look crossed her face for a brief moment. *Mother would have advice in this situation. I'm sure.* She heard Zercey ask a question. "Hmm?" She wrapped the bangle in a piece of cloth and put it back, looking up.

"I asked if you got the mission details," Zercey repeated, head tilting with curiosity.

"Some," Nyima responded, closing the trunk and locking it. "Chiyoko make me leader." She hadn't argued at the time, but she knew it was stupid putting her in charge when she still put words in the wrong order. What if she told the others to do something and got everyone killed? *I must think carefully before I speak.* "Let us go," she said to Zercey.

"All right. Is there anything I really need?"

She opened her mouth and almost replied in her native tongue. "— Rope and arrow anchors," she said, performing a quick translation.

Zercey groaned. "No, that means climbing! I *hate* climbing."

Nyima laughed under her breath. "We have Date helping."

190

Zercey brightened, then her expression fell again. "Great, flying and risking throwing up all over the place."

"You will not sick," Nyima replied in a stern voice. "Be brave." She gestured for Zercey to go ahead of her. "Let us go."

The location for the mission lay just outside the city. A vertical cave hidden in the valley connected to a larger cavern system below. Somewhere inside was their target: a dragon hoarding something Chiyoko wanted.

"Date, fly us down," Nyima instructed. "Lair at bottom—*the* bottom."

"There's a dragon," Date cautioned, staring into the mouth of the cave.

Nyima nodded. "It like it warm. Sleep in winter." She'd been startled to learn there was a dragon living in the valley past the farmers fields. According to Chiyoko, they left it alone and it left them alone. *If they never bother it, why must we now? How did they learn the dragon has the treasure they want?* All good questions, to which she had no answer.

"So, you're going to freeze it?" Zercey asked, as they made careful progress into the cave.

"Keep it asleep," Nyima replied, nodding. Some of the beads on her braids clicked and she tutted. Even the smallest sound could alert the creature. She grabbed hold and knotted them up away from her face.

"And the rope?" Zercey adjusted the long coils draped over her shoulder and crossing her torso.

"If it gets too cramped, I can't use my wings," Date told her. "I have a twenty-three-foot wingspan."

Zercey's brows furrowed. "How do you hide that under a tunic?" Date raised a feathery brow. "It's just how it works." He glanced at Nyima and she shrugged. Magic didn't need explaining, so why would any of them try?

"So, you need me to be an archer, just in case?" Zercey addressed Nyima. "That doesn't sound too bad."

"You're not here just to be an archer," Date corrected, and Zercey's face dropped as he held up his bow.

"He is right," Nyima admitted. "Plant magic," she said by way of explanation.

"I'm only part venin, though," Zercey whined. "Nyima, since when have I ever done anything remotely close to magicking plants?"

"It was Lerki's suggestion before he left," Date said, with a casual inspection of his black nails.

It was only then Zercey noticed he had stubs where each of the little fingers should be. The comment he'd made about cutting off pinkies took on a new meaning. "He seemed to think you could do it."

"Lerki is *way* too optimistic," Zercey groused. "What am I even supposed to do?"

"Tie down dragon; we slip by," Nyima replied, as they reached a ledge and looked down. It was a long drop, with a pool of water at the bottom. A thin stream of light behind them reached the surface, making it shimmer. The way would be much darker going ahead.

"A-and, if I can't?" Zercey questioned, looking fearful.

"Try," she said in a firm voice.

"If the dragon wakes up, you will be soper," Date pointed out. "Think of it as motivation to try your hardest."

Zercey's eyes narrowed, but neither budged. She realised she'd paired with two people who wouldn't endure complaints.

"Date, take me now," Nyima stated in a blunt tone.

The unintentional double entendre resulted in him choking, and Zercey smothering a giggle. It did much to cut the tense atmosphere, though Nyima was in the dark about what was so funny.

Looking from Nyima to Zercey, Date said, "You wouldn't be much heavier than Seth. I might be able to carry you both."

"We might surprise you," Zercey protested, not wanting to risk it.

"I can wait here alone," she reassured. Visions of his wings giving out, or one of them slipping from his grip and meeting an unfortunate end against the rock face danced in her head. "I'm good."

"It will take a bit," Date informed her, unfurling his wings and wrapping an arm around Nyima's waist. His hand stung as he pulled her close, his more protected arm and side numbing soon after from the chill. "You're colder than I expected." He was more used to Tundra's half-blood temperature.

"Am I?" Nyima responded. To her mind she was warmer than usual. If she had her full power the top layer of Date's skin would have frozen.

He shrugged and dropped over the edge.

Zercey gasped, clapping a hand over her mouth. She didn't breathe in until they shot past her, carried up on an updraft.

Dangling forty feet up in the crook of a bird-man's arm, Nyima couldn't think of worse positions she'd been in. Tensing and trying not to show fear, she clenched her teeth.

"I won't drop you; you're not *that* cold."

"Quenno," she muttered, falling back on her native tongue without thought. She forced her fingers to relax the death grip on his shoulders. "I not flying often."

"Not many do," he replied. "You're not that bad. I'm used to worse."

They touched down on a smooth platform in front of another cave mouth. Heat and cold alternated, like it breathed. The fetid sting in the air made Date's eyes water and Nyima blink rapidly. They both backed up and covered their noses.

"Stink worse inside," she murmured, steeling herself.

"I know, I'm not looking forward to it." Date's oversized nose was burning like he'd wiped it with pepper oil.

"Get Zercey."

Date gave a short salute and flapped his wings, taking off.

Do your best. For their sake. With a firm nod, she forced away the reminder she wasn't supposed to lead. Chiyoko was very clear during the briefing that Tundra, Magnilla and Lerki were the preferred trio, but since none were available, Nyima's team were second best.

You can do this, Nyima. You are a trained warrior. You have hunted beasts in the deadly green. You have led armies and brought down kingdoms. You can face one stupid, fire breathing lizard. She fisted her hands, forcing them to stop shaking. It was the fire bit that scared her. Ice elementals weren't fond of it in the first place, but the devastation it wrought her tribe left her with a paralysing fear. Even Date lighting torches for them to see by frightened her. *You must do this for the others. They're relying on you. Be strong.*

The smell was putrid. It got worse as she edged into the cave. Something scored grooves into the wall, two finger widths wide.

Claw marks? She stood in the centre of the opening and stretched her arms wide. She could just about touch each wall. *It is not wide, but long.* Drag marks in the floor from its body and tail supported the theory. *Short legs, too.* It was closer to a snake. *I can kill snakes. We can bring it back for dinner.* A smile tugging one side of her mouth up, she clasped her hands together. A gold glow appeared between, and she opened them to reveal a large orb of mana. Splitting it in two, she tossed one into the cave. It shattered as it hit the ground, sending ice skittering over the surface and up the walls. The other she blew on gently. It dissolved into blue dust, chilling the air. Snowflakes floated down the tunnel.

"Wow!" Zercey exhaled an icy puff. She stepped forward and paused. "Ew. The smell is almost as bad as the eye burning." She pinched her nose.

Nyima hid her amusement. If Zercey arrived sooner she would have complained more.

"What does this thing eat?"

"You don't want to know," Date murmured, with wry amusement.

The tunnel was shorter than Nyima guessed, and they arrived at the dragon's den to see the creature in a deep sleep upon a bed of gold. Long and thin, its scales gleamed like thousands of new copper coins in the firelight. It looked like a large snake with legs. What Nyima hadn't expected were bull horns on its forehead. It didn't have wings, leaving the question of how it got in and out of its home a mystery.

Nyima used more mana to freeze the walls of the den, further lowering the temperature and putting the beast into hibernation. This accomplished, Zercey set up a sentry point, her back hugging the furthest wall, while she and Date moved closer inside.

"What are we looking for?" he whispered, as they reached a secondary chamber.

"Pot," she replied, not knowing how to describe it fully.

"Fine, but which one?" Date pointed at two. The look on his face said she needed to explain more.

She scowled and thought of how Chiyoko said it. "An emerald pot with golden handles," she said after a pause.

Date nodded and turned to look, leaving her to sigh with relief.

"Found it," he crowed in an undertone. He dug through a small treasure mound and located it. "This thing is gaudy, even by rich family standards," he muttered. "They probably used it as a companion's water bowl."

That was easy. Nyima shook her head, determined to stay focused. "Let's go."

"I'll carry this," Date offered, mindful of his volume. "However, one of you will need to hold it when we fly back up."

Really? Nyima gave him a bland stare.

He held her gaze, then sniggered.

She rolled her eyes and gestured for him to go ahead.

They entered the main part of the den to see Zercey bobbing about and gesturing to the dragon. Steam poured from its nostrils and it appeared on the verge of waking.

Nyima nodded and directed her to the entrance. Something dripped on her head and she looked up. Her ice was melting. *I hate this planet.*

There was a clatter as Zercey dropped an anchor-tipped arrow. She was trying to slot one in her bow and aim it at the dragon's eye; her best target.

Groggy, the dragon swiped its tail.

Nyima and Date leapt over. "Run!" she hissed, shooting past Date towards Zercey. She pulled Zercey's arm, spinning her around, and lost her grip. "Zercey!"

Date didn't need telling twice. "Catch!" He threw the bowl to Zercey, causing her to drop her bow and arrows. "Ooof!"

The dragon's eyes snapped opened.

"Idiot!" Zercey turned and staggered a few paces, feeling a shove from behind.

"RUN!" Date snatched an arrow from her hip quiver, turned and fired.

There was a roar, followed by a strange indrawn breath. The dragon jerked its head up and belched, bathing the cavern with intense heat. They fled the backwash, the dragon hot on their heels.

Nyima lobbed icy orbs in rapid succession, aiming for the walls and ceiling. The rock groaned, splitting apart and raining debris. Jets of heat blasted down the tunnel. The cave glowed red, melting the ice clinging to the walls and ceiling. Her heat kissed skin turned blotchy. Patches changing from cobalt to glacier. She gasped. *No!* She fled.

"Jump and I'll grab you on the way down!" Date called, as she caught up.

"What if you miss?!" Zercey kept pace beside Nyima, spying the mask of terror on her face.

"Give," she ordered, holding a hand out for the pot.

The dragon smashed through fallen rock. It roared and slithered along the cavern, leaving gravel and stone powder in its wake. Zercey threw the pot to Nyima and yanked off the length of rope she wore. "Date, jump!" She threw it behind, hoping to tangle the beast's legs.

The end of the tunnel was in sight, with a drop waiting.

Nyima grabbed Zercey as her pace faltered. She shut her eyes as she jumped. The wind whistled in her ears as they plummeted. Date yanked them both into his arms. The sound of his wings flapping echoed, and they ascended to the top.

"Guess we're safe," Zercey said, pointing at the sheer drop.

Nyima and Date looked at each other.

"Dragon," she said.

"No, we're not," Date added.

Zercey threw her hand up, exasperated. "It doesn't have wings! How is it going to fly without wings?!"

"Trust me, it flies!" He grunted with effort and commented in a wry voice, "You might have been right about more than one trip." The dragon bellowed.

"Almost there," Date puffed. "I'm going to have to drop you. It'll chase—I can't outfly it like this."

"Fine," Nyima agreed. "We attack from ground."

"You'll strike it from below," Zercey corrected. "My bow is still in the cave!" Peering past Date's shoulder, her stomach lurched. "It's coming!" Zercey panicked.

"Not helping," Nyima said, letting go of the pot with one hand to rain shards of ice.

The gleaming serpent twisted and coiled, rising after them. Once again, Illthdar laughed in the face of logic and made a mockery of physics.

The trio shot out of the cavern. Date dropped Nyima and Zercey into the grass, along with the pot. The dragon sailed over their heads into the sky.

Like a winged mongoose tackling a horned snake, Date weaved through the dragon's copper coils.

Nyima and Zercey sat up, shaking off their aches from the rough landing.

"Nyima, give me that, I have an idea." Taking the pot, Zercey stood and whistled. "Hey, did you lose something?!" She looked at Nyima. "Running again."

The pair took off, leaving Date wondering why the dragon wasn't chasing him. When he spotted what happened he went after it.

Nyima slid to her knees in the long grasses. As the dragon flew over her head, she flicked her hand up, piercing its underbelly with icy spears.

The dragon roared at the sudden cold snap, twisting around and flailing.

Date barked right in its face as he flew by.

The dragon dove into the ground, scoring a large groove, then shot up again. Its tail snapped into Date, slapping him down. A twisting meander had it heading in the vague direction of its hole, slinking away with a roar.

"Yaa!" Zercey hopped up and down, holding the bowl aloft like a trophy. "We won!"

Date's pathetic gasps silenced her. *"Ow!"*

"Date, are you okay?" She dropped the pot and ran to him.

Nyima brushed herself off and joined them. "How bad is hurt?" She crouched and looked him over, not wanting to touch and make it worse. "Where?"

"Basically everywhere," he groaned, lying down. He whimpered for a moment, then took the offered hands and clambered to his feet. "Tengu have no durability," he revealed, hugging himself and grimacing. "You two look fine." Both women were grazed and dirty, but otherwise unharmed.

"You really are part bird," Zercey concluded, amazed. "Your bones are probably hollow on the inside."

"Mostly," he admitted, as Nyima and Zercey put him between them and helped him walk. "Nothing's broken," he complained in a grudging voice. "But—*ahhh,*" he groaned and hissed, "I kind of wish it was. It might not hurt so much. I don't have Tundra's pain tolerance."

"He can take a hit?" Zercey guessed. "With his muscles I'm surprised he feels anything."

The mention of Tundra's muscles put colour in Nyima's cheeks, but lucky for her no one noticed. *Scyanatha is right, I should get that under control. So stupid.*

"I admire him," Date revealed. "Seth too. Though, if you tell either one, I'll deny everything. Even Lerki is impressive when he's mad." A small smile flitted across his lips. "They can take a good beating; I try to avoid it."

"You are smarter," Nyima said, agreeing avoiding a hit was better than being able to take one.

Date let out a dry, but strangled laugh. "It doesn't feel that way at the moment, but thank you."

With two of the men's team effectively out of commission, Abaddon, Seth and the women found themselves busy again. This didn't bode well for Tundra, because it meant he had the immense pleasure of spending more time with Date.

A cooped-up Date, nursing a recent reminder people who were supposed to be dead ought to act like it. The letter didn't make it until the end of the week. To Seth's surprise, Tundra did it in before he could get his hands on it.

"You could exercise," he suggested, one afternoon.

Date flapped a hand and continued pacing.

"It would burn off that excess energy you have." It'd also amuse him, but he didn't say that.

"Can't," Date muttered, still pacing. "I don't want to strain and cause real damage, instead of being sore."

"It's been a week—quarter-whatever-you-call-it—already," Tundra pointed out, resting his elbows on the table. "You're being over cautious and you know it."

"I could break your other leg!" Date shot back. He gestured to their surroundings. "This is Quartz barracks, why are you here again?"

"It's a dirty job," Tundra quipped, smirking.

"Fuck you, too."

They chuckled, and Tundra took it as a sign Date was in a better mood. At least to have a conversation that didn't end in him cussing out every single person he knew. "What do you think?"

"A lot of things, mostly how helpful it would be if you'd complete a full sentence," Date snarked. "About what?"

"The new Acolytes," Tundra replied.

Date snorted, wondering what the real purpose of the conversation was. *Tundra never cares about other teams.* He shrugged. "They're all reasonably dependable, given their levels of experience. Scyanatha and Nyima seem to be the best." He paused and added, "But, I haven't seen all of them at their best form yet. What are your thoughts?"

Tundra nodded. "Too soon to say, really." He shrugged and added, "Scy's hot, Abaddon's shy and Nyima's... cool."

Date's gaze grew sharp at Tundra's hesitation. "Is that so?" When it came to women, Tundra was chased and didn't express much opinion in who he dated beyond the requirement they be female. Now, he conspicuously refused to make eye contact. *What have we here?*

"Enough about what I think, what does Seth think?" Tundra said, throwing his teammate to the wolves.

Date fussed with some papers on his desk, letting the silence stretch. "I don't think he likes the push to get them to standard," he replied at last, letting Tundra off the hook.

Tundra seized the topic like his companion did a bone, or shoes, or anything it shouldn't have in its mouth. "Chiyoko doesn't have a choice, otherwise she wouldn't rely on half-bloods as much as she does. I think it took her by surprise so many of us survived the horde."

Date snorted. "Depending who you listen to that is down to one of two things: dumb luck or cowardice." He shook his head and turned on Tundra again. "Why are you interested, anyway? Are you done pretending none of it matters to you?"

"It's nothing personal," he shrugged, expecting the familiar complaint. "The sooner Leigong steps in, the sooner I get back to what's important." He raised an eyebrow at the challenging look thrown his way. "What?"

"I'm remembering when you first met Seth," Date teased. "You almost killed him because you thought he was your Lord Leigong."

"I was impulsive." Tundra excused his angry, fourteen-year-old self. "They have similar powers. Leigong wasn't exactly forthcoming about why he left me here. He deserved a punch." *Or fifty.* "I still can't believe the Order made me wait till I was eighteen to join." He shook his head with disbelief. He hadn't met Seth again until they were both trainees on the same team.

"You were only slightly less of a loose cannon than Seth." Date enlisted right away, having followed a group of celestials on pilgrimage. Seth and Tundra were already problem recruits, and Date made them a trio, having hung up his mantle of blade for hire. He had a habit of saying the wrong thing at the wrong time to the wrong person. Tundra had a habit of saying nothing, getting all the girls and driving everyone insane. Seth was a showoff; typical, awkward half-blood, who couldn't control his powers. Nobody wanted to work with them. When Lerki arrived, that made the trio a foursome. People thought venin were insane, and Lerki was no exception. How they learned to get along was a tale of blood, sweat and lots of arguments. Each found a way to relate, often sharing exasperated looks at something another did. They grew close. Like brothers.

So, it annoyed Date when Tundra kept saying he didn't care. "You haven't changed a bit; you're still a dick."

"Ditto," Tundra replied in a calm voice.

They glared at each other, then laughed.

CHAPTER TWELVE

Calling himself immune was a level of deceit Lerki found acceptable. Only because the truth was more complex and took too long to explain. When it came to poisons, being long winded upset people. They cared about what it did, or how to stop it.

He tried hard to make Phanuel happy, though he was often met with lukewarm results at best. Elves didn't see plants the way venin did. Lerki learned to keep his mouth shut, rather than argue; tidying and tying loose ends when Phanuel's back was turned. He learned a great deal working with the Order of Mana.

There came a hum and he cracked his eyes open. "Just a bit longer," he told the tiny eitercopp. He didn't understand her, but pretended he knew what the hums meant. She sang, so he named her that: She Sings—Ka-Teamose. Little buzzing tunes to keep him alert, keep him awake. He was almost there, he could tell because he could feel his fingers again.

Resting against a large rock, a soft breeze whispered by his ear. "I don't want to," he protested. "I shouldn't listen now; Date told me that's why I can't do much in fights. I never build a reserve like he, Seth and Tundra do. Because I listen to you, Earth, Water and

Fire..."

The wind blew again. Ka-Teamose's buzzing turned frantic when Lerki sat up. He reached for the stinger embedded in his neck and pulled it out, along with the drained venom sack. "Bag, bag... Ka-Teamose, my bag." He swayed, feeling sluggish. "Back to Las. Hurry." His hand fisted the dirt, and he stared at the grains and grit slipping between his fingers with open mouthed awe. Blinking, he cleared his thoughts once again and repeated his instructions to the insect. "No time, can't stop and see other venin. Back to Las. Earth agrees. Back to Las..." On his feet, he took three strides before he remembered why he was there. "Recluse leaves! Get the leaves, then go back to Las." Grabbing a fistful off a bush, he shoved it in his bag. Departing once more, he took a faltering step, then another. "Oh dear," he muttered, locking his knees. The way wouldn't be as easy as he hoped.

In another part of Greenwood forest, Scy held a branch aside for the other three members of her party to pass.

"Laurelium, don't forget what we're doing," Vyxen called.

It cooed and leapt onto another tree branch.

"It'd be really nice to understand animals," Vyxen commented, wistful. "I used to pretend I could as a child. I scared my mother a lot." Her brows pinched for a moment, then her expression smoothed. "I wonder what it's like?"

"I cannot, but my understanding is it's different to how some wolves communicate telepathically with their kin," Scy said, trying to think of a good example. "Others have described it as something vague and intangible. Animals and companions do not speak in words, but images and ideas."

"Like daydreaming?" Abaddon guessed, tripping over a root and letting out an exclamation. They breathed a sigh of relief and smiled when they were caught by arms of conflicting temperatures; one cold, the other warm. "Thank you."

"You're welcome," Nyima replied.

This was followed by Vyxen asking, "You all right?" from their opposite side.

"Yes, I'm okay."

Seeing Abaddon was still upset, Scy sought to distract them. "Are you still training in the evenings, Abaddon?"

"Yes, but only when I don't have a night assignment." They smiled, having been enjoying their sparring sessions with the many different fae, demons and half-bloods.

With Munin flying overhead, and Maggy and Laurelium among the branches, Cypher hopped along next to Vyxen's feet.

"It snow soon," Nyima stated, closing her eyes and breathing deep. "I feel it."

"Heavily?" Scy stopped. "Should we turn back?"

"No; is fine," Nyima replied, pleased and smiling.

Scy shook her head, also smiling.

Nyima raised an eyebrow. "No?"

"No," Scy replied. "We're here." She pointed at Laurelium, cooing and bouncing on a tree branch.

"Now what?" Abaddon asked, pulling out a small collection of decoy mice. "Do we use these?"

"Yes, but not just yet. We must send the companions to draw the trekadisk," Scyanatha instructed. She turned to Vyxen. "You should have an idea of what to do; you've done it before."

"Not with trekadisk, but I caught Cypher," Vyxen replied. "Is it any different?"

Scy shook her head, then brushed a loose lock of red hair back into place. "It is the same. You go with Nyima and I shall with Abaddon. It might be easier to cover more ground if we split up."

The team of four divided in two, with Munin and Maggy going with their owners. Laurelium and Cypher joined Nyima and Vyxen.

Dusk setting in, the pair moved at a fast pace, wanting to capture the creatures before nightfall. Both light footed hunters knew how to avoid disturbing the foliage. The problem for Vyxen was she grew bored if nothing happened. It didn't take long for her to need a distraction, which turned out to be questioning Nyima. Something she hadn't done since the two met.

"I heard you liked hunting. You were assigned to a lot of teams after the horde came," she began in a conversational tone. "Guess you did lots of hunting growing up? Was it like this? In the forest? You like the cold. Was it cold?"

Nyima's eyes slid to the side, then forward again. "It was fine."

"Just fine?"

Nyima sighed, struggling as she tried to recall the right words. "My—father was—uh—leader—Chief." She nodded once. "Yes, Chief. He was Chief *uv dra C'deney.*"

"C'deney. Didn't you say that when you introduced yourself?" Vyxen frowned, trying to remember the string of words Nyima recited.

She nodded. "Yes."

"Huh. And you're an executor or something, right?" She hopped over a fallen branch and turned back.

"Aetumuh," Nyima corrected, lips twitching in amusement. "Title: Aetumuh. Tribe: C'deney. People: V'neketyh." The language was littered with voiceless vowels.

Vyxen hummed, chewing on her lower lip as she thought. "So, it's like my people!" she said, brightening. "My people are Native American, my tribe is Sitka, but I don't have a title." Her smile was cheeky as she added, "Unless you believe my brother when he says I'm an official pain in the butt."

Nyima nodded. "I think so. We travel."

"Oh, so like nomads?"

Nyima shrugged, not having heard that word before. "I—chose to become Aetumuh. I must fight for cissuhan." She left out so much, but couldn't even think of the time between being with her tribe and becoming an Aetumuh. It stuck in her throat like a hard lump, unable to swallow and too big to spit out.

"You're like a gladiator," Vyxen proclaimed. "They had to fight a battles to win their freedom, too."

Nyima shrugged, not wanting to speak more about it. "You have brother?"

"*Ehn, nisayenh*," Vyxen replied. "My family lives in Alaska; much of it still isn't really developed, so there's lots of wide-open spaces. I have two brothers, one older and one younger. My dad would have a fit about this place. He always knew all the best fairy tales."

"You miss them," Nyima stated, empathising.

"*Ehn,* a lot. Me and Salem are the ones who bring home the bacon. With me gone—" She stopped and sniffed. "I'm going back home the second I find a way."

"We will help," Nyima promised, nodding. Her pale blue eyes fixed onto a point in the distance and she found herself saying, "I must go home. I must." She was taken aback when Vyxen threw an arm around her waist in a one-armed hug, shying away in case her chill hurt. Vyxen hugged harder and Nyima felt a smile tug her lips, touched at the gesture. "Thank you."

"It's okay," Vyxen replied, squeezing and then letting go. "We'll find a way back. It'll work out." Her tone was reassuring, but she couldn't help but wonder if she wasn't trying to reassure herself more.

Cypher chirped, bouncing into the brush.

"Cypher!" Vyxen called, surprised by the sudden behaviour. "Cypher, come back!" Chasing after she said, "Nyima, stay there with Laurelium, we'll be right back!"

I won't disagree. Content to stay put, Nyima took in the expanse of the forest around her. It was dark, the ground covered in a thin sheet of damp that blanketed her bare feet with mist. From her perspective it was like being covered in a death shroud. "I hate nature," she muttered, lip curling. Glowing, orange blooms strung across tree branches and hung in spikes of green algae. The atmosphere turned from the familiar cusp of winter to eerie. The veiko beside her cooed and puffed its body up. "You like?" She shook her head and rolled her eyes.

A screeching yowl pierced the air and sent Laurelium skittering away in a panic. Nyima took a step after it, but then remembered Vyxen said to stay put. The animal would return to Zercey, but if she got lost she'd wander leafy hell until the others found her. She sat on a rock and drew her feet up. A growl came from behind and she strained her eyes trying to see what it was. *I'm not afraid of you.* She gathered mana in her hand, keeping the magic looser than usual. Tossing it into the bush, it scattered across the leaves and along the branches, covering them with frost and driving the thing out. It lunged, and she overbalanced, toppling to the ground.

Abaddon and Scyanatha were having as much luck finding the trekadisk as the others.

"What will you wear to the solstice celebrations?" Abaddon asked, remembering Vyxen raising the subject before.

"A good question," Scy commented, thoughtful. She took Abaddon's hand to guide them over a gnarly patch of ground. "Do you wish to know for the first day, second or third?" She tittered. "The first starts with the yule pyre, so nothing flammable."

Abaddon chuckled, recalling an event from a previous year. "I like the drums and lutes playing while everyone dances around the bonfire. It's exciting."

"That is a prelude for all-twilight. The ball is far more important." She already had a partner in mind to escort her. All she needed to do was capture him. "We could engage in the masquerade and change outfits," she suggested.

"I think I could shift enough to mimic you," Abaddon replied, reaching up to try and see how tall Scyanatha was. "I will end up very thin," they chuckled.

"Then we shall match perfectly," Scy declared, laughing.

"Culvers and Trenfal are named Winter and Spring Kings," Abaddon whispered, pausing as they heard a noise.

"Yes, we must watch that before the final dance of the cloven fruit," Scy decided. "Culvers will have to lose, as his role dictates, but it should be entertaining."

"I wonder who will be matched," Abaddon replied, deciding the noise was nothing.

Cloven fruit were nothing more special than citrus tied up with ribbons and cloves, but for those who gave the fruit to the object of their desire, the reaction was key. If the fruit was returned, they were rejected. If a clove was removed and the fruit returned, friendship was all they wanted. If the fruit was kept, the one keeping it signalled they were romantically interested in the giver.

"I have intentions," Scy whispered, conspiratorial. She put her finger to her lips as Maggy let out a coo. "It appears we have some luck at last."

Creeping forward, the pair crouched low to the ground. With hand signals, Scy had Munin circle. "We need those mice now," she whispered, holding her hand out.

Abaddon pulled several from a pouch on their hip and passed them over.

Tossing a toy to both Maggy and Munin, Scy and Abaddon waited as they lured the trekadisk from their hiding place.

The cat-like animals came in multiple colour blends. Some striped, others spotted. All had orange eyes and a deep furrow on their brow that opened when they used their telekinesis, revealing a third eye.

Following Maggy and Munin after convincing a couple of young trekadisk to come with, Scyanatha and Abaddon ran into Nyima and Vyxen, both with catches of their own.

"Nyima, what happened?" Scyanatha pointed to the scratches up and down her arms.

"D'nagytecg," she replied, dipping her head to the odd-eyed creature in her arms. It was making a sound between a purr and a growl, as though it couldn't make up its mind.

"D-d-nag-gie…" Abaddon tripped awkwardly over the new word.

"Dee-naah," she said, pronouncing the word again. She stopped there, realising five syllables might be a bit of a mouthful. "He is D'nag."

"Are you all right?" Vyxen's hand hovered by the cuts, which were oozing blue blood.

"Fine." Nyima nodded.

"This is Rhys," Vyxen said, pointing to her feet, where a regal looking black and purple striped cat sat washing its face. "Isn't he adorable?!"

The cat grew still, looked up at her and sniffed.

"Where is Laurelium?" Scyanatha looked around, but couldn't spot the veiko.

"Ran to Zercey," Nyima guessed. She didn't blame it being spooked.

"How did you catch D'nag?" Abaddon asked, hearing the odd sound it made.

In answer, Nyima turned her hands out to show more scratches.

"Hands," she said for Abaddon's benefit.

"You must have wanted to be caught," Scy said to the trekadisk, who meowed.

Nyima raised an eyebrow at this, finding the suggestion unlikely.

"We know their location now, and it's getting late. We should head home," Scyanatha said, taking Abaddon's arm to help them on the way. Fat snowflakes began falling as they exited the forest, with it growing heavier as they neared Las.

Nyima was the only one pleased by this and dragged her feet to enjoy the weather.

Piling into the barracks, three of the four headed for the stove to warm themselves up, while Nyima set to making a bed of furs on the top of her trunk for the brown and yellow spotted cat.

"I heard some great news everyone will like," Vyxen declared, warming her hands. "You'll never guess what."

"Not without hints, at least," Scyanatha answered, nudging her.

"Okay, it has to do with the Order," Vyxen hinted, making it a game.

"Does it have to do with the High Elders?" Abaddon guessed, rubbing their hands together to chase the chill from them.

Vyxen shook her head and made a buzzer sound.

"Not the High Elders," Scy mused, tapping her lower lip with a finger. "Does it have to do with missions?"

"Hmmm, kind of, but not really," Vyxen replied, before offering another clue. "Everyone has been asking for it for a long time."

"Not free days," Nyima nixed the idea before anyone else could think of it. "Queline say the Order has not enough people."

"No, it isn't about time off. Okay, if you don't get it after this last one, I'm unfriending all of you," Vyxen joked. She leaned forward and said, "Everyone has something that needs it."

"Is it a mattress?" Abaddon guessed, and Vyxen made a bell-ringing noise to indicate they guessed correctly. "Oh," they were surprised. "I was sure I was wrong."

"There's going to be a new shipment in a few weeks. We're all going to be proud owners of sweetgrass mattresses. The barracks are going to smell amazing!"

"Sweetgrass?" Nyima asked, unfamiliar with the plant.

"It has the same name here as it does on Earth," Scyanatha said. "It is called sweetgrass because of its smell."

"My people use it to smudge and make baskets," Vyxen was quick to add.

Game over, Scyanatha fetched a first aid kit from a shelf. "Nyima, you need to clean those cuts. Trekadisk claws can carry nasty things. You don't want to get sick."

"I not getting sick," Nyima stated, unable to recall the last time she even had a fever or was the slightest bit unwell.

"You haven't had half the things that float around Illthdar," Scy replied, voice stern as she pointed towards a chair. "You have no resistance to anything; no immunity. Now, sit."

Nyima sat. She felt like a scolded child, and the others' giggling didn't help.

"It's a small miracle one of us hasn't caught something," Vyxen wondered. She understood the possibility better than some; her people suffered from diseases on top of a host of other unsavoury things when Europeans immigrated. Out of principle, she would never forget the tribal history books she poured over in the homestead kitchen as a child.

"Staples in the rations are fortified to boost the immune system," Scy explained. Her fingers dipped into the salve, which she smeared across the claw marks on Nyima's hands and arms. "It's partly why we have group meals and cook individually. A person could easily end up with delirium, bends or any number of things that kill without treatment."

"Well, that sounds fun," Vyxen said, going to her ration pack and looking in it. "Does it matter that we swap them about?"

Scy shrugged. "I assume the most benefit comes from something everyone would eat."

"Drink," Nyima suggested, pointing at the small pot of coffee grounds and tea bags.

"The Order must expect it, so I think we can trust them to do what's best for us," Abaddon said in a hesitant tone.

"Well, enough about boring rations and stuff!" Vyxen closed the box with a firm snap. "What's everyone wearing for this party that's happening?!" She grinned and added, "And who's taking a date?!"

Zercey and Raemina completed their patrol and said goodbye at the gate. As she passed though she heard her name called. "What is it?!"

"I said, have you anything to report?!"

"Nothing! All quiet!" She cupped her hands around her mouth, but still had to repeat herself when the person didn't catch what she said. "We need cell phones, or radios. Cups on string would be an improvement," she muttered, adjusting her hood to keep the wind from tickling her neck. *Illthdar is so much colder than Terni… the drafts alone will kill a person!*

It was a dull day, and she was tired. The cold reduced her to hugging herself, as she tried to stop her teeth chattering. Snow was the icing on the cake, coating the ground like fine, sugar crystals. If she was younger, she would have loved it, but she grew out of romanticism with her first wisdom tooth. All she wanted now was to sit down, put her feet under the stove to warm and slurp a hot drink.

Coming in through the butterfly-wing patterned doors was a relief, and she divested herself of her many layers as she trudged up the winding staircase.

"Hi everyone," she greeted, her voice slow and sighing. Or it was, until she noticed her bunk was empty. "Where's Laurelium?"

"She not with you?" Nyima asked, getting up.

"Careful!" Scyanatha was forced back a step to avoid a shove, still in the middle of applying salve.

Zercey threw her cloak and scarf back on, pinning both in place. "No. I'm going to look for her."

"Me, too," Nyima said, following.

"I'm coming, too!" Vyxen snatched her mulberry coloured cloak from the stand and rushed after them.

"Veiko are fat. Stay warm," Nyima consoled, as they hurried out of Las and towards the woods. She'd explained how D'nag frightened

Laurelium into running away.

It wasn't Laurelium being cold that worried Zercey, but the predators thinking she looked like a tasty meal.

Snow came down in heavy, feather-sized globs, but still struggled to break past the forest canopy. The ground was a mix of frozen and muddy patches. It made the way hard and slippery.

"LAUURRRELIUUUUM!"

"LAURELIUM!"

"LAUREL! HERE GIRL!"

Zercey's cries grew more desperate, the deeper into the woods they went. "I've had her since the test. She's my baby. I can't lose her!"

Vyxen patted her on the back. "I know. I've had Baya forever, too. Let's hope Laurel is hiding somewhere and waiting for us to come get her."

Zercey nodded and sniffed, feeling the cold burn a path up her nose.

"I'm sorry," Nyima said again. "I think she gone home." As the weather grew colder her skin reacted, turning a darker shade of blue. She was a walking thermometer reminding them veiko preferred warm climates.

"LAURELIUM!" Zercey's voice grew hoarse. About to admit defeat, she turned to her friends, when a familiar coo reached their ears. "Laurelium!" She whipped back around, just in time to catch the grey and black ball of squish as it launched itself into her arms. "What happened to you? Did you get lost? That's not like you!" Laurelium continued to squirm and coo.

"Hey, Zercey," Vyxen said, a faint frown on her brow. "I think she wants to be set down."

Laurelium turned and gave a distressed coo.

Zercey released her and the veiko flapped short wings, scampering back the way she came. She turned and cooed until they followed.

"She must have found something she can't carry back," Vyxen reasoned. "Baya does the same thing."

Not having a companion, Nyima asked, "They do this often?" She

214

was in the lead, speaking over her shoulder.

"Laurelium, don't get too far ahead!" Zercey called, as they almost lost sight of her.

Laurelium cooed and bounced, waiting for them to catch up before bounding off again.

"It's only happened once or twice," Vyxen confessed. "One of those was something I think Baya thought was a staff, but was actually just part of a tree. She was like: staff, stick, they're totally the same thing." She was upbeat and laughing as she acted out the veiko's train of thought. "Aren't you happy, mommy?! *Ehn,* I did a good job!" She made a heart-shape with her hands, and the others chuckled.

Laurelium scaled a tree and hopped from branch to branch, leaving the trio to follow. The ground was riddled by dormant, thorny vines, and would have taken too long to cut through. Not to mention Nyima was barefoot.

A few tree branches later they were able to climb down, while Laurelium cooed to announce they were at their destination like an Illthdar satnav. Late as it was, weak moonlight filtered through the trees, reflected by the snowfall, giving some illumination.

"Do you see anything?" Zercey asked the other two, looking around.

"No." Nyima sighed. "Nothing."

"Laurelium, can't you take us closer?" Vyxen said, crouching to talk to the creature.

Laurelium's response was to jump up and down and flap its stubby wings in frustration.

About to question it further, Vyxen stopped short when she heard ripping. Turning, she saw Zercey removed a strip of cloth from her scarf and was in the process of wrapping it around a tree branch. "Making a torch?"

"Veiko can see in the dark," Zercey noted, pinning one end of her makeshift torch between her knees and freeing her hands to use her flint and steel to light it. "Laurelium can probably see something really close by, but it's too dark to tell. We might be able to if there's more light."

A spark catching, Zercey gently blew on it to coax the fire to life. She waved the torch about, looking for whatever Laurelium found.

"I hope it's not a dead body," Vyxen whispered, crossing her fingers.

"Dead body, in the dark, with us. What are the odds?" Zercey replied in wry amusement.

"There," Nyima said, pointing.

Zercey moved the torch back. "What did you—" She gasped and rushed over to look.

Obscured in part by dancing shadows cast by the torch light, there was still no mistaking a face down figure covered with snow. Whoever it was had bright yellow hair, held back by a large clip. The person wore typical Illthdarian garb: untanned leather and unbleached linen, though the lack of layers implied they were unprepared for the change in weather.

"He alive?" Nyima called, keeping watch in case he'd been attacked.

"He's like ice," Zercey murmured, as she checked for a pulse. "He's still breathing."

"Nyima!" Vyxen called over her shoulder. "He's alive! We're going to need help moving him!"

"I go to Las and getting people!" Nyima called the reply and hurried off.

A muffled, frantic buzzing could be heard coming from underneath the man.

"Zercey, help me roll him over. I think he's lying on something," Vyxen said, already pushing at his shoulder.

"We might make an injury worse if we move him," Zercey replied, worrying her lower lip with her teeth. The buzzing grew louder. Shaking her thoughts away, she found her courage. "Let's be careful and not move his neck or spine anymore than necessary."

"Right," Vyxen agreed with a nod, reaching to gather up the long,

216

vibrant strands of hair. She dropped them when Zercey gave an abrupt gasp. "What's wrong?"

"It's Lerki!"

CHAPTER THIRTEEN

“Lerki?” Vyxen echoed, moving to check. “It is! What's he doing here?”

“Dying if we don't do something!” Zercey panicked. Nodding to Vyxen, she gave the count, “One, two, three,” and they rolled him onto his back.

Lerki made no protest, but the eitercopp that crawled its way from the collar of his tunic buzzed, happy to escape being smothered. “Poor Ka-Teamose,” Vyxen said with pity. She noted the outline where Lerki laid and said, “He’s been here for a few hours. He either fell when the snow just started or before.” Shaking her head, she added, “He could have died of hypothermia.”

“We're not out of the woods yet,” Zercey replied, distracted enough that she failed to catch her own pun. Shaking his shoulder, she tried to rouse him. “Wake up, Lerki!”

“Can't you do that harmonising thing or something? Would it help?” Vyxen suggested as she stood and pulled a jag-toothed knife from a sheath on her hip. She looked for suitable branches to make a stretcher.

“It should be working now,” Zercey replied, brows furrowing. “I never had to do anything before; it just happened. Could that really be it, though? I mean, everyone talked about how he'd be away for months at a time, but no one said how long he could stay. I don't know if this is normal or not."

"No way is lying face down in the dirt normal," Vyxen quipped.

"Reinforcements reporting!" Seth's boom accompanied the heavy step of his boots as he thumped through the undergrowth. He used his massive axe to cut through branches and clear a path. "You could freeze them, or something. Make it easier for me," he joked to Nyima, taking the lead, who sprung like a rabbit avoiding the thorny ground.

"You doing good," she replied, vaulting over a log which Seth smashed to pieces.

"Seth!" Zercey brightened. "Nyima, you're a mind reader! Seth, it's Lerki!"

Seth's eyes widened, and he hurried over. "What did he do to himself?!"

"Your guess is as good as anyone's. Maybe better," Vyxen said, tying branches together. "You know him more than we do."

"I've never seen him like this before," he confessed, unstrapping a set of long planks from his back. "Don't worry about that, Vyxen. When Nyima said you found someone unconscious I thought to grab these."

"Good thinking," Vyxen said, abandoning her task and putting her knife back into its brightly beaded sheath.

Zercey bit her lip, volunteering, "He doesn't look hurt, but we can never be too sure. We only turned him over when we realised Ka-Teamose was trapped under him."

The insect companion buzzed from her hiding place in the folds of Lerki's clothes when her name was mentioned.

"We'll have to ask when he wakes up, then," Seth decided, moving the stretcher into position, while the girls rolled Lerki onto it.

It wasn't the first time Lerki ended up face-down on the ground, but it was the first where he'd been far from help. According to Lerki, he was gifted with a certain amount of luck thanks to his venin tree: the gold birch.

"I'm going to love hearing this one, I can feel it," Seth said in a sarcastic lilt, strapping his axe to his back. He hefted one end of the stretcher, while Vyxen and Zercey took the other. Nyima assumed a guard detail, with Laurelium acting as sentry, and they returned to Las.

News travelled quicker than Queline. It was bound to be a topic of conversation when a person dispatched over a moon ago returned on a stretcher. Seth ran to find his friends, returning not long after with Date and Tundra in tow.

"This idiot..." Date rubbed his hand over his face, outward appearance irritated to disguise concern.

"And another one bites the dust," Tundra remarked, detached. "Better watch out, Seth, you're next."

"Man, if you don't shut up—" Seth balled his hand and shook it.

"Lerki, you better wake up; I can't keep these hotheads in line without you," Tundra said, ignoring Seth. When Lerki gave no indication he heard, he added, "Plus, you need to get this cast off." The trio clustered around the bed, moving aside when healers approached.

Awkward as she felt, Zercey loitered in a corner of the room, making herself available to resonate. Vyxen and Nyima sat either side. Her other friends, by now friends with Lerki in their own right, filtered in as news reached them.

It was hard to say how many hours ticked by. Zercey knew her eyes itched from tiredness, and Vyxen's yawns triggered hers and Seth's.

Fed up, Date tried ordering them out. "Go to sleep. You're not helping him exhausted."

"Follow your own advice," Seth retorted, slouching against a wall with his eyes closed. "If you can't do that, shut your damn pie-hole and leave me alone." His tone was sharper than any of the women or Abaddon heard before.

"We haven't been working all day," Tundra supplied, though not without shaking his head at Date when he opened his mouth to retort. "We're already rested. Seth, you're worried and that's fine, but Date's right; you're not going to achieve anything like this."

"Fuck sake, I know that already!" The windows rattled and Seth lowered his voice. "Sorry, guys. Look, I know, but I can't, okay? It's not a thinking thing. I know I'm being stubborn, but you two need to let me right now, got it?"

Date sighed and scrubbed his hand over his face again. "All right," he relented, voice clipped, "but we're hauling you out the second you fall asleep and start having a nightmare." Discussion over, silence resumed its reign over the infirmary.

Stifling another yawn, Vyxen felt her eyelids droop. A hazy thought drifted up from the recesses and she found herself musing about the one place she wanted to be most. The temperature took a sudden and sharp dip. "Nyima, you don't have to check on me, I'm awake," she said, guessing the cause.

"...What the fuck?!"

"Wh-what?!" Zercey chimed after Seth with alarm.

Vyxen opened her eyes. The medical room was gone. Abaddon, Date, Lerki, Nyima Scyanatha and Tundra were gone. In their place was a cold, deserted cave. Outside was dark, with thick snow on the ground. "What in the world?" She stood and saw the other two looked as bewildered. "Where are we?"

"Well, it isn't Las," Zercey noted, moving to the mouth of the cave and looking around. She hugged herself, not dressed for the bitter cold. "I can't see the Order anywhere. It's easier to see the spire in the dark," she added, as she ventured out and looked in all directions. She concluded with a shrug, "I have no idea where we are."

"There's got to be an explanation. I'm going to assume we're still in Illthdar," Seth said, following suit.

Vyxen fell in beside him, taking two steps for every one of his. "Any sign of the others? It'd be weirder if it's just us that's been picked up." She added in an ominous voice, "Unless something is targeting half-bloods. It wouldn't be the first time that's happened."

"Wouldn't this place be teeming with people if that was the case? It's not as though we're in short supply or anything," Zercey noted with no lack of sarcasm.

Seth shrugged. "Just going off experience on this one."

"So, uh, how many times have you been drifting in and out of sleep and woken up in a completely different place, Seth?" Vyxen asked.

"It tends to happen when you're dreaming," he shot back, defensive. "Anyway, we've got to get somewhere warm pronto, or we're going to end up like Lerki, or worse." Clicking his tongue, he muttered, "Man, next time I see Jingyi I'm punching him in the face for jinxing me."

Vyxen snickered. "Speaking of which, if someone was after half-bloods, wouldn't he be in the same boat as us?"

"Donno," Seth admitted. "He's from Earth, sure, but apparently a different version. It's confusing."

"Is this the part where I start pinching myself?" Zercey asked. "I don't think I've dreamt anything so realistic before." She touched an icy puddle and felt chill seep into her fingertips.

Seth growled in frustration and scratched his head. "This is making even less sense than usual," he said with a sigh, forcing himself to calm down before he summoned a thunderhead by mistake.

"I agree," Vyxen replied, as she squinted in the dark, trying to take stock of their surroundings. She brightened and said, "But, for once I really don't mind."

"Why's that?" Zercey prompted her, crossing her arms.

A slow smile lit Vyxen's face. "I think I know where we are." She scampered up the hill, kicking snow with each stride.

Seth and Zercey paused to look at each other before chasing after. Zercey called, "Vyxen, are you planning to explain before we get to wherever you're leading us?"

"We're not going to scare the daylights out of someone coming unannounced, are we? Which is okay, if that's the goal, but if it's not we need to talk about this before we do anything else!" Seth puffed, struggling to keep pace.

They came upon a well-worn path made of long, thin trenches of compacted snow, with hundreds of divots between, painting an image of the most common method of travel.

"SALEM!" Vyxen picked up her pace, racing towards a log house. Lights inside produced a warm, yellow glow. "MASON! MOM!" Several dogs barked at the disturbance.

"Mom?" Zercey repeated, steps faltering.

Eyes wide, Zercey and Seth shared looks.

"This isn't Illthdar," he said, voice shaking. "Is it?"

Seth arrived in Illthdar seven years ago, and never gave up the dream of making it back home—like most half-bloods. He never imagined part of it involved winding up halfway around the world. He struggled to remember his Arabic, which he hadn't used since he was twelve. The chances of being able to grasp English in the

222

fifteen minutes they stood on the doorstep while Vyxen had the life hugged out of her were remote. Seth felt like a creepy stalker, watching the family reunite, but they had nowhere else to go, so he and Zercey stood there. *Awkward.*

Vyxen's mother was a tall and proud Native American woman, with smooth, dark brown hair pulled into a ponytail. She had high, sculpted cheekbones, and faint creases around her eyes and lips from blissful years of laughter.

Her grandmother had hair as white as her granddaughter. She stood calm and firm like an ash tree, punctuating conversation with wicked quips, as befitting her sharp mind and tongue.

Salem, Vyxen's brother, was a tall and broad man, three years older than his sister. He had the same grey eyes as her, but a darker skin tone. His haircut stood out: shaved on one side and braided across the centre in a relaxed mohawk, it flopped over to touch his chin on the opposite side.

Bouncing around like a bunny between them was her little brother, Mason. He was about five and looked at everyone with a mix of awe and glee.

"Do you know what they're saying?" Seth whispered to Zercey. The look on her face said she caught something. He watched her mouth words and was reminded of Nyima and others doing the same thing during conversations. He tried to think what he'd heard about Vyxen. He was sure she said she was from somewhere cold. *Alaska?*

The family clustered around, asking a million questions, with him catching a few familiar words in Anishinaabemowin. He saw them gesture to Vyxen's outfit and he wanted the ground to swallow him whole. He never felt out of place wearing his battle gear before, but he did now.

Vyxen's mother kept touching her hair, unmindful of the tears running down her face that Vyxen kept trying to wipe away.

"Mom!" Vyxen sobbed, the sound hiccupping. She threw herself at her mother.

"Zercey, can you ask if we can come in? I'm starting to lose the feeling in my hands." *And my nipples could cut glass.* They all stopped and looked, caught by the strangeness of the Illthdarian tongue.

"Buhhh..." Zercey began, trying to translate the request in her head. "I-is right to enter here?" Her English was broken and childish. "Outside is cold."

"Of course!" A chorus sounded and the pair were yanked into the warm kitchen. Mugs of steaming, hot chocolate were passed, with mimes to drink.

Vyxen did all the talking, making huge actions as she told her story. Now she was home, she felt kinder towards Illthdar, if the smile she wore was any indication.

Seth and Zercey nodded weakly whenever she looked to confirm something. As a child, he wanted to go to America. He studied hard to make his dream come true. Then Illthdar happened and everything he learned was useless. He didn't know how he felt about being back on Earth, besides a sick nervousness in his stomach. *What do we do now?* It was the biggest question weighing his mind. His family had phones, but he didn't remember their numbers. His old home address was lost, too. His brow creased as he tried to recall pieces of his childhood that might help. He jumped when Zercey tapped his arm. "Uh, yeah, what is it?"

"They're trying to come up with sleeping arrangements," she said. "Vyxen's older brother wants to know if it's okay to share his room."

Seth agreed. "Sure. I'll sleep on the floor if there's nothing better. Thank him for me."

She nodded, twisting a strand of hair around her finger. "He say, 'thank you, that's good'."

"Okay, so it's settled," Salem declared. "You and Vyxen can share her bomb-site, and I'll bunk with Seth."

Vyxen's grandmother got up from the table saying, "I'll go find some extra sleeping clothes, and some blankets and pillows."

"Have you eaten yet?" Vyxen's mother asked her daughter. "Salem brought elk home, so there's plenty for the time being."

Turning to her friends, Vyxen re-asked the question in Illthdarian. "I'll pass for the moment," Seth replied, then went for a joke which felt weak. "I'm still trying to digest what just happened."

"I can try eating something," Zercey agreed. "Some comforting food sounds really good right now."

"Seth is okay, but Zercey said she'd have some," Vyxen relayed the information to her mother, who smiled and set about dishing stew into bowls. "Has everyone been okay, Mom? I'm sorry I disappeared; it was an accident and I was so worried—" Her voice failed. Tears flowed. Her eyes and nose turned blotchy and she sobbed again.

"Baby." Vyxen's mom embraced her and rubbed her back as she cried.

The night passed as expected.

Rousing and deciding to tickle her friend awake, Vyxen's eyes widened. The ashy quality of Zercey's hair brightened overnight, as though it never was. *Did I imagine it?* Shrugging, she launched her attack.

"Vyxen, get off me!" Squeals of protest and girlish laughter filtered down the hallway.

Breakfast consisted of eggs and potato fritters. Afterwards, Vyxen, dressed in normal clothes, declared she was going to throw herself back into her routine, starting by going on a hunting trip with her older brother. "You guys can come along," she offered and Zercey shook her head.

"No bow, and we'll stand out too much like this," she replied.

"There's no one else but us for literally miles!" Vyxen widened her arms to emphasise her point. "But, suit yourself. What about you, Seth?"

"I'm not much of a hunter," he admitted. "I'll find something to do, don't worry."

"Hmm, in that case, since I know for a fact you know which end to hold an axe, why don't you chop firewood?" she suggested, with a cheeky wink.

The task, normally relegated to Salem, was one Seth grasped with fervour.

Meanwhile, Vyxen's grandmother drafted Zercey into cleaning out the chicken coop with Mason.

"Where are you from? Why do you talk like that? What do you do? What's your family like? How long are you staying?" The little boy peppered her with questions. Seth's chuckles echoed from around the corner, separated by sharp thwacks of an axe splitting wood. He heard her hesitant answers and wanted to help, but

Mason already figured out Seth couldn't understand him.

"You curious." Zercey laughed.

"How does your hair do that?"

"Do what?"

"Isn't the colour different?"

An excitable fluffy dog shot between them, making Zercey jump. Not waiting for Zercey's answer, Mason ran after it, screaming, "TUNDRA!"

"That's going to give me a stroke every time he does that," Seth said, coming around the corner to see her with a hand clutched to her chest. "I'm really confused; the longer we're here, the more Illthdar feels like some weird dream."

"One look at what you're wearing should clear that up," Zercey said, lips twitching. "We look like we escaped from Imogen's circus."

Seth gestured to his eyes and hair. "I should be grateful they haven't pointed out the most obvious features. That's always a favourite of mine."

"Vyxen's related to them. Call me crazy, but I think that makes them used to weird hair and eye colours," Zercey remarked.

"Good point," he agreed.

"I need to pick your brain for a minute."

The sudden change in topic, had him frowning. "Sure. What is it?"

"This can't be real," Zercey started and Seth laughed.

"I know, it's unbelievable—"

She waved a hand to cut him off. "No, I'm not being poetic; it *can't* be real."

His reply was slow and thoughtful. "Okay, why do you think that?"

"Because my hair is still changing colour."

Seth's expression turned stony.

Zercey looked over her shoulder to see Vyxen mobbed by their pack of sled dogs.

As though having the same thought, Seth crossed his arms. "We've got to say something to her." He frowned, hating the idea of crushing Vyxen's happiness. "Are you sure? One-hundred percent positive?"

Expression matching his, Zercey nodded. "You mark my words, by this time tomorrow my hair will be greener than pezzat."

"How, though?" Seth said, running a hand over his scalp.

"I don't know, but unless I'm in two places at once, there's no way I could be resonating. I'd have to be with another venin." She made a show of looking around. "I'm not seeing any green haired people, are you?"

Nodding, Seth went into mission mode. "We've got to be careful. We don't know what lengths this thing will go to keep us here."

Zercey rubbed her hands up and down her arms in comfort. "I'll talk to Vyxen tonight before bed."

The night drew in fast in winter. Not wanting to upset Vyxen, Zercey stalled for time. She insisted on more card games and movies until everyone else drooped from exhaustion.

When she, Seth and Vyxen were the last ones standing, Vyxen said, "Okay, what's going on? Both of you are acting like you're expecting something to jump through the wall and murder us."

Seth gave a mirthless laugh, the irony not escaping him. About to answer, he was stopped short when Zercey raised a hand.

"Vyxen, have you noticed anything weird about us?"

Vyxen's face darkened. "Yeah, I did."

Seth's eyebrows rose. "Well? What do you think?"

She took a deep breath. "I believed it at first. Then, I realised Mason hadn't grown any—he's still the same height as when I last marked him on the kitchen door frame. Three times in a row, my grandmother brought up needing to get the roof fixed next week. She told me she was going to before I disappeared." Expression wreathed in pain, she added, "And Salem's been nice—that never happens. *Never*. I expected him to push me into a snow-bank and accuse me of trying to get out of doing real work when I saw him."

"So, you knew..." Zercey trailed off, biting her lip.

"I've been playing along," she admitted, eyes welling with tears, "because—I miss everyone so damn much!" Her voice cracked, and Zercey leapt to give her a hug. "I didn't wanna not believe it!"

"I'm sorry. I'm so sorry..." Zercey held her until it seemed like she calmed down.

Sniffing and with a hardness in her tone, Vyxen stated, "We should go back to the cave. It's probably half snowed in by now, but that's where we arrived, and the best way I can think of to get back. That or the thing I didn't know I walked through to get to Illthdar in the first place, but we won't see that until the snow melts, which is a long way off."

"Did you want to say goodbye?" Seth asked, and Vyxen shook her head.

"They aren't them." She looked like she wanted to cry all over again. "I need to go before I'm tempted to change my mind."

"Okay, let's get our things and go," Zercey instructed.

They tiptoed down the hallway headed for the front door when a small voice called, "Where are you going?"

Turning, Vyxen's shoulders slumped at the likeness of her baby brother, rubbing drowsy eyes, dressed in Bugs Bunny pyjamas with his pudgy belly peeking under the hem.

"Vyxen, where are you going?"

Her heart gave an agonising twist. "We're going to check on the dogs," she tried, but her brother—or thing that looked like him—didn't buy it.

"You're going to disappear again," he accused. His eyes shone with unchecked tears. "Those people are stealing you away."

"*Kaa,* Mason, listen—" She crouched, wanting to reason with him.

"Watch out!" Seth yanked her back as the floor warped and shifted under her feet.

"Quick, outside!" Zercey got the door open.

Seth pulled Vyxen out and lodged a shovel under the door handle. The dogs let out a series of angry barks.

"Come on," Vyxen said, voice trembling. She shook herself from her stupor. "Let's hurry."

"Do you know the way?" Seth rubbed his arms to ward against the cold.

Vyxen shrugged. "If it's still the same as the real thing, I should, but it knows we know now."

"Should we be glad or worried that it doesn't look like it's chasing us?" Zercey queried, eyes darting towards the house.

"It's an illusion," Seth commented. "If we see the way out, what do you want to bet we end up debating if it's the real deal or not?"

"Think you can stir something up, Seth?" Zercey asked. "If my hair is responding, maybe—?"

He interrupted, "Not sure; I can try."

228

Vyxen shook her head. "Don't do anything just yet," she instructed, leading as they trudged down the path. "We may need it later."

Lerki opened his eyes and inspected his surroundings. He was warmer than expected, and drier. Hands moved into his peripheral vision and he reared back. "No!" He toppled off the bed. "Stay back! It's all over me!"

"What's all over you?" Tundra went to lean on the bed.

"Don't touch it!" Lerki waved his hand back and forth.

Tundra retreated and pulled Date away too.

"Don't touch anything I've touched. At all! In fact, don't move!"

"What the fuck?" Date muttered. "Lerki, what are you on about this time?"

"Pollen—recluse poison," he replied, clawing his way onto the mattress. A goose egg sized lump was forming on his forehead, and he winced to touch it. "It makes people retreat into themselves."

"That why Seth, Vyxen, Zercey collapse," Nyima stated, gesturing to the other beds.

Lerki made a strange noise in the back of this throat.

"What is the antidote?" Scy queried in a stern voice.

The noise intensified.

"There *is* an antidote, isn't there?"

"Lovely," Tundra remarked, sitting again.

Date sighed. "The rest of you stay put, I'll get Phanuel—"

"Y-you don't need to do that." Lerki sat up and started peeling his clothes off, oblivious to the women in the room. "It will wear off. It's just, that's when it's most dangerous."

"How?" Nyima questioned, gaze fixed on her friends.

Lerki stood and went to inspect them. "Cold fingers, hands, limbs..." he listed, recalling symptoms from memory. "It fills the arms and legs first, then when it fades from those it goes to the heart—"

"And if they cannot endure it, the heart fails," Scy finished in a dead tone.

Lerki nodded, lips a grim line.

"This is bad," Abaddon deduced. "Very bad. They're only half-bloods..."

Date's chair made a startling scraping noise as he shoved it back. He stalked from the room and slammed the door, hard.

"Just needed air," Tundra said in a throwaway tone. "Ideas, Lerki? Also, keep your pants on," he added, spotting Nyima blushing and not knowing where to look.

"I need to clean," he protested, rubbing his hands to warm them. "I can't touch anything until I have."

Abaddon looked concerned. "Does it spread that easily? Is there anything we can do?"

Scy shook her head, informing everyone, "Recluse—not to be confused with the spider—is better known for being a hallucinogen. Those who are poisoned are said to fall into three categories: recovery, addicted and dead."

"Good one, Lerki," Tundra said in a bland voice, slow clapping. He made his way to the door. "I'll get bath water."

"I'll come," Abaddon volunteered, following. "I can carry it back easier than you."

"Thank you," Lerki called, busy stripping sheets from the bed. *Two cloaks?* He held the other one up.

"Zercey's," Nyima supplied, eyes sliding towards the bed again.

"We need to wet these," Lerki instructed. "Once wet, it can't carry." Looking down, he debated ignoring Tundra's advice. Amethyst eyes flicking towards the women, he remembered other races didn't see nudity like venin.

"It's an airborne pathogen," Scy deduced, filling the silence with relevant small-talk. "Are you sure you're well enough to move? You were exposed as well."

"A-ah, I am fine," Lerki stammered. "Much better now. I was impatient, so I didn't wait long enough before I came back." Correcting her guess, he said, "No, it cannot move in the air, or stick if it is wet."

"Why do that there?" Nyima demanded in an accusing tone.

Lerki shrugged and couldn't meet her gaze. He turned his back and fussed with the bedding some more, humming to Ka-Teamose sitting at the head of the bed.

Date stood some distance from the infirmary by the stairway
leading to the lower halls. He leant against the railing, head
bowed, taking fortifying breaths.

Tundra and Abaddon approached from the opposite direction,
heading for a supply cupboard.

"You might as well come," Tundra told him, pausing to rest. "We'll
need a lot of water and it'll take less trips with you." He jerked his
chin towards his crutches to emphasise his point.

Sighing once more, Date pulled himself upright. "All right, I'll
come."

"Did something happen?" Abaddon queried, surprised by his
reaction in the infirmary.

He grimaced and said, "The last time I saw recluse poison in use it
did not end well."

"Who was it?" Abaddon heard his footsteps falter. "Sorry. You
don't have to tell me if you don't want to."

Tundra raised an eyebrow in silent challenge.

Date scowled. "No, I'll tell you. It was the first son of Lord
Naigubu of Mount Takao." Bomb dropped, he breezed ahead, so
they could take their time absorbing the information.

Abaddon's brow furrowed, putting puzzle pieces together. The
fourth born son of a tengu lord had a grudge against anyone who
was an heir. He was so hated they disowned him. All facts pointed
to the most obvious conclusion: the oldest brother was dead.

"I know what you're thinking," Tundra said. "You won't solve his
issues overnight."

"I wasn't trying to solve them," Abaddon disagreed. "I was trying
to understand them."

"I don't think you'll manage that overnight, either," he quipped,
moving to hold the supply room door open.

"He sounds like he wants someone to," they concluded.

Tundra hummed, thoughtful. "I think everyone wants to be
understood, even if they're afraid of what comes after."

"What comes after?" Abaddon's head cocked.

"Sometimes acceptance; sometimes rejection," he replied, spotting
buckets in a corner. He raised an eyebrow when Abaddon went
straight to them. "I thought you were blind?"

"I am, but I remember where things are, and there are other ways
to see." Aware they were down one person, they asked, "Where did

he go?"

"To get more air," Tundra said, not missing a beat.

"Do you know what happened?" Abaddon queried. "To his brother, I mean."

"I've heard bits and pieces." He shrugged. "But, he hasn't said outright from start to finish in the whole time I've known him. He's not dead, if that's what you're wondering. I know that much."

"Huh..." *So what is the answer to the puzzle?*

Returning with buckets, Lerki took one, filled it and, without hesitation, tipped it over himself. He then filled the other bucket and stuffed the bedding and clothing in. Water sloshed across the floor. He was heedless of the slip hazard. That done, he doused himself one last time before going to Seth's bedside and putting a hand to his forehead.

"Careful, he wakes up swinging," Tundra reminded.

"He remains cool," Lerki noted. "It will be some time yet before he might wake." Turning to the rest of the company, he cast his gaze over them. "It's not safe to touch them until they have been cleaned properly." He went on to advise in a calm and serious voice, "You must wash before and after. No clothing that touches them can leave this room."

"A full quarantine," Scy said, as she moved to take a closer look, raising her hands when he tried to stop her from coming too close. "I won't touch," she told him. "Can't I check for myself?"

With some hesitation, Lerki relented and moved aside.

Date returned with another bucket to see Scy leaning over Zercey's bedside. Spying the mess Lerki made, he remarked, "You would do it that way."

"It was fastest," Lerki replied, in the process of bathing Ka-Teamose by running the taps and sprinkling her with water.

"They weren't on fire, you could have taken your time," Date argued, with a shake of his head, heading back to supplies for a mop.

"I'm getting colder," Zercey observed through chattering teeth. Their progress along the snowy path slowed to a crawl. She stopped shivering. "Huh? It's not so bad now."

"That's worse," Seth noted, sighing as he came to a stop. "I'm feeling the same way. Pretty sure that means we're beyond help. Vyxen, are you okay?"

"Sure, I feel great," she replied, mock cheerful and enthusiastic. "I can't think of a single reason why I wouldn't be perfectly fine."

They walked longer than they should have. She thought they were lost, but she was positive it was intentional. For whatever reason, the thing responsible didn't want them to reach the cave.

"Great, that's one of us," Zercey played along, ignoring Seth when he gestured wildly at Vyxen's back. "I wonder if we can hurt it?"

"If we can, sign me up," Vyxen said, making a fist. "I'll give it a hurting it won't *ever* forget."

"I'm just desperate enough now," Seth said, dropping his arms to the side. "I'll try anything. What are the chances I can use mana like this?"

"Let's find out," Zercey agreed, moving to stand on his left, while Vyxen took his other side.

He looked between them and chuckled. "Man, if this is what it takes to get a girl on each arm no wonder it's so hard to get a date." Cracking his knuckles, he shook his fingers out. "Any requests?"

"I like thunderstorms," Vyxen commented. "Got anything beyond fire and rain?"

"Well locusts won't do anything, I don't think," Seth mused aloud. "Solid electrical; I could also have it rain lava."

"Sounds good as anything," Zercey answered, shrugging.

"Go for lava," Vyxen said, eyes dull and apathetic. "I want this thing to burn," she added, forcing herself to ignore the image of the homestead going up in flames. *It's an illusion.* The knowledge did nothing to stop her trembling.

"Okay, then," he said, taking a step forward and raising his arms, drawing clouds together.

It's okay, it's not real. It's stopping me from going home for real. It'll just be like watching a movie. A horror movie. Starring everyone I know and love. "Stop!" She couldn't do it. She wanted to escape, but not like this. Vyxen covered her eyes.

Seth dispersed the gathering clouds, and Zercey ducked around him to hug her.

"I'm sorry, but I can't, I just can't—" Vyxen bit back a sob.

"Hey, it's okay. We get it," he reassured. "No one wants to see that."

A stabbing wind whipped into their faces. They shielded them and covered their eyes. It was then the world changed.

CHAPTER FOURTEEN

❝ What's happening?!" Scyanatha pointed to the beds, where Seth, Zercey and Vyxen convulsed. Lerki rushed to check, as she stepped back.

"They're going into the last stage," he stated, running to a shelf lined with jars and bottles. Picking a few, he shoved them into her hands, along with a mortar and pestle. "Make these into a paste, please. Thank you." He turned away without waiting to see if she complied.

Date, having finished cleaning, snatched the partially filled bucket before Lerki tripped over it. Raising an eyebrow, he withheld comment.

Lerki snuffed out a lamp on the wall, and healers arrived soon after.

A brown eyed, fox-demon carrying a musical instrument took the pestle and mortar from Scy. "Thanks for your help."

Lerki engaged in a quick conversation with the healers, then drew everyone aside. "We go out and wait. Only rest can help now."

After a quick stop in Fluorite barracks so Lerki could change clothes, the group wound up sitting in the Quartz men's barracks waiting for news. Looking for a distraction, Lerki removed Tundra's cast, while the women examined their surroundings.

"Tundra, keep using your crutches for the next few months," Lerki advised, watching him flex his leg. "It has only just healed and may not be strong enough yet."

"Sure thing, mom."

Job done, Lerki needed something else to do. His amethyst eyes drifted to a pile of books and note paper, and he didn't hesitate in leafing through them.

"I was expecting something a bit grander for Quartz," Scyanatha admitted, wine-coloured eyes drinking in the details.

The bunks had turned and artfully styled spindles, and matching trunks. There were separate tables for dining and eating, but no drawers to store clothes. Though, they had more space than the Jasper women did.

"The budget is put towards the women's side," Date answered without missing a beat.

The women chuckled, unsurprised.

"How you know?" Nyima raised an eyebrow.

Date flushed. "I did not spy, if that's what you're suggesting." He spotted Lerki fussing with his papers. Unable to resist, he put the lop-sided pile to rights. With excess care, he focused on tapping the pages against the tabletop until they were square, before returning them to the stack.

Tundra snorted, attempting to smother his mirth at the obvious play for time.

"I did not," Nyima countered, watching with amusement. "You did. Did you?"

Tundra shook his head, smirking at how Nyima had him over a barrel. "Trick question, Date. Stab yourself for safety," he quipped, referencing his favourite line from Ryan Sohmer and Lar DeSouza.

237

They fit so well with Date's less than awesome feats, he sometimes had trouble deciding which quote to use.

"Don't start." Date was unamused by the inside joke and sent a dark look Tundra's way. To Nyima he said in a throwaway tone, "They told me." He went back to rearranging things Lerki's fussing put out of place.

"Did they?" she replied, doubtful and enjoying his torment.

"What?"

His flush deepened and he refused to answer.

"I'm glad I am in the women's barracks," Abaddon mused, letting Date off the hook. "The men's has a funny smell."

"Fluorite doesn't smell," Lerki shared, as he walked over to one of the windows and pulled it open.

"Lerki, it's cold!" Date squawked.

Lerki ignored him, saying, "Well, not like this; it smells like potions."

"With the ingredients those potions have, that's not much of an improvement," Tundra pointed out.

Date walked over and slammed the window shut. "Stop. Touching. Things." He pointed to a seat.

Lerki sat, smiling.

"What of Jasper's male barracks?" Scy hinted, looking to Tundra.

Without missing a beat he said, "Smells like sweaty men that sleep without showering first."

Scy, Nyima and Abaddon all grimaced.

"Exactly," he said, crossing his arms with satisfaction.

Merriment curtailing, Abaddon asked, "Do you think they'll be all right?"

Lerki made a concerned noise in the back of his throat, but said, "I think so. Mostly. Recluse poison leaves its scars. Not marks on the body, but deeper."

Date slammed a drawer with more force than necessary.

"People become obsessed with it, wasting away in the process," Scyanatha explained. "It's said it makes people see their desires

238

realised." She shrugged, lacking the understanding needed. With her status and connections, she had few desires she couldn't realise without help.

Someone rapped on the door, and Date answered. A short conversation ensued, ending with him nodding. He closed the door and turned to the group. "They've woken up."

By the time everyone reached the infirmary, Zercey relocated to Vyxen's mattress.

Seth waved. "Look who's come to visit."

"They still need to get cleaned, up," said a healer, a ghostly figure of a woman, transparent enough the shelves behind were visible. "It's okay to speak for a bit, however."

"Thank you, Lyz," Lerki replied, crossing the room and seating himself between the two beds the trio were on.

"Jingyi, check you out," Seth commented, spying the freed leg. "Now I can punch you without feeling guilty."

"It was coincidence," Tundra dismissed, standing by the door.

"Coincidence," Seth repeated with a snort. "You damn jinx." He laughed and added, "Good seeing you looking better, dude."

"Is anyone going to tell us what happened?" Zercey sat close to Vyxen, their arms linked.

"Poison on his clothes," Nyima said, pointing at Lerki. "Got on you."

"That's the last time I do you a good turn," Vyxen joked in a weak voice.

Seth nodded and chuckled. "You're looking better than when we last saw you, Lerki. Gotta tell you, man, yellow? Not your colour."

"No, I very much dislike it." Lerki laughed, the sound whistling and echoing. The others joined in, worry and tension easing.

"What happened while you slept?" Scyanatha asked, noting Vyxen looked strained.

"We kind of dream jumped a bit," Zercey replied in a cagey voice.

"You were in the same dream?" Abaddon was surprised. "Is that

239

normal?"

"Illthdar," Vyxen said with a shrug. "Forget logic, anything is possible here."

"Phanuel needing that stuff is a new level of disturbing," Seth stated, concluding Lerki was coated in what he meant to collect. "You're not denying it," he pointed out to the silent room.

Tundra shrugged. "I'd trust him with it over Uwe, and Culvers would probably poison himself without realising, like you." He smirked and edged back when Seth tried to smack him.

"Thanks, dude, that makes me feel awesome. Really," Seth dead-panned.

"Anytime," Tundra replied, just as sarcastic.

The healers brought in buckets and sponges for Seth, Vyxen and Zercey to wash, and the others left them to get comfortable for the night.

Lerki was the last to leave, advising, "You should stay quarantined for one night. By tomorrow the poison should have worn off completely." When they tried to argue he was up and leaving the infirmary, he added, "Half-bloods are weaker than faeries."

That evening, while Seth was unable to join them, Date and Lerki met with Tundra in Jasper barracks.

Lerki sagged in his seat, thudding his head onto the tabletop. A long pause, then a muffled, "I'm tired," was heard.

Date, in the middle of sipping mulled wine, choked and spat into his cup. "You just—" He shook his head, laughing.

"And you're relieved it didn't end badly," Tundra noted in a dry tone.

Date's laughter cut off and his back straightened. "Any one would," he returned in a hard voice.

Lerki whined, "Stop, my head hurts."

"It would after that," Tundra said, grabbing hold of Lerki's head and wiggling it from side to side.

Lerki swatted him away with a limp hand.

Tundra patted Lerki's back. "So, what's really going on?"

"First erdepth seeds, now recluse leaves," Lerki hissed in frustration.

"Is the doppelgänger linked? Phanuel has their essence, too," Date reminded them.

"I'm no McGiver," Tundra stated, shrugging. When all he got were blank stares he said, "I don't know what he's thinking."

Date hummed, reasoning, "Common poisons. He could be replenishing stock."

"He's never needed them before," Lerki stated, drumming his fingers. "There are many uses, but I'm tired of getting them."

Date tutted, sympathetic, though judgemental. He let Lerki be and turned on Tundra, pointing. "You, either be all in or all out. Stop pretending interest in our affairs because it's something to do."

"You're just saying that because you already know I can't walk away," Tundra countered. He wasn't phased by Date, used to his confrontational behaviour.

Lerki whined again.

"You should return to the infirmary." Concerned, Date rose from his seat at the suggestion. "Come on." He forced Lerki up and

shoved him to the door.
Moving slower and using a walking stick, Tundra followed.

In the infirmary, Seth sat cross-legged on his bed, while Vyxen and Zercey shared the other. None had any intention of sleeping and were playing cards.

"Do you have any sixes, Seth?" Zercey asked, cards fanned out in front of her nose.

"Ha! Go fish."

"Vyxen, I'll take that two you had," Seth stated, holding out his hand and wiggling his fingers.

"D'ooh," she said, as she passed the two of wands over. Inspecting the oddity of the cards, she asked, "Why are they different from Earth cards?"

"They represent four out of the six royals that used to rule Woodralan," Seth supplied. "The names are different, and the shapes, but they're basically the same as Earth's suits; coins for diamonds, swords for spades, cups for hearts and wands for clubs."

"Why only four suits if there are six queens?" Zercey frowned.

"Because chess pieces are white and red here—they're already covered."

Vyxen fanned her cards out and looked at the suits with more interest. "Who were the six queens of Woodralan?"

"Besides all being completely dead? They're daughters of Queen Carnaphen and King Birthgou. The White Queen, Dirthgna, was the oldest." Seth had to pause to get the rest in the right order. "Eurdyce, Freymina, Gwenamitz, Hertenzia and Inani are the rest." He flipped cards over to illustrate which queen went with each suit, but Zercey slapped her hand down on the pile.

"Game," she reminded, smothering a laugh.

"Right," Seth said, chuckling. "Any sevens?"

"Go fish," she answered, and he drew a card from the deck. "What about the rest of the royal line?"

"The kings are still alive, best as I know." And better off not mentioning. They had spies, and nobody wanted to risk getting on the wrong side of one. "The White Prince, Las, has been missing

243

basically forever. The Red Prince, Raighbheart, is still around. He'd probably be a sure thing for king, if his mother wasn't a complete psychopath, and the Stewards of Woodralan weren't completely against it."

There wasn't much to say to that.

"Vyxen, do you have any nines?"

"Yeah, here..."

"Seth, do you have any fours?" Zercey frowned, thoughtful. "All those queens and there are only two princes and no princesses?"

"Yep," Seth shrugged. "Don't ask me. Some faeries have a hard time reproducing."

Zercey took the card away from him. "And threes?"

"Go fish."

"Drat."

About to take her next turn, Vyxen was drawn from the game as the door opened. Her eyes widened when Lerki and Date entered.

"Whoa, what happened?" Seth looked from one to the other, as Tundra followed. "Whatever it was, he didn't deserve it," he said in mock admonishment.

Date rolled his eyes.

"No one decked him," Tundra told them. "He wasn't feeling well."

"It's just a headache," Lerki protested, but sat on one of the vacant beds anyway.

"And we were just talking about what the girls were going to wear for solstice," Seth said with a shake of his head, earring clinking.

"Women or ladies." Date sighed.

Vyxen and Zercey wondered if all his quips were improvised.

"Don't let us stop you. We know how much you love talking about dresses, Seth," Tundra replied, the subtle hint telling him to continue the bluff at his own risk.

Seth chuckled awkwardly. "I'm still better dressed than you."

Tundra laughed. "Sure, Rupaul."

"Hater."

"Fu— "

"Lerki, what's wrong?" Zercey interrupted before Seth and Tundra spiralled into banter. Climbing out of the bed along with Vyxen, she headed towards the men gathering around Lerki's borrowed bed.

"I'm tired and my head hurts." He sighed. "It's nothing, but they made me come."

"If I were them, I'd have done the same," Seth said, standing up. "You were poisoned, too."

"You're not secretly one of those people who is good at looking after others, but terrible at looking after yourself, are you?" Vyxen's eyes had a shrewd glint in them.

"He is." His three friends answered in one voice.

Date added, "He definitely is."

"I am not," Lerki protested, shoulders rolling as he tried to sit taller. "I mean, I take care of myself..."

"I think they're just teasing," Zercey reassured, hand raising, though she stopped short of touching his shoulder when he slumped again, looking defeated. His head hung, a few wisps of green hair falling over his face. She spotted his lips twitching, and he gave a split-second wink. It seemed Lerki was playing a game. Flustered, Zercey turned to Vyxen to see if she saw it, too.

Vyxen's lips stretched into a smile, letting Zercey know the move wasn't missed.

Lyz appeared in the doorway. She took one look at them and sighed. "What now, Lerki?" She moved to check him, concluding, "Take something for the headache and go to sleep."

He shot Tundra and Date a smug look, and Zercey giggled. His body language told how unimpressed he was for being hauled in for something so trivial.

Tundra was unapologetic, crossing his arms and levelling Lerki with a stare.

Date kept shaking his head and laughing under his breath.

"Get out of here, clowns," Seth scolded. "I bet your last coin you're going to get put to work tomorrow."

"All right, we're going," Tundra said, turning and opening the door. He dodged to the side when someone almost collided with him. "Excuse us." Date made a gagging sound behind him and he shot him a bemused look.

"You're still awake," Magnilla greeted her friends. She nodded to Tundra and came in, hips swaying. "The others told me what happened, so I thought I'd check on you. How are you feeling, Vyxen, Zercey?" Rose tinted lips stretched into a concerned smile. She brushed a long lock of honey blonde hair over her shoulder, eyes flicking to Date. She was pleased at his regard, not taking in the disagreeable glare.

Zercey made a strangled noise in the back of her throat.

"Magnilla," Vyxen greeted, with an insincere smile. "How are you doing? When did you get back?"

Recognition crossed Tundra's face at the name.

"Just arrived," she declared, stepping close to the bed. "Training didn't take as long as I expected, but I'm happy to report I'm back and better than ever."

"Good for you," Zercey congratulated in a dull voice.

Lerki's head twisted back and forth at the exchange, expression unreadable.

Vyxen made small talk, asking, "Where's Thijs, waiting in the hallway?"

"He is," Magnilla simpered. "Do you want me to get him?"

Zercey jumped in. "No! No, that's okay! We're going to sleep soon."

Seth raised an eyebrow at this.

"I know you must have feelings for him, Vyxen," Magnilla stated, throwing her a look of utmost sympathy. "He's an attractive man; one of the most prized in all of Thies."

Vyxen gaped, wanting to fall off the bed and die laughing. She couldn't exhale without giving herself away, so sat there looking allergic while Magnilla went on.

"Only the strongest and greatest are allowed to become one with

246

my line, and I don't think you could hold up against a Thies." She reached over and patted Vyxen's hand. "Please, give up for your own sake; I wouldn't want you to be hurt."

Vyxen spluttered, *"Kaa*, no problem!"

With a satisfied nod, Magnilla said, "I came to see how you're both doing. How are you?"

"Never better," Zercey said, trying to hide her horror at the mental leaps Magnilla's mind took.

Vyxen disagreed and shook her head. "We've been better, but we'll be out by morning."

"It must have been a shock. I can't imagine what it must have been like. With our healing abilities that poison wouldn't have been a problem for anyone in my clan," she said, voice dripping sympathy.

Lerki jostled a table and knocked something on the floor, disrupting the conversation. "I'm sorry. It was an accident."

Date motioned for Lerki and Tundra to follow him out, already bored of Magnilla's preening.

"Interesting," she concluded, before returning to her favourite subject. "Training was exhausting, and I'm desperate for rest. Don't be surprised if you catch me sleeping in the oak tree."

"We won't," Vyxen answered with a cheerful lilt.

"No, we won't stop you," Zercey remarked. She added under her breath, "The snow might, though."

"I'm only here for a few days. My clan has a celebration it hosts with the first full winter moon. It's important I attend." Pausing for breath, she lowered her voice to confide, "It isn't my favourite thing, as the oldest bachelorette in attendance." She scrunched her nose and shook her head. "I'd invite you, but it's very, *very,* rare for outsiders to be allowed to take part."

"That's a shame." Zercey's comment was bland as white bread.

"So, I guess you came back when you heard the rumour," Vyxen said, inspecting her nails.

Magnilla paused. "What rumour?"

"Oh, just that Trenfal is supposed to be the spring ki – "

"Trenfal is Spring King!?" An uncharacteristic exclamation escaped at the news, her eyes dancing with excitement. She then remembered herself and coughed. "No, I hadn't heard. Thank you for telling me; I might have missed it otherwise."

Her eyes flicked towards Seth, who stared back, unblinking. "What?"

"I'll say this," Magnilla stated, seeming to decide something. "I'm an excellent judge of character. My mother and I can see into the souls of others. My clan calls them the eyes of God."

"Uh-huh..." Zercey droned, circling her hand for Magnilla to get to the point.

"You don't have to believe me, but remember what I told you when I left, Zercey. Date Toshiiro and Lerki of Gold Birch aren't honest people."

"You got a ton of nerve!" Scowling, Seth stood, towering over her. "You like being frank? Here's one: in a choice between Date and Lerki over you, I'll take their corner any moon!"

"I don't say this lightly!" Magnilla squared up to him. "If I thought for an instant you were like them, I would have waited. You haven't scrutinised who you call your friends, Seth Storm-Bringer; maybe it was time you did. God as my witness, I have always told the truth."

"Fuck your truths and get out!" Seth pointed at the door.

Magnilla shot the girls a sympathetic look, adding, "Don't forget, I'm never wrong."

CHAPTER FIFTEEN

With everyone as healthy as they could be the following week, the official kick off to solstice began. The first of the three days was a celebratory dance around the yule pyre. There wasn't a moment's rest for anyone in the Order of Mana. With potions and spells to prepare, construction to complete and decorations to hang, their days were loaded with every task imaginable.

"Scyanatha!" Seth waved. "Can you make the ground here tiered for the ice sculptures?"

Cheeks pink where the chill air kissed them, Scyanatha looked pretty and festive with her red hair curling over her fluffy, white hood. She smiled, flirtatious, and sauntered over to him. "Oh, I think we can manage something," she said in a pleasant voice, mindful how to play the game. "How many do they need?"

"Three, tops," he replied, chuckling and trying not to look too obvious at the ruse for her attention. "I don't know about Nyima, but Jingyi?" He made a face and shook his head. "He doesn't have much of an imagination."

"I would not write him off just yet," she cautioned, tapping her fingers in a playful rhythm against Seth's forearm. "Jaspers are fighters, yes, but we are also crafters. He may surprise you."

"The only way he surprises me these days is when he comes up behind me and waits for me to notice." He wore an endearing smile as he rubbed the back of his neck.

Scy's smile stretched and her red-wine eyes slipped to a point past Seth's shoulder.

"He's there right now, isn't he?" Seth spun around, swinging and missing as Tundra ducked, chuckling.

Scy tittered, covering her mouth with her hand.

"You're getting better," he said. "At least you know I'm doing it on purpose."

"Man," Seth swatted his shoulder, "I'm starting to miss you hopping."

Tundra shook his head. "So, you need me a leg down before you can get a leg up?"

"You're an asshole." He chortled. "Scyanatha's getting your tiers, anyway. How many do you want?"

"For me, none, but Nyima seems to have plans enough for three," he said, brows pinching when Seth slapped his knee.

"Ha! Called it!" He pointed at Scy, then grew bashful. "Err, called it."

"I should be able to manage something," she offered, amused and smiling. "How big did you want them?"

"First one: knee height," Nyima said, approaching and gesturing to her bare leg. "Next, go up the same." She brought her hands up to her bare waist to illustrate her meaning. "And top," she concluded, repeating the action and touching her bare shoulder.

Tundra nodded, adding, "It'll be in rings, but people will need a path to the pyre through the middle."

"That sounds simple enough," Scy reassured them, tapping her lip in a thoughtful manner. "Maybe carved arches..."

"Each tier is— " Nyima paused and spread her arms wide. "— This."

Scyanatha nodded, trying to keep her amusement from showing at the sight of Tundra's eyes tracking Nyima's actions. "I see why you are asking me to make them," she concluded. "That will take a lot of mana, and you will need yours for the sculptures and chill flames."

"Other ice and water casters are helping," Tundra disclosed. He

gave an impressed nod to Nyima and said, "She's our ringleader."
"You'll be in good hands," Scy stated, beaming at them.
Addressing Seth once more, she asked, "What are you doing?"
"Not a lot, for a happy change," he replied. He added in a stage
whisper, "Just don't tell anyone I said that, I want to keep it that
way." He raised his voice to finish in a normal volume. "I could
make snow, but there's enough people who can make their own.
Abaddon asked me to get iron bars to melt down and bend into a
cage. It's gonna be the framework for the ice dome over the pyre."
"They should be happy with that," Scy enthused. "They find
pleasure in metalworking." The others returned to their tasks,
leaving Scy musing to herself. *Today is shaping up nicely. I
thought we might have to put more effort into encouraging some
people, but it looks as though they are making strides on their own.*
She smiled at a shaggy haired goblin and less fuzzy, but springy-
footed puck faery who came to help erect the raised rings of earth
Nyima requested. It wasn't an easy task, even with the three of
them and Scy cursed the lack of mana for making her so weak.

Once, the barrier between Illthdar and worlds like Earth was
thinner than the whispers between lovers sharing a pillow.
Scyanatha was the younger of two children born to an iron falloy
queen and her beloved husband, an air puca of the Unseelie court.
An Unseelie princess should be stronger, but several hundred years
trapped on the wrong side of the veil withered her power. She
didn't despair of the time spent on Earth, it was an education and
enjoyment. She had her brother, his dragon lover, their uncle and
her dear friend, Maraxis, to keep her company. Between them,
they'd seen empires rise and fall—and helped a few along—
amassed a fortune she couldn't spend in her lifetime, broken more
hearts than she recalled and travelled to the most obscure and
bedevilled places the planet had to offer. Humanity gave her much
sport and she saw no reason not to play. With her own set of the
most delicious rules, too. How could she resist? *I wonder what
trouble they're causing now?* Over time, she and Maraxis went
their own way and lost contact. Her family would be delighted to
learn she'd found a way home, but the state of Illthdar gave less
reason to celebrate. The moment she stepped through the veil at
the stonehenge, Scyanatha thought she'd walked into a nightmare

land. The ground barren and dead. Scavenger faeries and things which feasted on death and fear overran the forest. The hair on the back of her neck stood on end. She transformed into her steel-wolf and fled. For days she ran, passing burned or abandoned villages, until she drew close to the coast and recognised the location as the Isle of Illthdar. Though others would call it a curse, Scyanatha was pleased to run into Uwe, who brought her to Las.

With one final effort, and more grunting than she deemed necessary on the part of the goblin, the job was done; the earth tiers were level and the precise height asked for.
I'm pleased. Scy located Abaddon to employ designing archways over the paths leading to and from the pyre. The central column, already in progress, had large timbers set in a square, overlapping pattern. They would build it high enough for the fire to burn throughout the night. A cage framework went over the top, with flowers and decorations woven through. Thick ice concealed them, revealed as the fire melted it, symbolising the defeat of the Winter King by the Spring King.
For yule pyre and all-twilight the Winter King presided events. On the third day, came the crowning of the Spring King, emphasising the dawn of a new ruling era.
For a land suffering rationing, the celebration managed to provide an obscene amount of food. Anyone who couldn't craft or build was sent hunting in Greenwood forest or to prepare meals in the brewery.

Drafted as an unofficial co-ordinator, Scyanatha made rounds to check everything ran to precision timing.
She found Date in the ballroom, tutoring "uncultured swine" in the ways of yule pyre and all-twilight dances.
"Unless otherwise stated, all moves start on the left side of the body. Left foot, left hand, to the left side, the left shoulder and so on," he said, waving his hand about like a conductor with a baton. Scy stopped by the doors to observe. The women wore looks of excitement, while the men looked resigned to their fate. These were the ones Date kept thumping when he passed, making scathing comments about a lack of form and disappointing their partners. *Sly devil. He doesn't only mean dancing.* Scy tittered at

his wit.

"Ladies, you are on the right. Gentlemen, remember: the lady is always right."

Polite chuckles sounded for the weak joke.

Date ignored them. "Most steps are in strings of two, three, six or eight," he said, before commanding people to pair up. There were male-female couples, male-male and female-female. No one batted an eye. Once they decided who led, Date continued. "For yule pyre, the first dance is— " he shot a warning glare to the usual suspects "—colloquially called the 'wench toss'." He made a point of clearing his throat to cover the ensuing sniggers. "It is, in fact, called the official bransle. We begin in a circle around the pyre with a double step to the left, then back to the right."

Scy nodded, wondering how Date learned court etiquette. *Perhaps it is not only a title he throws around when he says he is the fourth son of a lord.* His bearing marked him as a figure of distinction, and there were plenty of tengu families inhabiting the Juichi mountain range where the peak of Takao lay. She watched the dancers step in time, with Date moving to correct poses and footwork. She smiled and tapped her foot, anticipating his reaction to the upcoming climax: the wench toss.

"Those being led, place your hands on your partners' shoulders...if you can reach them," he quipped, raising a feathery eyebrow at some of the dramatic height differences. "And hop on the count of three. Partners, you are going to place your hands on your partner's hips and *pass* from left to right, then *set them down.*" He gave beady-eyed glares to sniggering people. "You have one job and that is to not sling them about like a sack of flour. Put them down properly or you will *never* dance with them *ever again!*"

Scyanatha laughed at this, covering her mouth with her hand.

"This brings back memories," she called to Date, as the dancers finished and left. "You're a good teacher."

"It's an easy dance," he commented with a dismissive shrug. "What do you need?"

"Nothing, just checking on things," she replied. "They think I'm a coordinator."

Date snorted. "It always happens to someone." He drank from a bamboo flask and wiped his mouth. "How are the others?"

"Who?" she teased, guessing what kind of information he wanted.

"Lerki, Seth and Tundra," he replied, brows pinching for a moment, before he raised one in suspicion. "Who else?"

Scy smiled, ambiguous, before answering. "Seth is putting his charm to good use running errands, and Tundra is playing in the snow with Nyima." Date nodded at this, seeming satisfied. "I haven't seen Lerki. He could be with one of the hunting parties."

"Lerki isn't a hunter." Date shook his head. "He's probably hiding."

"I'll go look for him, then," she said, taking her co-ordinator role seriously. "We need everyone helping."

"Good luck trying," he said, gesturing to the doors, where his next group of dance students entered.

Scy hummed as she debated where to go next. "I just came from outside, so they wouldn't have time to get much done. The hunters have their own supervisors, and the court enactment is Bracken and Queline's job." She nodded once, deciding, "The brewery."

In the brewery, with her arms buried past her elbows in dough, Zercey half-listened to outfit descriptions for the all-twilight ball. "It is tight through here," a woman with lilac coloured hair said, gesturing to the torso area, "and flares around my knees. It is a dark shade, but the moon and star motif were too perfect to resist." "Oh, Raemina, it'll look like you're dancing through a galaxy!" an enthusiastic faery replied, getting dressing on Raemina's pale arm when she grabbed her. "Is there anyone special you're giving your fruit to?"

Zercey didn't hear Raemina's reply, as a louder voice spoke up from the workstation across from her.

"Mine will be full of ruffles and lace. There'll be buttons up the bottom half of the back, but it will be open to the neckline. And my shoes are to die for!"

Both Raemina and the green-skinned, shoe fan were from worlds different to Earth and Illthdar. Both arrived after falling through strange portals.

Zercey kept quiet about her own dress choice, feeling like she didn't measure up after hearing how Magnilla's dress needed an armed escort to deliver it. The outfits hanging up in the barracks ranged from daring to scandalous, and she'd begun thinking she'd fade into the background in comparison.

"You look like Cinderella pre-ball," Vyxen said, as she tapped Zercey on the shoulder. She giggled and wiped flour from Zercey's nose.

"Ugh, thanks." Zercey tried using her elbow but wound up wiping more flour on herself. She gave in and said, "What's up?"

"Bored." Vyxen shrugged. "Today's hunting party has plenty of people, so I thought I'd come here instead." She looked around Zercey to the dough. "What are you making?"

"Just bread," she replied. "Come help me."

"Ehn," Vyxen said, getting stuck in.

Several minutes passed in amiable silence.

"We need to talk to the others about what Magnilla said," Zercey broached.

Vyxen nodded, aware she'd been hiding from the topic, and her friends. "I think it's okay. We've only had time to work on dresses and fall into bed, anyway, so no one noticed."

"Thanks for letting me crash with you," Zercey said. "I can't tell you how much of a relief it is just to have a place to go. You know what I mean?"

Vyxen nodded, then flicked flour at her. "Don't get mushy or I'm tipping this bowl over your head."

Zercey gasped, "You wouldn't!" She tossed a fistful back.

"Ehn, I would!" Vyxen crowed, laughing.

"Behave!" Elder Winsky snapped, glaring from across the room. Face equally dusted in white powder, cheeks threatening to dimple, the effect was ruined somewhat. Non-binary, they served to train the male Acolytes of Jasper on a normal day, but their love of fig pastries drove them every Solstice from the courtyard to the brewery.

"Knock-knock!" Scy rapped on the door frame and entered, smiling. "How is everything?"

"Good!"

"Great!"

"Eh, not bad."

"Better now you're here."

Scy waved at those she knew and headed to Zercey and Vyxen. "You two look like you're having fun."

"The best!" Vyxen slapped her hand on the counter and sent up a cloud of powder.

"As long as everything gets finished," she said, waving a teasing finger from side to side.

"Yes, ma'am!" Vyxen saluted and giggled as she got flour over her face.

"Now, has anyone seen Lerki? I heard he prefers to hide instead of pitch in." Scy's smile turned wicked as she added, "I wanted to have a word with him."

"I saw him," Zercey admitted, wondering if Scy was joking or serious. "He was heading for Phanuel's laboratorium."

"I guess it's safe to say he'll be working. Whatever Phanuel comes up with will be worse than any task I could think of," she concluded, with a wicked titter.

The mystery of Lerki's whereabouts solved, Scy wasted time discussing outfits and hairstyles for the upcoming festivities before venturing on. She thought she'd given Nyima's group enough time to get something completed, and given Nyima and Tundra time to strike up conversation. The former's Illthdarian had come on in leaps and bounds since Tundra developed a habit of engaging her in conversation whenever he saw her. She also seemed more relaxed around the rest of her team, as though a worry was no longer as pressing. Or perhaps, she set it aside for a time when she could do something about it.

Standing at the base of the tiers surrounding the log tower of the pyre, Nyima put place markers for where sculptures would stand. She earmarked several for herself, and shared others among those who expressed interest. She already knew which Aetumuh she wanted watching over the festival.

"Guess that's everything," Tundra chatted, coming to stand beside her. He crossed his bare arms from habit, not because he was cold. She slanted a glance his way, curious. "Yes."

"Did you get enough people to put up sculptures?" The smile he gave her was boyish and charming.

"Yes."

Tundra shrugged. "Guess that means there isn't space for one more?"

"Yes. No." She replayed the sentence, but still wasn't sure which short answer was the right one. "You may have one."

"Great," he decided. "Pick a spot next to one of yours and I'll work there."

"Fine." Her brows pinched with the turn of the conversation. She wondered why next to hers specifically. Pointing to indicate the spot, she said, "There."

He chuckled and nodded. "Thanks. I decided if we're having Gods, Leigong should be among them."

"Who is he?" She assumed he looked after Tundra's home world.

"He protects Warren," he replied, confirming her hunch. "It's the Earth dimension I'm from." He shifted, looking awkward.

Nyima felt a bubble of amusement at his expression. *He doesn't know how to explain it? I know how he feels.*

Clearing his throat, he continued. "He's a thunder God, whose job is equivalent to Chiyoko's." He grew grave as he added, "He leads a resistance against world A and the other worlds it's defeated."

Multiple versions of one world sounded more complicated than what Nyima was used to. Questions wanted to pass her lips, but she held them back, uncertain how to broach it when he appeared to regret confiding already. She laid a hand on his brawny forearm. Tundra looked at her, askance.

With an inch height difference between them meeting his gaze was comfortable. Yet, she found herself growing flustered as the silence stretched. She had nothing to fill it with, so fumbled for something to say. "You have only one?" She took her hand back and pointed at the tiers.

"There are others," Tundra replied, staying where he was. "None I've any interest in honouring or serving."

It was another curious statement. She wanted to ask more about his world, but Abaddon called her name. Disappointed their chat was cut short, she called, "Yes, here." She turned to where Abaddon made their way towards her. "What is it?"

"I finished the ironwork, and Nixx is welding them together. Scyanatha asked me to make archways next. What do you want them to look like?" Their colourless eyes were bright with joy, their cheeks and nose tinged a darker shade of red from exertion. She considered the question, and Tundra raised an eyebrow, watching her expression change from thoughtful to conclusive. She held one hand out and produced a small sample of twisted ice and spirals, with bits of crystal leaves shooting off. "Something like this."

Abaddon touched the ice, running their palms over the design and committing it to memory as it melted. "I like it," they agreed with a sweet smile. "Can you show me where they need to be?"

Nyima pinched the cuff of their shirt between her fingers and led them to the pathway. She stepped back and stood beside Tundra, watching as Abaddon took measured steps along, touching the tiers and making a note against their body.

Tundra glanced from Abaddon to Nyima, skimming her form again at the echoed action. The white crop top and ribbon skirt were typical garb, and he'd seen women in far less before, but still, the flashes of cobalt blue legs contrasted with the white fabric and drew his eye. *Nice.* He looked away once he had his fill.

"Should the arch slope with the steps, or be level?" Abaddon asked, turning to the pair.

"You pick," Nyima replied, trusting their judgement.

"Can you remember all of that?" Tundra's brows rose when Abaddon nodded. He couldn't recall what he had to eat last, and the idea of anything more complicated seemed impossible.

"I have a good memory," they confessed with quiet firmness. Abaddon spoke of having a good memory the same way a human spoke of having a heartbeat.

It sent Tundra's mind back to the point they collected buckets. There was no telling how long ago they last needed one, but they remembered.

With Abaddon set to their new task, Nyima and Tundra returned to work crafting.

That evening, Abaddon and the women clustered around a table in Jasper barracks, picking over a meal.

"Despite the intel, I never did see Lerki in the end," Scyanatha chatted, in an amiable mood. "Date was right to wish me luck."

"He was probably hiding in a tree," Zercey mused aloud. At their confused looks, her cheeks pinked and she added, "It would work well for him." She drew a breath and said in a hurry, "Speaking of him, Magnilla, what have you heard, exactly?"

There was a sense of surprise from everyone but Magnilla at her being addressed by Zercey.

"He's not completely honest," Magnilla said, oozing pity. "I'm not sure how, or what, but he's hiding things. He apologised in the infirmary, but there was something very off about it." She tossed her hair and added, "I didn't feel threatened. I could take him in a heartbeat, but for a split second, he had a murderer's intent."

There were quiet snorts at this.

Zercey shook her head, finding it hard to picture an intimidating Lerki. "And Date?"

Nyima nodded, recalling what Magnilla said to her and Scyanatha when she arrived back. "You said he had not four sons."

"The only way there are four children is if you count the eldest's wife," Magnilla replied. "According to my father's messengers, Lord Naigubu of Mount Takao's wife died in childbirth and the fourth baby was stillborn."

Abaddon leaned back in their chair, a thoughtful frown on their brow. "Something happened to the first son with recluse leaves, but Tundra said he didn't die."

"When is this?" Nyima said, reaching to tap them on the back of the hand.

"When we were getting buckets."

"I don't suppose your father informed you of the household members, Magnilla," Scyantha said, steepling her fingers in a business-like fashion.

Magnilla nodded. "First of all, the family name isn't Date, it's Takayama. Lord Naigubu's *three* sons were called Matataro, Daijiro and Kinsaburo." She drew breath and added in a smug voice, "If Date is the fourth son, following their naming traditions, he'd be called something-shiro."

"Okay, so his given name is Toshiiro. That's not exactly off,"

Zercey said, fussing with the ends of her hair. "He said he was disowned."

"We must ask for truth," Nyima said, not liking the atmosphere the talk generated. "He has done no wrong."

"That's the whole problem, isn't it?" Abaddon queried. "Date might not tell us the truth?"

"It's easy to see how someone of lower social status could benefit from a farce," Scyanatha commented, bringing silence to the table. "What good would it be for a high-born family to deny the existence of one of their children?"

"It makes more sense to kill him than let him smear their good name," Magnilla stated.

Nyima nodded, agreeing, "He is happy when told they upset."

"Who's writing to him?" Magnilla's fine blond brows came together. After Abaddon informed her, she said, "How do you know he doesn't write and send them to himself to boost his credibility?"

No one answered.

"The tengu have renaming ceremonies," Scy said, breaking the silence. "What are their names now?"

Magnilla rolled her eyes and said, "Matataro became Nobumasa; Daijiro became Takamori; Kinsaburo is now Yoshikazu. When the current Lord Naigubu dies, Nobumasa will be renamed Lord Naigubu." She snorted and added, "My clan gives their children one important name to live up to and doesn't feel the need to change it like shrugging off a winter coat."

"Great, but that doesn't prove anything, besides you spent a ton of time nosing into the family background," Vyxen pointed out, tapping her fingers on the table. Her nails were painted bright blue, though the polish was chipped. "It doesn't prove he isn't son of lord whoever, either."

Magnilla tossed her head. "He has everything to gain from exploiting a noble household. They stand to lose more if it's proven they threw out one of their princes."

"True," Scyanatha said, wanting to drop the conversation, since it was going nowhere. "I assume the fourth child is the daughter-in-law. What's her name?"

"Inoshi: the second daughter of Lord Daranibo of Mount Fuji," Magnilla replied. She paused and looked from Scyanatha to

Vyxen, who were gaping at each other. "What?"

"That's...the name of his companion," Vyxen whispered, eyes wide.

Over in Jasper male barracks, the men were ignorant of the revelations being unwrapped on the opposite side.

"I'm going to call you blister, with how frequently you show up as soon as work is done," Date said as Lerki peeked around the door. "I'm sorry, Date," he replied, shutting the door and taking a seat at a table. "I was busy."

Date blew out a long puff of air. "Busy dodging work."

"Don't worry, Lerki, we saved you some food," Seth said, lifting a plate cover. "It's a bit on the cold side, but it's still better than any swill you'll get from Fluorite."

"Our food isn't that bad," he said, sniffing the lingering aroma. "Thank you."

"You're still here, eating ours, so it can't be that good," Tundra pointed out, shaking his head.

"Hey, Jingyi, those sculptures are shaping up," Seth commented, changing topic. He chuckled when Tundra threw a bread-roll at him for the pun. "You mad, bro?"

"Hand slipped," Tundra replied in a bland voice.

"Yeah right," Seth shot back, unconvinced. Moving along he asked Date, "How's teaching going? Any twinkle-toes out there?"

"They aren't going to crash into anyone," he answered, turning back to Lerki. "Scyanatha was looking for you."

"I saw her too," Seth volunteered, withholding he didn't mind that one bit and he owed Lerki for it. Spending time with a woman out of his league like Scy was a dream come true.

Tundra raised a hand. "Same. Did she find you?"

"No," Lerki replied with a shake of his head. "I didn't know she was looking."

"Well, that's a lie. What had you busy?" Tundra's gaze narrowed.

"I was helping Phanuel," Lerki replied, taking a bite of food.

Date snorted into his soup. "You were turning his room upside down, you mean," he corrected. "I know how you help."

Lerki smiled, as Tundra and Seth chimed, "Guilty, very guilty."

The grin dropped from Seth's face. "Speaking of that— " he addressed, making eye contact with each in turn, "—someone's been saying things."

"Someone's always saying things," Date responded, with a dismissive flick of his fingers.

Seth shook his head.

"Okay, it's bothering you," Tundra concluded. "What is it?"

"That Date and Lerki are dishonest, for one," he replied, growing annoyed again.

Tundra began a slow, sarcastic clap.

"Dude, really?"

"What am I dishonest about?" Lerki queried, green brows pinching.

"I was almost convinced you had something new to say," Tundra said, leaning back in his chair and crossing his arms.

"Jingyi, come on, man."

"Well, thank you for that," Date huffed. "So good to know who trusts one."

"Hey!" Seth argued, his drop earring clinking against itself as he whipped around to face Date. "I defended your ass, I'll have you know."

"So, he's a snake in the grass, and?" Tundra remarked.

"Really," Lerki demanded, "what am I dishonest about?"

"She didn't go into details," Seth confessed, sagging in his seat when his ire fizzled.

"Then it's a basic observation anyone with two good brain-cells to rub together could figure out," Tundra declared. "Nothing to get upset over."

"I should punch you," Date remarked to him.

Feeling better now it was out, Seth said, "In fairness, dude, you kind of go around with a sign on your back saying, 'Shady'."

"You're not making me feel better," Date informed, intent on brooding over the matter.

"Okay, you're not incredibly shady," Seth reiterated in a teasing voice, "but still shady. Like the kid that brings their pet to school without permission, shady."

Date shook his head, not comprehending Seth's turn of phrase.

"Who is saying these things?" Lerki asked, eyes wide, fingers drumming on the table top.

"Magnilla," Seth replied, and Date threw his hands in the air and cursed. "Hey, I'm just the messenger."

"I should have guessed," Date groused, crossing his arms.

"Fucking figures." Turning away from the conversation, as though trying to blot the unpleasantness of it from his mind, he cast his gaze over their barracks.

With so many men, space was at a premium in Jasper. The shaved, timber bunks staggered in multiple rows, had no more than a foot between them. The largest free space focused around the stoves used for heating and cooking. The tables set up along the center aisle looked more like tall benches than tables, and were bracketed by shorter, skinnier, benches to sit on. Given the time of day the majority were occupied, with people elbow to elbow. Some gave up the notion of having table space and dined on their bunks or closed trunks.

"Okay, so you make sense," Tundra concluded, pointing to Date, who huffed again in response, "but she's also saying Lerki's lying to people."

"No, she didn't call him a liar," Seth corrected, thinking back to the conversation. "Just that he wasn't honest."

"There's a hair's breadth of difference between the two," Tundra stated. He adjusted his position, snagging the bread-roll from a distracted Lerki's plate. "One isn't far from becoming the other."

"I haven't done anything to her, yet," Lerki said. His choice of words had them turn in unison. "I haven't," he insisted.

"'Yet'," Date repeated. "Which means you thought of it."

"Three little letters," Seth added. "So much pain."

Tundra nodded in solemn agreement.

"I didn't do anything," Lerki protested, stammering and leaning away.

"If I had a coin for every time you came out with that line," Seth remarked with a shake of his head, "I'd have a lot of coins, let's put it that way."

"But I didn't..." Lerki trailed off, shoulders sagging in defeat, as Tundra shook his head at him. He looked at his plate, then at Tundra eating the roll. "That's mine."

"Not anymore," he mumbled. "And like you said, you haven't done anything, yet."

"I wasn't going to feed her spotted corobane," Lerki defended. "Or anything!"

"That's quite specific for someone trying to maintain his innocence," Date pointed out.

Lerki made a noise in the back of his throat.

The trio laughed, and Date clapped him on the shoulder for good measure. "We believe you," he said. He leaned forward and added in a quieter voice. "I'm just a little disappointed."

CHAPTER SIXTEEN

Tundra roused at the telltale *thunk* of a head colliding with a night stand. "Another one?" He winced in sympathy, rolling onto his side and looking down.

Seth sat on the floor, rubbing his head and casting evil looks at his bunk. "You know me," he replied, grimacing. He prodded the large lump and hissed.

"Yeah, I know you." Tundra sat up and rubbed his hands together. "Get up, I'll get that iced for you."

"Thanks, man," he replied, grateful for the portable ice pack that was his friend. Standing and resting his elbows on the top bunk where Tundra slept, Seth's eyes closed when frosty fingers chilled his injury.

"What was it about this time?" Tundra prodded, encouraging Seth to air the skeletons in his closet.

"Uuuh..." He rubbed his forehead, dredging the memory from the murky depths. "I fell into a river and it swept me downstream." Words slow and choppy, his brows pinched in concentration.

"You were still a kid?" Tundra probed, keeping his tone even.

Seth hummed. "It was early on. I was twelve? Maybe thirteen. It was close to my birthday when I got here."

"So, you fell in and got picked up by the current," Tundra

repeated. "Then what happened?"

"What happened in the dream, or what really happened?" Seth countered. "They didn't go the same way."

"Oh. No wonder." Tundra could guess.

"In the dream, I missed the branch that saved me from going over the waterfall." Seth shuddered. "I was plummeting towards rocks when I hit the floor."

"Yeah, done that," Tundra admitted, with a relatable nod. "It's no picnic." Withdrawing his hand, he said, "That should help keep the swelling down."

"Better than a bag of frozen peas," Seth joked, sitting on his bunk. "I'm just glad that happened after you got your cast off. Falling from the upper bunk could've cracked my head open."

"Your head?" Tundra quipped. "Not likely."

"Fuck you, too." Seth chuckled. Times like this, he often wondered how he survived arriving in Illthdar as a small boy with no survival skills, lost in the wilderness. He wouldn't have lasted five minutes on Earth, let alone a planet with sentient plant life. If the flowers didn't torment him, the trees attacked. It was a relief when animals chased, even if they did look like they escaped a mad scientist's lab. Nightmares were a small part of his lingering trauma.

He wouldn't admit it, but he looked up to Tundra. A seasoned assassin before he arrived in Illthdar, he'd been there, done that and lost the t-shirt. He was nonchalant, with a natural confidence that drew women like bees to nectar, and a set of skills that made him a force to be reckoned with. He understood Seth's insecurities and concerns without judging. Because he knew what being chased by monsters was like. Cornered, thrown from cliffs and swept downstream. He never went into detail, but it was comforting someone got it. Even if the nightmares never stopped, he knew Tundra would take it all in his stride.

"It's a normal reaction to an abnormal situation," Tundra reasoned. "Your brain's trying to process everything. It's a lot to figure out, so it'll take a bit."

"Man, I'd just like to know if it's ever going away," Seth replied, fishing the chessboard with white marble and red tiger's eye pieces from under his bed. "Red or white?"

"You pick." Tundra shrugged. He cleared a space at one of the long tables in the middle of the room. "Some people learn to ignore their trauma, and others deal with it."

The way he said it had Seth asking, "Do you get nightmares?"

"Probably, but I don't remember. I don't think I sleep deeply enough." He shrugged again, unbothered. "Qiang would wake up swinging, too," he said, trying to placate Seth.

"Your big bro?" Tundra didn't mention him often. "He'd have nightmares?"

Tundra nodded. "Everyone's got something." His thing was blood. He could take someone's head off, or rip their spine right out their back, but if he saw their blood coating his hand or someone lying in a pool of it, he got sick and dizzy. Ironic for an assassin.

Resigned to being short of sleep for the night, the pair settled down to play chess until the sun rose.

"No." Date's voice was firm and toneless.

"It's an order, Date," Uwe countered, rust coloured eyes narrowed, daring him to argue. He had his feet on his mahogany desk, muddy boots staining the expensive wood. There were also teeth marks in the back of his luxurious armchair—whether his or made by someone in the throes was up for debate. As a man of status, Uwe showed disdain for all things by destroying them. It was a direct contrast to how he cared for his clothes. Today's outfit was a matte grey houppelande. The floor-length, baggy robe had full, flared sleeves. Lined in black fur inside and out, the wide cuffs and tall collar had a gold inset pattern of fluer-de-lis and artichokes running from his throat to his boots. Which, as muddy as they were, had large inset rubies and gold buckles. He accented it with an overstuffed hat and his grey, broad scarf—the ittan momen. Clothes were power, and ruining objects was power. Destroying people was the most powerful thing of all.

With the curtains closed against the glare of the morning sun, Date was forced to peer at his High Elder through the gloom. "All right, let me rephrase; no, *sir.*" Of course he dared disobey; always would. Uwe was the exact type of person he had the most experience dealing with and knew how far to push things.

Coming to Las was a last resort. The last place to turn to save the tattered scraps of his soul. Still, Date would saw his wings off before he bowed to anyone not worthy of his respect. He made it a point to test Uwe at every turn, making note of each failure.

"Is there a problem with escorting the damsel?" Uwe queried in a singsong.

Somehow, Date managed not to sneer at the term of address. He would not call the lady a damsel in any sense of the word. "She's not a damsel, for one," he listed. "Two, she's not fond of me; three, I'm even less fond of her and four, I'm positive she doesn't need or want my escort."

"You're going and that's final." Uwe pulled his feet off the desk and stood. The show of dominance failed: he was five-feet-seven-inches and about as intimidating as a pillow cushion.

Date ignored the display, much like he ignored the faint glow in Uwe's eyes. "I'm going to murder her if you send me."

"Don't be ridiculous. Nobody plans murder aloud. Besides, if she is as capable as you claim, it would be impossible." Uwe strolled to a shrouded aquarium in one corner of his office, sliding open the mesh door at the top and making show of rolling back his expensive outer-sleeve. His hand darted in and fetched out a peach-coloured roserat. With it wriggling by the tail, he tossed it in the air and caught it in his large mouth. A sharp bite. A crunch and squirt of blood. He drew an embroidered handkerchief from his sleeve and dabbed his mouth.

"There's a first time for everything," Date muttered in a dark tone, flexing his wrists to test the position of hidden knives in his wrist guards. The power-play didn't motivate the way Uwe wanted.

"Date, you're going on that mission." Uwe's tone was final and accompanied by a dismissive wave of his hand.

Two days before yule pyre and drafted on a mission with Magnilla, of all people. Date would fall to his knees and thank the Gods if she chose to leave without him. "Fine, but I pick the rest of the team."

With a nod of agreement, Date left to collect those he wanted. He hoped being difficult would result in Uwe washing his hands of the mission, but fetching a crystal shard beat personal dislike of Magnilla.

Date thumped his fist on the door to Jasper barracks.

A woman with dark skin and black dreadlocked hair stuck her head out and glared. "What?"

"Uwe sends me," he said, mock bowing. "I'm to collect Magnilla, Zercey and Vyxen." He hedged his bets the latter hung out in their room than her own.

"Wait." The woman slammed the door.

Tabitha. Date rolled his eyes and tutted. *I wasn't planning on coming in.*

The door reopened and the women exited, accompanied by Magnilla's brother. Date raised an eyebrow and sent a pointed look into the room.

Thijs kept his gaze on Magnilla, uncaring he shouldn't be in the women's barracks. With how his hand lingered on his sister's hip, Date questioned how familial they were. "Come on," he urged, setting aside the disturbing implications. Turning, he headed up. "Let's hope Lerki isn't hiding this time."

"I don't need an escort," Magnilla postured, pulling her shoulders

inside. I honestly think she wants to return to Thies and never come back."

Pushing her way between them, Nyima gave Vyxen and Zercey a chance to slip out from under Thijs' domineering presence. Arms crossed, she squared up to him. "She want to be a coward? Let her run," she stated, unimpressed and jutting her chin. "Warriors lose. They learn from it. If she cannot, she *is not.*"

Whether Nyima's scathing declaration made it back to Magnilla no one learned, but there was no further mention of her departing Las. On the surface, she appeared dedicated to facing dishonour with dignity. Though, Nyima kept a watchful eye for any subtle changes in demeanour until the day of yule pyre, when other things eclipsed Magnilla in importance.

"Black or brown?" Zercey held two pairs of boots out for Nyima to inspect. "I have no clue what I'm doing."

"Yes," she agreed, amused. "Why do you asking me?" She pointed at her bare feet. Her outfit for yule pyre consisted of magenta fabric, wound into a halter top, and a matching ribbon skirt. She included gold chain for trim, a lot of bangles and a delicate pair of anklets. The vast drop in temperature brought out a lustrous radiance to her cobalt skin and made her pale blue eyes look even brighter.

"Will you just pick a pair? I can't decide," Zercey demanded, shaking the boots with impatience. "It's snowing, and you're going to have a blast, but I'll die if I'm not dressed properly."

Scyanatha intervened, dressed in red with a tartan sash and horned headdress. "Zercey, we shall be dancing around a *fire* inside a shelter made of ice several inches thick." She took the boots and set one down. "With the exception when you're standing at the doorway, you won't feel the cold, I promise." She handed over the brown pair.

Still leery, but pacified, Zercey slunk to her bunk to finish getting dressed.

The anticipated and dreaded night commenced at sunset. The sound of drummers, strummers and wind instruments already echoed all the way up to Amber barracks in the tower's rafters long before the sun dipped below the horizon.

Zercey, and others, resorted to ingenuity in coming up with something suitable to wear. The Order didn't pay much, but everyone was expected to dress fancy the following night for the ball. That in mind, she took a pair of scissors to the dress she'd arrived in, having discovered it bagged and sagged where it used to fit. "Zercey, your mother would go bananas for the new fad Order training diet." She giggled, biting a loose length of cotton thread with her teeth. She gathered the excess fabric into pin-sized pleats and removed the top portion of the dress. With it, she made a waistband and wore a peach shirt and brown bodice. "It'll do," she decided, slipping into it.

"You look cute!" Vyxen grabbed Zercey's flailing hand and helped her pull the outfit on. She had on bright-pink, cable-knit leggings, with a burgundy miniskirt that had leather ties up either side. She paired this with a matching geometric-patterned, crop-top hoodie and flat boots.

"Someone's been delving in lost and found again," Scy commented with a knowing smile. "Only you could find something so Earth child of the eighties and make it work, dear."

"Miigwech!" Vyxen beamed and played with the toggles on her magenta hoodie. "I heard Culvers is being chair lifted into the party." She giggled at the thought.

"Plenty of opportunity for the carriers to have a feel," Scy quipped, feeling a modicum of pity for the too attractive High Elder. "Uwe was brought in on a silver throne, and never stopped bragging," Scy continued, eyes laughing.

"A frat boy entrance does sound more like Culvers," Zercey noted, fishing through her things for kohl eyeliner and tinted powder.

"It's the same every year," Abaddon said, adjusting the clasp on their cloak and fussing with their pink hair. "Not everyone will be happy. I heard lots of complaints about how he has to lose the fight."

"Speaking of Culvers," a nymph on the next bunk set over began in a loud voice, nudging her friend, "you certainly came back from the shower looking *very refreshed.* Working off some of that sexual frustration?"

"Shhhh! Why would you say that?!" The half-blood girl turned several shades of tomato.

Gales of laughter broke out. It was no secret the showers were used for things other than washing. A solo trip was as common as a shared one, with men, women and those of neither gender slipping in under "ignorant" eyes.

"Tasteless and base," Magnilla sniffed, turning to admire herself in the mirror. She smoothed a tiny wrinkle in her heavy, velvet green dress. She then ruined the demure effect by hiking the skirt up over her knee so she could lace her black boots. "As for the duel, it's only right that Trenfal win. He is full faerie, more senior than Culvers and more respected." She straightened her skirt again. "Next year they will have to have the High Elders and Order of Amber swap around anyway."

"It seems kind of sexist," Zercey mused, having given up the search for anything to make her look less pasty. "Hasn't there ever been a winter or spring queen?"

Nyima looked up from where she'd been using a hand mirror and dark blue pencil to line her eyes. "That interesting."

Scy hummed and nodded. "There may have in the past. The story is an old one, after all."

"I would have liked to compete for one of the positions," Magnilla noted twisting a golden curl between her fingers so it sat just right, "but, it wouldn't have been fair. Had I been here at the time I would have helped officiate."

Behind her Vyxen and Zercey made a show of trying not to gag.

"Is it true some people trade outfits for all-twilight?" Zercey asked, wanting to confirm a rumour.

"They do, dear," Scy confirmed. "It's all part of the masquerade. Some go to even greater lengths, using potions to change their appearance for the night."

"It isn't something I could do," Magnilla commented, bringing the conversation back to herself again. "Not with the outfit my clan has arranged. There are just as many people who don't hide their faces, as ones that do."

"Have you, um, heard the story about wh-why people wear masks and trade outfits on all-twilight?" Abaddon asked, ducking their head and fiddling with the buttons on their vest.

"You'll have to tell us on the way, Abaddon," Vyxen said, as she stood up. "I really want to hear it, but if we don't leave now, we're going to miss the kick-off."

"Once upon a time, high in the mountains, lived the Winter King in his Winter Kingdom. He wasn't well-loved. Because of the cold, his people always suffered. One day, the Winter King's family received a threat. A member of the royal family would die at the all-twilight ball; murdered, unless he changed his ways. To avoid their fate the Winter King had everyone attend wearing masks, and the royal family traded places with the servants for the night."

"The Winter King sounds like a tool," Vyxen commented, skipping down the stairs ahead of everyone. "He basically made it so his servants die in their place."
"Why do we celebrate this?" Nyima dead-panned, finding the idea ridiculous.
"There's more," Abaddon chuckled, holding tight to the railing and taking careful steps.

"The Winter King's son, the crown prince, was betrothed to the second princess of autumn. She was secretly in love with the second prince of winter, an ambitious man after the crown."

"The story hasn't got any better," Vyxen said in a sing-song. "Now we have creepy lovers killing their own family."
"Right?" Zercey laughed, shaking her head at the court theatrics.
"Hush, just listen," Scy scolded, though her ruby painted lips tilted up with amusement.

"The autumn princess and second prince devised a plan. Each night the princess put a small amount of poison in the crown prince's wine cup. Over the following weeks he grew ill, but no one knew the cause. Just when they thought they'd succeed, the youngest prince learned of it. The autumn princess used her charm to trick the prince into thinking she fell in love with him, and his older brother coerced her into killing the crown prince."

"Whew! This girl really gets around! She's messed with three princes all in the same family. Did she love any of them?" Zercey said, as they paused on Quartz barracks landing, so Magnilla could fuss with her gown.
"Shh!" Nyima and Scy said together, interested in the story.

286

Abaddon smothered a chuckle and continued.

"The problem was the youngest prince was already in love with someone else—a servant, so they could never be together. Suspicious of the princess, the youngest prince asked his beloved to serve the princess and uncover the truth. The servant watched from the shadows, as the princess and second prince shared a passionate love, while she tricked the crown prince into thinking she loved him. When the servant told the youngest prince he asked her to send for him on a day the second prince arrived for a tryst with the autumn princess. He would catch them together and reveal their affair and plot to his brother and father."

"So," Zercey rolled her hand, "what happened to the second prince and the princess?"
Nyima shook her head, beads on her braids clicking together. "The prince should of tell his father."
"And the servant?" Vyxen prodded. "What happened to her? Did she follow the prince when he was exiled?"
Nyima frowned at Vyxen, wondering how she knew the ending.
"I don't know," Abaddon replied. "I never heard that part."
"Let me think," Scy went to tap her lip, then remembered she had paint on it and stopped. "Maybe I can remember."

"The plot was revealed and the crown prince saved. The princess was thrown before the court. The king demanded why she tried to poison his beloved eldest. She fell to her knees, tears rolling down her cheeks. 'The youngest prince made me do it! When I said I wouldn't, he said he would tell everyone I had an affair with the second prince.'"

Scy's altered pitch as she mimicked the treacherous princess was met with laughter and disbelief.
"What? *Kaa!* Are you serious? Please tell me they catch her in the end?!" Vyxen stepped backwards down the last flight of steps, caught up in the tale.
"This is a faery tale with a sad ending," Scy replied. "The king decreed the youngest prince have his hand removed and be banished from the land."

"What the hell?!" Zercey's eyes were wide. "How is that even fair?! He probably starved to death, what with being pampered and missing a hand."

Nyima nodded, then spotted the men waiting at the bottom of the staircase. "Hello."

"He died and became a vengeful spirit," Date concluded the tale, putting a hand on Vyxen's shoulder as she nearly walked into him. "The Winter King was eventually overthrown by the Spring King. Just about every native Illthdarian knows the story."

"You're right," Vyxen said to Scy, turning to smile her thanks at Date, "it was a faery tale with a sad ending."

"Illthdar," Scy said, with a blasé shrug, more interested in looking over the men's outfits.

Of the four men, Tundra was least dressed, wearing a light-blue, sleeveless yukata, split at the waist on both sides. Underneath he wore dark, velvet leggings, the silvery hairs shimmering in the light as they made their way outside.

Date was most overdressed in a heavy, black coat made of layered, black feathers. One might have mistaken it for his bird form if his arms, face and boots weren't visible. One arm fitted through the sleeve, while the other sat in a sling, leaving the sleeve flapping like a broken wing. The clothes beneath were a sooty greyish-black, as though faded from too many washings. He had a red-beaked face mask perched atop his head to complete the look.

Seth's robes had an almost-Christmas feel to them, with alternating bands of red and dark green, and thin threads of gold dividing each ribbon-like stripe. His collar was high and flush against his neck, and he traded his dangling earring for a twisted, gold dragon that wound itself around the lobe. Instead of sandals, he wore brown boots with calico fur trim.

Then there was Lerki, who swapped his cloak for a heavier, red poncho. The sleeves of his chocolate brown shirt, with tight-fitted laces, ran from cuff to elbow. The shirt, much like Tundra's, split at the sides. Though, it ended where the lower waistband of his trousers began, to show a second set of jewellery along his hip line. He ended the outfit with tasselled boots.

Foregoing a greeting, Magnilla's lip curled as she stated, "This is

288

the exact problem with arranged marriages. It's a barbaric custom that allows for infidelity and loveless relationships. It is strictly forbidden among my clan."

"It would depend on the arrangement," Nyima commented in a clear and concise voice, raising an eyebrow. "I had one."

"You're married?" Zercey looked at her, surprised.

As did Tundra, though his expression twisted with an awkward grimace; infidelity wasn't his preference.

Nyima shook her head. "No, it was broken," she replied, declining to elaborate.

"That's appalling!" Magnilla was disgusted by the notion. "That someone would force you to marry like that! It's all for the best it was broken off."

"I was not forced," Nyima stated, narrowing her eyes at the accusation. "It is for my tribe. He was not too older than me, and my father was friends to his. I did not have minded, but I found out after it was no more."

"It's disgusting!" Magnilla shuddered like she heard something vulgar. "I don't care how, why or whatever excuse they make! Arranged marriages are revolting and only cause grief for everyone involved!"

Nyima usually held her tongue whenever Magnilla made sweeping proclamations, but she would not this time. She was insulting Nyima's people and family and she *would not* allow it. She opened her mouth to tell the arrogant female exactly what she thought of her when—

"Don't knock it until you've tried it," Date muttered, loud enough for everyone to hear.

"It's best you change the subject," Thijs cautioned, hands moving to his sister's shoulders to calm her. He massaged gently, lest her upset over the topic get out of hand. She was such a strong and overpowering woman, he didn't want the weaklings she teamed with to end up hurt. His brow glistened with a thin sheen of sweat, despite the snow falling outside.

"Thank you, *dear* brother," Magnilla simpered, seeming to think his statement won her the argument.

Having taken a deep, fortifying breath, Nyima returned to the topic of the Winter King's story. "Why people swap outfits?" she reminded them, allowing her irritation with Magnilla to transfer to her statement.

A strange look on her face, Vyxen turned to Date. "Do you know?"

"The masquerade ball, where servants were forced to dress as royals, so assassins could kill them instead. They made the servant, who loved the youngest prince, dress up as the autumn princess as punishment. The spirit of the youngest prince tried to save her, but they killed her. In his grief, he whispers to the Spring King to overthrow the Winter King." His voice remained toneless, expression blank, as he spoke.

"People dress up and change outfits because it is said every year the spirits of the prince and servant return to try to correct the tragedy of long ago," Scyanatha simplified. "It's a better version of Romeo and Juliet."

"Okay, that's slightly better, but it still sucks," Vyxen decided. With a wicked grin in place, and much to the confusion of her friends, she added, "And what happened to the sasah?"

Date raised an eyebrow at the peculiar question. "Sasah?" he questioned back. "There's no sasah in the story."

"Huh... I wonder how I got that mixed up..." she trailed, devoid of subtlety, as her friends shared comprehending looks with each other.

"Someone must have been inspired and decided to embellish his version," Magnilla noted in a scornful voice.

"Maybe," Date shot back, sharp enough to understand her suggestion. "But, they'd be an idiot. The story is almost as old as Illthdar."

"It is a very old story," Scyanatha agreed. "It wouldn't surprise me if there were different versions."

"Oh wow," Zercey remarked, craning her neck upwards to take in the decorations as they left the Order, and crossed under the iron-bound, ice arches. Blue flames in lanterns hung from the centre cross-beam illuminating the path. "God, look at that!"

"Who thought of the strings of lights?" Scy wondered, not recalling assigning it to anyone.

"Tundra," Abaddon replied. "He came and asked how."

"We've outdone ourselves this year," Tundra agreed, redirecting attention from himself. He leaned closer to Nyima, pointing at the tiny lights on strands of cable connecting each statue's hands to the chimney leading to the ice dome below. "It's come together better than I thought."

"Pretty," she said, smiling at him.

"Yeah," he agreed, though his eyes were on her.

Seth gave a long, slow whistle, as his eyes flitted about trying to take in everything at once. "I'm speechless," he confessed. "This is some kind of awesome."

"Everyone has done an excellent job with the amount of preparation time," Magnilla agreed. "It's almost as good as something our clan could produce."

Unnoticed, Nyima rolled her eyes at the non-compliment.

"Look, Seth," Scy said, looping a fair-skinned, lithe arm around his darker and broader one. She waved with her other hand towards the towering vestige of ice statues. The different styles were easy to pick out, with Tundra's no exception. "I told you Tundra might surprise you," she murmured in his ear.

Leigong, with staff in one hand and conical hat in the other, was crafted with careful attention to detail.

"Dude, you been holding out on us," was all he could think to comment. Half—most—of his attention was on the fact Scyanatha kept blowing fruity scented breath in his ear.

"Abaddon, you have done good," Nyima complimented, patting them on the back.

Everyone circled the tiered rings, admiring the statues.

"Abaddon, you're a genius!" Zercey gushed, with them giggling awkwardly at the praise.

"I have no idea how long it would have taken you guys to make these by hand," Vyxen said, captivated by the grace and sense of movement in each figure. "They look like they could spring to life."

"We could do something like that," Magnilla noted, tilting her head to the side as she considered it. "It wouldn't be hard."

A tense, feminine sigh was the only sign anyone was unfortunate enough to hear her.

"The feast begins," Lerki declared, quickly ushering everyone towards the terrace to enter the ballroom. A gong sounded a second later. He beamed as the women and Abaddon looked confused at how he knew. He winked, a quick spring in his step, looking excited for the feast.

The ballroom was host to both the yule pyre feast and the all-twilight ball the following night. Since previous yule pyre feasts decorations hadn't survived to the following night, the hall had minimal adornment. The crystal chandeliers suspended in the centre of the room were polished to a high shine. The waxed floor was an intricate mosaic in cobalt-blue, gold and red, and sealed with a heavy varnish that made it smooth as glass. The velvet curtains concealing the terrace doors were brushed and tied open, so people could enter and exit through the gardens. The upstairs gallery, reached by concealed stairways, gave guests an overview of the tables. The graceful slopes and curves of the large pillars made them look deceptively delicate, with ornate, crown moulding at ceiling and floor level.

Long rows of tables and chairs were set out. The china and cutlery polished to a high shine that refracted light stronger than the moon. Gold leaf was applied to many archways and pillars surrounding the vaulted windows, and the excess of candles and pillar torches added a festive glow.

While most peeked at the decorations leading up to the event, there was something about the atmosphere of candlelight that made it more magical. There was no limit to what the eyes could feast on while they waited for the guest of honour, Culvers, the Winter King, to arrive.

A fanfare sounded and the High Elders, High Priestess and Order of Amber appeared, dressed as members of the Winter King's royal family. They were followed by a hand-picked procession; Elders and Acolytes who proved themselves through the year to the High Elders.

Each was decked in bright blue velvet, white leather and silver. Pearl, jewelled accessories encircled wrists, necks and adorned their hair. Heavy, dark blue capes, with white fur trimming kept them warm, secured at their shoulders by glittering, chain cord.

"He looks uncomfortable in that," Seth muttered, leaning to his right to talk to Scyanatha. He watched Culvers shift his shoulders to adjust the number of adornments encapsulating his dominating presence. He threw off his cape the second he sat at the head table, with Chiyoko to his right-hand side in the role of winter queen casting disappointed looks his way.

"He may be more uncomfortable with so many people staring," Scy reasoned. "I didn't think he would like being the centre of attention, even if it is for two days."

"So, where's Trenfal hiding?" Tundra questioned, scanning the crowd. He'd noticed him missing from the line up early on.

"Would the Spring King make an appearance tonight?" Zercey craned her neck, trying to see over people's heads.

"In some versions he's a member of the court," Date disclosed, keeping his voice low so he wouldn't detract from the Winter King's opening speech. "He could show, but won't be dressed as the Spring King."

"No, he shows up incognito and observes the scene," Trenfal said from behind Magnilla and Thijs's.

As Seth, Scyanatha and Zercey turned in their seats, Magnilla's smile widened. "Trenfal," she simpered, "I knew you were there. You'll need to work on your stealth." She spun around to face him, arching prettily.

"I'll be stealthy next time," he replied without pause. "Is everyone enjoying the festivities?" He looked around, taking in nods. Gone was his normal butterscotch robes. Tonight, he wore a light green, button-down vest, with scalloped, cream coloured sleeves, and paired with grey breeches, tucked into calf-high, black boots. A simple slate coloured coat, draped over his shoulders, completed the look.

"It has only just started, so there's more to go," Scyanatha pointed out, keeping one ear on the speech. "But, so far it has been wonderful."

Applause broke out, signalling Culvers' finished. Everyone settled at the long row of benches, while Trenfal vanished into the throng. Simple, hearty dishes were served: stews made with lentils or wild game, fresh bread, root vegetables mashed, roasted or fried with animal fat, and all washed down with frothy beers and sweet meads. There were no desserts on offer; confectionery and sweet pastries were reserved for all-twilight.

Suggested by a cheeky faced Vyxen, the group played twenty questions while they ate. However, the game had marked differences in that the questions all came from her and all were required to answer. There was much merriment and laughter around the table as everyone tried to dodge giving a full reply to her probing queries.

Afterwards, they filtered out into the courtyard again to watch Culvers light the pyre and signal the start of the dances.

The ice dome was large, but not so big it could fit everyone inside. Instead, there were four rings of dancers that circled the yule pyre once it was lit. With two inner rings inside the dome and two larger rings on the outer, dancers zigzagged among them; partners either moving closer or shifting further out depending on the dance.

After his efforts to prepare others, Date remained far outside the outer ring, sat on the lowest statue tier. His feathered cloak was insulated enough he didn't feel the chill. Though, he still glared when two producers of it made their way over. He wanted Tundra to monopolise Nyima's attention, since it was clear the idiot had taken interest in her. *The last thing he should be doing is passing up chances to impress the lady.*

"Not joining in?" Tundra commented, taking a seat next to Date. Nyima sat on Tundra's other side, and he hid a smile, which Date caught.

Ah, that's his plan, is it? Bring her over here and send me off. Date schooled his features before pointing out a fatal flaw. "I can't perform lifts one-handed."

"So, you're going to sit here, pouting and sulking, instead," Tundra summarised, giving him a sideways glance.

Date raised a brow. *You mean you're going to sit here pouting and sulking if I remain.* "If it's my choice, it's my choice," he returned, fussing with his red mask. "Aren't you two going to take part in the outer circle, at least?" *Get lost and go dance with her, idiot.*

"I don't mind watching with this leg," Tundra replied, flexing his knee for emphasis. "And it's not a bad view over here, either." he added, leaning back and making a show of turning to look around, blue eyes skimming the fetching figure in pink beside him.

Date snorted, rolling his eyes at lack of subtlety. Yet, Nyima seemed oblivious as she kept her gaze trained on the dancing.

The official bransle was not a dance for couples in the truest sense. With the number of pairs in each circle, it was impossible for the orchestra to play enough times to ensure every pair started and ended with the same person. This made it the perfect dance for anyone looking to snag a set partner for all-twilight. It was also where many, despite Date's warning, showed off their strength by snapping their partners up into the air with spins and flourishes. There were predictable screams and the corner of Date's eye ticked with each one. "Uncultured swine," he muttered under his breath. "Careful," Tundra pointed out, having heard anyway, "I'm pretty sure at least one of those 'uncultured swine' is Seth."

"You made that too easy, even for me," he replied with a mocking glare, ignoring his friend's chuckles. Having a crafty thought, he rose from his seat. "I'll teach you two a galletta. The music is wrong, but it's better than nothing." *If he won't take the initiative, then I shall make him.*

The galletta was a dance for three people that the casual observer might mistake for holding hands and skipping in the snow. With Nyima bookended by Date on the left and Tundra on the right, he showed them the steps first, before beginning in earnest. Date pranced forward, stopping for Nyima to catch up, then Tundra followed. They bowed to her, then repeated, leaving snaking trails through the snow around the tiers. "...fourteen, fifteen, sixteen. Movamente. Bow...and done," Date said, dictating the finish. Tundra shook his head and remarked, "I'll never appreciate this like you, but—" he shot another sideways glance at Nyima, "—with the right company, it's okay."

Date made a suspicious and calculating sound in the back of his throat.

Catching the intent, Tundra cautioned, "Don't start."

"It is better with people you actually *like,"* Date agreed, ignoring Tundra's eyes narrowing. "It's better to know it and never need the skill than be caught short."

"Why do they do these dances?" Nyima gestured at the circles with the hand Date was holding. She then lowered it to her side and waited for the burning sensation to subside. He was *very* warm blooded. She left her other hand in Tundra's, not thinking how it looked, but acknowledging his body temperature was more to her taste.

"Courting," Date replied, ignoring Tundra giving him death glares.

"And entertainment," he added, begrudgingly. "Nobles, royals and such have limited means that don't include the degradation of others."

"It's more than Illthdar," Tundra reassured. "I've seen a few places where it's the same thing, and worse. Power corrupts too easily."

"What they do to others they will say is their right," Nyima agreed, recalling a valley bathed in blood and flames. A shudder passed through her.

Tundra blinked, surprised. "Are you cold, Nyima?"

"Yes, I am," she replied, misunderstanding.

Date shook his head, crossing his arms at the exchange.

"You should move towards the pyre. Date and I can come along, if you'd like," he prodded, willing to escort her anywhere.

"No, thank you. I like it here." The last thing she wanted to do was move *towards* the fire.

"Oh. Okay."

Date looked to the heavens for help, as Tundra made an excuse to leave, and Nyima sat back on the lowest level of the tier enjoying the rest of the festivities. He thought she wasn't bothered by the disappearance, but he caught her looking in the direction Tundra fled every so often, and this gave encouragement she wasn't uninterested. *If only that idiot hadn't run off.*

The night ticked on, the roaring fire melted the ice and left the ironwork exposed, allowing for light and heat to radiate beyond the ice dome.

The sky lightened with coming day break. When the logs reduced to embers and ash, Culvers addressed everyone again, planting his feet among the smouldering ashes at the centre of the pyre.

"Friends!" His booming voice caused those closest to jump with fright—he never needed to raise his voice, so when he did it shocked. Projecting clearly, he looked more impressive than usual, and likely did it because people talked during his dinner speech. All fell silent.

Culvers cleared his throat. "Every year we gather to celebrate our ascension," he proclaimed, waving his arms in grand fashion.

"And every year they come to destroy what we created to make this nation prosper!"

Those unaware of the history behind the celebration were informed during dinner, so they weren't confused—as long as they listened to Culvers earlier speech. Those who didn't pay attention looked lost, much to others amusement.

"Every year we give no mercy. This year is no exception. For though they, like liubul'k undeserving of their masters, bare their fangs to bite the hand that feeds them, we will not lock our doors and cower behind curtained windows!" Culvers pierced a few individuals in the crowd with his steely, silver gaze. Murmurs of how frightening he looked bounced around the pyre. It was the point where fiction and reality blurred, and, in that fleeting moment, he was the Winter King. Tall, powerful and assured he had no equal. "Let them come," he crowed. "Let them come, and we will show them we are not p'ake for their slaughter, but dragons in our den awaiting their strike!" He punched the sky at the same moment the sun crested the horizon. Back-lit by the burning dawn, he cut a terrifying figure standing among smoking ashes.

CHAPTER EIGHTEEN

The cloven fruit trading hands during the all-twilight ball was the Schrödinger's cat of gifts. It could confirm affection for that special someone, or shove an attempted escapee back into the friend-zone. The fact people could hand out more than one fruit further served to complicate matters.

Having retired to the barracks with leftovers from the feast to pick at, Zercey spotted the basket of clove studded fruit on a table near their bunks. "How is this supposed to work, exactly?" she asked, picking up a lime by the attached lavender ribbon, and staring at it as though she had a dead mouse by the tail. "You said you could give it to anyone, but it both matters and doesn't matter at the same time—how?"

"Yeah," Vyxen chimed in, eyeing the basket with renewed distrust. "Nobody wants to get accidentally engaged."

"When in doubt, pass it out." Scyanatha repeated a well-known saying, before launching into a more in-depth explanation. "If you're given a cloven fruit, it's customary to take a clove from it, but afterwards you have three choices: keep, return or pass it to another."

"So, a clove means friendship. The whole fruit means a house and

two-point-four kids?" Zercey reiterated, raising her eyebrows.
Scyanatha laughed. "Nothing so dramatic. It means you might
have the last dance with them on greenman."

"Might," Nyima echoed, setting out a length of fabric to wear later
that night. "Might not?"

"That's right; if the person who gave you fruit gave more than one
out—which is very common, might I add. They may well have
more than one option for the dance." Scy picked at her meal and
tittered at their dismayed looks.

"Ugh. Suddenly I'm flashing back to secondary school gym class."
Zercey sulked, resting her chin in her palm and leaning her elbows
on the table.

"It's a popularity contest. Great," Vyxen concluded in a flat tone.

"It is all rather tiresome," Magnilla noted, with a delicate yawn.
"I'm not the type to play the field." She gestured with a flippant
wave of her hand. "That doesn't stop them from trying. I don't
expect any of *you* to have a problem, but if you can't pass the fruit
on fast enough just throw them in the fireplace. Normally, I'd say
give them to Thijs, but you won't see him; something came up."

"There must be honour," Nyima assessed, ignoring Magnilla. "Or
how to know someone got someone else's fruit?"

"Friends often dance with each other at the cloven fruit dance,"
Abaddon pointed out. "It isn't a strict dance for couples."

"But," Scyanatha added, lips tilting up in a wicked smile, "it is
where a lot of people make the first step towards being more. I
highly recommend picking a clove with your teeth while keeping
eye contact."

There was laughter and cries of, "I couldn't!" though Scyanatha
ended with a few words of caution. "Sometimes, in an act of
desperation, people will resort to stealing. Be on guard."

"I said something came up," Magnilla repeated with a delicate
sniff.

Everyone turned to look at her, waiting for further exposition.

"It isn't anything I'm at liberty to share," she said, gathering her
long blond hair in a ponytail.

"Ehn, okay," Vyxen answered for them. Nobody cared enough to
pry into Magnilla's business when chatting about the ball was more
fun. "The circle dances around the pyre were great," she said,
rejuvenating the conversation. "I had a wild time getting tossed up

in the air like a popcorn kernel." She made a popping sound amidst laughter. "Seth's a good dancer. I thought I was gonna hit the ceiling!" She giggled until she was almost sick when people forgot the steps Date tried beating into them, resulting in pile ups and tangled footwork.

"He has a certain something in his hips," Scy agreed, licking her lips.

Catching the sultry look on Scy's face, Vyxen teased, "I bet I know who you want biting your fruit."

Scy tittered and replied, "He can bite more than that, if he likes."

"Oh, stop!" Zercey laughed, covering her cheeks as they turned red. "You two are terrible!"

Uncomprehending, Nyima tilted her head to look at the citrus on the table, asking, "They should eat it?"

There was more laughter at this, but Magnilla sighed and said, "She's not talking about fruit. It's a cheap metaphor for sex."

Stung, Nyima hummed and turned away, mouthing the conversation back to herself and nodding.

Atmosphere bludgeoned to death, everyone fell silent and ate their food or grew busy preparing for duty later. Magnilla remained where she was rolling her eyes. She'd only been helping out ignorant Nyima with yet more language struggles. Why did everyone always have to act like she was the villain?

Down one floor, on the opposite side of the hallway, four men divested themselves of every chafing, too tight article of clothing. "I'd never wash this arm again if I wouldn't end up smelling like our barracks," Seth commented, holding it in front of him.

"Why?" Lerki's sage brows pinched.

"He's a complete idiot, that's why," Date stated, slumping on his bunk. He had a damp towel in one hand, which he wiped over his face and feathers crowning his head. "And that's just the sort of thing idiots say when they're feet-over-head stupid for someone," he added.

"Who pissed in your coffee?" Seth glowered. The moment of romanticism broken he hazarded a guess. "You didn't like being compared to the youngest prince?"

Date set his towel aside and rolled to face the wall.

Seth laughed, "Called it."

"The question is," Tundra said in a calm voice, taking a seat. He leaned back, balancing on its back legs, "how much we'll have to throttle him before he explains this time?"

Date raised an arm and pointed at Tundra. "Explain your moon-eyeing Nyima first and maybe we'll talk."

"Moon-eyeing?" Lerki repeated, turning to look at Tundra who shook his head in return.

"There's nothing to explain. I was cleanly shot down. Period. Dot. End of." He was still nursing the cold rejection.

"I take it back," Date remarked, sitting up and facing the trio.

"Seth is the smarter one, after all." At least Seth remained with the person he carried a torch for.

"Careful," Tundra returned, though his words lacked real venom, "I can think of at least six different ways I can remove one or more of your limbs and beat you to death with them."

"What am I not understanding?" Lerki asked. "Everyone is talking in codes again."

"These two numb nuts," Date responded, pointing to Seth and Tundra in turn, "have crushes. Satisfied?"

"No. I mean you. Were you pair-bonded?" Lerki asked, hands busy untangling knots in his hair. His fingers caught and he grimaced.

Date laid back down. "Married? No."

"You seemed to have strong opinions of it earlier," Lerki replied, pausing his finger combing when the knot refused to undo.

"I've seen every which way a marriage can come and go," Date said in a dour voice.

"What is that supposed to mean?" Tangle free at last, Lerki secured the tresses once more in the ball clasp and let it fall behind his back. "Date, you have not made anything easier," he noted. "I thought you were doing it on purpose; it was very misleading." Around them, Acolytes milled about chatting, creating a mellow but steady buzz in the background. Having fallen into a strange silence for a moment, the four took in their surroundings: excitement from small groups over handing out fruit and whether the object of their affection would keep it; others fussing with outfits or face paint; some eating or sleeping.

Then. "So, which brother was it?" Tundra asked, crossing his arms.

"Which brother was what?" Date questioned back with a snort.

"The one that got screwed over in *this* story."

Date's slate eyes narrowed. "All of them, if you must know. That thrice damned, contemptuous minx."

"Minx? Which one was that supposed to be again?" Seth prodded, and was rewarded with a dark glare in return.

"We're. Not. Talking. About. It."

"Inoshi was the minx," Lerki guessed. His chest puffed, pleased with his recall. "Is that right?"

Date turned away. "No," he corrected, toneless.

Tundra set his chair square again, as he contemplated the facts. There was no other conclusion: Inoshi wanted Takamori—Date's older brother—to be next in line for the throne. Much the same way the autumn princess had. To that end, she took a page right out of the story of the Winter King. Yet, Date insisted it didn't fit.

"Okay, so how is it supposed to go, then?" Seth demanded.

Date sighed, giving in and deciding to tell them. "Tatsuko orchestrated the whole thing, probably from the first day she was presented to Takao's esteemed— " he rolled his eyes, words steeped in sarcasm "—and most noble family. And the only reason she's called Inoshi now is because both Takamori and the real Inoshi are dead."

With undern finished, everyone had duties that day. A yawning
Zercey regretted her life choices for not taking a nap before her
shift on top of the wall. At least Illthdar had coffee. "I can't believe
we have to be on high alert during this thing," she moaned,
sagging. "How do people do this?"
"I don't know, but I've decided I couldn't care less. If someone
wants to steal some dumb fruit, they can have it," Vyxen droned.
She'd been awake since dawn the day before and was having
trouble stopping her eyes from crossing.
"Isn't sleep deprivation a form of torture?" Zercey grouched.
"What made the Winter King think this was anything close to a
good idea? No wonder rebels stormed the castle!"
"To people like the Winter King and his family, your suffering was
another part of the entertainment," Date said, gruffly. Having
dropped a bombshell on his friends, he exited before completing
the tale. "Your pain equals their amusement, and remarkably little
has changed since then."
About to comment, Zercey spotted a pair of figures approaching
the gate from the outside. "Oh, hey," she pointed them out, "there's
Scy and Lerki." Waving, she called, "Hey! Anything new?!"
"All is calm, and all is bright!" Scyanatha returned, laughing.
Vyxen and Zercey booed the joke.
"How is everything up there?!"
"If it was evening, I'd joke about it being a silent night," Vyxen
muttered, before yelling a less imaginative, though no less accurate
response. "Boring!"
Date moved to stand beside her and saluted.
Scyanatha chuckled. "I shall see you all later!"
Lerki waved one last time, before adjusting the satchel strap on his
shoulder, and they continued into the city.

"I did not understand what was wrong," Lerki admitted in relation
to Scy's summary of their patrol. "That was a strange choice of
words. Was it a joke?"
"It was more a play on words. The line was part of the lyrics from
a human song," she explained, smiling at his curiosity.
"Humans have songs?" At Scy's hum and nod of confirmation, he
admitted, "I never knew. Seth has never spoken of it."
"Humans can be surprisingly creative," she remarked, giving him a

reassuring pat on the shoulder, before expanding on the concept. "Every culture, every tribe I've met has music in some form. All of it is beautiful in its own way."

"Sancata Zercey said— " Lerki began, a look of melancholy crossed his fine features, but dissipated as quickly as it had come "—that humans were beings she would never regret knowing, even in her final days."

"Sancata," Scy murmured, having heard the word before, but unable to place it.

Taking her echoing of the word to indicate she was enquiring, Lerki said, "Ah, yes; only one Zercey left into the veils. She was Sancata Zercey of..." he trailed off, his face contorting into one of frustration and irritation.

"Can't think of the name in Illthdarian?" she guessed, and he nodded.

"Sungiphi." He gave the name in Clek, trying to describe what it meant. *"Sungiphi* dances in wind, stretches to touch the water and hugs the earth on the banks."

Scy patted his shoulder in comfort. "I'm sure it will come," she said, though not without making a note to contemplate it later. Just as her own wording hadn't escaped his notice, his hadn't escaped hers.

"If you pass by, I'll start a snowball fight," came a new voice to their conversation.

The pair turned their heads.

"Seth, Tundra!" Lerki greeted his friends, as his eyes travelled to the others in their company. "Abaddon, Nyima and Magnilla..." Considering the mix, the smile on his face faltered. "You have a mission."

"First one in awhile," Tundra admitted, glad to get out of the city. "I'll manage, though." He swung the walking stick in his hand like a baseball bat.

"And they're sending me along to carry you back if you can't," Seth declared, chuckling. "You mad man."

"Okay, but don't be late," Scyanatha cautioned. "All-twilight might last until dawn, but it's better to attend the whole thing."

"We'll be okay," Abaddon stated, relaying their mission brief at Nyima's nudge and Magnilla's pointed cough. "A coastal village sent word that raiders attacked. The Order wants them dealt with."

It was a simple task and a common one. Magnilla remained silent throughout the account, staring at a point in the distance as though she weren't part of the group.

"Lerki, you're in charge of our fruit," Seth said, pointing.

Lerki nodded, tight lipped.

Tundra added, "We'll say hi to Date as we go past, so he'll know what's up."

"Vyxen and Zercey are on the wall, as well," Scy informed them.

"Good luck and we shall see you tonight!" The smile she gave was reserved for Seth, and the look on his face said he knew it as he chuckled and tried not to fidget.

Nyima led the team towards the coastal village, which wasn't part of the usual patrol path. Boats arrived from another island late in the night, and the occupants wasted little time stirring trouble for the fishing village. News came to Las thanks to a corvazneo carrying a message.

Curls of black smoke snaked into the sky, as the group crested a hill and looked at the village. The wind aggravated the waves lapping the shore, making them sound like vicious slaps. There were no signs of life or movement. It was eerie.

"I-I think we're too late," Abaddon murmured, taking in the lack of stimulus.

"Must check," Nyima replied, foreboding colouring her tone. The team hurried along the pebbled pathway.

"What the fuck?!" Impotent with fury, Seth flipped an overturned handcart out of the middle of the icy road. Its wares spilled out covering the dead driver. "What the fuck happened here?!" The sky gave an ominous rumble.

"Fire magic of some kind," Tundra assessed, crouching and examining the burns marks on the body. At Nyima's nod, he scouted ahead, then returned. "Small foot prints all over. A lot of them."

"Fire, small feet, travels in groups," Abaddon listed, brows pinching. "Sounds like imps."

Nyima kept her icy blue eyes trained on the horizon, an air of caution about her. "What are imps?"

"Demons," Abaddon replied. "They like warmer islands like Don, Bien and Mu." It was strange they chose to leave their home to come to the much colder island of Illthdar.

"That answers why Chiyoko thought we'd need ice magic, plus Storm-Bringer." Tundra added his friend's moniker with a sarcastic lilt. "And the demon encyclopedia." He indicated Abaddon, who flushed at the comment, unsure about being considered the go-to fountainhead for demon information.

They split and searched the village for survivors.

What remained was a sorry sight. The houses, made of thatch and mud-packed timber frames, became ideal kindling. There was a lack of spilled blood expected from a massacre, but imps primary offense and defense was fire magic. They killed and cooked their

306

prey at once. The bodies the group found that hadn't crumbled to charcoal had limbs hewn from their torsos. From the scatter, death hadn't come fast enough. Many charred alive as they fled.

However, for a busy fishing village, the number of corpses didn't tally with the amount of huts.

Tundra booted in a still smouldering door, blackened and splintered from a fire blast.

"Anyone in here?!" Seth ran into a burning building on the other side of the street and was driven back, coughing.

"No one's here," Magnilla informed them, expression blank. "No one alive, anyway."

"Like Ifrit," Nyima bit out, with a deep inhalation and disbelieving shake of her head. "No mercy," she said, voice shaking, hands fisting at her sides. She squeezed her eyes shut, unable to bear looking.

For Aetumuh of Ice, Nyima uv dra C'deney—a v'neketyh from the planet Vaosynlr—the course to Illthdar was more straightforward than others. Though the sense and reason of her arrival was not.

Tall and slender, with blue-toned skin and dressed in a white camisole and ribbon skirt, she appeared in a crack of thunder prepared for battle. *"Cissuhan?"*

No one came from within the forest to meet her. Not that day or any since.

After some weeks spent roaming the forest and coast, overhearing grunts, clicks and trilling that meant nothing, her luck further soured. A group of warriors accosted her. With no common language to demand answers, she had to defend herself.

Ramming an elbow into the cheek of a short one, she brought a knee into the stomach of another.

Harsh cries and commands sounded. Men and women formed a circle, preventing her escape.

No! Leave me alone! She tried to flee.

Sticky ropes appeared from inside the sleeves of one. He lashed her arms, bound her legs. Pulled.

She resisted. *Go away!*

Another wrapped a length around his arm. A hard and sudden tug. Off balance, Nyima fell to the ground. She turned her head, spitting dirt.

A tall man in plaid, with two-toned hair and silver eyes looked down.

She couldn't break the ropes. Struggled to gain her feet.

The man dropped, driving his knee into her back and pinning her. He spat a command. Body language said he wanted her to stop. She couldn't. She had to fulfil her duty. *"Fru yna oyi?! Fra'na ecso Cissuhan?"* Who are you? Where is my master? When this failed to produce anything besides nonsensical gibberish she tried threats, then curses. *"Oyi'ddylg sa: Efemm tacdnuo oyi! Syo oyi c'fymmuf haa'tma puhac yhtea luikrehk!"* How dare you attack me! May you swallow fish bones and die choking!

So was Nyima's ignominious arrival to Illthdar. An embarrassment. She wasn't much further along in finding Cissuhan since then, either. *What can I do? Nothing until Cissuhan arrives. I must be patient. The Order is good enough for now. I still have time.*

"You okay?" Tundra stared at Nyima, noting the strain and abstraction on her face. "I've had the pleasure of meeting them," he said, referring to the creature she mentioned. If it was the same one.

Nyima opened her eyes and managed a reassuring smile. "Yes, thank you." She doubted it was the same. Ifrit was unmistakable.

"There's always someone," Seth argued with Magnilla, running a hand over his orange hair. As she strutted past, he said, "Uhhh, where are you going?"

"I want to thank you all for escorting me this far." She spoke in a voice so quiet everyone strained to hear. "I'm afraid this is where we part." She launched into a sprint and didn't look back.

"What? Wait for us, Magnilla!" Abaddon unsheathed their axe and chased after her. "We shouldn't split up! Come back!" They stumbled and fell, crashing to the sand and crying out.

"I got you," Seth said, hauling them onto his back. "What's with her?"

Tundra passed, putting on a burst of speed and rounding the head of the bay.

Nyima, jogging at a slower pace, knew there was no point trying to catch her. *She has run away like a coward.*

The group lost sight of Magnilla and slowed to a halt as they caught up with Tundra.

"Of all of the stupid—!" He bent over to catch his breath. His leg throbbed a reminder he wasn't in top form.

"You've got to be kidding me," Seth puffed, readjusting Abaddon so they sat more secure. "Did an eitercopp creep down her back or something? Why would anyone just take off like that?!"

"I don't know," Abaddon replied, white knuckled from clinging to Seth. "We can't know un-until we, um, find her."

"No," Nyima ordered, trying to ignore the unpleasant, wet sand squishing between her toes. "The village is being more important." She put her hands on her hips and surveyed their surroundings. "This path is no good." She shook her head. "No tracks. No people. Let us to looking the other way." She pointed the way they came.

"Magnilla said there were no survivors," Abaddon reminded, chewing the inside of their lip. "I'm worried about her," they added.

Nyima's eyes narrowed. "Always one left," she said in a dark and bitter tone.

Tundra's brows pinched at her comment, finding it curious, but the timing inappropriate to ask. "She's right," he said, taking his cane from her and leaning on it.

"Well, okay," Seth commented, incredulous and gesturing at Magnilla's footprint trail. "There went our tracker. How we supposed to find anyone without her?"

Nyima scoffed. "Not the *only* tracker."

"Let's go to the village, and I'll take a look at the prints in the snow," Tundra said, validating her statement.

"The coast is to the left." Abaddon oriented themselves, drawing the location up from memory. "The way we're going will take us along the cliffs of Gilquay. They wouldn't have come this way for safety."

Nyima nodded once, pleased with how the team adapted being down one "vital" member.

"The only other way would be towards the forest or risk skirting the edge of the coast and hope they aren't spotted," Tundra reasoned, using the new information.

"I don't know why they would come now," Abaddon stated, their voice just above a whisper, brow creasing. "Imps don't like water, and, er, they hate c-c-cold more than anything." They had a hunch the imps came from Don or Bien. The conjoined islands lay to the west of Illthdar, while Mu was to the east. "But why?" they murmured under their breath.

"Why come with boats in winter?" Nyima voiced, gazing at the rough waves.

"I'll bet anything it has to do with that fissure," Seth determined, face rigid.

Nyima frowned, looking around the group in turn. "What fissure?" All the barracks gossip was about dresses and sex, so she tuned it out. Had she missed something important?

"Like a festering and infected wound, it lies across the face of the land, weeping and throbbing. Like a beacon, it calls things towards it; dark and menacing."

"You do have a way with words, Inari," Tundra said in a dry voice, naming the figure approaching from behind.

Inari had white hair cut in an extreme bowl, cropped just above the ear on one side, but dropping past their chin on the other. They dressed in many layers, the innermost pearl white, with each outer layer a shade darker than the last; the topmost glossy silver. Much how Seth dressed in long robes, Inari's ran to the ground, pooling at their feet. The hem was decorated with ornate, crimson flowers, delicate leaves and a magnificent grey crane covered the back, beak pointed skyward.

"I was called away from the events of the night," Inari said, tucking their hands into the long, drooping sleeves of their junihitoe. "My task was to close the fissure, but my efforts were fruitless."

"That explains why we didn't see you last night," Seth noted. "I figured you weren't a fan of dancing."

"Dancing is not a fan of me," they corrected in a gentle voice. They had a feminine facial structure, though their tall build was angular and masculine. "I never appreciated tripping."

"What is the fissure?" Nyima demanded, a sense of urgency latching onto her heart and squeezing it. If the imps were related, then resolving one problem could eliminate the other.

"It radiates a hideous, yellow light," Inari described with rancour. "The rocks are jagged and tooth-like. It bears an aura of a

310

necromancer's workbench. Which, suffice to say, is unpleasant."
"So, after waving your arms in the air and saying every spell you
have up your sleeves you decided to come back this way
because...?" Tundra held his hand, palm out, waiting for Inari to
give him a reply.
"Because High Priestess Chiyoko sent a floydrake while I was in
the middle of waving my arms in the air, reciting every incantation
I know," they replied in a similar mocking tone. "It bore a letter
which advised me to meet with another party. I assume it must be
yours."
"Great! We could actually use your help." Seth jumped in, literally
putting himself in Inari's way. "Abaddon's twisted something," he
explained, turning to reveal them clinging like a baby red panda.
"Think you could fish anything out of that mallet space you call
sleeves that'll fix them up?"
"It isn't that bad," Abaddon protested, as Seth lowered them to the
ground. "It's almost healed as is— "
"Abaddon," Inari repeated their name, as though attempting to
recall. "Ahh, I do know you, after all." They turned to Seth. "I do
not have healing magic, Seth, but we might have some remedies."
"The fissure dragging things to it?" Nyima questioned, while
Abaddon sat on a rock so Inari could tend to them.
"They come as though in a trance," Inari replied, poking and
prodding Abaddon's bare ankle. "By the time they arrive, nothing
is able to draw them from whatever spell they are under. They
throw themselves in without acknowledgement or awareness of the
world."
Tundra mused, "No one will argue it's strange."
Applying salve to the inflamed muscle, Inari worked it in with
smooth, circular motions.
Abaddon flushed. "I-I—" They pulled their leg away. "I think
that's good enough." They redonned their sock and boot. "Thank
you, it feels better."
"Good," Nyima stated, drawing the group back to the importance
of their mission. "We should going to the village. There are
survivors." She was sure of it.

CHAPTER NINETEEN

"It would surprise them to know they have more than a few people interested," Scyanatha said to Vyxen and Zercey when she met with them for metelaf. They sat at the bottom of the steps leading to the battlements, passing sandwiches and drink back and forth. Talk soon turned to dating and who might be asked to dance at the ball later that night.

"It has to be harder for them than us," Zercey considered, pausing to sip mead from a bottle. "Some people are hung up on the whole non-binary thing."

"I'd love to see them with someone," Vyxen agreed. "Abaddon's just so cute. They're sweet and quiet, but they're totally not a pushover."

"I would hope they have someone who isn't confrontational," Scy reasoned. "They do not like arguments for many reasons."

The other two hummed their agreement.

Zercey wiped her mouth and said, "What about Nyima? She must have gone somewhere because I never actually saw her dancing last night."

A slow, knowing smile spread across Scy's face. "I saw her, and she was dancing, but it wasn't around the pyre."

"Ohh?" Vyxen leaned forward, taking the chance to snag fruit and cheese to go with her crackers. "Just what kind of dance was she doing?" Her white eyebrows waggled.

Scy threw a grape at her and laughed. "Not that kind! She was with Date and Tundra."

"Buhh," Zercey shook her head, laughing even as her own face flushed, "I don't think that helped get our minds out of the gutter." Vyxen snorted and tried not to choke on her food.

"You two." Scy shook her head like an indulgent big sister. "It was a normal dance, thank you. Out of the way and a fair distance from the fire. I only spotted them once when Seth happened to toss me."

"And speaking of Seth," Vyxen reached over and tweaked Scyanatha's cheek. "You've got some slick moves there, girl. I saw what you did."

"I don't know what you're talking about," Scy replied in faux innocence, eyes laughing. "It's a pity he only shows his arms in battle gear. They are *very* nice."

"Ohhh, haha," Zercey began, leaning back and pointing.

Vyxen beat her to the punchline. "It's more than just his arms you'd like to see," she said, with a suggestive purr, and the three dissolved into giggles.

"You may be right about that," Scy admitted. "He's certainly easy on the eye. I wouldn't have minded if he'd have stripped down like Lerki— "

"Whoooaa, wait." Zercey cut in, making a T-shape with her hands. "When did Lerki strip down?"

"Yeah. How did we miss it?" Vyxen chimed in, with a sideways glance.

"That's not what I meant," Zercey protested, blushing furiously.

Scy laughed. "It was when you were exposed to recluse poison," she explained, retelling the event in full. She noted at the end, "That jewellery really is just about everywhere."

"Stop! Please stop!" Zercey's face was deep pink. "I don't want to think about Lerki naked! Oh my god! You two are incorrigible!"

"Unfortunately, he kept his lower half decent. I will forever wonder what would have happened if Tundra hadn't pointed out modest people in the room," Scy teased one final time before changing to a safer topic. "On our way back to headquarters earlier, we ran into Magnilla and the others."

"We saw them leave," Vyxen confirmed. "It seemed important; the

High Elders don't normally send that many people at once."
Zercey counted the team off on her fingers. "Abaddon, Nyima, Tundra, Seth and Magnilla…five does seem to be pushing it. Six in total if you count Thijs—he's always a step behind her somewhere. The largest parties we've had so far have always been four or less."

"Magnilla did not seem like her usual self," Scy shared.

Vyxen and Zercey began packing up, sighing.

Scy gave them a reproachful look. "She is our friend, and I'm worried about her."

Zercey rolled her eyes but decided to indulge. "Okay, how was she not herself?"

"She wasn't as talkative as usual," Scy admitted. "Normally, she would reassure everyone they would return in time, listing reasons why she had a vested interest in making it happen. Today," she shook her head, "she let Abaddon speak for her."

"Okay, fair enough," Vyxen remarked. "I haven't a clue beyond the obvious things she could be upset about. You're going to have to ask her." She added under her breath, "Or Thijs, since he's always *so helpful* that way."

"You know," Zercey grinned, nudging her, "you could ask him, too. I mean, what a chance it would be since you have a crush on him, eh?"

Vyxen's mouth fell open and she repressed a shudder. "EWWWW!"

"What is this?" Scyanatha looked confused. She grew more amused as the explanation unfolded.

"*Kaa!* No way do I want to be with Magnilla's creepy, little brother!" Vyxen shook her head and made an X sign with her arms.

"You two could try a little harder to get along with them," Scy said.

Vyxen shook her head and Zercey's nose wrinkled at the suggestion.

"I really can't," Zercey mocked. "See, Imogen would snap herself in half if she tried, and she's double-jointed!"

Scyanatha sighed, but finished packing away the meal, waving them off as they climbed the stairs back to the battlements.

"Sorry if we kept you waiting," Vyxen stated, breezing over to Date and Lerki, who huddled together.

On seeing Lerki, Zercey fumbled trying to do the same. *His jewellery's everywhere?!* She knocked over a supply rack of arrows and stubbed her toe on a raised stone on the walkway. Vyxen bit her lip, trying to contain her giggles. "Thanks for agreeing to keep watch, Date."

He raised an eyebrow. "It's fine. Nothing's happening, anyway."

"So, Lerki." Vyxen nudged him.

Lerki blinked at her, rubbing the spot she elbowed.

"What brings you up here? You don't have anything else to do for the day?" She was subtle as a sledgehammer.

"I brought tea to Date for his pain," he replied, simply.

Mess tidied, Zercey patted her hands against her hips, unsure what to do with herself. She looked a complete idiot, but collecting the scattered arrows and returning them allowed her time to twist her head back on. "Has it really been all quiet?" She addressed Date, unable to trust herself speaking to Lerki. She couldn't stop thinking about him topless. "Did the away team return yet? Scy's worried."

He nodded, then shook his head. "Not yet." He looked past her to the horizon, narrowing his eyes. "There's still plenty of daylight, so they may return before our shift ends."

"I worry," Lerki admitted, wringing his hands. "Tundra's leg is only just healed and he's already going into full duty."

"You can't stop him," Date pointed out. "That's how he is. I'm more surprised we kept him off it as long as we did."

"Bit cavalier, is he?" Zercey teased, laughing.

"That is an understatement," Date replied, straightening. "This may be them now."

Lerki, Vyxen and Zercey gathered along the wall and peered out. In the sea of white, several ant-sized figures appeared.

"There are more than just five," Lerki noted. "It looks more like—" he squinted "—twelve or fifteen?"

Date shook his head. "There are fourteen, and how is it they ever let you go on wall duty with eyes as abysmal as that?"

Lerki smiled. "I don't need to see as far ahead as you," he stated off-hand.

Zercey agreed, able to pick out the shapes on the horizon. "You might be near sighted, Lerki." Her eyebrows pinched when he gave a mysterious wink, leaving her to wonder if the bad guess was intentional. *He likes trolling his friends.*

"Well," Vyxen reasoned, pointing, "in his defence, it looks like Seth is carrying at least one person."

"I'd fly there to confirm, but I'm grounded until further notice," Date said, shaking his head, feathers swishing in the breeze.

"Guess that leaves us," Vyxen concluded, tagging Zercey on the shoulder. "Come on!" She bounded away, passing them all as she headed for the stairs.

Nine survived the imp invasion. Though, it might have been a different story without ice magic on the return trip to Las.

A band of six fire imps doubled back to the main road to finish off the villagers. Abaddon, Inari and Seth protected the civilians, leaving Nyima and Tundra taking offensive action.

Nyima had no mercy, dispatching four with jagged spears of ice that turned them into pin cushions. Tundra finished the remaining two with a punch to crush one's windpipe, which he over-arm hurled into the other, breaking its ribs.

"You strong," Nyima complimented.

"Thanks. Not so bad yourself."

For Nyima, the mission had a certain amount of catharsis. Gone was that lost child, huddled in a snow-bank while ifrit reduced her tribe to ash and bone. Now, she was strong. The imps were feeble caricatures next to the towering ifrit. There was no satisfaction giving them an icy death, but she'd brought justice to the dead villagers. There would be no closure until the ifrit chief's head was stuck atop one of her spears, but she felt a little more confident in fighting her fear of fire. As their friends greeted them outside the gates, she vowed to increase her training.

"Boozhoo!" Vyxen called, bounding to a stop in front of them. "Is everyone okay?"

"Does anyone need a healer?" Zercey chimed in, as she arrived beside Vyxen. Her lilac coloured eyes swept over the Acolytes and noted one missing.

"Fortunately, everyone's just shaken," Seth replied, carrying a small child on his back and another in his arms. He winced when a pair of hands grappled with the chain on his earring. "Ow, ow, ow…"

One of the women came to his rescue. "Pagak!" she scolded, taking the child's fingers in her hand and easing them off Seth's ear. "Careful, or you will hurt the kind man."

Earring released from the the child's grip, Seth rubbed his earlobe as he balanced the other kid on his hip.

"I'm so sorry, he doesn't know his own strength yet." The woman wagged a finger and smiled.

Seth grinned. "Nah, it's okay. Not going to say it didn't hurt, but no real harm was done, so it's all right."

"You look like you left in a hurry," Vyxen noted, seeing the lack of possessions. "Come on in and we'll get you set up with a change of clothes and some bedding."

"Vyxen, if you can help with that, I can ask around to see about getting food and places for everyone to sleep?" Zercey suggested.

"Good plan!" She bounced and waved, beckoning them forward. "Come on, everyone! Follow me!"

That left Nyima, Seth, Inari, Tundra and Abaddon to the task of reporting to Chiyoko.

"You're dismissed," Chiyoko said, waving her arm in the direction of the door once the group finished speaking. Her long, yellow sleeve covered her hand, making it seem as though she didn't have one. As the group turned to leave, she added, "Not you, Inari. You have another report to give."

They hadn't moved. Nodding, they said. "Yes, and we might advise that you seek your comfort before we begin. It's most perplexing…"

The door shut behind them, and Seth shook his head. "That's not how they explained it to us."

"They may have more detailed information for the High Priestess," Abaddon replied, taking a position at the rear. Seth assumed the front, with Tundra and Nyima next to each other between the two. Tundra shared his observations of Inari, having previous experience with them. "They're probably dragging it out, so they can hide from the party. They like to be fashionably late when it isn't business."

"You know them well?" Nyima slanted a look at him.

317

Humming, Seth answered, "They helped our transition once we completed training. We worked with their team a lot in the first year." He waved his hand about in a general manner. "Doing the same we're doing with you guys."

Nyima's eyes narrowed a fraction at his back, and she nodded. "I see."

"What happened to the rest of their team? There were five originally." Concern marred Abaddon's fine features. "Inari is always with at least one member."

"That—" Tundra drew a breath and shook his head. "It's a difficult subject."

Abaddon caught the hesitation in his voice and let the subject be. "Do you think Magnilla made it back yet?"

"Hmph." Nyima didn't want to discuss it. Magnilla running away to appear once the job was done wouldn't make her look good. This left her to conclude Magnilla ran away and that was all.

Since neither man answered either, Abaddon tried for a more convivial topic. "We have to get ready for the all-twilight ball."

"It's gonna be a blast!" Seth rubbed his hands together. "The fruit will be flying!"

"It flies?" Nyima's brows pinched. She thought it was passed out. *Is this another sex thing?* She didn't want to ask and get belittled like earlier.

Tundra chuckled and said, "It depends. With how some people react, it winds up on the other side of the room."

She smiled and chuckled, realising the joke.

"I wonder if Lerki has ours ready yet," Seth wondered.

"We'll find out when we get to the barracks," Tundra replied, as they paused at the bottom of the stairway leading to the barracks.

"So, we'll see you there?" He looked at Nyima as he spoke.

She nodded. "Yes."

"It's only the event of the year that everyone's going to," Seth joked, snorting with mirth.

Tundra shoved Seth by the shoulder. "See you, then," he said to Nyima and Abaddon.

"I think he likes you," they whispered, as they headed to the barracks.

Nyima was glad Abaddon couldn't see her blushing.

Walking in, they found Scyanatha sat crossed legged on her bunk, stone beads floating around her head as a reference guide for a headdress, with a mirror propped at her feet. Spotting them, she called, "Welcome back. How did the mission go?" Taking in the pensive look on Abaddon's face she grew concerned. "What happened?"

"Magnilla run away," Nyima replied blandly, moving towards the bolt of fabric she intended to make her dress with.

"Uh, it w-wasn't quite like that," Abaddon corrected, explaining what happened. "Did she, er, c-come here?" They looked in Scyanatha's general direction with hope.

"No, dear. She will probably turn up at the ball," she soothed. "She was supposed to sing, after all."

Abaddon was pacified by this and began feeling around for their things.

Nyima had reservations. It wasn't the first time Magnilla ran off after being embarrassed by a setback. The difference between then and now was she'd done it without packing first.

"*Boozhoo,* everyone!" Vyxen entered with Zercey following close behind. She was laden down with a puff of multi-coloured fabric and accessories. "Got all those people settled and now it's time to par-tay!" She put her stuff on Magnilla's empty bed and began stripping off her leggings, pixie skirt and light-weight sweater.

"I'm starting to regret my life choices," Zercey stated, as she looked at her dress hanging from her bunk. She'd chosen a one shoulder, mid-thigh length toga made of silk, with a longer, sheer layer going over the top. Her eyes darted to the window, where it was still light enough to see snow falling outside. "This isn't going to be particularly warm." She'd look pretty in pink, for sure, but would it stand up to the outfits other Acolytes were wearing?

"The ball is indoors and it will be plenty warm with the turn out," Sky reassured her, helping Abaddon secure their hair—which they'd changed for the night to long and red—into an updo. "You may find you need to escape to one of the balconies or the terrace."

Nyima pulled a face at this, resigned to feeling like she'd been shoved into a forge for the night. Naked, but for a pair of panties, she had her back to the room to concentrate on designing how she wanted her dress to go. The sheer, white fabric she'd bought was to be the skirt, which she wrapped around her waist and gathered by her hip, creating a split. This was kept in place with a series of ice crystals that became a belt and clasp. As for her upper body, she crossed her hands on either side of her waist, then drew them up and over her breasts, leaving a path of crystals behind. She flicked her fingers wide at the shoulder and spikes jutted out. There was no need to add a back and, thanks to her icy aura, she was in no danger of anything melting. She had shoes for the occasion, also made of ice, and her braids were tied up with bits of decorative chain to keep them off her neck.

"My god, you look amazing, Nyima!" Zercey gestured to all of her as she turned around.

"Thank you," she replied, testing to see if all the crystals were in the right place by moving her hips side to side. She nodded, satisfied.

"That could well be a stand out outfit," Scy determined, a twinkle in her eye. "Though, you may be beaten by some of the men. They do tend to go over the top for these things." She patted Abaddon's shoulder. "Your hair is done, dear."

"Thank you." They reached to feel the result. The long, red strands were pulled back from their face into a single, centre braid. It was pushed up, giving them extra height, then left loose and flowing once it reached shoulder point. "I love it," they concluded with a smile.

"Perfect," Scy chimed, pleased. "Do you need help with your things?"

"No, thank you," they replied, then frowned. "Unless it's been moved..."

"Everything's on your bed how you left it," Vyxen answered, from the depths of her ball gown.

"Thank you." Abaddon went to their bunk and stripped off. By touch alone they found their dress. It was two-toned, with a hooped skirt, fluted sleeves, and a fashionable hood that draped over their back. A decorative, mock-bodice, with lacing, criss-crossed over their stomach. It gave the impression the solid, lavender side panels were secured over the shimmering, steel grey gown. They teamed it with calf length, leather boots and a complicated choker that had a moonstone in the centre and stars and moons set along the neckline.

"You look like a steampunk princess!" Vyxen enthused, as she managed to get her head out of her dress and pull it on.

"I do?" Their face flushed. "Thank you."

"Does anyone have anything for dark circles?" Vyxen made a face at her reflection. "I look like a moving corpse with these bags."

"You're not alone," Zercey commented, adjusting a metal laurel leaf crown on her head. She put a foot on one of the bunks to tie her brown, lace-trimmed boots. "I'd be surprised if anyone looks rested tonight."

"More powerful, higher-ranked nobility would have free time to rest during the day after yule pyre, but that did not extend to lower ranked servants." Scy shrugged, unable to excuse history. "There were executions following the ball of anyone who fell derelict of duty."

"Viva la revolution, then," Vyxen cheered. "Down with the Winter King! I didn't want to see Culvers lose, until now."

Abaddon giggled and hummed in agreement, then looked curious. "Vyxen, why aren't you dressing in Quartz's barracks?" They noted it was unusual for her to be changing with the Jaspers. "No one minds, but—"

"Because Uwe threatened a surprise inspection and I didn't want to give myself more reasons to punch him," she replied, pulling a face and shuddering. The action sent a strap off her shoulder and she righted it. Vyxen's dress was a further expression of her bright and cheery personality. She'd chosen something that would flutter when she spun, and had a dusting of stars and glitter all over. The top half was dark and sparkling. The colour washed out as the eye moved down, going through the spectrum until it reached the hem, which was pink. She looked like the night sky and the dawn all at once. Upon her wrist was a bracelet made of tiny, gold stars, which matched the circlet adorning her head. "This thing is amazing, but I have babies—" meaning companions "—to feed. I can't believe I spent so much on an outfit I'm only going to wear once!"

"You may find another occasion to wear it," Scyanatha reassured. Her hair was twisted and plaited into several braids, wrapped about her head, with some tendrils falling free. Having swapped outfits with Abaddon, she wore a daring, black dress. The skirt was split up to her hip on one side, with a V-shaped front that plunged almost to her navel. Her modesty was spared by a sheer panel, and

321

bejewelled black gemstones. The straps were thick, but it was otherwise sleeveless, with black fur trim. She paired it with high-heeled, stiletto boots in a simple, black suede with buckle decoration and front lacing. She stepped back and whistled as everyone gathered together. "We are a stunning looking group," she complimented, giving them short applause. "If we don't collect a string of hearts tonight I shall be shocked."

Vyxen guffawed when Abaddon and Zercey stammered. She then pointed at Nyima, trying to look elsewhere. "You people suck at keeping secrets!" She linked arms with them both, as Nyima brought up the rear. "You're gonna get a dance with that special someone if it kills me!"

"Kill her," Nyima said in a wry voice, causing more laughter.

"Now, now," Scy waved a teasing finger. "I'm sure we're all grown up and mature enough to catch our own fish." And if they weren't, she would just have to throw a net over them to make sure. "The ball awaits."

Up one floor and across the hallway, in the Order of Fluorite barracks, the men were having less success getting ready.

"Give me back my coat, you fucking plant!" Date pulled at the curled leaf bed with his good arm. He'd left the coat there, so he could fold it open and make it easier to put on. However, the leaf had a mind of its own and decided it was heavy enough to tuck in for the night.

Lerki rushed to his aid before Date resorted to violence. "Shhh," he soothed, stroking the large, thick stem. "He didn't meant it."

"Serves you right for putting it there," Seth told him, shaking his head. "I can't believe you forgot they did that."

"He could always go with it as an overcoat," Tundra joked, straight faced.

The leaf opened and Date wasted no time snatching the garment with a huff.

Lerki attempted to placate him. "Should I help you?"

"No, I am past the age of being helped to get dressed," he snapped. "And you two, shut up," he said to Seth and Tundra.

They both sniggered as they returned to dressing.

Inari sat at one of the tables, chuckling. "You four are the same as always." Decked in an elaborate headpiece with black horns, their white hair was obscured by draping layers of red and orange fabric, trimmed in beaten, copper coins. More fabric flowed down across their shoulders and back to form a cape. Their junihitoe followed the same colours. Their sleeves, full and billowing, gathered at the wrists, studded with black jewels. The robes dropped to the floor, fanning around their feet, which were clad in curl-toed shoes. A black and orange sash wrapped around their slim waist to hold the ensemble together.

"Unfortunately, you're not wrong, Inari," Tundra agreed. He'd changed out of his habitual style of black and baby blue and into sleeveless tang-style, white jacket. He left it unbuttoned, revealing a grey shirt with a high collar underneath and left the hem untucked from his straight-cut black trousers which he paired with his day to day boots. He helped himself to some cubes of spicy melon that Lerki laid out in preparation as a natural anti-sleep aid, and added, "Boys will be boys."

"Hey, I'm loads bigger than I used to be," Seth protested, flexing a bicep for emphasis. "I worked hard to get these babies. You're still a lunatic though, Jingyi."

Eschewing his usual style for the evening, Seth had on something inspired by Pharaoh Taharqa. A gold headdress covered his orange hair, with a two-headed cobra decorating the front. He was bare chested, with a spotted, animal print pelt thrown over one shoulder and arm. With it, he wore a twisted necklace made from a thick band of gold wire, and a cobra earring curled around his earlobe, fanged jaws poised to strike. Both his upper and lower arms were decked with more gold bands. Polished to a high sheen, they gleamed against his dark skin. Though his ankles were adorned with more of the same bands, on his feet were plain sandals made of leather. Around his waist he wrapped and pinned a simple, white muslin cloth to complete the effect.

"From you that's flattery," Tundra returned, tone calm and even.

"Thanks, man, I can tell you really mean that," Seth dead-panned, picking up on the sarcasm.

"Anytime."

The pair chuckled at each other.

"Well," Inari commented, their eye colour flickering between amber and mustard yellow, "at least you have enough fruit." They nodded towards a high mound of citrus inside a basket, each covered in cloves.

"Those are for Fluorite," Lerki replied, before pointing towards a more simplistic group of limes, lined along the windowsill. "These are ours."

By the standards of many Illthdarians, Lerki's uniform was the most formal thing he owned, but it was stiff—he wore it only as long as he had to. This restricted its use to when he worried his High Elder might want him. Appearances, for reasons he didn't understand, mattered to Phanuel.

The undershirt was least of his concerns, though it forced his jewellery down, pinching skin and making him suffocated. It was deep aubergine, trimmed in tan, with tight sleeves that ended in points at his middle finger. His trousers were tan and cut into his waist, but the coat was the worst. It had an off-centre, V-cut collar that pressed down on one side. It was kept closed by a long line of buttons across one side of his chest. It split and flared past his hips, stopping at mid-calf. It was two shades of purple and bore a velvety texture. His boots were also purple. Starting with a thick band of dark purple at his knees, and turning amethyst from his shins down. They were finished with vine decoration in tan thread. "Are you sure you're gonna to be okay in that?" Seth caught him fidgeting.

"It's only for one night," Lerki stated, trying to convince them both.

"It's an all-nighter," Seth reminded him. "The longest night of the year, at that. That's a lot of hours."

"I know. I should be fine." He'd probably be fine. Maybe.

"Think of half the getups the women sew themselves into," Date interjected, irritated at the suggestion Lerki consider wearing anything comfortable. "They do not get the luxury of being able to slip out of things so easily. He'll wear that all night; I'll make sure. Out of basic respect and duty as a gentleman." It was a trick and a dance, but Date managed to dress himself after removing the sling and enduring sharp reminders why he needed it.

His jacket was slate grey and was—what Seth called—a modern-style with two buttons at the waist. Under it, he wore a black-feathered shirt, that he'd turned and folded the collar of down over the jacket. With matching straight-cut trousers, his garb was complete with shiny, toe-pinching black shoes. The final touch, his large, black wings poked through vents in the back of the shirt and jacket. The effect was spoiled somewhat by the sling, but he couldn't help that.

"Don't eat so much melon," Lerki cautioned, watching them chow down. "It has side-effects."

"Yeah, I remember from last year," Seth remarked with a laugh. "The bends lasted for two days. *Two days!*"

"You're half-blood," Date reminded him. "You would feel it the worst."

"I'll tell you both something," Seth said, looking them in turn. "I never hated you guys more than when my colon wanted to come out through my windpipe."

Tundra put down the piece of melon in his hand, swearing off it from then on. "That was the last for me. I'd forgotten about that. I didn't like the aftertaste to start with."

"Oh, it tastes great," Seth argued, tone mild. "I like it too much and that's where the problem starts."

"Before we leave," Date stated in a stern voice, looking towards each of his friends in turn and pointing with a black-nailed finger. "You, you, and you will ask someone to dance, or I'll do it for you."

"Yes, master?" Tundra retorted, raising an eyebrow, finding the return of a dictatorial Date to be unwarranted and unwelcome.

"Hey, man, what gives?" Seth chimed in, equally surprised. "It's just a party, not a war-zone."

"If I'm going out there, you're coming with me," he stated, putting it in terms of misery liking company.

"For all of your sakes," Inari commented, as they produced a red fan from their sleeve to cool off, "do not *ever* put it in those terms when you're inviting anyone to dance. If you do, we would expect to see you bathed in their drink. Possibly your nose may end up swollen, though that would depend on who you ask."

"Why is this so important now?" Lerki frowned, confused. "It has not been in the past."

"Well," Date admitted, deciding Lerki hadn't shown any interest in anyone to be pressured. "You're free, but these two idiots are not."

"That really makes us want to rush off and do it, Date," Seth bit back. He was working up his nerve already, without his dumb friend sticking his beak in.

"I've thought of two more ways I can beat you to death with your own body parts," Tundra stated, scowling. "Try to refrain from insulting us." He'd been shot down and didn't want to make a fool of himself twice in the same week.

"It's not an insult if you're being legitimately stupid," he countered.

"Man, you going to back off or what?!"

"This is why everyone punches you."

"Stop being difficult!"

"Stop!" Lerki and Inari spoke in unison.

Lerki added, "Nothing is made clear. Date, please explain yourself."

He waved a belligerent hand at them. "As I said, these two are smitten. I'm being kind; it is a punishable offence to fall in love, and equally punishable to do nothing." The memories were forever fresh in his mind, as well as the cost. "I've seen every way love is capable of building dreams and dashing them," he said, expression growing grave. "It is the only force I know that is both pure and corrupt enough to bring ruin to every person around them, and yet they still remain ignorant of its abuses."

Seth and Tundra looked at each other, passing an unspoken communication that ended in them both sighing and nodding.

"Okay, Date, I'll make an effort," Seth said, feeling like a death row prisoner waiting for his time in the chair. It was stupid because he wanted to offer Scyanatha his cloven fruit and have her keep it. His friend was killing the mood and his will.

"Oh, was that what we were going with?" Tundra said to him, shaking his head. "I thought we were going to tell him to stick that big nosed mask from yesterday up his ass."

Date shot him an evil look.

"You heard her," he said, crossing his arms, a stubborn look on his face. "She wasn't interested."

"Oh, of course not, master assassin and keeper of all the secrets," Date replied, sweeping a bow and wincing when his arm hurt. Straightening up, he added, "And that is why she spent much of the latter part of the evening waiting for you to come back, you puce-faced, deep-sea roach."

Tundra's eyebrow ticked. "What?" He'd thought her earlier pleasant attitude to him was because they had to work together, but maybe it was more.

Lerki, assuming another fight was about to break out, intervened with, "It is getting late. Shouldn't we be on our way?"

Date glanced at the clock, which said it was sometime between soper and rusten. "Yes. They should have finished dressing by now." He ushered them out of the door and down the stairs.

"And we're late," Seth stated, spotting Abaddon and the women clustered around the entrance to the ballroom looking in. He crossed his arms and looked to his friends. "You can't tell me we aren't."

"No one's trying to," Tundra said, with a slight shake of his head. He looked at Nyima, wondering if what Date said was true, or if it was him playing matchmaker.

"Think of your excuses on the dance floor," Date muttered, taking point with the others bringing up the rear.

"Good evening," Inari greeted, slipping from their place to address everyone when it looked like the men forgot how to say hello.

"They didn't expect you to wait."

"We didn't," Nyima replied, straight-faced.

The sight of Tundra and Seth's faces falling at this had Vyxen and Zercey smothering giggles.

Vyxen regained her composure first and cheerfully asked, "We were just wondering what you were all gonna be wearing, and now here you are." She looked them over. "So, what took you?"

"Lerki's bed ate my coat," Date returned, without missing a beat.

Abaddon, Nyima and Scyanatha looked bemused.

Knowing what she did about Fluorite's barracks, Vyxen snickered.

"It wasn't going to eat it," Lerki protested, breaking rank, as everyone seemed intent to mingle.

"Good thing, too. Probably would have given it indigestion," Vyxen snickered, thinking Date looked a bit like a feathery, mafia member.

"Ha, ha," he dead-panned, as his friends let out more heartfelt laughter.

"Am I seeing double?" Seth looked between Scyanatha and Abaddon. "Date and Jingyi almost traded this year, too."

"Not almost," Tundra corrected, gauging how smothering Date's clothes were. "He couldn't pay me enough."

"Yes," Scy replied to Seth's question, giving him a look with heavy-lidded eyes that bordered on sultry, "and if you guess right, you'll win a prize."

Zercey whispered to Vyxen, "Guess Scy got her wish after all." She giggled as she took in the lack of actual clothing that made up Seth's outfit.

Tundra chuckled at the banter, commenting to Seth, "She's fiery."

Seth's smile broadened as he offered Scy his arm. "I like it hot." He managed not to blush as Scy winked at him and stroked his bicep. With high heels on, she was three inches taller than him and every bit the seductive faery.

"So do I," she purred into his ear.

As though the pair gave an unconscious signal, the rest fell in line, pairing up to enter the ballroom.

When Nyima took the initiative and put her hand on Tundra's arm he looked surprised at the unexpected move. He took her fingers away, noting her eyes widen with dismay, but replaced them through his arm instead of on top. "You don't want to hear Date complaining about protocol," he joked, feeling awkward.

She smiled and nodded, but didn't reply.

Inari stepped up beside Abaddon. "Shall I escort you in? There is much to catch up on, don't you agree?"

"I—" Abaddon stammered, taken aback by their forwardness. They gave a firm nod. "Yes, I think so."

Zercey caught a glint of mischief in Vyxen's silver eyes and shook her head. This further served to embolden her and she hooked Date's good arm in hers and pulled him towards the door to the ballroom. Leaving Zercey with little choice but to pair up with Lerki.

Which was how Vyxen planned it.

CHAPTER TWENTY

A single, long table pressed back against the right-hand wall, with another standing perpendicular that almost reached the terrace. With chairs on the far side, it marked itself as the head table, reserved for the Winter King's family. The other table was laden with sweets, pies, cakes, pastries and deep bowls full of chilled, floral-scented punch. Across the hall chairs hugged the wall.

Scy nodded at them, commenting, "They wouldn't have them in the past. Everyone was expected to dance or drop before His Majesty."

Date snorted, adding from experience, "Some still do. Improvements never happen without enforcement."

Testing her footing on the floor, Zercey's boot slid against the polished surface. "Wow," she breathed, grabbing Lerki to steady herself.

He looked down at her. "Are you all right?"

"This floor is treacherous," she declared. "If anyone spills anything, it'll become a *sala da bowling,*" she said, reverting to Italian when she didn't know the Illthdarian equivalent.

"Selada bolin?" he echoed, testing the feel of the strange words on his tongue.

"I'm impressed," Inari said, addressing the group as they reached into their sleeve. They withdrew cloven fruit for Date and his friends and handed them out. "The outfits this year are very pleasing to the eye."

Abaddon hummed a few bars of the song playing, commenting, "The music is also very good this year." A playful, bouncing tune, it made them want to dance.

"Oh bother!" Scy said, making Abaddon jump. "We left our fruit upstairs!" She tapped her forehead.

"I go," Nyima offered, eager for an excuse to escape the sweltering room.

Vyxen stuck her hand in the air. "I'm coming, too!"

"If you hurry, you shouldn't miss anything," Scy said, though she glanced towards the head table and frowned.

Date turned to Tundra. "You and I will accompany them."

Nyima shook her head. "No need; not dangerous."

"I insist," he stressed. "It isn't proper etiquette to go without escort."

Nyima raised an eyebrow, unimpressed.

Tundra shook his head and shrugged, helpless.

"Like anyone's gonna see us," Vyxen pointed out. "The whole Order's here. Who's going to care?"

"I do, and that's more than enough," Date replied, levelling her with a look that brooked no argument.

Nyima rolled her eyes. "Very well. Let's go."

"You'll get your beak flattened before the night's over," Tundra prophesied to Date, still shaking his head.

"And it will be worth it," he retorted, resting his good hand on the centre of Vyxen's back to propel her out the door.

As they exited, Lerki made a long-suffering sound in the back of his throat.

Seth hung his head in embarrassment. "That guy…"

Scyanatha tapped her lower lip. "Well, if he's thinking traditionally, it wouldn't be wrong. Guests at the original Winter King's ball wouldn't let anyone go out alone. Least of all courtly women."

Seth let out a heavy sigh. "Maybe, but he's being more of a pain about it than last year. No one here asked for an accurate recreation of the story." Date's mood was fraying his nerves, so he sought to improve it. "All of you look great, by the way."

The women and Abaddon murmured their thanks.

"I'm surprised there aren't more people wearing masks," Zercey commented, casting her gaze beyond their group.

"Who's to say they aren't?" Scy proposed. "Not all masks hide faces, and not all are easily visible."

"Shape-shifters find this season a delight," Inari chimed in. They passed around cups of fragrant punch from a bowl on the table beside them. "This is where they might showcase their talents. Hie liked this day more than any other."

Scyanatha's brows rose at the name. "Hie? A good friend of yours?"

"Yes," they replied, their eyes fading to an aqua shade. "One I knew before I joined Chiyoko's Order of Mana. We knew him since he was a three-tailed fox. That was over half a millennia ago."

Zercey's eyes widened. *Half a millennia?* How old are you?" With how youthful everyone looked, along with how childish they acted, she sometimes forgot faeries had centuries on half-bloods.

"We could not say," Inari confessed. "We have seen islands born, and nations disappear into sea foam. I wonder myself at times. In truth, we haven't the slightest idea how much time we have existed for."

"Is it so strange?" Lerki shifted from side to side, feeling more surprised by Zercey's shock than Inari's admission.

"You never visited the other side of the veil," Scy noted with an indulgent smile. "Compared to some, humans live for a very short time."

"Oh, I see…" Lerki replied, growing thoughtful. "That explains some things." It was curious watching how much Seth and Tundra changed in a single year.

"Yeah," Seth chuckled, seeming to read his friend's mind. "Like how my voice cracked and when I grew facial hair."

Lerki shook his head. "I meant how you grew. Are human voices fragile? Didn't you always have hair on your face?"

"People's voices change as they age. For some men, it happens quickly when they hit puberty; it's called cracking," Zercey offered, with Lerki nodding. "Facial hair also comes with it."

"What happened to Hie?" Abaddon cut in, bringing the conversation back to the original topic. Like when the girls spoke of their development, they found the conversation awkward.

"He died this summer," Inari answered in a sombre voice. "Consumption."

Scyanatha hummed, empathetic, and patted their shoulder.

"Oh. Er, I'm sorry," Abaddon said, ducking their head. "I didn't know."

"It's fine." Inari's smile was sad. "He was a private man. I didn't have the slightest idea until the end."

"Hie would trade places with your team throughout the night," Seth remembered, chuckling.

Inari laughed, a light and bubbly sound spilling from their lips. They nodded. "No one could tell who was the original by the time dawn broke. The others return." Inari lifted their arm to direct Date's group over after spotting them through a break in the crowd.

"We made it in time," Date puffed, approaching with Nyima, Tundra and Vyxen. "They're playing the Winter King's waltz."

"It a sign the Winter King coming?" Nyima guessed, as she

handed over Abaddon, Scyanatha and Zercey's fruit.

"Actually, no," Scy replied, toying with the ribbon on the end of her orange. "It is a song foreshadowing his demise, and played when the Spring King arrives."

"So, Trenfal's somewhere in the crowd," Tundra murmured, blue eyes flitting about trying to pinpoint him.

"It also means the Winter King isn't far behind," Date added.

"They may be gathering in the room of worship as we speak." Unlatching from Lerki's arm, Zercey grabbed Vyxen, laughing as she spun her around. "Come on, I need a word with you real quick."

"Don't leave the ballroom," Scy called in caution. "Or, if you must, stick to the balconies or terrace."

"That sounds like a good idea," Tundra commented, changing visual target. "I'll stake out one for the group. We'll need it."

"Before that," Date plucked four cloves from his lime and presented them to Inari and his friends. "To another year." He tossed them back like he was downing a shot.

"To another year," Seth echoed, copying the action with his lime. Inari, Tundra and Lerki followed suit.

Nyima raised an intrigued eyebrow. "This is tradition, also?"

"Well, it's one way friends share cloves," Scy answered, somewhat disappointed at the lack of ceremony.

"Did you want to share, Scyanatha?" Abaddon asked, holding their fruit aloft.

A slow, sly smile crossed her lips. "In a moment, Abaddon. Once Vyxen and Zercey return."

Date made a pointed cough behind his hand and Seth's posture stiffened.

"Uhh, in that case, do you want to dance?" Seth requested, in an over loud voice.

"I was wondering when you would ask," Scy replied, a flirtatious smile flitting about her mouth. She placed her hand in his. "Yes, please, I would be delighted."

"Don't break a leg, Seth," Tundra called, mocking.

"Back at you, Jingyi!" Seth shouted over his shoulder.

"No throwing her like a rag-doll, either," Date ordered, eyes narrowing. "You great, lumbering behemoth." He sniggered when Seth shot a rude hand gesture in response.

"You three are like watching Hie, Xiao Li and Cthul," Inari said, laughing behind their fan. "They all said they liked that about you."

"And you, wringing your hands the whole time, just like Lerki." Tundra chuckled when there was the expected protest.

"I don't." Lerki's attempt to defend himself fell short, as both Tundra and Date laughed.

Nyima looked to each man, but without knowing the ones being compared to, she was lost with how accurate they were. "Who are they?"

"Inari's old teammates," Tundra answered, twirling the lime in his hand by the ribbon end.

"Yes," Inari replied in a sage voice. "Quetzal and I from Fluorite, Hie from Jasper, and Cthul and Xiao Li from Quartz."

"Balanced," she commented on the fair spread across three Orders.

"Our team is unusual," Abaddon confessed, wincing. "We should have someone from Fluorite, but we don't, and we only have Vyxen from Quartz."

"They're right," Lerki stated, pulling at his coat collar. He stopped when he caught a disapproving glare from Date. "There are missed skills without different people."

"I see," Nyima replied, knowing the reason they'd banded together was kinship, not logic.

"We can't take on anyone else, though," Abaddon lamented. "There are already six of us; that's the upper limit."

Inari advised, "Your only option is to broaden your knowledge within your team."

"That idiot." Date's sudden hiss drew attention towards the dance floor. "He's trying to pick a fight with me."

335

"Seth's misbehaving," Tundra assumed, unable to find him in the crowd. "With how you baited him, I'm not surprised."
The music was a simple waltz, yet Seth laughed it up, making uncoordinated movements out of time with the music. A laughing Scy let him lead where he wanted, enjoying his daft sense of fun. A muscle in Date's jaw clenched and unclenched in irritation, positive it was intentional.

"Did we miss anything?" Vyxen returned with Zercey in tow.
"No." Nyima scrutinised them, but was unable to discern from their body language the reason they left. Vyxen bore an uncrackable straight face when she put her mind to it. Zercey was the more obvious choice if one wanted a hint about their conversation, but she made a point to avoid eye contact.
"Scyanatha and Seth are dancing together," Abaddon offered.
Vyxen beamed. "That's great! If they didn't, I wasn't going to forgive them," she declared.
One of Date's eyebrows went up at this. "Speaking of unforgivable—" he began, only to be cut off by Tundra.
"I'll go find that empty balcony." He slipped away before another word was said.
Date shook his head. "The hard way it is," he concluded, as the rest swapped looks with mixed curiosity.

There was no time to question him, as a fanfare announced the Winter King and his entourage. They entered the ballroom in pairs. The procession garb altered little from yule pyre: the mens' fur lined capes replaced with shorter, blue velvet ones, revealing royal-blue doublets, trimmed in silver, and bright white breeches secured at the front by polished, silver buttons. Chiyoko and Queline had no capes at all; their outer layer sideless surcotes— with wide and deep arm holes showcasing their figures—were identical in colour to the doublets. The inner kirtle was lighter blue and decorated with silver vines.

336

The sea of dancers parted to allow them straight passage across the room. Many got into the spirit of things and bowed or curtsied as Culvers and Chiyoko swept by.

Uwe's head swivelled towards their group as he passed.

Date blinked when he felt something—*someone*—duck between his folded wings.

While the rest of the procession took their seats at the table, Culvers stood before it. A tall and striking man, he wore his salt and pepper hair swept back from his face and looked at ease in his role compared to the previous night.

No one spoke. Few dared breathe, as suspense built.

"Esteemed friends and family," Culvers said, voice cutting clean across the ballroom. "The curtains are open, the windows cast wide!" His tone was sardonic, mocking. "We have even taken the guard from the city gates. Let them come, let them strike. We will meet them, measure their worth, and dispatch them to the cradles from which they came!" He threw his arms wide, cape falling from his shoulders to the floor. "Dance! Drink! Show them how little we think of the snapping teeth of small beasts!"

There was a round of applause. Culvers blinked, breaking character long enough to nod and look humble. He rounded the table and took his seat between Chiyoko and Queline.

The music struck up again, and while many of the dancers resumed, Seth and Scyanatha returned to where their friends gathered.

"He's got the pride and arrogance down," Seth said, impressed. "I didn't think Culvers had it in him to be an actor."

"Aren't you done back there?" Date tried twisting around, but couldn't see more than a flutter of white hair between his wings.

Vyxen's voice sounded muffled among the plumage. "Mmm, I don't know. I thought I might just live here now." She tweaked a feather.

"Ow, hey!" He twisted again, trying to shake her free. "What is this about?"

"Uwe doesn't like the word 'no'," she replied, disgust clear in her voice. "In fact, I think he takes it as a personal challenge if a woman isn't interested."

Date groaned and rolled his eyes. Uwe *would* confuse hard-to-get with forget-about-it. Before he could comment, Lerki made a sound in the back of his throat. Turning to look, Date expected Uwe, but was surprised to see Phanuel. "What did you do, or not do, this time, Lerki?" he asked in a bland voice.

"Nothing I know of," Lerki replied, putting his weight onto his heels and leaning back.

Date wasn't convinced, and his suspicions grew when Phanuel planted himself right in front of them and addressed Lerki in a strict tone.

"Tomorrow morning report to my office. I need you to retrieve something for me. Preferably before the snow melts." The way Phanuel's lips twisted it could have been a joke. It wasn't.

"Ahh…Yes, sir," Lerki replied, flapping his hands, anxious.

As fast as Phanuel came, he left.

Off to terrify the next person was Lerki's guess, as his shoulders sagged.

"You could have got killed on that last one," Zercey commented, scowling. "What's he thinking, sending you back out so soon?"

"That is unfortunate," Scyanatha said, slanting a sympathetic look Lerki's way. "Hopefully, he'll wait until after greenman."

"Something tells me priss-face won't be that generous," Seth remarked before sticking his fingers in his mouth and whistling. "Hey, dude! Over here!" He waved at Tundra.

"You didn't need to call," Tundra said, amused, as he came over. "I remember where I left you."

"Dude," Seth shook his head, "with you, it's better safe than sorry." He grinned, satisfied he'd caught his friend short.

"Shit." Tundra chuckled. "I walked into that one."

"Speaking of greenman," Scy said, getting Abaddon and the womens' attention. "Everyone, gather into a circle and pass your

338

fruit to the person on the left."

"Okay, sure, but why?" Vyxen queried, as she slipped out of her hiding place and moved to stand beside Nyima.

"Custom is for friends to be sharing cloves from their fruit," Nyima volunteered to Vyxen with a shrug.

"Um, Inari and the men d-d-did it earlier," Abaddon added. "There are lots of different ways."

"We always miss the interesting stuff," Zercey remarked, taking Scy's fruit and passing her own to Abaddon, who gave theirs to Vyxen. "So, what do we do?"

"Well." Scyanatha's smile grew foxy. "Now we each have another's fruit, we shall kiss them." She made a shushing noise when Vyxen and Zercey giggled. "Bite a clove out with your teeth, then pass the fruit over. We repeat the process until we have our original back."

"Why?" Nyima wasn't keen on putting those things in her mouth, despite wanting to take part.

"Blessing the fruit," Scy replied, sending Seth a saucy look. "For good luck and good hunting," she finished, raising her eyebrows and lowering her voice.

Seth tried to keep his cool as he said, "You know we can hear you."

Unlike the men, Scyanatha wasn't one to let any opportunity go to waste. Raising one shoulder in a shrug, she locked gazes with him and let a slow smile creep across her painted lips. "I know."

Seth glanced away, covering his mouth to hide a grin.

"I feel kind of stupid doing this," Zercey muttered, planting her first kiss on Nyima's fruit. She cracked up watching everyone make awkward attempts to get cloves out of the fruit with their teeth. Her first attempt was just as clumsy. *I would pick one stuck tight.* She twisted and turned her head trying to pinch the dried flower bud and pull it free.

"Do we need to eat them?" Vyxen asked, talking around the one between her lips, while the men sniggered.

Deciding to further fox a few male egos, Scy said, "Chewing is optional, but in the choice between spitting or swallowing—" she paused when she heard choking "—I recommend swallowing, so you only have to taste the clove once." Her feigned innocence fooled no one.

"My mouth is numb," Nyima noted, growing worried. "Should it?" The clove was pungent; an unusual combination of sweet, spicy and peppery. Judging by the expressions and commentary, she wasn't alone in not enjoying them.

"It is, though it will last only for a little bit," Scyanatha reassured. She couldn't resist adding in a cheeky tone, "Plus it will sweeten your breath if you need it."

Nyima's expression remained neutral, which Tundra wrongly assumed was due to lack of interest.

"Ugh," Zercey pulled a face, "I forgot how much I hate crunching these things on Christmas Eve."

"It's better to swallow them whole." Abaddon felt the different pattern on their ribbon and stopped passing.

"There, done!" Vyxen did a triumphant shimmy.

The men laughed and gave them a round of applause for their efforts.

"Now no one look likes they lack suitors," Scy concluded. "Which is another reason friends take cloves."

"This is more custom?" Nyima inspected the fruit with renewed interest.

"Something like that," Date answered. "Only someone without friends or prospects would have unspoiled fruit." A face came to mind and he snorted.

Vyxen shook her head and sighed. "Only Illthdar could create social outcasts by counting how many empty holes there are in an orange."

"But, we have to pass these things around all night, right?" Zercey was befuddled and anxious. "How does that even work?"

Scyanatha, ever the calculating hostess, said, "We have need of a visual aid."

"Tundra." Date snap volunteered him before anyone else spoke. Tundra's jaw dropped and he looked panicked for a moment.

"Go on," Date insisted. He would stick those two together if he had to. The attraction was obvious, but neither seemed willing to follow through. *Commencing operation: doing it the hard way.*

"All right," Tundra muttered, chuckling at being caught. "Nyima, if it's all right by you?" It was better to get it out of the way fast with his pride intact. If he didn't, he was certain Date would resort to more obvious, nay drastic, measures—tying him and Nyima together and locking them in a cupboard being top of the list.

Nyima raised an eyebrow, lips pressed into an irritated line. *Is he asking for a partner for the example, or permission in general? He and this whole thing is confusing. Why can't people be more straight-forward?* She nodded and took a step forward. "Yes." She hoped that was enough encouragement.

"Perfect," Scy chirped, clapping her hands. "Now, Tundra offers Nyima the fruit." She narrated as they performed. "Nyima now has two—technically three—options. One: they trade fruit."

Tundra and Nyima swapped fruit, awkward smiling at each other. "Now, they have a clove from each and keep the fruit." A clove was duly taken and swallowed whole. "Two: they take a clove and return the fruit to its owner."

Nyima interrupted at this point. "I no do not want to be eating more of these. Must I?"

"No, dear, we all understand that part." With all the work Scyanatha put in helping them they didn't need further confusion. Everyone nodded, and Nyima shrugged, keeping hold of the citrus—an action not unnoticed by Tundra.

"Three," Scyanatha continued, recalling she liked this one best, "is more secretive and involves some deception. They trade like in option one, but then give the fruit to someone else."

Abaddon summed up, their voice forever soft and low-key, though no one struggled to hear. "To keep the fruit and not give it away means feelings are mutual. To take a clove and return the fruit means friendship. To give the fruit away to someone else means unrequited feelings."

"So, it's all up to the person who's offered the fruit," Zercey concluded, not reassured. "Great."

The musicians struck another tune.

"Rufty-Tufty," Date said, narrowing his eyes with intent at Tundra and Nyima. "It's your type of dance."

"Subtle," Tundra muttered in a sarcastic undertone. "Doesn't that take two couples?"

"You have two couples." Date wasn't letting Tundra slip away. He offered his hand to Vyxen and said, "Might I?"

Hurrrr, dance? Really? Me? Vyxen's eyes widened before she recovered. Snickering, she said, "Sure!" She'd get a front row seat watching Tundra and Nyima's adorable awkward crushing on each other. Date spun her under his arm, as she took his hand. She squealed with delight as her floaty skirt flared. That was where her amusement ended; she didn't know the dance.

"It's simple," Date murmured under his breath, explaining.

Beginning with a quick step to the centre, the couples greeted each other. A double step out again. After this repeated, came a step to the left, then right. Each partner span in place. Then came the spurning, where the partners swapped. Date led Nyima, while Tundra led Vyxen. Returning to the middle once more, they span in place and rejoined their original partners. With one arm out of action, Date had to rely on Nyima escorting herself back. The dance concluded with a final spurn-and-turn and bow to all.

Vyxen found it easy enough in the end. The hardest part was remembering when to spurn and when to return to her partner, laughing whenever she collided with someone. It made it impossible to split her attention long enough to watch Nyima and Tundra. Gathering how they escaped to the terrace together the moment the song ended she guessed things went well. She and

Date shared satisfied looks. Mission accomplished.

CHAPTER TWENTY-ONE

Passing the threshold dividing the ballroom from the terrace, a sigh of relief escaped Nyima's lips. She checked her dress for signs of melting, but it survived so far.

Tundra ran both hands over his face and through his short, jet-black hair, spraying drops of perspiration from the ends. Understanding looks and smiles passed between them.

Musicians staked out sections of the terrace, providing background music to those who wanted a break and chat. Tables sat at intervals, occupied with people eating and drinking.

It was within the Order of Mana's means to set out torches, but instead the three-quarters full moon did the job of lighting the space. Its gentle glow painted everything bluish white, adding an intimate atmosphere. In the gardens below, snowflakes coated the ground glittering like stardust.

"Beautiful," Nyima breathed, resting her elbows on the terrace wall and cradling her chin in her hands. If not for the architecture, she could fool herself she was home.

Tundra stepped up beside her. "You're not bad, either." At her frown, he gestured to her dress. "How long did that take, so they don't stick together?"

"Not long," she replied, looking at her dress as though just remembering it. Backless, only the front needed attention. "I had to working quickly."

"That must be the secret, then," he concluded, nodding. "My brother was more skilled than me; I'm not nearly as fast." Unused to confiding, he surprised himself with the admission, but it felt natural telling her.

Nyima's brows pinched, picking out the key part of his sentence. "Was?"

"He died," Tundra supplied, eyes narrowing as he recalled being told after the fact. "I don't know who, but I'm going to find them and make them pay."

She recognised the undercurrent of violence in his tone, having heard similar from her own lips. "I understand," she replied, a fleeting look of pain crossing her face. "I must also." Her tone was coloured by sadness and regret.

He knew consolation meant nothing, but— "I'm sorry," he said, resting his forearms on the railing and staring at his hands. "It isn't a journey I'd wish on anyone."

Touched, Nyima thought Tundra might be the first person she could genuinely relate to. "Yes—No," she replied, still unsure which short answer was right in these situations. She wouldn't want anyone to follow her path, either.

One side of Tundra's mouth went up in amusement, but he nodded. Nyima laid her hand on his forearm. "I am sorry for you." She didn't ask further questions. There would be other times to share, and she wasn't willing to spoil their growing intimacy.

Once again they fell silent, and Tundra had a need to fill it. "It feels better out here," he said, wanting to kill himself for his lack of conversational skills. "I need to train harder, so it doesn't get to me."

"The heat?" At his nod, she hummed and said, "Me, too." Again, she did not elaborate.

Now what, Jingyi? You said she looks nice, you talked about the weather, goals and... You're out of ideas. We can't stand out here in silence all night. He blinked, fighting tiredness. As he yawned he thought to make the best of it. "We've got a shift after greenman in the morning, too," he said, shaking his head and stretching.

"Yes," she replied, pausing. "This...celebration is being very strange," she confessed, shaking her head. "The need for why these fruit?" Her chuckle was soft, but bemused. "My people, they travel. Very far to find each other." She illustrated her point by parting her hands in front of herself. "Not so very many tribes." Her expression grew pensive. "Seeing other tribes is great joy. Trade, dancing, marrying." She shook her head a little, her nose scrunching at the corner. "Can't be slow or not so sure." It was more than she'd intended to say. She was surprised with how much she'd spoken, but it seemed to be habit forming when they were together. He didn't judge or make fun of her verbal mistakes, and seemed interested in her answers.

"Two nights and a morning of partying," Tundra commented, echoing her feelings. "I've spent longer awake, but not like this. It's good experience for times I'll need to push past the point of exhaustion, but there's no arguing doing it for the sake of it is stupid." His lips twisted wryly, as he contemplated the differences between her mindset and his. "Maybe that's a problem of mine. I spend so long weighing and assessing situations the time to strike passes, and I only realise too late. I need to train to react more instinctively."

Nyima smiled, amused by the amount of times he'd brought up training in the conversation. "Training is very much important?"

"Here? It is," he admitted, with a nod. "Leigong put me here for that specific purpose. I'm not nearly skilled or experienced enough to do what Arctic—Qiang—couldn't. Fortunately, I was told time isn't linear to Warren."

Nyima frowned, intrigued. Time not passing the same way in Illthdar as opposed to other dimensions? It sounded plausible, but wasn't something she picked up overhearing other conversations. "Qiang your brother?"

"Yeah." He chuckled. "Though, I have to keep reminding myself that. We're so used to calling everyone by code names in the Lim Tu. When I was younger I'd sometimes forget my own name, unless the masters were scolding me."

The place he came from sounded awful. "You Tundra there, too?"

He nodded, then paused and looked at her, eyes crinkling. "Try that again."

"What?" Her head tilted and she met his gaze, seeing amusement in it.

"Say 'Tundra', again," he said, one corner of his mouth lifting. The way she said it bore repeating.

Her eyes narrowed, suspicious after Magnilla's "helpful" corrections, but she indulged him because he was nothing like Magnilla. "Teun'dra."

Thought so. Her accent put emphasis on different sounds. "Not quite." He had another thought. "Say 'Tonne.'"

Nyima wasn't sure what his point was, but he seemed to be enjoying himself. "Deun."

Oh boy... He tried not to smirk. "Say 'Dra' again."

"Dra," she repeated, the creases in her brows deepening with each attempt. After the fifth, she said, "Why do I say it again?"

346

"Because..." he said, trailing off as inspiration failed; he didn't want her to take insult. Her Ds were almost non-existent, making an almost G-sound. It made his code name sound like Tongue-ra. He couldn't remember her having said his name before, otherwise he'd have noticed before now. The way this was going, he was dangerously close to having a porn-star name. "Try it like this: Tey-un-De-rah." He looked and felt like an idiot.

Nyima stifled a laugh. She'd figured out there was something amusing in how she pronounced his name. She didn't know what, but Tundra looked cute and awkward trying to correct it. "Teyundrah," she said, elongating the sounds like he wanted. "Why do they call you Teyundrah?"

He chuckled, seeing how daft he'd sounded. "It's as good a name as any," he replied, with an unhelpful shrug. "I was never the same calibre as Qiang, so they gave me a name that showed it." Anticipating the question, he gave the pre-emptive answer. "Tundra's a good enough name, but it's never going to be the same degree as Arctic." A scowl marred his face. "But, I'm not going to let anyone shoehorn me into a predetermined destiny." Guessing her next question, he volunteered, "It's a word we use to describe a frozen wasteland."

Nyima turned introspective. The word was a cruel way that could describe her whole world, but she would not ever call it that. She decided she wouldn't call him that, either. "You name is Jingyi," she said, remembering it from their introduction, and raising her eyebrows to encourage information.

"It's embarrassing," he confessed, chuckling and ducking his head. "Most mistake it for feminine, but it can be both, depending on the characters. It means 'quiet joy.' It's a big difference from my brother's. His meant strong or energetic." Even his original name didn't stack up.

"It's nice," she said, smiling and imagining the thought that went into picking it out. "Your parents were happy."

"Anyway," he said, diverting back to the original conversation, and avoiding the tough topic of his family, "that name came to mind more readily than my own when I first got here." There was a light chuckle from her, and he raised an amused eyebrow at the sound. "Something funny?"

"No, not so much. I was having the first thought to using my best attack."

"Oh, so that's what Teysuht is. It made sense for you to have a moniker, but…" He trailed, unsure how to end the sentence without unwittingly insulting her.

"It not a person," she stated, shaking her head and frowning. "It means—"

She looked away, brows pinching, as she tried to think of the word in Illthdarian "—ice that's not melt," she settled for in the end.

"Permafrost," he supplied. "I've heard worse. Nyima fits you better, though." He paused again, curious. "What does Nyima mean?"

"It our Goddess: hunters and warriors." A common name among the tribes.

"It *does* fit you better." With her strong and shapely figure, he doubted any other name would do her justice.

Scyanatha had advised that when given a compliment, Nyima should pretend she was unaware and act modest. She couldn't do that, although she felt a bashful blush creep across her cheeks. Maybe because it was Tundra complimenting her. She replied with a simple, "Thank you," and changed subject before things got awkward. "You people are called Lim Tu?"

Tundra hesitated, face twisting. Not the best topic for a romantic evening's chat. Still, he found himself answering. "Not quite. I was trained and raised by them, but I wouldn't call them my people." Though he didn't want to discourage her, he also didn't want to continue the heavy discussion.

The strains of a new dance filtered across the terrace.

Tundra paused, listening for a minute to work out what it was, then asked, "Is it all right to ask for another dance?" It was better than talking, and kept them together for a while longer.

"Yes." Nyima smiled, adding in an amused tone, "Not in the oven."

Tundra laughed. "Same." He held his left hand out and took her right. Drawing her into his arms, he rested the other hand against the base of her spine, fanning his fingers wide. He held in a smile as he heard a short inhale. *Maybe Date was right.*

Nyima placed her other hand on his shoulder and they began moving in a quick-step, more his speed than the Rufty-Tufty. For someone who went around barefoot all the time, she managed high heels well. Though, if he wasn't as confident and secure as he was, the extra height might have been intimidating, having put her eyeline two inches above his. Still, Tundra *was* confident. He had excellent command of his body and spatial awareness. Without prying eyes—and dictatorial tengu—watching his every move, he didn't mind dancing. It helped that his partner had rhythm, so their bodies moved in perfect sync. In the back of his mind he wondered what other activities they'd move in perfect sync.

The music slowed as the piece ended. Nyima breathed faster than he expected for someone that fit. Their breath mingled and Tundra caught the scent of cloves. He kept looking from her earnest eyes to soft lips. The chilly aura emanating from her felt fresh and inviting, like the first winter snow. There was a sense of expectation, though his question was *un*expected. "You don't mind acting in the spur of the moment?" His voice was hushed and intimate.

"'Spur of the moment'?" she half-whispered back, unfamiliar with the term. Curious and wanting, she inched closer. Tundra was unlike anyone she'd met. She liked him. He was steady and strong, and more fun than she knew existed. She tried to calm her rapid breaths, afraid he didn't feel the same way.

"Being impulsive," he reiterated, hopeful. His heart thudded hard in his chest. It seemed he waited eternity for an answer. Anticipation thrummed in his veins. He held his breath.

At Nyima's shy nod, he felt her suck in a surprised breath when his lips closed on hers. *Shit. Wrong move.* He pulled back again just as quick, debating the likelihood he was about to get slapped.

A clear debate flashed across her face, ending with Nyima drawing her lower lip into her mouth and moistening it. She slid her hand from his shoulder to the back of his neck, and the other she released from his grip and placed against his cheek.

Tundra waited, sensing innocence in her actions. He edged closer, encouraging, so the space between them grew smaller. With rigid self-control he held still, letting Nyima take the next step. He hadn't asked to kiss her, so this was his way of making up.

She planted a tentative kiss to his lips and remained for a count of three. Tundra put his other arm around her, drawing her flush against his body. He followed as she drew back, placing butterfly light kisses on her mouth, urging her lips apart. She was soft and willing, her skin like cool satin under his palms. He couldn't help stroking up and down, as she wrapped both arms tight around him and they got lost in each other.

Zercey returned from a turn on the dance floor with Lerki, cheeks flushed pink from exertion and embarrassment. After stepping on a wayward clove she'd gone skidding a quarter of the way through the dance, nearly taking him with her. All she could do was find humour in it. She noticed their time together deepened the colour of Lerki's hair, making it a more lustrous pine-needle shade, which she preferred over sickly yellow. Yet, his movements remained slow and constrained. By the time the dance finished he was winded, pale faced and tugging the collar of his jacket.

"Lerki, are you okay?" she asked, as he doubled over, fighting for breath. When he shook his head, she tugged at his jacket, taking several tries to release the tiny buttons.

Lerki gasped a breath, then exhaled stale air from his jewellery.

Their remaining teammates gathered around.

"Dude, you okay?" Seth's brows furrowed with concern.

Lerki looked choked and distressed. He could breathe in through his mouth, but not let out half as much air as he wanted.

"Shit, let's get you sat down." Seth hooked Lerki's arm over his shoulder and got Date to take the other side. They helped him to a chair on the other side of the room.

Once seated, Lerki took the coat off. "I'm not suffocating for fashion," he said to Date.

"Agreed," he replied, not willing to take etiquette to the point of death.

Scyanatha fetched a cup of water. "How you feeling, dear?"

"Better," Lerki admitted, with a grateful smile. "Thank you."

"That was a near thing," Inari noted, inspecting him, their eyes cloudy-grey. "I would advise against wearing that coat again."

"I am *never* wearing this outfit again." He dumped the coat on the next seat with a hateful glare.

"You damn well nearly swooned like a maid in a new corset," Date commented, feeling guilty for forcing Lerki to endure it.

"I was just about to ask what this thing's made of." Vyxen lifted it up by two fingers. When it didn't lose its shape she added, "but it's obviously the same stuff as straight-jackets."

Lerki sounded fatalistic as he said, "I learned things about myself, or I realised things I wouldn't have thought of before this."

"You will know to be more cautious in the future," Scy agreed.

Deeming Lerki out of danger, and having a strong desire for the mood to lift, Vyxen gave Zercey's cheek a playful tweak. "Besides the slow strangulation part, that looked like fun," she teased, returning the exact comment Zercey gave her when she and Date returned earlier. "You were dancing like Seth."

Zercey laughed. "I think I'd have better luck on ice skates." Although, knowing her luck, she'd end up slipping and breaking her nose. She noted Tundra and Nyima were still absent. "Wow, guess they were really hot."

"Or they're getting that way." Seth chuckled, winking. "Venus here with the matchmaking win." He put his hand out to Vyxen, who high-fived him with glee.

"Venus?" Date shook his head, raising his eyebrows. As though he'd done none of the work.

"Yup," Seth said, in a cheerful voice. "Goddess of matchmaking. Our girl, right here."

"Girl?" Date's eyebrows rose higher.

Seth rolled his eyes. "Lady. Woman. Whatever."

There were sniggers all round, which gave Zercey time to think of an ice breaker for Inari and Abaddon, as she'd promised Vyxen she would. "Is it true you can't dance, Inari?" She went with the most obvious.

"We can do little. We are an impotent cannon of glass." They sighed, frustrated. "As such, we only go where investigation is required. That is all we are useful for without a team."

"You shall join ours," Date stated, mood improving. Pleased with his work for the night, he began to relax. "It was about time we took a fifth."

Inari's eyes turned a bright gold colour, as they raised a hand to their chest. "The rumours of the curse haven't reached you?"

Seth barked a laugh, throwing his head back.

Date rolled his eyes. "Who hasn't heard?"

"What about a curse?" Vyxen piped up, proving Inari's point.

"All of their old team is gone," Scyanatha said in an undertone to her. "When there is only one survivor there are often rumours stating that person is the cause of misfortune."

Seth clapped Inari on the shoulder, a jarring motion meant to reassure them as he said, "How dumb do you think we'd be if we believed something like that? We heard, we just don't care."

They smiled and inclined their head. "Thank you. We accept and are flattered."

With Lerki sitting out a good part of the night, the others engaged in several more dances. There were many for groups, as well as pairs and couples.

351

Finishing another set with Scyanatha, Seth grasped the nettle. "Is there any point where you're going to offer me the fruit, or are you just leaving all this in my court?"

"I didn't want to insult your masculinity by taking the initiative," Scy commented, lips stretched into a wide smile. She wiggled her hips in time to the music, despite them standing to one side of the hall for a break. "Do you want to try my fruit?" she teased, voice low and suggestive.

Seth's brain stalled. Every answer he tested sounded like it belonged in a porno. Scyanatha might find it amusing, but he wanted more than a bunk up. "Only if you're willing," he replied in the end, feeling lame in comparison.

"I'd very much like to taste yours," she continued, in a seductive voice, reaching for his waistband.

Seth sucked in a breath, as her fingers skimmed his hip and he felt something loosening. *Hot shit.* She drew her hand back, and he chuckled when he realised she unknotted the ribboned lime from his belt. Her foxy smile said she knew exactly what he'd been thinking, as she pressed the fruit to her lips, flicking her tongue out to lick a clove. She closed her mouth over and drew it free, tipping her head back and swallowing.

Seth fumbled to pull a clove out of her lime with clumsy fingers and stuff it in his mouth.

"Delicious," she concluded, cradling it to her bosom. "I think I'll keep it."

"It's all yours…" he said in a faint voice, mouth *very* dry. He questioned if he had the stuff to keep up with such a woman, but one look at Scy's saucy smile and he knew he'd have a damn good try.

"Finally cooled down?" Scyanatha cooed, spotting Tundra and Nyima returning, and deciding to let Seth cool off also. She noted Nyima's flushed face and the smug look Tundra wore, and concluded, "No, definitely the opposite." They weren't holding hands, or even standing very close together, but the air crackled between them.

"Food and drink," Nyima said, keeping the reason for their return short.

"Worked up an appetite," Tundra added, unable to refrain being suggestive. He was lucky double entendres went over Nyima's head.

"Yes," she agreed, nodding.

Seth struggled to keep a straight face, as everyone joined them—bar Lerki, who still sat in a chair.

"I think the next dance is for the women only," Date noted, as the musicians paused for a break and singers took their place.

Scy named the piece, as the first harmonising soprano notes rang out.

"The song of Niamh."

"The song of who?" Zercey repeated, watching dancers take their places.

"It's about a water nymph who fell in love with a human: Oisin. She takes him through the veil, where one hundred years passes for each year he stays with her. When he returns home after three years, he finds his home and people have faded into legend. He grows old in an instant and they are separated forever."

"Well, that sucks," Vyxen proclaimed, eyes wide. "Will that happen to us?"

"It's just a story." Scy shook her head and touched Abaddon's forearm. "Will you join us for this one?"

"Yes, I'd love to!" Their smile was wide and bright.

The group took their places on the dance floor, leaving Inari and the men standing by the terrace doors, near Lerki.

"You're not fooling anyone hiding here," Date said, sitting beside him.

Tundra and Seth swapped relieved looks they weren't targets anymore.

"I'm not hiding," Lerki protested.

"No, you're right, I used the wrong word," Date admitted. "I meant cowering like a spineless beetle."

"I'm not cowering," Lerki argued, lips pulling down.

Date drew in a deep breath and let it out slow. "You and Tundra…always arguing with me for the sake of it."

"Leave me out of it," Tundra commented. He crossed his arms and shook his head, then went back to his conversation with Seth and Inari.

Lerki drew Date's gaze back from glaring at Tundra by asking, "What is it you think I'm cowering from?"

Date's dark eyes narrowed as he inspected Lerki's face. Eyebrows rising after a pause, he concluded, "Perhaps I was wrong. You're clearly fine, so unless you have some burning problem with the rest of your clothing, there is little point in shying away any longer."

Lerki opened his mouth to question further, but was interrupted.

"Might I borrow Date for a moment?" It was Trenfal, dressed in pale mint, with a long duster coat in a darker, forest green, trimmed in gold draped over his shoulders.

Date turned to look through the terrace doors, trying to pinpoint the position of the moon.

"I'm in a bit of a rush, unfortunately; I'm not as old as I used to be," he chuckled.

"Man, you look like you've been botoxed," Seth commented, pointing at the smoothed lines and disappearing crow's feet.

"One of the benefits of being a lios elf," he replied, sweeping a hand through his bright, golden hair, "is a renewal cycle. Anyway." He looked at Date with an air of expectation.

"I'll fetch Vyxen and we'll be along," Date said, raising his eyebrows at Tundra to do the same for Nyima.

"Don't be long." Trenfal left as fast as he came.

"So, you were caught after all," Inari remarked, as Abaddon and the women returned and had plates and glasses handed to them.

"Who?" Abaddon was confused, then their frown cleared. "Oh. Date, Nyima, Tundra and Vyxen."

"Yes," Date replied, as the latter pair said goodbye to everyone and exited first, with Tundra's hand lying flat to the small of Nyima's back. Date and Vyxen followed, with him drawing her to a halt before the threshold.

"Behind these doors," he gestured with his good hand, "is the end of the celebration for us, so before we go," he presented her with a cloven lime, "I'll take the opportunity to give you this."

"Oh, thanks," Vyxen replied, taking it like it was cursed. She was hoping to avoid the whole fruit thing. It was all right sharing with the girls and Abaddon, but she didn't feel like she could commit to someone since she was going home. "Friends?" she prompted, passing hers over.

He replied, voice calm and steady, "That suits me."

The Spring King's rebel army attacked without warning. With sparing use of mana, the magic thrown around the room was for effect more than damage. Dramatic deaths and excited screams echoed throughout the ballroom.

Nyima and Tundra teamed up to isolate people on the balconies and terrace, sealing them from the rest of the room with ice walls. This also cut them off from the mock battle—a "happy accident" they took full advantage of.

Vyxen and Date's job was tying up prisoners in the main hall—befitting their weak and injured states.

Meanwhile, Trenfal battled his way across the room, throwing people aside, then calling apologies. He soon had Culvers pinned to his seat with the tip of a blade against his throat. "Your tyranny ends here, Winter King!"

Drawing his feet up against the table, Culvers pushed back, toppling his throne.

"C-culvers!" Concerned, Trenfal leapt the table, but Culvers was already up, sword in hand.

Their blades clashed and Chiyoko screamed.

"Do it over there!" She pointed to the middle of the hall, as Uwe yanked her out of her seat.

"I think we're better off over there, m'lady."

Phanuel was heard scoffing as he crawled under the table.

Queline brought her elongated rabbit feet up and booted Trenfal's backside, showing buck teeth in a huge grin when he looked at her like she betrayed him. "Winter King's team." She then had to defend Bracken when Hok'jai swung a meaty fist at his head.

Trenfal leapt onto the table, thinking he had the advantage. Until Culvers tipped it over, sending him crashing to the polished floor, ears ringing from the impact. Culvers followed, chasing Trenfal around the room. Several people stopped fighting to laugh at the display, and were then caught and tied up by Vyxen and Date.

"Steady on!" Trenfal dived to one side.

"Come then, old man," Culvers laughed, slashing the air with his sword.

Trenfal's green eyes narrowed. Snatching an abandoned tablecloth, he whipped it at Culvers, who snagged the trailing end. A tug-o-war ensued. Blades clashed. The battle made more complex when Culvers whistled and a small army of spiders crawled from his sleeve down the cloth to clambered over Trenfal's fingers.

"Ugh, yuck!" He let go and flapped his hand.

Culvers laughed and lunged again.

"This is all part of the act, isn't it?!" Zercey couldn't keep distress from her voice. Despite her attempts to duck and dodge, she was knocked to the floor by a male dwarf wearing a tightly-fitted, red skullcap concealing part of his ginger hair. "Ack!"

"Inari, beam seeds!" Lerki called, holding a hand out.

"Here!" They produced a small pouch from their sleeve and tossed it. Lerki drew a seed and made a shushing noise. The plant germinated, producing a long, wooden rod, with tangling roots at one end and a fouled canopy on the other. With it, he batted the dwarf away.

"Lerki, pass me that!" Seth's knuckles were raw from punching people's metal accessories.

"Inari, what else have you up your sleeves?" Scy asked, amused and thoroughly enjoying herself.

"It would depend on what you need," they replied, eyes molten red. "If it's something small—"

"Stone beads might be nice, otherwise, I'll accept anything small and round," she replied, regretting swapping accessories with Abaddon; it meant hers were not to hand. Ducking low, she picked up and vaulted a goat-faced borrower, sending him sprawling across the glassy floor with a grunt.

Inari produced a handful of amber shard necklaces and tossed them to Scyanatha. "Will those do?"

"Better than nothing, dear," she said, snapping the string. "Many thanks!" She summoned a current of air and swept the beads into a mini tornado. When four Acolytes came at her, she winked and flicked her fingers, striking all and making them cower.

"Uhh, Scy, they're supposed to win, you know," Seth said, impressed and trying not to laugh.

"I know," she called back, smiling, "but I don't have to make it easy."

"Easy?" Zercey echoed, hiding behind Abaddon and Inari. "They outnumber us, and most people are running out the room."

"Do you have weapons, Inari?" Abaddon asked, turning their head to better catch sound vibrations.

"Knives are our limit," they replied. "The largest we have is a dagger."

"I'll take it," Abaddon said, decisive. "Maybe t-two, if you have another?"

They passed a pair of jewel-studded ones.

"Thank you." Abaddon charged issuing a war cry. Trenfal's troops had blunted training weapons, so they felt daggers evened their odds. Quick as they were, Abaddon's movements were hampered by the dress. More than once, they debated splitting the skirt, but it belonged to Scyanatha.

"Is it usually this chaotic?!" Zercey ducked behind Inari again. They hadn't been touched the entire time, making them the perfect shield.

"Not usually, but perhaps they have the right combination of people this year."

"They have that winged snake, Date, for one!" Seth barked, having good sense to blame his friend for the tactics on display. "They also have two ice magic users, who are at their strongest in this weather."

"Don't forget Vyxen," Scyanatha cautioned. "You would regret it, if you did."

"My, my," Inari said as the battle reached a slow and messy climax. Their eyes turned amber when two masked ogres seized them. "There is no need to be so rough."

"Ah shit!" Seth was knocked down by a blow to the back of the leg. "Ghenha!"

The blonde dwarf grinned and gave him the middle finger, teaming with two gnomes to tie him up.

"Ugh, I always hate this part," Seth complained, wincing as rope bit into his wrists. "I'll remember this, Daygo and Inwash!"

"It's Dagaz!"

"It's Yngwaz!"

"My bad."

"Zercey!" Lerki called, twisting to look for her as a dark-skinned beauty shoved him towards the other prisoners. A kongamato, with leathery folds of skin that spanned from her long arms down her sides.

"Sit," she snapped.

Unable to pinpoint Zercey in the crowd, Lerki blasted air through the openings under his jewellery, making an echoing screech next to the woman's ear to throw her off.

"Oh no you don't, plant-man!" She reared, thumping him hard on the back of his head with the butt of her club. "I'll gag you the next time you try that!"

"Tabitha, that hurt!" Lerki rubbed his head, eyes pricking with tears.

"Honestly," Scyanatha remarked, with arms bound and a blindfold fitted over her eyes, "I'm all for light bondage, but this has turned excessive."

She heard Seth choking for air beside her. "Are you all right?"

"Fine!"

"You did it to yourselves, boss," chimed one of the gnomes, and echoed by their friend. "You got rough, it's only fair we escalate."

"Lerki, I'm over here!" Zercey stood, waving. Wearing Lerki's coat over her dress, she was forced back down.

He let out a relieved breath and stopped struggling with Tabitha.

Despite their efforts, the chaos was over in minutes, concluding when Trenfal had Culvers on his knees, disarmed. "It's over for you, dishonourable king!" he declared to the crowd. "Glory to the people!"

"LONG LIVE THE SPRING KING!" The rebels cheered, applauding as dawn began to raise twilight's curtain in the windows. It shone through the fractals created by Nyima and Tundra, melting the thin layer in a perfect metaphor for the defeat of the Winter King.

With the party over, everyone returned to their barracks to rest or change for greenman.

Zercey hung up her dress and said, "I'm confused. I thought there was supposed to be a fight between them today?"

"There is," Scyanatha replied, easing her fingers through her plaits and shaking her hair out. "That is a final effort by the Winter King to reclaim his throne at the Spring King's coronation."

Nyima listened with half an ear, rubbing a finger back and forth across her lower lip. She would hold the memory of that night close no matter where she wound up in future. *Jingyi.* With a fond head shake, she folded the gauzy fabric she'd been wearing. Her trekadisk, D'nag, crept forward to see what she had. Nyima shooed him away. He swiped, missed and slipped into the fabric box with a yowl.

"Did you see how many people were rebels?" Vyxen giggled. "It was hilarious watching everyone run out the room!" She cuddled Baya and Cypher, then smothered a yawn. "Are you sure we can't just sleep through the last bit?"

"You have made it this far, I don't think you want to miss the conclusion." Scyanatha's persuasion skills were waning with the long hours. It was fortunate she had back up.

"It was fun," Abaddon said, running their hands over the decorated handles of their borrowed knives. "I had a good time."

"I don't think you were the only one," Vyxen sang, giving a pointed look and wide smile towards Nyima and Scyanatha.

Scyanatha's laugh was carefree. "Who could resist? It would be a crime to let such a delicious man escape."

There were murmurs of agreement at this. Seth had the kind of personality that made him easy to be around and augmented his good looks.

"Nyima?" Vyxen edged into her personal space, feigning innocence. "I almost forgot you were at the party. Wherever did you go?"

The others smothered their laughter as Nyima's cheeks turned a deep shade of blue. "I do—was—be going—nowhere! And Jingyi—he wasn't—isn't—not going—coming, too!" She struggled to come up with the right words, growing more flustered with every mistake.

Coming to her rescue, Zercey diverted the conversation. "Date seemed to like your company, Vyx."

"Pft!" She waved her hand. "We're just friends."

"You never know," Scyanatha argued in a silky tone. "Many people are 'just friends' for years before they decide to become something more."

Vyxen got the message and changed targets. "Abaddon, did you speak with Inari? You knew each other before, right?"

"Yes, err, we did," they replied. "On b-b-both counts. We were in the same training year, um, originally, before my injury."

Zercey pumped them for more information. "So, you must have known their old teammates, as well."

They hummed and said, "Yes, I did, but they were on the men's side. Only ones like Inari and I could travel between."

"That's handy, then," Vyxen said, shooting Zercey a look. "It means you can go into their barracks with Zercey when she gives that jacket back to Lerki."

Zercey looked at the coat she was petting like a companion. "Oh! I totally forgot I had this." Her cheeks turned pink at the falsehood. "I didn't want my dress falling down in the fight, so I put this over the top."

"Zercey, if you keep going you'll be redder than a tomato." Scyanatha tittered, going over to Nyima and untangling a piece of chain stuck in her braids.

"No, seriously!" Zercey grew louder and hugged the jacket tighter. "I don't even like it!"

"How red is she now?" Abaddon giggled, wriggling into a long sleeved top.

"You too? The betrayal!" Zercey threw the jacket over her head to smother her laughter.

"Let's hope she is never interrogated," Scyanatha said in an amused whisper to Nyima, who nodded.

Across the hallway, Inari and the men were holding a similar conversation.

Seth laughed and said, "If she threw another innuendo at me, I swear, dude, I was going to die!"

"That looked like her goal, from what I saw," Tundra joked back, setting his party clothes aside and getting out a clean set of duty wear.

"Man, with how little we actually saw you, I'm surprised you saw anything." In that respect, Seth guessed the rumours about Nyima being a complete ice queen were exaggerated.

Tundra shrugged, but couldn't keep the smug smirk off his face. "I'm not one to kiss and tell."

"Dude, you just did."

"Well," Date said, cutting through their chuckles, "I'm pleased with your results. A bit disappointed in your execution, but you managed not to fall on your faces and that's what counts." Giving Tundra a sideways stare, he added, "I didn't have to do it the hard way, after all."

"You'd have been better off leaving us to it," came Tundra's counter argument. "I wouldn't have wanted to kill you half as often as I have."

"It was still worth the effort." There was no arguing with him. He got the result he wanted. Mostly. "Now, remember to treat them with the respect they deserve."

"Do you wanna kill him or should I?" Seth punched his fist.

"Maybe Scyanatha and Nyima will do it for us, now," Tundra countered. He bet they hit hard.

"Ow." Lerki winced as he prodded the tender spot on the back of his head.

"Tabitha got you good, didn't she?" Seth came over to look, hissing through his teeth. "You going to be okay?"

Lerki's reply was slow and undecided. "Ahh...I should be. It just hurts."

"She always was quick to violence," Inari shared their observations, "but when we aren't behaving, it is to be expected."

"Last person she went all out with ended up blind. Which is why people give her a wide berth," Tundra stated, as the others nodded. He looked around the room and saw everyone was ready. "Greenman, shift, then sleep. Nearly done."

CHAPTER TWENTY-TWO

With a change of clothes and carrying cloaks, the group reconvened in the hallway and descended the spiral staircase laughing and chatting.

In the courtyard, the ironwork that surrounded the yule pyre was repurposed as a cage for the match between the Winter and Spring Kings. Ashes blackened the snow under their feet, turning it to grey sludge. The vines wrapped through the metal were removed for better visibility. Spectators crowded the tiers holding the ice statues, rubbing arms, clapping hands and stamping feet to keep warm.

Both Culvers and Trenfal were present and dressed in polished armour: Culvers in silver with gold accents; Trenfal in gold with silver detailing. Each had a buckler strapped to his forearm and carried a sword.

"Shall I gut this liubul'k where he stands?!" Culvers pointed his blade at Trenfal and laughed when the people booed and cheered.

"Nay, good people!" Trenfal swept his arms wide. "Do not be fooled by this tyrant! I shall liberate you all!"

There was laughter at this. Trenfal chuckled and shrugged.

A horn sounded, signalling the start of the match. Swords clashed and it was a repeat of the previous night. Those who missed the bout sat up and paid attention. For the rest, they chatted among themselves creating hypothetical matches with the rest of the Order.

"Phanuel versus Uwe?"

"Tough, they're both conniving and slimy."

Seth nodded to where Culvers got a sneaky left under Trenfal's guard. "Looks like spring is gonna be late this year."

There were winces and sighs of sympathy when Trenfal shook his head, dazed.

"He isn't a High Elder for nothing, I guess," Zercey said, impressed. "I guess all the faeries thought a half-blood versus an elf wouldn't be a good match." She looked around at the rapt attention on people's faces and concluded, "They were so wrong."

"A half-blood arachne from Don," Date said, marking the difference. "He's lived here since he was ten, and their kind is stronger than most." He cheered as Culvers dented Trenfal's shield and the latter threw it to the ground.

"Half-bloods are tougher and scarier than you think," Vyxen said, tweaking his cheek. "Go, Culvers! Sic some spiders on him like last time!"

There was a united gasp from the crowd as Culvers blade came within a hair's breadth of slitting Trenfal's throat.

"Culvers, for Mana's sake!" Trenfal leapt away and rolled to put distance between them. He then closed it and shoulder barged Culvers into the ashy snow. "Yield!" Raising his sword to make the final strike, Trenfal's victory was delayed when Culvers tossed a fist full of grit and powder in his eyes. "Damn you, Culvers!" Trenfal reared back and Culvers sprang to his feet.

The crowd began to turn. Support for Trenfal grew with each underhand act Culvers performed. The Winter King would fall and the Spring King would rise.

Emboldened and urged on by those chanting his name, Trenfal struck, darting forward with each lunge. He pressed Culvers back to the cage walls. A block. A feint. Culvers' sword went flying and the point of Trenfal's was against his throat.

The chatter of the crowd that buzzed during the first part of the fight was gone. The silence was deafening.

Trenfal panted, green eyes bright. His hair shone in the sun and he looked thirty years younger than he did a few moons ago. "Yield!"

Culvers' lips thinned and he nodded, once.

Cheers went up. People stood, stamping their feet and clapping.

Trenfal blinked at the applause and stepped back, grinning. He thrust his sword arm up and cried, "GLORY TO THE PEOPLE!"

"ALL HAIL THE SPRING KING!"

Musicians struck a lively tune and the sedate atmosphere turned to organised chaos.

Seth already had his hand out for Scy, who tittered and simpered as she took it, playing demure.

Tundra glanced at Nyima, who smiled and nodded.

They, along with other couples, moved to surround the cage and take part in the cloven fruit dance. Others rushed around looking for their prospective partners from the night before.

"Ironic, isn't it?" Date remarked, standing to one side with those not dancing. "History says the Spring King wasn't much different. Soon enough, he was overthrown and Illthdar was under the control of the Queen of Arcana."

"So, they were real people?" Vyxen watched the couples twirl and sway, beaming as she spotted her friends.

"It's debatable," he replied, blowing on his hands to warm them. "The Winter and Spring Kings were inspired by rulers of a darker age. The mother of the six Woodralandian Queens ultimately overthrew the Spring King."

Vyxen nodded. "Huh, the Spring King was a bit like Robin Hood. Only, he ended up being a jerk, too."

"Who?" He turned to regard her. "I'm not familiar with that name," he confessed, shaking his head. Hazarding a guess, he said, "They must be human."

"Ehn," She gave an abridged version of the Disney tale.

Having been lost in thought as he watched the couples, Lerki piped up with, "Do you suppose anyone has considered undergoing the twelve nights?"

"Twelve nights? What's that?" Vyxen seized on the topic like a liubul'k with a bone.

Lerki's mouth fell open, as his face flushed.

"Wait, don't you mean twelfth night?" Zercey's eyebrows went up. "I thought that was only a celebration of the Anglican church."

"No, ahh…that…" he struggled.

Inari chuckled and came to his aid. "No, he means twelve nights. It begins in Prasiolite and is normally a celebration of lovers."

At this information, Vyxen's eyes widened and her smile stretched wider.

Behind her, Date buried his face in his hand and let out a low groan.

"Really?" she drawled, shifting with excitement. "And how does someone celebrate twelve nights?"

"I forgot I have to see Phanuel!" Lerki's jewellery whistled in panic.

Date rolled his eyes. "He's still busy with greenman," he stated, snaring Lerki by his poncho before he could escape.

Calming somewhat, Lerki breathed deep and nodded. "I am sorry, I forgot."

"I haven't participated in it before, either," Abaddon shared. "It's during Imbolc."

"So, is it called twelve nights, or Imbolc?" Vyxen demanded. It sounded cute and she needed to know the thing, right now. Especially if she could convince her friends to take part.

"That is the last day of the event, yes." Inari nodded to Abaddon when they referenced the celebration's alternative name. "While most will celebrate the last day, the eleven preceding are something less engage in these days. Let us simply say that it holds some added stipulations."

Zercey declared, "With how everyone went on about solstice, I thought Illthdar didn't have any more holidays."

"It isn't a formal holiday," Date admitted, releasing Lerki. "Don't tell that to the fanatics, though."

"So," Vyxen repeated, gesturing for more information, "how does it work?"

"Well," Inari began, only to be interrupted by Lerki.

"It isn't as important as Year Turning." Lerki tried to remedy the situation before escaping. "Did you want to learn the cloven fruit dance, Zercey?"

"Buhh…Sure, I guess…" she trailed, taking his hand and passing Vyxen the coat she was yet to return. Peering behind him at the gathering dancers, she didn't think it looked any more difficult than other dances. It was primarily doubling forwards and back to one's partner, arming and siding punctuated with sets and turns in between.

Date sniggered under his breath, ducking his head at the less than subtle ploy Lerki utilised. He had no understanding of how women talked amongst themselves. What Zercey didn't hear now, she would obtain from her friends later.

"He's so cute," Vyxen tsked once the pair were out of earshot, using a babyish tone of voice. "I just wanna pinch his widdle cheeks!"

Abaddon giggled.

"Ugh." Date made a nauseated sound. "It's times like these I'm reminded he only pretends to be an educated man."

"So, Inari," Vyxen bounced beside them, wanting to get back to the topic before someone else found a way to divert it again, "twelve nights?"

Inari smiled with endless tolerance as they answered. "There are a few ways to go about the ritual. One is the couple exchange gifts; another is they alternate giving gifts. Some may try to woo their paramour by surprising them each day."

"It's a longer Valentine's day," she summarised. "How expensive do these gifts have to be?"

Inari shook their head, deigning not to respond. They produced a small bottle of rose-coloured liquid from their sleeve. "Could I interest anyone in berry mead?"

"That much, huh?" Vyxen guessed, and they laughed.

"Is it yours?" Abaddon queried of the liquor, and Vyxen raised an eyebrow at the odd question.

"Unfortunately, no. Our last batch was ruined with the incident in the barracks," they replied, brows pinching in irritation.

Date coughed, turning his head.

They revealed to Vyxen, "The gifts vary, but they centre around a theme for each of the twelve days."

"I know what you're up to," Date challenged her. "It's more complicated than you think. Give me a day and I can write it down for you."

"Thanks, but I can just ask Scy instead; she'll know and I won't have to find someone to read it to me." Vyxen beamed at him.

"You really can't read Illthdarian?" At the time, he'd thought she was avoiding writing letters to Magnilla's clan.

"Ehn," she replied, shrugging. "I'm not staying here forever. It wouldn't be worth my time to learn something I'll never use."

Date grew pensive at this.

"Year Turning is exactly as it sounds; it is a day to mark the change in the years," Inari volunteered. "Many come to pray and give their respects to the crystal of Vvekw."

"Oh, okay," Vyxen said, slightly disappointed. While a New Year celebration would hold some opportunities, she was left with the impression the potential fun factor was minimal. "Any other holidays I should know about?"

The reappearance of their friends forestalled an answer, signalling the end of the solstice festival. At its close, the Acolytes were forced to return to duty. Everyone was sleep deprived, so shorter shifts were organised in consideration—the smallest of mercies Chiyoko afforded.

Lots drawn, the group separated. Some to take their positions, the rest to their beds.

CHAPTER TWENTY-THREE

Lerki wobbled on his feet, tiredness making him clumsy. He straightened and tried to pay attention while Phanuel droned on. The lab was dark and humid. The perfect environment for putting someone to sleep. His attention waned and his gaze flitted to the table, where a row of potted plants sat. "Those need watering," he murmured. "By the stars, Lerki, pay attention!" Phanuel slapped him on the head with a sheaf of papers.

"I was," he replied, in mild reproach, repeating back the mission parameters. "However, that's at the northern tip of Illthdar. It would take me months to travel there and back on foot."

Phanuel placed his hands behind his back and leaned forward, making his hunch more pronounced. "Take a rathe and return in one month," he said, in a condescending tone.

Lerki's brows pinched. "The resonance will only last for a month at most. Even with a rathe, it would take at least that long to get there. I would be unable to come back with what little time I have left." Unless he ran into a necromancer who reanimated him. He shuddered at the thought. He also didn't want to leave Las. Since Zercey arrived he was able to stay for extended amounts of time without needing to rush to his tribe and resonate with them. He'd been able to take part in events and spend time with his friends. Now, Phanuel wanted him to go away for months to collect some snake venom? *It's not fair!*

"Then I guess it's a good thing we have a venin half-blood at our disposal you can take with." Phanuel moved to the table and sat. The unpleasant, satisfied look on his face suggested he'd been planning this for a while. "Problem solved."

Lerki looked around for inspiration. Like Fluorite barracks, the laboratorium teemed with life in containers and jars. Shelves full of ingredients and reference books lined the walls. In the room's centre was a workstation, suspended from the ceiling by nimbus clouds that rained into a tank below to keep aquatic ingredients fresh. The table was cluttered with bottles, books and a strange cauldron made of green crystal.

"Problem not solved," Lerki argued. His voice rose an octave. "She's half-blood and has no resistance. If she made it to the peaks, one boreal bite would be the end of her."

"Oh, that's simple: don't let her get bitten. Leave her at a base camp beside the mountain while you finish the last leg of the journey alone," Phanuel replied, tone bland. "I fail to see the issue."

Lerki struggled to contain himself. Phanuel was someone he admired in a lot of ways, but his temperament left something to be desired. That was basic common sense. Venin avoided dangerous things, but it seemed every other species charged in head first. "There are half a dozen other things that can kill her in the north! Not least the melano-khole, seven types of poisonous flower, birds of paradise and worse! There's also everything else between here and there—which includes Sleepy Forest and the fissure!" Waving his arms with incredulity, he added, "And all during the coldest time of the year!" It wasn't just a bad idea, it was terrible!

"Then take a team," Phanuel bit out between clenched teeth. "I don't care what your complaints are, Lerki. We need that venom and you know how to get it." He stood and bored holes into him with a fierce glare. "And do not raise your voice at me."

"I'm sorry, I forgot myself." Lerki's shoulders sagged with defeat. "I need time to think of who to pick," he said, tiredness seeping into him once more and stealing his will. "How many others may I have?"

"Two should be sufficient," Phanuel estimated, motioning for silence. "Ah-ah-ah. *Two,* Lerki. Chiyoko won't allow more if they're full-blooded, and I don't want to endure the ringing in my ears if you try. My advice is take ones that don't use ice magic—the beasts up that way adapt to cold."

"Ah…" Lerki nodded slowly. "Yes, sir." *It seems I have no choice.*

RACHEL GARCIA

A rustle disturbed Scyanatha's slumber. Her eyes cracked open at the squeak of hinges on a trunk. Stone beads flew from her bracelets to scatter over the person's back. "You are not Magnilla," she said, blinking to clear her sleep fogged eyes.

"Her Highness, Princess Magnilla, sent me to collect her things. She's decided she won't be returning." The female werewolf grabbed the pack and placed a letter on top of the trunk lid. "She sends her regrets to be leaving you without a team leader." The woman nodded once and left. Scyanatha sighed and got out of bed, reaching to shake Nyima awake—the only other team member present. "We have post."

"Post what?" Nyima pulled herself onto her knees and leaned over the side of the bed.

"A letter," Scyanatha restated. She used a fingernail to slice off the wax seal and open it out. Her ruby eyes scanned the contents at speed. "I see."

"She do being what—hrr—" Nyima paused and let out a frustrated breath. "Coward?"

"Not in so many words," Scyanatha said, holding the paper up so Nyima could see the long and flowing script. "But, that is one interpretation." She folded it again and sighed. "It's a pity she couldn't set her ego aside to work with others. Even in leaving, she says she left us without a leader."

"Leaders do not be cowards," Nyima spat, annoyed at being woken for this.

"That is true," Scy replied. "I don't think she gave it a real chance, either. It was Rhodochrosite when we met." She settled back into bed. "Nothing to be done about it now, I suppose."

"Hmm." Nyima's non-committal hum spoke volumes.

"Careful," Tundra cautioned Zercey, grabbing her as she tilted to the side. "You're falling asleep."

They were on the battlements on watch. Though, with how sleepy the city and surrounding area was, they doubted there was anything *to* watch.

Zercey groaned and scrubbed her face. "I'm never doing this again. How do people here *do* this every year?" She felt resentful of the others rotated to sleep first.

"When you grow up doing something it becomes second nature," Tundra shared, stretching his muscles to keep busy and alert. Beside him, Seth was peeling off layers, using the bitter wind to keep awake. "You're not me," he cautioned. "You won't appreciate going without a coat for long."

"I'm tired enough to risk a cold," Seth returned, orange eyes opening wide, then squinting. "My brain feels like it's made of p'ake fur."

"I always suspected—" Tundra began, smirking.

"Kiss my ass," Seth shot back.

"I'll defer that to Scy," he returned, chuckling as Seth flushed.

"I'm telling her you guys said this," Zercey teased, giggling.

"Just as long as you don't tell Date," Seth said, sharing a look with Tundra. "He doesn't get the difference between playful banter and misogyny."

"I think it depends on if the woman takes offence," she replied. "Knowing Scy, she'll one up the pair of you and laugh the whole while."

They both nodded, knowing their limits.

Seth grew introspective as their amusement faded. "Man," he whistled slowly, shaking his head, "sometimes it feels like I've lived here all my life." He leant against the wall and looked in towards the city. He appeared forlorn as he revealed, "I don't think I could go back, even if they did find a way."

"I didn't even think about that," Tundra stated, patting Seth on the back. "You don't have the choice anymore."

Zercey looked around, panicked at the idea this was her forever. "That's *horrible!* I was waiting to start my university course back home. I mean, eventually people will stop looking and write us off for dead, but that doesn't mean we shouldn't keep trying to get home."

"I don't know what to say to you," Seth told her. "I want to give you hope that maybe it'll happen, but I've been here nearly eight years."

"I don't think they're really trying, Seth," Tundra said, crossing his arms. "It isn't in Chiyoko's best interests to rush the discharge of people bolstering the ranks."

"It probably helps some that half-bloods are more adept to living without mana," Seth murmured. "It makes us more hearty than full-bloods."

"So, that's why there are so many of us and so few full-blooded people around," Zercey said, eyes widening with realisation. "I thought it was just because so many came all at once."

"Nope. We're just unlucky enough being born in places with little or no mana. Our bodies are used to going without, so that's what makes us valuable."

"More or less," Tundra agreed. "And, for people who world-jump—"

"Meaning you," Seth said, sniggering.

Tundra shrugged but didn't deny it. "We have experience using mana, but there's less here so we have to adapt. When we get home, we'll be God level."

Zercey snorted, expression souring. "I bet there are exceptions to that rule."

"Or they were exaggerating," he replied, guessing who she thought of.

"What? Exaggerate? Never!" she gasped, clapping her hands to her cheeks and laughing.

"Hey, here comes Lerki," Seth said, watching a head of green hair sprint through the gate. "And there goes Lerki."

"He's still awake?" Tundra remarked, walking over to the edge of the wall and peering down. He heard him call out to Abaddon and Date, returning from patrol. "He's crazy. He and Inari have to swap with those two next." He gestured to the returning pair.

Seth joked, "In the list of crazy, it goes: Tundra, Lerki, me and Date."

Zercey's lips twitched as Tundra shot him a dirty look.

"Well, none of *my friends* are crazy," Zercey replied, fighting to keep a straight face.

"That's good news for you, buddy," Seth teased Tundra, giving him a playful shove. "At least you know you're not hooking up with another lunatic."

"You're an idiot, Seth."

"But, I'm not the only one," Seth returned, levelling him with a smug stare, as though pleased with his comeback.

Tundra shook his head at him.

"Here comes Lerki," Seth said, happy for the distraction. "And there goes Lerki, again. At least he isn't running this time."

"Wonder what he wanted with them?"

The men and Inari found out Lerki's intent late that evening, sat around a table with a map spread out before them.

"This is the safest route," Lerki said, tracing the trail skirting the coast that snaked around the Sleepy forest. It ended at the base of the North Mountain.

It's also the longest," Tundra pointed out.

"This way is faster." Inari cut a line through the forest.

Lerki recoiled. "I want to avoid bad things, not go through them!"

"I had safe passage this far," they noted, as the other three sniggered. They tapped a manicured fingertip at an unmarked spot. "The fissure is here and little else. Everything has fled from its presence."

"Nothing is something," Lerki reasoned, face stony. "The forest and the elements should never be frightened from their nature."

"I would not use such strong words," they disagreed. "It did not feel subdued."

Lerki countered, holding his ground. "It feels normal to you for wild things to be tamed. To me, it is very unnatural."

"Okay, so, whatever path we take, we skirt the fissure," Seth said, intervening before things got heated.

Inari calmed, nodding. "It is best to avoid it until we are able close it for good. It has a pulsating beat like a heart and with each thud, life around it is choked and smothered. Every soul thrown into its abyss only strengthens it further."

The men were silent, digesting the doom-laden statement.

But, Inari wasn't finished.

"The time when normal magic could hope to seal it has long past. We fear that, unless something is done soon, it may swallow Illthdar whole."

To be continued...

RACHEL GARCIA
ABOUT THE AUTHOR

Rachel Garcia was born and raised in the Land of 10,000 Lakes: Minnesota, USA. She had a modern romance, falling in love with a British man living in the UK and flew 8,000+ miles with all her worldly possessions stowed in three suitcases to ultimately live in West Yorkshire with him and their two children. A Latina-American, she is an advocate of positive change and anti-discrimination, Rachel's passion is to write stories that mirror real life in a world of fantasy to help highlight and address inequality.

Lightning Source UK Ltd.
Milton Keynes UK
UKHW010630140122
397142UK00001B/189